THE COWBOY AND THE CHICKEN HOUSE -LOVE BEHIND ENEMY LINES

Behind enemy lines, hunted by the Gestapo, rescued by brave agents of the Belgian resistance, Fighter Pilot, "Cowboy" Jack Dodds, meets the love of his life in a place called "The Chicken House"

LEE LEVENSON

outskirts press

The Cowboy and the Chicken House: Love Behind Enemy Lines

v2.0

Outskirts Press, Inc.
http://www.outskirtspress.com

ISBN: 978-1-9772-7955-2

PRINTED IN THE UNITED STATES OF AMERICA

For Alice

This story is dedicated with heartfelt gratitude to the Airmen of the Mighty Eighth Airforce, many of whom were teenagers and young men, and to the brave and dedicated young women and men of the Comet Line and the resistance movements of France, Belgium, Holland and Spain who risked their lives to rescue downed Allied airmen and provide safe refuge for them.

A NOTE TO THE READER

This story is not intended to be a detailed, all-inclusive day by day historical account of the events surrounding the German occupation of Belgium, France, Holland and Europe during the Second World War.

Every library, bookstore and online bookstore is full of detailed books offering far greater detail and historical accounts of WWII. My effort is to take you back into this time, permitting the characters to speak for themselves and to see their lives through their eyes.

Dialogue of everyday conversations occur between the characters help to create perspective of the events and situations that confronted them during this period. All are woven into the story to enhance our understanding of the point of view of the characters themselves, to see things through their eyes. Unless otherwise quoted from actual sources, all are to be considered derived from the imagination of the author.

The major events presented in our story are true and put us into the lives of our characters and what they had to deal with. Events like the Mighty 8th Airforce Missions, dates and losses that Jack Dodds finds himself flying. Such things as the tragedy and loss of life of the V-2 Bombing of the Rex theatre in Antwerp, Belgium killing hundreds of innocent civilians. The murder of Pharmacist Henri Charles in Bouillon, Belgium by Pro-Nazi Rexist assassins. All these things and more were a part of the lives of our characters and the real-life people of their time.

It provides insight into the lives of men and women, some young, some very young, some old who were dealing with an unbelievable crisis of their time. A crisis that took the lives of over 50 million people. It is the story of two young people who were thrust into each other's lives by a crash landing in an open field in the Ardennes Forest in Belgium.

In the end, it is also a love story. The story of two young people, a story shared by many others who found each other and joined together for a lifetime. It is also about the "Greater Love" of the brave men and women, civilians, clergy, religious, military who were willing to lay down their lives for their friends. My effort here is to offer you a good story, which will provide insight into a generation of people who are not so very different from us, but who were confronted with a crisis that truly formed the future of humanity. I hope you enjoy the adventure!

Lee Levenson, December 2024

"The chickens are coming home to roost, and you happen to have just moved into the chicken house." Douglas MacArthur

CHAPTER 1

Highland Beach Towers Highland Beach Florida Decorated WWII US Army Air Corps Fighter Pilot John, "Jack" Dodds, takes on a New Mission to Visit His Local Dentist.

It had been a long while since Jack had driven his ten-year-old Buick LaCross. *"What was it? Two, three weeks?"*

He didn't remember.

He searched for the keys which normally would've been in the kitchen counter drawer right near the coffee maker. He went through every drawer in the kitchen… nothing. *Ellie had gone and done it again!*

She had hidden his keys again. Ever since they had that argument, or as Ellie preferred to call it *a mild disagreement* about his continuing to drive, she had been hiding his keys.

He concentrated with all his might to remember exactly when the last time was that he had driven the car. That might give him a clue as to the key's whereabouts.

He smiled as he recalled overhearing Ellie's telephone conversation with his son, Lucien. Ellie was growing increasingly hard of hearing and tended to put calls on the speakerphone. It made it easier for her to hear who she was speaking with, and of course everyone else within a three-block area.

"*Mom, I can't believe you're asking ME to fly down from Charlotte to tell a decorated World War Two combat pilot that he shouldn't drive his beloved Buick. The LaCrosse that he drives through the car wash every other week? No thanks!*"

He could still feel the embarrassment and irritation when Ellie pushed Lucien,

"*Lucien, he's getting older honey. He's not the fighter pilot you put up on a pedestal. He's your dad, he's changing, we're both getting to be old, honey. He sometimes loses his balance and becomes more and more forgetful. I'm worried*"

As he reflected on this conversation, he became a bit irritated but then shrugged it off. He remembered Lucien telling Ellie to take the call off speaker and guessed that Lucien, the sharp airline pilot suspected that he, along with everyone living in the entire high-rise condo complex might be able to hear their conversation.

After that call ended, he kept his nose buried in the morning paper, pretending that he didn't hear a word as Ellie walked slowly by,

"That was what? Three, four weeks ago?" He couldn't recall.

Laughing to himself and shaking his head he snapped his fingers as he suddenly remembered a spare set of keys tucked away in the desk drawer in his study and office. Excited, he turned to his right, almost lost his balance, corrected by grabbing onto the back of the nearby sofa and moved toward his office study.

Jack walked quietly past the spare bedroom in order not to awaken Ellie or her caregiver, Jackie, both of whom must still be asleep. Ellie would be in the hospital bed that had recently been installed, Jackie would be in the Lazy-Boy recliner. He would leave a note for both that he was heading to the nearby dentist's office and would be back soon.

Rummaging through his desk drawers, he let out a low sigh of relief as he found the spare keys to the Buick and spare front door key.

Tip-toeing quietly past Ellie's room, he grabbed his wallet. Letting himself out the front door of the condo. Locking the front door, he turned to take in the early morning Atlantic Ocean view, deeply inhaling the smell of salt air and carefully looked over the guard rail to survey the parking lot four stories below him.

Spotting a likely area of the covered parking areas below him, Jack walked to the elevator and pressed the down button.

CHAPTER 2

Highland Beach, Florida, Jack Seeks His Buick

Arriving at the ground floor, Jack stepped off the elevator and moved towards the array of covered parking spaces looking for his ten-year-old Buick LaCross. The condo owners were assigned parking places, and he quickly spotted his section and walked slowly towards his car.

Most seasoned pilots will start their "preflight" while walking to their parked aircraft. A good pilot would notice something out of the ordinary even from a distance as he or she approached the aircraft: tires inflated evenly, landing gear struts equally extended, windshields intact, bullet holes and shrapnel damage repaired, etc.

Jack, by force of habit did the same for his parked Buick. He scanned the vehicle from a distance at first and then with ever more scrutiny as he drew closer. Everything seemed okay to him: tires appeared evenly inflated, no "parking lot" dings, just a little cleaning for the windshield and mirrors and he would be good to go. Could use a little washing and cleaning though, he thought.

"When was the last time I had this thing through the car wash?" he wondered aloud, as he backed out of the parking space.

As he started to roll forward, he suddenly remembered that he had failed to leave a note for the nurse, Jackie. He decided he wouldn't be gone that long and would explain his absence later.

Jack pulled out onto A1A, the beach road, turned left, drove about a half mile and turned towards busy US1. It felt great to have escaped the confinement of the condo, to be on his own, behind the wheel and free.

Now if I can only get this damned toothache fixed!

CHAPTER 3

Delray Beach, Florida Jack arrives at the Dentist Office

In a few short minutes, Jack turned into the parking lot in front of the dentist's office. He smiled when he saw an empty parking space which was in the shade underneath a large tree.

Perfect, he thought to himself, "My Buick will be a lot cooler when I come out! Sure, it's a bit of a walk but I'll be damned if I'm going to hang that damned handicapped sign from my mirror. I'm not handicapped and it's a short walk.

With that, Jack parked his car and opened his glove box. Sorting through papers, cards, and other junk, he located a crumpled face-mask and put it in his shirt pocket. He made a mental note to get a new supply afterwards as there were no more left in the glove box.

Getting out of the car, he slowly stood until he was able to stand completely upright without losing his damn balance, took a deep breath and made his way across the parking lot to the front door of the dentist's office.

Just before entering the office doors, he put the facemask on and removed his sunglasses. Much to his surprise, there was nobody sitting at a table, blocking the inside entrance to do a forehead temperature scan and check for facemasks.

As he moved slowly into the office, he noticed he was the only one wearing a face mask. *Strange,* he thought.

A young receptionist looked up at him and smiled, "Good morning, Mister Dodds, I'm Lisa. I recognized you from the recent article in the *Sunshine Times* about your World War Two experiences. It's a pleasure to meet you in person. You're a lot more handsome and distinguished in person! No need to hide your face behind that mask unless you're not feeling well?"

Jack was momentarily caught off guard, but responded, "Thank you, Lisa. I'm okay, just this nasty throbbing in my lower jaw. I thought it was required to wear a mask."

"No, sir. Since Covid's risk has pretty much been reduced, masks are no longer required."

Lisa looked at her computer then continued, "I spoke with you this morning when you called, and Doctor Siegel is ready to take care of that nasty toothache. I just wanted to check on a few things."

Lisa looked down at her computer, then back up at him, all business now,

"Mister Dodds?"

Jack smiled and interrupted her, "*Mister Dodds* is fine, my friends call me Jack. *Mr. Dodds* is my father. You can call me Jack"

She smiled, and continued, "It's been a while since we've seen you, while the staff is preparing an exam room for you, I'm going to have you fill out this form which will update your information. I see that you are ninety-nine years old. That's amazing! You don't look at all like you're ninety-nine!"

Jack laughed, and said, "Yeah, I know. I don't look a day older than ninety-eight."

Just as the two of them laughed together, Doctor Siegel happened to walk by the reception area, spotted Jack and smiled. "Jack! Greetings! I just overheard Lisa, You're ninety-nine?"

"Yup, ninety-nine."

"Wow! That's great. How did you get here?"

"What do you mean, how did I get here?"

"Did someone drive you? Or did you Uber? Just wondering, that's all."

Jack frowned, *Ellie must've given them a head's up, I'll have to have a word with her when I get home.* Then he looked directly at Doctor Siegel and asked,

"I'm sorry, Doctor, could you repeat the question?"

"Sure, I was just asking how you got here, just curious."

Jack looked at the dentist and then at Lisa before smiling, "Buick."

And the day went downhill very quickly from there.

CHAPTER 4

Delray Beach, Florida Jack In The Dentist Chair

Jack was guided into a chair in a room marked "Imaging" where a technician took a series of dental X-Rays. When that was completed, he was led into another exam room by Sarah, a young dental assistant with an absolutely dazzling white smile.

Sarah quickly adjusted his chair position and placed a dental bib over his chest. She set out dental tools and other implements on the tray and then adjusted the overhead light. "Doctor Siegel will be right in, Mr. Dodds. Are you comfortable?"

Jack nodded and smiled at her. "Thank you, Sarah. I'm fine."

She paused and seemed about to say something to him but paused for a moment.

"Did you want to tell me anything else, Sarah?"

"Well, I just wanted to tell you that I happened to see the recent article in the *Sunshine Times* about your time spent behind enemy lines in Nazi occupied Europe and that entire amazing story."

She smiled and went on as she continued setting up dental tools and adjusting the lighting. "My dad flew in Vietnam and showed me the article. We are so proud of you and of your entire generation."

"That's very kind of you, Sarah. Thank you and please thank your dad for his service. That Vietnam war was brutal."

She beamed and went on, "Doctor Siegel told me this morning that you were one of his patients. It was a very nice story and made me very grateful for you and your generation. The article also said how devoted you had been to your wife, putting her name on your airplanes, and, well," she paused, seeming to hesitate before she went on,"

"Was there something else, Sarah?"

"Well, I just lost my grandma, and she and my grandpa were very devoted like you and your wife. I was very moved by how dedicated you two were throughout your beautiful marriage. That's all I wanted to say."

"Well, that's very nice of you, Sarah."

She seemed to be getting emotional, which surprised Jack. Then she patted his shoulder and looked to the entrance of the surgery room and, as if on cue, Doctor Siegel came in, smiled at him and turned on a monitor that displayed Jack's mouth in all its glory.

"Well Jack, for a guy who's ninety-nine years old, you have a very good dental profile. One for the books. You do have an abscess forming under your lower tooth on the right side and we will have to perform a root canal to take care of it. Is that okay with you?"

"Yes, of course, Doc. Let's get this damn thing out so I can sleep at night."

Siegel smiled, "We're not going to extract the tooth, Jack. We're going to perform an endodontic procedure better known as a root-canal and get rid of that pesky nerve that's decaying and causing you this discomfort. I'm going to numb you up, okay?"

By this time, Jack was starting to feel very weary and just nodded his approval. As the dentist started a brief series of injections in his lower jaw, something that Sarah had said started to bug him. Something about "*losing her grandma?*" What was that all about?

Doctor Siegel finished the injections, patted Jack on the shoulder, and smiled, "I'll be right back, Jack, we'll let you get good and numb. I must check on another patient in the next room. Oh, and a nice story in the *Sunshine times* the other day. My dad served in the Navy in World War Two out in the Pacific. He and my mom were very devoted right to the end also. Be right back."

With that, he disappeared out the door.

CHAPTER 5

Delray Beach, Florida, Jack Flees the Dentist's Office

Jack felt the lower jaw numbing and was growing sleepy. He hadn't been sleeping all that well lately and fatigue was setting in. Then, suddenly the last comment by Siegel about his own mom and dad hit him,

"*He and my mom were very devoted right to the end also.*

"*Right to the end also?* What the hell was he talking about? Had something gone wrong with Ellie while I was on my way over here?

He looked around the room to ask Sarah what was going on, but she too had left momentarily. Jack sat up and moved his legs off the chair in one slow motion. Standing shakily, he started down the hall and out into the front of the reception area. *He had to get home!*

He barely noticed the startled expression of some people that he pushed past as he headed towards the parking lot, still wearing his dental bib. Fumbling for his keys, he started towards his Buick when he heard his name shouted behind him.

Turning around, and becoming dizzy with the effort, he saw Doctor Siegel and Sarah running towards him. Siegel called out to him,

"Jack! What the hell is going on? Where are you going?"

"I've got to get home and see to Ellie."

Doctor Siegel and Sarah exchanged a quick, surprised glance. "It's okay, Buddy, let me take care of that molar for you, and we'll let you get back home right away. Do you have any family or friends at home who can come here and drive you? Because I see you're upset, and I think you're having a little reaction to the Lidocaine."

"Just Ellie and her nurse, Jackie. But I've changed my mind, I....."

Jack's voice died as it suddenly dawned on him that maybe Ellie wasn't home, she wasn't anywhere! "*What the hell is wrong with me? Where's my Ellie?*"

With that, the entire parking lot started spinning and he started to go down.

Doctor Siegel moved quickly towards him, but Jack fainted, collapsed, hitting his head on the pavement before the dentist could get to him.

Siegel cursed, "Shit! He hit his head! Dammit!"

He turned to Sarah, while at the same time deftly removing the dental bib and placing it under Jack's head on the pavement. "Call 911, tell them our patient may be having an adverse reaction to Lidocaine and has fallen with a possible head injury." He gently rolled Jack onto his side into the recovery position and continued,

"I'm checking his airway right now, Sarah. Get some of the other staff out here right now to help me get some shade over him and keep traffic away from us in the parking lot so the paramedics have clear access. Bring the portable O2 out here right away. Tell the other patients in the waiting room to please reschedule and check on whoever's in the other exam room, right now, I cannot get to them."

Sarah nodded, placed her cellphone to her ear after dialing 911 and took off at top speed back into the office.

Within a few moments, almost all the dental office staff were gathered around Jack as the sound of sirens grew ever closer to the parking lot.

CHAPTER 6

Thursday, 25 May 1944- European Theater of Operations (ETO) Strategic Operations (Eighth Air Force): Mission 370:

Twenty-two-year-old 2nd Lieutenant John "Jack" Dodds took off with his squadron of P-51 Mustang fighters as they climbed out gaining altitude over the English Channel. They formed up to join other members of the 357th Fighter Group escorting a massive flight of Mighty 8th Airforce B-17 and B-24 bombers on mission number 370.

Allied command's intent was to destroy German military assets and infrastructure in anticipation of the looming invasion of France. Mission 370 included 406 bombers and 604 fighters who were dispatched to make visual attacks on rail installations and airfields in Belgium and France.

Having completed four missions so far, Jack was becoming a rising star. In after-action reports, his squadron Leader noted Jack's very capable flying skills and incredible marksmanship. On just his first mission, he shot down a Heinkel bomber and on his second mission, Jack scored two "Kills," a Junker 188 and, after a brief dogfight, a formidable ME-109 fighter. He was also credited with destroying several Luftwaffe aircraft on the ground during a fighter sweep in Belgium.

Two more in the air and Jack Dodds would be declared an "Ace" with five kills. His fellow squadron mates teased him about getting a bigger helmet to fit his ever-growing head, but it was all good-natured kidding.

They all felt pretty good at having a "sharpshooter" among them when things got tough. Jack credited his shooting skills to hunting in the forests and woodlands at an early age while growing up in the mountains of Western North Carolina.

He was half joking when he said that learning how to "lead" a fast-flying duck or goose, translated to his targeting skills while flying the ferocious P-51 Mustang. Instinctively he understood that he needed to fire his six .50 caliber Browning machine-guns slightly ahead of his target aircraft allowing his target to fly into the path of his lethal fire.

Jack was unassuming, low-key and didn't "strut around" all full of himself which endeared him to his squadron mates. He was a "team Player" and liked to crack jokes and laugh along with the best of them.

They all looked forward to this mission which would be focused on destroying Rail and ground transportation facilities and airfields in France and Belgium.

On this 25th day in May, Jack's fighter squadron was assigned to protect 247 B-17s as they proceeded to attack marshalling yards at Brussels/Schaerbeck Brussels/Midi and Liege/Guillemines.

CHAPTER 7

May 25, 1944- Jack & Murphy Spot Hidden Airfield Near Liege

Once this flight of B-17s were safely on their way back over the English Channel, Jack's flight of P-51s were cleared to conduct ground sweeps on targets of opportunity. All the vehicle traffic on the road was fair game, even horse-drawn carts which could be carrying munitions or supplies.

The Nazis severely restricted civilian road travel which meant that anything out in the open was subject to being targeted. Railway stations, trains, locomotives, bridges, and infrastructure were systematically destroyed in anticipation of the Normandy invasion.

Jack loved this part of the mission and eagerly awaited the signal from his group leader that they could go out and "kick ass", wreaking havoc on the target rich environment of German occupied territory below.

Jack was flying "wing" on group leader, 2nd Lieutenant Bob Murphy's P-51 Mustang as they went in search of targets in the vicinity of Liege-Guillermins. Jack spotted what appeared to be a hidden airfield below. This field was not on any of their intelligence maps.

To keep radio conversation to a minimum, Jack pulled up abreast of "Murph" and signaled to look below. "Murph" obliged by rolling from side to side to get a better look. Once he spotted the target, he gave Jack a "thumbs up" and signaled to follow him.

Murphy rolled hard left with Jack tucked onto his wing and together, they pitched over into a high-speed dive. They descended to tree top level and aimed directly at the airfield. Sure enough, the Mustang duo were unwelcome guests to this small, poorly concealed Luftwaffe airbase. They saw men running towards several German aircraft hidden under camouflage tarps.

In the few seconds Jack had approaching at incredible speed, the hidden aircraft appeared to be several ME-109s and one or two Heinkel bombers. Jack slid right; Murphy slid left as they came in over the airstrip.

Both pilots opened with their six .50 caliber Browning machine guns with devastating effect, tearing into the hidden aircraft, men and equipment.

Murphy pulled up sharp left with Jack following closely on his wing. "Murph" made it clear they were going to circle around for one more high-speed pass. As they passed abeam the airfield, they looked down to their left and could see columns of smoke and fire from the effects of their first pass.

Still a little above tree-top level, they came in with Murphy again on the left, Jack on the right. Jack spotted some men pushing an ME 109 out from under a camouflage tarp and a pilot attempting to climb up on the wing. He quickly sighted in on this group and thought,

"Poor dumb bastards! You should've stayed put."

He opened with short, controlled bursts of his .50 caliber guns on this group, tearing them to shreds.

Just before they completed that second pass, Murphy broke radio silence with a terse, "flak tower your 2 o'clock!"

Murphy turned hard left as Jack turned hard right, heading directly towards the flak tower. He hoped that this would cut off the gunners' angle, making it more difficult to hit him. Jack opened with his .50 calibers just as the Germans opened on him with their 20 mm anti-aircraft guns. He scored direct hits on the gun position, obliterating the men and equipment but not before they scored direct hits on him at the same time.

Damn! These guys were good!

Jack cursed as he took the hits from the anti-aircraft guns, shattering his windshield, tearing into his right wing and fuselage and opening huge holes all around the cockpit. His Mustang shook violently as he zoomed past the now obliterated flak tower. Miraculously, he himself somehow escaped any hits to his body due to the armament protection surrounding his cockpit.

Black oil covered what remained of his windshield. The vibrations increased in intensity, and he realized he was about to lose control of the airplane.

With no time to think or communicate, feeling the controls stiffen up, and with limited control over the bird, Jack fought to maintain control. He was too low to attempt to bail out and had no choice but to look for a place to attempt a landing.

He could not see out of the front of the aircraft due to enormous clouds of black smoke and his shattered windscreen. He stuck his head out the right side of the shattered cockpit into the slipstream and spotted an open field further to his right.

His control stick only had partial movement left and right, restricting the ailerons and providing him with limited turning ability. Instinctively he used pressure on the right rudder pedal which allowed for a skidding right turn in the direction of the field.

Still at tree top level, with the engine coughing and spitting, he knew that he would have to belly it in rather than attempting to lower his landing gear, if they even worked.

Fighting with all his might to keep wings level, he crossed a small stream and aimed for a grass field which contained a border of what appeared to be chest-high grass and a length of recently mowed grass. The mowed grass would make for a safe landing spot if he could just make it. That's about the time his engine started to sputter and surge more frequently, and he knew it would quit soon.

Trading off his airspeed for a bit more distance, close to an aerodynamic stall, Jack attempted to hold off the Mustang just a bit longer trying to make the grassy portion of the field rather than the high grass border.

His engine coughed and quit just as he came over the field. He felt he was too fast, but he didn't have room to bleed off any more air speed as the end of the field and the forest beyond it were rushing up. Gritting his teeth, he allowed the aircraft to touch down on the soft, grassy portion.

The P-51 "pancaked" into the grass, bounced once and then started skidding towards the high grass at the end of the field. Jack braced himself for the impact and held on for dear life as the field went rushing by him and the high grass and trees loomed directly in front of him. He hoped he would stop before he entered the high grass or the row of trees. His last thoughts before entering the high grass

"Crap! Not going to happen"

CHAPTER 8

May 25, 1944, Crash Landing in a Grassy Field

Still skidding and sliding on its belly, Jack was feeling pretty good about getting the aircraft safely on the ground, tall grass or not. Just when he thought he "had it made", the notorious air intake shaped like a large scoop on the belly dug into the earth causing the aircraft to flip upside down.

Inverted, the Mustang's tail slammed violently into the ground then came to a complete stop. Hanging upside down, his face covered in shattered plexiglass and debris, Jack found and released his shoulder restraints and slid onto the ground. He crawled on his belly out from under the aircraft and knew he needed to get far away from the aircraft just as it caught fire.

He removed his goggles, tore off his helmet and struggled to his feet. He immediately felt dizzy and disoriented. His nose felt like it was broken from the sudden impact, and his eyes were now clouding up with blood from numerous cuts on his forehead. He staggered a few feet and looked back at the Mustang. The aircraft was now completely engulfed in flames with thick, black smoke pouring into the air.

Better get far away from here before….

He took a few more wobbling steps before being knocked to the ground as the burning P-51 erupted in a loud explosion. For Jack, everything went black.

MURPHY'S HIGHSPEED PASS

Jack's "lead", 2nd Lieutenant Bob Murphy looked intently over his left shoulder as he completed his hard climbing turn to the left. He was just in time to see that Dodds obliterated the flak tower, but not before his Mustang took some massive hits from the German gunners.

He winced as he saw black smoke and pieces of Dodds' aircraft flying off in reaction to the direct hits. Dodds' Mustang started to oscillate indicating possible control loss or that, *God forbid,* Dodds was seriously or mortally wounded.

C'mon Jack! He shouted out loud into his cockpit, *get control fast or get that bird on the ground!*

Just then, Murphy saw several tracer bullets fly past his own cockpit and realized that he was taking German machine gun fire. His experienced eye spotted the German gunners' position as he rolled his Mustang almost vertically to his left.

Back down at tree-top level he came in for a third high-speed pass, opened on the German Machine gun position, exhausting the remaining ammunition of his .50 caliber guns while sending the Germans and their guns into oblivion.

Satisfied that he had taken care of the threat, he continued to his left in a highspeed climbing turn, gaining some altitude while trying to find what had become of Jack Dodds. Shaking his head and cursing out loud, he spotted a fireball in a nearby field and knew that it had to be Dodd's P-51.

Murphy made a mental note, locating the approximate position of the crash site in a field in the Ardennes Forest and continued his climb, chasing after elements of his squadron returning to their home base in England.

Later that day, in Murphy's "after action report" 2nd Lieutenant John Dodds would be classified as MIA, "Missing in Action". His family would be notified by the War Department. Murphy himself presumed that Dodds was most likely killed in action.

CHAPTER 9

May 25, 1944, Coming to in the Grassy Field

Jack awakened to find himself sprawled under a clump of bushes in the high grass bordering the field. The air was full of the acrid smell of what was left of the burning P-51. He heard numerous voices speaking in German and, instinctively, he knew to keep quiet and remain motionless.

It might take these guys a while to realize there's no dead body in the aircraft.

He felt like throwing up and did everything in his power to avoid retching as it would reveal his whereabouts to the Germans. He took deep breaths, in through his mouth and out through his broken nose which helped overcome the nausea. After a few deep breaths, he mercifully slipped back into darkness.

Jack was not sure how long he had been out this time. He heard voices coming a lot closer to his position in the deep grass. Only this time, the voices were not speaking in German but what sounded like French or Dutch, he couldn't be sure.

"Hier!"

A large man who appeared to be in his late twenties or early thirties and a young teenage girl moved to Jack's side. The man spoke in accented English:

"Hallo, stay quiet. Don't move. You are safe. We want to check your injuries out."

Jack tried to speak but his throat was dry, and his jaw hurt like hell. The man smiled and shushed him,

"No, no it is okay. My name is Lucien, and you are safe. Just be quiet."

He signaled to the girl who produced a canteen of water.

Lucien handed the canteen to Jack, allowing him to drink but retained a strong grip on it.

"Okay, good! Drink some now but just a little until we check you out. Okay?"

Jack nodded but as soon as the cool water hit his mouth, he was ravenously thirsty and would have finished the entire canteen had Lucien not pulled it back out of his grasp.

"Okay, my friend, I know you're thirsty, but just a little for now. Can you sit up?"

Jack nodded and slowly sat up. He immediately felt dizzy, and Lucien helped him back down onto his back. He turned to the young girl and whispered some quick instructions to her. Then he turned back to Jack.

"It's all okay. I think from your uniform and your airplane that you're an American. We will get to know more about you soon, but first we've got to get you to a safe place, okay?"

Jack nodded his head in understanding. Lucien continued, "You're going to be fine. We just need to get some help to get you out of here before the Germans come back. It will be dark soon and then we can get you moving. What do they call you?"

Jack's voice sounded strange and foreign to him, like he had swallowed sandpaper, "Dodds, John Dodds, 2nd lieutenant US Army Air corps."

"Okay, Dodds, again my name is Lucien. I am here to help you."

Jack coughed, "Thank you, Lucien! My friends call me Jack."

"Okay Lieutenant Jack, you are with friends now."

Jack smiled and slipped back into the darkness as the rain increased in intensity.

CHAPTER 10

Lucien Evacuates Jack- 1800 Hours (6:00 Pm) Site of the P-51 Crash Landing

The rain was coming down intermittently as Lucien and Jan, his 14-year-old nephew, moved quickly and silently through the tall grass bordering the field and rejoined his niece. 13-year-old Elise covered in a dark black hooded rain gear had remained with the American airman.

Elise had been doing her best to shelter him with a waterproof cloth while all the while quietly administering small sips of water to Jack who was now sitting up and awake. Both Jack and Elise were soaked to the skin.

Placing his finger over his lips to indicate silence, Lucien gave Jack a quick going over. Then he smiled and whispered in a barely audible voice,

"Okay, Lieutenant Jack. We must be very quiet. The Germans have not yet posted a guard by your aircraft because they are busy dealing with all the damage you and your pilots did to their airfield."

At mentioning the airfield, Lucien gave a low chuckle, and affectionately placed his hand on Jack's shoulder.

"You pilots did a good job! *Les Bosches* thought they had hidden their airfield pretty good until you boys came down and sent a lot of them to hell. Goodbye Krauts, huh?"

Still smiling, but seeing no reaction from Jack who was shivering, he continued,

"Okay, now we will move you, but you must be quiet. Okay?"

He looked at Jack to make sure he understood. Satisfied by Jack's nodding head, he continued, "But they will come back soon, very soon to look for your body now that the fire is just about out, and the wreckage is cooling. They will try to identify your remains and will report your identification details to their headquarters. Understand?"

Jack nodded and Lucien continued, "Once they discover that there is no body, they will know that you have survived, and they will start searching for you. Understand?"

Jack nodded and attempted to talk but only a hoarse grunt came out of his parched throat. Lucien took this as a "*Yes.*"

"Okay, Lieutenant. We must take you to a safe place. Let's see if you can stand up without making any noise?"

Another nod and Jack attempted to stand. The two teenagers attempted to help him but quickly let go of him as he became nauseous. It felt like every bone in Jack's body was broken and coming apart. There was a searing pain in his right calf.

He immediately became dizzy and despite best efforts, vomited loudly several times before sinking back down to his knees, pitching forward onto his hands and now on all fours, he shook his head angrily.

Lucien quickly peeked out from behind the tall grass and was relieved that there was no one near them who would have heard the noise. He produced a clean handkerchief and wiped Jack's face, patting him on his back.

"Sorry! I am so sorry!" Jack croaked.

"No, Lieutenant Jack, it is okay. I expected even more of a reaction from you. You have been through a lot, but now we are moving. Okay?"

Jack nodded again and with the two young helpers on either side of him they stood him up on his feet. The pain and nausea became somewhat manageable as Jack took slow faltering steps and slow, deep breaths.

Lucien moved them through the tall grass into the nearby wooded area. There they were joined by two rough looking men who were armed with submachine guns.

It occurred to Jack that throughout the heavy downpour these men had been quietly standing guard over them, obviously prepared to intervene if anyone showed up at the wrong time. They slung their weapons over their shoulders and immediately took over supporting him much to the relief of the younger, smaller teenagers.

As the rain increased in intensity, the small group assisted Jack through the wooded area and emerged into a clearing bordered by a small stream. They waded through a shallow portion of the stream and led Jack up to a horse-drawn cart tended by another man. The cart had a large canvas top protecting whatever cargo it might be hauling.

The two men on either side of Jack easily and carefully hoisted him into the back of the cart and gestured for him to move towards the front of the cart and sit. Moving with surprising ease and grace, Lucien leapt into the cart followed by the two teenagers.

Jack was shivering from the damp and cold and starting to feel nauseous again. Lucien produced a thick woolen horse blanket and placed it around Jack's shoulders. He retrieved a military-style canteen and allowed Jack a few sips. The cold water from the canteen seemed to help reduce his nausea as Lucien leaned over to whisper into Jack's ear,

"We don't want to give you too much water, Lieutenant Jack until we get you checked over for internal injuries. It won't be long now. We are almost at curfew and will need to stop soon."

Jack nodded his understanding, turned away from Lucien and dry-heaved until he thought his ribs would break. With that, exhaustion and the gentle rocking of the horse-drawn cart, he slipped into a deep sleep.

CHAPTER 11

18:30 Hours (6:30 Pm) May 25, 1944, Jack arrives at a Safe House

The rain continued to come down in sheets, pounding on the soft canvas covering the cart. Jack awakened when they slowed to a mere crawl preparing to come to a stop. The horse gave out a low snort signaling that they had arrived. The men and the teenagers got out, and Lucien carefully assisted Jack towards the tailgate.

Once at the tailgate, the men quietly grabbed him under each arm and gently set him down on his feet as if he weighed nothing.

Jack saw that they were in front of a small stone farmhouse, typical of many on the Belgian countryside. Two young women who appeared to be in their twenties stood by the open front door which revealed a relatively dark interior save for a soft glow emanating from simmering coals in a central fireplace.

They all moved silently inside the farmhouse and the door was shut behind them. One of the women seemed to be in charge, quietly giving directions to the group. Once inside, several oil lamps were lit casting a warm glow over the rustic interior.

Shivering and still draped in the woolen horse blanket, Jack was led to a wooden armchair positioned in front of the fireplace. He felt numb and "washed out" as he was attended to by the two women.

Without addressing Jack directly, they removed the woolen blanket and carefully pulled his flight jacket over his head, unbuttoning his uniform shirt. The woman leader carefully removed his military "dog-tags" and made some notations on a notepad.

Jack started to come out of his "funk" and wanted to object, but she smiled and shook her head, reading from the dog-tags and softly said in perfect English,

"Sorry, John Dodds, DOB 07-20-1922. We will keep these for a while. You will be getting a new name and identification soon. It will not do for any of us, you especially for the Nazis to gain these dog-tags. Just relax for now. Okay?"

Jack nodded slowly as her meaning dawned on him.

Lucien stoked the fire and Jack started to feel much better as the heat from the fireplace increased.

Meanwhile, the men who had accompanied the group moved into a small adjacent kitchen area. They added charcoal to a cast iron stove and held their hands over it as the heat intensified.

They removed their rain-soaked coats and sat around a rough wooden table talking amongst themselves in low whispers. Elise, the teenager, had shed her rain-soaked cloak, and went into the kitchen.

She opened a canvas bag and produced some coarse black bread, some cheese and other food items and began to prepare hot water.

At the sight of the cheese and bread, Jack's stomach growled. He was no longer nauseous and suddenly realized that he was hungry, very hungry.

The woman who had made the notations about his military dog-tags quietly conferred with Lucien then turned to Jack and spoke,

"It's going to be okay, Lieutenant Dodds. We are so glad that you survived the crash of your airplane. I am Janine, Lucien is my brother and our sister in the kitchen is Denise. You've already met Denise's son, Jan and her daughter, Elise, my nephew and niece."

Jack nodded and tried to smile,

"Thank you, I am glad to meet all of you. Your entire family it seems."

Janine, still very serious, looked him directly in his eyes and continued,

"Where are you from, Lieutenant Dodds?"

"Uh, I'm from America, the United States of America."

"Yes, of course. But, where in America are you from? Where were you born?"

It dawned on Jack that these were not just questions of curiosity but an interrogation by a very attractive young woman.

"Oh! I'm from the western part of North Carolina in the mountains."

Janine nodded, making some notes on her pad and continued,

"Ah, that's interesting. The mountains. What city in the mountains of North Carolina? Or is that South Carolina?"

"It's Boone as the nearest town, but just outside of Boone in a place called Deep Gap. And it's North not South Carolina."

"Sorry, but these questions are necessary. What is your mother's first name and her maiden name?"

"Anna and her maiden name is Feldman."

At that, Janine looked up from her pad,

"Feldman? So, you're Jewish?"

"Jewish? No, I'm Roman Catholic."

"But Feldman is definitely a Jewish name. and under the Jewish tradition, the children take the mother's religion. This will also be the position of the Germans if you are ever captured."

Shocked, Jack responded,

"Look, all I know is that my family raised me Catholic, and my mother always seemed to be the one to insist we go to Church, so I don't know what you're getting at."

"Okay Lieutenant. say that God forbid, if you are ever in the hands of these Nazi bastards and they ask you for your mother's maiden name just make up one that is Christian. No offense."

"None taken. I understand. I guess I'll tell them Murphy"

Jack laughed to himself as he thought that he and his Wingman would be considered brothers with that change of his mom's maiden name.

"Okay. Just one or two more questions. What is the name of your current commanding officer, and how many aircraft in your squadron?"

Janine was attempting to prompt this American to respond according to the Geneva Convention and she finally succeeded.

Exasperated, Jack folded his arms across his chest and responded with his name, rank and serial number. This brought a smile to Janine's face as she made some notes on her pad.

She turned to the men in the kitchen and spoke to them in French. They nodded their heads, drained their coffee cups, put on their raincoats and headed out the back door of the cabin into the rain-soaked night.

Jack watched their departure and then turned a questioning eye towards Janine,

"What was this test all about? Your brother found me near my crashed and burning airplane, pretty obvious that that was where I came from. I assume these guys were here to make sure I passed the test, right?"

"Yes, Lieutenant, you passed the test. We cannot be too careful these days."

Janine made some more notations on her pad then continued,

"Yes, they are Marcelino and Gerard, good friends and very strong members of the Resistance who support those of us trying to assist our allies. If you had turned out to be, in my opinion, a Nazi impersonator, of whom we've had more than a few, it would not have ended very well for you to be sure."

Looking directly at Jack to be sure he understood, she went on,

"We have lost many wonderful people recently to traitors. Some of these traitors are collaborators, much to our disgust and some double agents posing as Allied airmen."

She paused to see if Jack was following her,

"The Nazis have placed English speaking agents in Allied uniforms taken from dead or captured airmen. These impersonators study the dog-tags and other information of captured or dead airmen and then present themselves to us seeking 'help' and many of our people have fallen for this betrayal."

"That is awful! How terrible!"

Janine nodded and then changed the subject abruptly,

"Lieutenant, I have some medical experience as a student surgical nurse in training before the Nazis invaded Belgum. Since that time, I have helped many of our own people and our allied friends who have suffered injuries during this war."

She said something to her sister, Denise who scurried into the kitchen as Janine continued,

"Sometimes, when a person has suffered a major trauma such as you did, serious injuries are not always so evident. I would like to examine you to make sure you have no serious hidden injuries. I am not a doctor, but as there are no doctors available out here, I am all you have. Is this okay with you?"

At that moment, Elise brought Janine a cup of tea which she handed to Jack, encouraging him to take a small sip. Satisfied when he nodded his understanding, she continued,

"Do you mind if we remove some of your clothing to look at your injuries? If you are shy, my sister and the two teenagers can step outside and join the men out back."

The warm tea did its magic, enabling Jack to reply in an almost normal voice,

"Thank you, very much, that is okay with me. At this point I am so grateful to be with all your company and to have survived. I am not shy, and I understand your concern. And there is no way that I want them to step outside in the cold and rain."

CHAPTER 12

May 25, 1944, Janine examines Jack's Wounds

Janine, assisted by her sister Denise, gently removed Jack's flight suit, stripping him down to his boxer shorts. The shirt, undershirt, socks were all removed and carried away by the teenage girl, Elise.

Janine said something quietly to the girl while pointing to Jack's flight suit pantlegs. Elise nodded her head in understanding.

Elise returned with some medical supplies and placed a bottle containing a clear liquid and some clean, white cloths on a nearby table. She then placed two packets removed from Jack's pantlegs marked "E&E Aids", then withdrew to the nearby kitchen out of sight.

\While Janine prepared to examine Jack, her sister, Denise carefully opened the two packets and placed the contents neatly on an adjacent table.

Janine produced a flashlight and carefully went over Jack's back, arms and legs. She noted several lacerations on his forehead that had been bleeding and used some tweezers to remove small shards of plexiglass imbedded in the skin of his forehead.

Smiling, she commented on the plexiglass,

"Luckily, you must have been wearing googles or you surely would have had some serious injuries to your eyes. You are lucky indeed. Lieutenant."

Next, she noted a flesh wound on his back near the shoulder blades. There was a long 6-inch trough on the surface layer of his skin. She deftly cleansed the wound and was relieved that it didn't appear to have penetrated very deeply.

She was very concerned about a deep laceration on his right calf that looked to her experienced eye to be a bullet penetration wound. The wound was no longer bleeding which indicated no likely arterial involvement. She took some time as she made some detailed notes on her pad.

Lucien had just reentered the kitchen through the back door with the other men and Janine called him over to look at the wound across Jack's shoulder blades and the wound on his right calf. Lucien clucked his tongue and laughed out loud,

"Lieutenant! Janine is right! You are truly a lucky man! There is a nice long path of a bullet or a piece of shrapnel that just barely touches your skin along your back. Another millimeter deeper, and you wouldn't be here with us now, we would have already buried you!"

He laughed and went on,

"The wound to your right leg looks to me like something similar to the wound on your back, made by a bullet or piece of shrapnel Those Bosch tried to kill you and they almost succeeded, the bastards!"

Jack laughed along with Lucien who smiled even wider,

"But you and the other P-51 pilot tore the hell out of that airfield. You not only destroyed most of their airplanes that were on the ground, but you killed a lot of Bosch who were caught out in the open. So, the hell with them and we are glad that we have with us a lucky American."

Jack smiled and nodded in agreement. He thought of his wing leader, Bob Murphy and hoped that "Murph" made it back to England unscathed.

Meanwhile, Lucien explained how close Jack had come with the wound on his back to Marcelino and Gerard who were again quietly sitting in the kitchen. They all smiled but said nothing out loud.

Serious bunch, Jack thought.

Jack figured some fragments of the antiaircraft .20 mm shells may have shredded and penetrated the cockpit armament somehow. Even so, he was grateful for the well-designed P-51 and its protective armor shielding. It was amazing that he hadn't felt a thing up until now.

He thought, "Adrenalin" I guess.

He nodded his agreement of being a "lucky American" and winced as Janine applied some type of anesthetic to his back and leg wound and his forehead.

"Lucien is right, Lieutenant. You are very lucky. Those wounds could have been far more serious. For now, we cannot do anything more than dress them. I have applied alcohol made from spirits to your wounds to help eliminate any infection, but I would much prefer it if we had Sulfa powder."

She swiveled around to look at the content of the two packets removed from Jack's flight suit, then turned back to face him.

"As you may imagine, Sulfa is in very limited supply here in occupied Belgium and is closely watched and regulated by the Nazis. I do have a contact closer to Brussels who may help us but that will have to wait."

Janine continued to look through the packets that were retrieved from Jack's flight suit,

"Unfortunately, some of the contents in your two Escape and Evade packets were damaged in the crash and some are missing. I was hopeful that there might have been aspirin in there, but there wasn't. There is a small roll of adhesive tape which we can use."

Denise handed her a small envelope which contained several front and side pictures of Jack. She smiled at this discovery,

"Excellent! These photographs of you were designed to be used to create false papers. I am hopeful that they will work when our expert gets his hands on them. So that is good news!"

Then, back to business she looked intently at Jack's forehead to make sure there were no remnants of the plexiglass still there before continuing,

"As I said, once we get closer to Brussels, I have a friend who can take a look at your wounds and who might be able to get us some sulfa drugs."

Jack nodded his understanding and asked,

"Was there a small box marked Horlicks Tablets in that packet?"

Janine looked at Denise, who raised her finger and went back to the flight suit. In a moment she returned with a small crushed cardboard container marked "Horlicks tablets"

Jack smiled and said,

"Please give these to whoever might like them. They are chocolate candies which may provide some energy and taste great."

Denise called Elise over and gave her the box. The young girl opened it, her eyes got wide, and she let out a small laugh. She handed one malted milk ball to her mother and then went into the kitchen to share with the others.

Denise cut the little ball in half and offered it both to Jack and Janine, who declined. She then unceremoniously popped both halves in her mouth with a big smile and moved into the kitchen.

Janine meanwhile looked carefully at Jack's nose which was slightly off kilter.

"Okay, Lieutenant, now that we've looked at your flesh wounds, let's talk about your handsome face."

Jack gave her a puzzled look,

"My face?"

Janine looked at Denise and said,

"Spiegel?"

Denise smiled, disappeared for a moment and returned with a small handheld mirror which she held in front of Jack's face. Much to his surprise his nose was not only lacerated but pushed slightly off kilter to the left side of his face.

It looked like he had been in a prize fight, and upon reflection later, Jack thought that indeed he had been, except in a prize fight with something in the cockpit of his P-51.

Janine and Denise both laughed as she continued,

"I can push your nose back into shape if you will let me. I've done it many times even on my brother's ugly face."

Lucien overheard this as he came into the room from the kitchen. He smiled and pointed to his big nose that looked like a typical prize fighter's face.

Janine stifled a laugh and went on,

"It may be a bit painful now, but it will only get worse if we don't do anything about it. Do you want me to try?"

Jack gulped and bravely smiled, "Sure. Why not?"

Janine didn't hesitate. She placed the fingertips of both hands on either side of Jack's nose and, in one swift motion, moved it back into its original alignment.

Jack tried, and failed to suppress a bit of a yelp, but then smiled and nodded his head in approval,

"Well, that was fun."

"You were very brave, Lieutenant. Now I'm going to complete my overall check of your body, okay?"

He nodded and put on his best stoic look as she poked and pressed on his back and ribs and made him move his arms in several directions. She looked over his legs and, other than the deep laceration on his right calf, was satisfied that there were no other visible surface injuries.

As she concluded her examination, Denise came back into the room carrying some clean, warm clothing which she handed to Jack. The two women pointed towards the kitchen indicating that Jack could have a little privacy to put his change of clothes on.

Marcelino and Gerard accompanied Lucien out the back door once again, giving Jack the room. In a few moments, he emerged fully clothed in a clean woolen shirt and heavy woolen slacks.

He slumped wearily into the wooden chair next to the fireplace. Janine smiled as her sister helped her pull a pair of woolen socks onto his feet.

She placed a pair of worn, leather boots in front of him, and again the two women helped him to slip them on. They both smiled when he acknowledged that somehow, they fit perfectly. She then gestured for him to get back up to his feet,

"Okay, Lieutenant, I know you're very tired. We want you to get some rest. First you will want to take care of your bathroom needs. Lucien will escort you to the place just out back. You must be very quiet. Lucien will have a flashlight but will not use it unless necessary. Understand?"

Jack nodded his head somberly, stood up shakily and moved towards the front door. The rain had stopped, and a heavy fog overshadowed the forest. Lucien was just outside and signaled to follow him.

In a few minutes, they returned. Janine smiled, handing him another small tin cup of tea.

"Drink this now, Lieutenant,"

She pointed to a quiet corner where some thick blankets were placed on the floor.

"Try to sleep now. We must be prepared to move in a few hours at dawn. Keep your boots on in case we must move quickly."

Jack nodded and moved towards the makeshift bed, he winced as he inadvertently touched his newly adjusted nose and then spoke earnestly to the group of his rescuers gathered there in the safe house.

"I want to thank all of you. I cannot find the words that say that sufficiently, but please know how grateful I am for your kindness. I also would like to thank whoever donated these clothes and boots to me."

At the mention of the clothes and shoes, Denise's face turned a bright red and she turned away briefly. Jack later learned that the clothes belonged to her husband, Martin Michel who, a year earlier had been arrested, tortured and shot by the Nazis along with other suspected members of the resistance.

Denise regained her composure and pointed towards the blankets,

"We are grateful for all of you who fight for all of us, Lieutenant. Now, get some rest."

"I will, but what about all of you and the others?"

"We will rest when this war is over. Now, sleep!"

Jack didn't remember laying down on those blankets. He didn't even remember slipping into a deep, dark exhausted sleep, nestled in the corner of a little cabin deep in the fog shrouded Belgian forest.

CHAPTER 13

May 26, 1944, Early morning Belgian Forest Safe House- Jack into the Pantry

Dawn found the occupants of the cabin busy packing up, dousing the fire in the fireplace. Jack noticed Denise pulling back the blackout curtain slightly and peering cautiously out the window.

Something's up, he thought.

Denise released the curtain, nodded to Janine who turned towards Jack with a sense of urgency in her voice,

"Lieutenant, to the right of the little kitchen here there is a pantry. Please go to the pantry *right now* and push on the middle shelf. The shelves will swing open and there is a space to hide back there. Be careful not to knock off the cans and jars on the shelves when you close it behind you. You should have enough room to sit on the floor back there. Do not come out until you hear me, or Denise. Do not respond to anyone else. Understand?"

Despite every muscle in his body crying out with pain, Jack got to his feet, moved into the kitchen and found the pantry. Just as he pushed on the middle of the shelves there was a persistent loud knocking on the door.

The shelves did not swing open as Janine had said. He pushed again. Still nothing. The pounding on the front door grew louder as Jack grew increasingly frustrated. *Come on! Open!*

Exasperated, he pushed hard with both hands resulting in two cans falling to the floor. Just then, the whole of the shelving unit swung open and several more cans teetered precariously on the edge of their shelves. He hurriedly pushed them all back into place, stooped over, picked up the two fallen cans and stepped inside the small space.

Carefully pulling the shelving unit behind him, he pressed his back to the rear wall of the closet and slid down onto his butt on the floor.

He heard loud, German voices directed at Janine and her sister but couldn't understand what they were saying. Janine seemed to be calm however and was responding in German in a quiet, calm manner. Then, Jack's blood ran cold when he heard the German words: "*Amerikanischer Pilot!*"

CHAPTER 14

May 26, 1944, Germans at the door,

Inside the pantry, Jack strained to hear what was going on. At first, there was some muted conversation which he understood must be in German. Still, he could sense the tension in Janine's and Denise's voice as a male voice spoke in rapid-fire words with an accusatory tone.

Another male voice interjected itself into the conversation and Janine responded calmly but in sort of a questioning tone. She laughed and engaged her visitor in what seemed to be a light-hearted conversation.

He noted that same German voice muted somewhat as Janine continued to speak interjecting a chuckle or two.

The tension in the room seemed to lessen somewhat as Janine and now Denise could be heard talking and laughing. Jack could have sworn there was a bit of flirtation going on there. Then, Janine changed direction,

"Vielleicht ein kleiner Tee?"

Jack understood that she was offering her visitors a cup of tea. The tone had changed from confrontational to friendly at that point,

"Nein, Danke."

Some more laughter, then the conversation ended, and the front door was closed. In a few moments Janine stood before the pantry.

"Okay Lieutenant, you can come out. Gently push on the middle of the door in front of you and it will swing open."

Jack came out, still holding the two cans he had picked up from the floor.

CHAPTER 15

May 26, 1944- Jack out of the pantry Janine a Leader of Réseau Comète

Jack, still holding the two cans that he had taken inside of the hideaway with him, looked at Janine. "What was that all about, Janine?"

She didn't answer at first but took the two cans from Jack's hands and placed them on the shelf in front of her. Smiling she said, "Ah! I see you like cabbage?"

Jack looked at the two cans marked "*chou*" which he took to mean "cabbage" in French. Janine and Jack laughed and let out a long collective breath of relief. That seemed to lessen the tension. She continued,

"The two Germans who came here are Corporal Karl Schmidt and Corporal Lukas Kohler. We get along with both quite well. We flirt a bit with them, make sure our friend who has a poultry farm and processing warehouse takes care of them with eggs and chickens."

She smiled, "Getting eggs and chickens during these days of severe rationing ingratiates them with their superiors. While they are not really a threat to us right now, they are still German military, and we must be careful."

She looked at Jack to be sure he understood and went on, "As friendly as they may seem to be, we have a saying about these Boche occupiers, 'they are either at your feet or at your throat', so we are always wary of them no matter how friendly they may be at the moment."

She glanced over her shoulder to see Denise nodding her head that the Germans had driven away from the cabin, then she went on, "That being said, we do have to worry about SS-Haupt Sturm Führer, Erik Hoeffner, the Commandant of the airbase you shot up."

That got Jack's attention as Janine continued, "According to Schmidt and Kohler, Commandant Hoefner is outraged that the airbase under his command was shot to pieces by Allied aircraft. He is even more angry that one of the planes, *yours* crashed, the pilot somehow survived and is on the run."

She went on, "The Germans know that this pilot is either hiding out somewhere near the crash site or is being protected by local people. Commandant Hoeffner is holding all his people responsible to find you."

At that point, the rear door of the cabin opened, and Lucien came in, his eyes full of concern. He came over quickly to Janine and looked at her expectantly.

Janine smiled reassuringly and spoke in English for Jack's benefit, "It's all okay, Lucien. You know those two corporals are harmless. They are just going to the homes around here looking for some American pilot."

She put her hand on Jack's shoulder with a big smile, "I wished them luck and assured them if I ever saw him, I would let them know immediately so that they could be in the favor of SS-Haupt Sturm Führer, Erik Hoeffner."

Lucien snorted, "I will one day kill that Kraut with my bare hands after what he's done to so many of our friends."

"I know, Lucien! There will be a time and place for all the Boche, but for now we must be careful. I have worked hard to establish a friendly relationship with those two, stupid corporals."

Lucien sighed and nodded as Janine addressed Jack, "Since the German occupation, I continue to serve as a rural nurse with the local infirmary, treating German military and staff who are in need. I also am called upon to help with dialect translations for the local people, as I speak German, Dutch, French and English. They think that I am a Nazi sympathizer, so this commanding officer tolerates me."

Jack spoke up, "Doesn't being considered a sympathizer put you in danger with the locals and with the Resistance?"

"Yes, normally that would be so, collaborators are hated and one day they will pay the price, but you see, Lucien and the men who you have met *are the resistance*! They know how important that cover is for us, they know what I am doing and why I am doing it."

Lucien nodded his head in agreement then turned towards Jack,

"Lieutenant, we have lost so many dedicated people who are devoted to defeating the Nazis and for hiding Allied airmen. Many of them have been betrayed by traitors and collaborators and Nazi spies. So many of them have been tortured, sent to concentration camps or executed on the spot by the Gestapo."

Lucien continued with a serious look on his face, "Most of the effort up to now comes from the group known as the Réseau Comète or Comet Line as it is known in English. As one leader of the group is captured or killed, another steps forward to take on the job even though it may mean a terrible fate awaits him or her."

He paused for a moment, fixing his eyes on Janine and continued, "Many of these leaders and their "helpers" are women, young women."

Jack's eyes grew a little bigger as he realized where Lucien was going. Lucien turned towards his sister with a grim, tight-lipped smile on his face,

"Lieutenant Jack, meet the one who has taken over as a leader of Réseau Comète."

CHAPTER 16

May 26, 1944, Janine-Jack-Lucien taking stock

Janine seemed a bit embarrassed and waved her brother off, turning towards Jack,

"Yes, it is true that I, along with other "helpers" have been doing our best to keep Allied airmen from falling into German hands. We have lost so many brave women and men. I was very close to my friends the founders of Comet Line, "Dedée" who is Andree de Jongh and her father, Frederic de Jongh, both fallen to the Nazis by way of a traitor. But when one falls, we others step forward. It is what we do, Jack."

Jack was at a loss for words, so he just nodded his head and remained silent.

Lucien smiled, put his hand on Jack's shoulder, kissed his sister on the forehead and went back out through the kitchen door.

Janine watched Lucien disappear out the back door then turned to Jack,

"Okay Lieutenant, Lucien and another friend will be evaluating a British airman to see if he's legitimate. If he checks out okay, then we will figure out the best time to move you both from here to a safe place closer to Brussels or Paris. We were thinking about this evening, but now tomorrow at the earliest."

"Janine, I do not want to continue to endanger you and your family. Eventually the Nazis will come back here and before they do, I should move on."

Janine smiled, "Move on? My dear Lieutenant where will you *move on to?"*

Jack shrugged, "I'm serious, Janine. You are all at great risk hiding me. I do not want to put you all in any additional danger."

"That's very thoughtful and kind of you, Lieutenant. But it's a bit late to worry about that. We are all in danger each day that these bastards are in our country. Yes, you will move on, and we will be assisting you in moving on."

She paused to make sure he was following her, then continued, "The Comet Line was very successful in using the rail system in moving downed allied airmen through occupied territories, particularly Belgium and France. Then with the help of Basque guides who escorted us over the Pyrenees into Spain. From there we "Helpers" would get them on to Gibraltar where they could be repatriated back to England. You must have known of this, yes?"

Jack nodded, "Yes, of course I've heard of it. We were given "Escape and Evasion E & E" training. We were aware of Resistance groups that might offer us safe houses, and safe escorts. I was certain, based on your tremendous care and help that you and your family are involved somehow."

Janine smiled, "Yes, it is true. But you know that the Allied bombings, ground attacks, strafing attacks such as you just participated in have intensified throughout the occupied territories of France, Belgium and Holland. We all are sure that this is in anticipation of a coming invasion, but it also means that our primary means of exfiltration, namely the rail system and overland travel through the Pyrenees into Spain and on to Gibraltar is no longer safe."

This got Jack's attention, "So where does that leave us? I can see now that travel through France down south into Spain must be extremely difficult and dangerous."

"Not only difficult, Lieutenant, not only dangerous, but impossible."

"Yes, of course, I can see that. So, what is the plan then?"

"We are working with our intelligence Allies in England on a new plan that will provide safe shelter to you and your fellow airmen."

"A new plan?"

"Yes. It is certain that the Allies will be launching a large-scale invasion of occupied France and territories. We don't know exactly where or when this will occur, but the thinking now is to find a safe haven for allied airmen like yourself until they can be liberated by the Allied armies."

"What do you mean by a 'Safe Haven?'"

"All I've been told is that more information will be coming soon. In the meantime, we must prepare some identity papers for you and find you another safe house. Most likely this will happen in the next few days. We will know more soon."

"Okay, understood. You mentioned another airman, but you seem to have doubts about his legitimacy? What's the reason for that?"

Janine nodded, "All I can tell you right now is that this individual does not claim to be an Allied airman. We are not sure who he is and so Lucien and his friends are going to carefully check him out. We think he's British but, again as I told you before we must exercise extreme caution."

Jack nodded his understanding.

Janine shrugged her shoulders and moved on to another topic: "Lieutenant, I am concerned that your two open wounds may become infected without the Sulfa drugs. So, I would like you to bathe which will help clean any wounds and help your recovery. Denise is preparing some warm water and soap in the kitchen as we speak.

She looked over at Denise, who nodded and pointed to the heated large basin of water which she had set on the kitchen table. Janine smiled and said,

"We will put a blanket over the doorway into the kitchen to give you some privacy. After you've bathed, I suggest you try to get some rest. Any questions?"

Jack gave a slightly twisted smile

"Yes, what happens if I'm in the middle of the bath and there's another pounding on the door?"

Janine smiled, "Then the Bosch will have an excellent view of the backside of a naked American running into the woods."

CHAPTER 17

4th Day at the Safe House Belgian Forest May 1944

Just before dawn, Jack stirred awake, still nestled under thick blankets on the floor in the corner of the cabin. He felt slightly feverish. His right calf was throbbing and felt sore. He knew that this was not a good sign and most likely meant that an infection was setting in.

He became aware that Lucien stood next to him with a cup of black ersatz coffee,

"Good morning, Lieutenant. Time to get up. We've got things to do."

Jack had been hiding in the cabin for the past four days awaiting further word as to the Comet Line's plans for his escape. The women were nowhere to be seen. Instead, Lucien was accompanied by his young nephew, Jan and his two men, Marcelino, and Gerard.

He noticed a strong, familiar odor coming from the opposite side of the room. He accepted the coffee cup and sat up, looking around the room.

In addition to Marcelino, Gerard and Jan, there was another man sitting quietly in the corner opposite the fireplace. He appeared quite a bit older than the rest of the men. He smiled and looked directly at Jack.

He stood up when Jack looked in his direction and gave him a wave which Jack returned. This man seemed to be the source of the odor.

Lucien smiled and introduced him, "This is Emil, he is here to escort you to a new safe house."

Nodding towards this stranger, Jack put his coffee down and turned to Lucien, "Thanks for the coffee, Lucien. What's going on?"

"Something's happened that makes us want to move you out of here sooner rather than later. Our leadership are meeting with other advisors to discuss the best way to protect you and your Allied airmen colleagues."

Lucien looked intently at Jack who nodded that he understood, "One thing is for certain, however. We no longer can go through the Pyrenees into Spain and then to Gibraltar. We primarily used the rail lines to escort our airmen to the Spanish border. That option is no longer available to us, I'm sure you know why.

Jack did indeed. The Allied bombers and fighters were tearing up the rails, marshalling yards, bridges and infrastructure in France, Belgium and southern portions of Holland. In fact, he himself had taken great joy in shooting up airfields, numerous locomotives and railway infrastructure.

At this point in the conversation, Emil spoke up, "I'm afraid that we must get a move on, Lucien. The sooner the better."

Jack looked between the two men, "Okay I understand, but what about the increased surveillance by the Germans that Janine talked about?"

Lucien looked first to Emil then to Jack, "Well to answer your first question, yes, there most likely will be increased security checks and searches. Nevertheless, we must take the chance because we think there will be another visit here by the Germans and this time it won't be by the two Kraut idiots who are easily manipulated by my cute sisters."

"Okay, makes sense. Where are your two 'cute' sisters?"

"They are taking care of some very important business for you and your brother airmen who will be entrusted to our care."

Just then, outside of the cabin, there was the distinct call of a very loud rooster which startled Jack and made the others laugh.

Jack stood up, went over to the front window, pulling the blackout curtain aside. Parked directly in front of the cabin was a large, black cargo truck.

The business name emblazoned on the side of the truck in large, gold lettering stated, "Emil Delacroix, Kippen" which Jack assumed meant *chickens* especially since there was an image of a large chicken painted on the side of the truck.

Jack noticed that the sides of the truck had several screened windows which revealed hundreds of screaming, clucking white chickens absolutely crammed inside.

"Whose truck is this outside?' he inquired.

Lucien pointed to Emil.

"This belongs to Emil. He is one of us. Emil is a well-known poultry farmer who is licensed by the German authorities to supply their commissaries with poultry. This gives him quite a bit of safety in moving about the area. Emil is going to drive you to his place until we can get you into another safe house."

"Okay. I understand. But I'm wondering what happens if we get stopped by the police or Gestapo on the way. I still don't have any identification papers."

Lucien led Jack out the front door and up to the chicken truck as he continued, "Well, we know it's a risk. But past experience has shown us that neither the police nor Gestapo seem too interested in opening a truck filled with over five hundred smelly, noisy chickens. And, my American friend, since you will be inside the cargo area, they will not look in there other than from the outside."

Lucien smiled, "And of course once you receive some proper clothes you might not smell so bad."

At that, Jack suddenly realized what Lucien was implying, "Wait! What? I'm getting into the *back of the truck* with all those chickens? Janine just last night insisted I bathe and get cleaned up. Why the change?"

Lucien turned very serious, "I'm sorry, Lieutenant Jack. But there have been some major arrests over the past few days that have just now come to our attention. It seems that there is another traitor somewhere in the Comet Line and we are not taking any chances."

Emil chimed in, "Okay, Lieutenant, time to get in with the chickens."

He handed Jack a facecloth dipped in oil of camphor. "This will help you a bit with the smell."

Jan, Lucien's nephew, was standing by a door on the side of the cargo van and opened it to allow Jack to climb in. The air within the truck was thick with the odor of chicken feces and urine and the smell was overpowering.

On top of all that, the noise from the chickens was deafening, causing Lucien and Jack to have to shout over the din. Jack held the rag to his nose and tried not to gag.

He was somewhat relieved to see that there was a space protected by a wire mesh barrier which prevented the chickens from entering and climbing over their human occupant. He noticed a small pile of burlap bags that he could presumably sit upon.

Lucien looked in, his own rag over his face and pointed to a latch on a screened doorway on the barrier that divided the cargo space and prevented the chickens from intruding on his space.

His eyes watering from the atmosphere within the van he shouted, "Okay, Lieutenant. If Emil is stopped by the police or the Gestapo, he will pound three times on the back of his cab. You should hear his alert, or at least, feel the vibration of his fist pounding the cabin. With me so far?"

"Yes, of course."

Lucien continued shouting, "Good, to keep appearances of a normal day, Emil tells me he will make at least two stops to deliver chickens and eggs so don't be confused by those stops. If it's a routine delivery stop, Emil will only pound one time on the back of his cab, if it's an inspection, then three hard pounds on the cab. Okay?"

"Yes."

"Good. Now if you do get stopped for an inspection and hear or feel the three pounds on the cab, meaning some Krauts want to inspect the cargo, then you must loosen the latch over here and allow the chickens to come in and block the side access door. You will have time to cover your body with those empty burlap bags next to you, then move to your right and put your nose to that little opening to the outside. Understand?"

Jack looked across his space and spotted a very small, screened porthole which would allow fresh outside air to come in. He nodded as Lucien continued,

"It is nasty but necessary. We've used this method before and had no problems. This outside access door will have a padlock, and Emil will take his time unlocking it if the authorities demand it. This will give you time to release the chickens and cover yourself up. Understand?

Again, Jack nodded "Okay Lucien. You mentioned that you've done this 'chicken thing' before?"

"Yes. With an Australian RAF navigator."

"Okay and so that worked out all right I assume?"

With a straight face Lucien nodded, "We think so."

"You think so? What do you mean?"

Again, with a straight face, Lucien explained, "Well before the ride into town, this Aussie was very talkative and bragged a lot about how great Australia was, so much better than his British brothers or his American cousins. He never shut up."

"And after the ride?"

"We are not sure, but after the ride all he did was make clucking sounds and run around Emil's chicken yard chasing the rooster. We think he was confused."

Silence. Then with a loud roar, Lucien burst into laughter and pointed towards the side entrance indicating for Jack to climb in.

Grumbling and shaking his head, Jack limped over to the side door, climbed in, pressed the rag to his face, gagged a couple of times and scooted his butt over to the far side of the compartment.

Still shaking his head, he managed to tear off two little strips of cloth from the camphor-soaked rag and stuff them into each ear which helped with the cackling and crowing.

As Emil drove away, Lucien made a mental note to check on the American's right leg as soon as possible. He and the others watched the truck go down the dirt road and turn out of sight. He sighed, shrugged his shoulders and said in English,

"Our American friend is on the move. Our very smelly American friend."

They all had a good laugh. Then Lucien, with a serious look said, "Go with God, Yank." They all returned to the cabin, went through and removed everything that might prove to be incriminating. In a few short minutes they too departed the cabin nestled in the Belgian woods.

CHAPTER 18

MI-9 Safe House Paris 30 May 1944 Janine & Denise meet with MI-9

It was becoming apparent to many in the Comet Line that exfiltration through the southern border of France over the Pyrenees was becoming extremely dangerous and close to impossible. This was, in large part, due to the increased bombing and destruction of the railway system by Allied forces in anticipation of the upcoming European Invasion.

Janine, and Denise had been summoned to Paris to meet with MI-9 Agent Albert Ancia and Baron Jean de Blommaert to discuss plans to deal with downed Allied airmen. At the last minute de Blommaert would not be able to join them as he was still in Brussels making alternate arrangements for saving Allied airmen.

They were also planning to meet a Comet "Helper" code-named "Enri Dumont." Dumont had been recommended to them by associate, Pierre Boulain, who had helped with the exfiltration of allied airmen and had earned the trust of Jean de Blommaert.

Both young women were growing concerned by the betrayal and arrest of many of the Comet line helpers. This loss of key members of their organization was certainly due to Nazi double agents who had infiltrated their ranks.

One of the biggest losses occurred in January 1944 when the Gestapo on a tip from a double agent arrested British Intelligence Agent, Jacques Legrelle, code named "Jerome'.

Perhaps the most painful for Janine and Denise was the capture and imprisonment of the principal founder of the *Réseau Comète,* Andrée de Jongh better known as "DeDe". Soon after DeDe's arrest, her own father, Frederic de Jongh also fell prey to Nazi double agents.

No one knew where the Germans were holding DeDe or even if

she was alive. With all of this in mind, Janine and Denise were understandably nervous about a newly hatched plan to meet a new member of the Comet Line.

Pierre Boulain, a trusted "Helper" arranged for the women to meet "Enri" at 14:00 hours (2:00 PM) at Le Perroquet, a well-known café next to the palatial Bayonne city hall. Boulain recommended that they bring other Comet Helpers with them to the café.

Boulain explained that this way they could effectively coordinate and update the changes necessary for future operations with "Enri" and his contacts in Paris. Boulain assured them that the café was a popular gathering place and a larger group would not attract attention.

This did not sit particularly well with either woman who were becoming increasingly cautious about exposing any other members of their organization to arrest and torture by the Gestapo. Janine voiced her concern with Blommaert while they were both in Brussels.

Blommaert understood Janine's concerns and told her to do what she thought was best. He would join them in Paris in a day or two and they could discuss their meeting and its implications at that time.

The Nazis were very effectively closing in on the *Réseau Comète*, and so, relying on her instincts, Janine decided that just she and Denise would come to the first meeting with "Enri."

They did not know what Enri looked like and he, of course, did not know them. Pierre Boulain suggested two ways they could identify each other: Enri would be reading a newspaper, wearing a red necktie with a lavender boutonniere in his lapel, and Janine and her group of helpers should have small lavender-colored ribbons subtly worked into their hair.

Janine instinctively did not like this idea and decided that she and Denise would separate and approach Le Perroquet café from two different directions, looking casual and disinterested, with no lavender ribbons anywhere to be seen.

Thoroughly "put-off" by this whole arrangement, Janine planned to carefully examine the situation at the café and might even cancel the meeting altogether. She made a mental note to discuss this in greater detail with Blommaert or the other MI-9 agent, Albert Ancia when she and Denise met in Paris.

On the day of the rendezvous with Enri, Janine arrived 45 minutes prior to the planned meeting time and found a sidewalk bench one block away from the café at a little corner park. Across from the park at another series of sidewalk benches sat Denise, her head buried in the local paper. From their two different vantage points, they casually observed the goings and comings at the café from afar.

Janine, ever observant, noticed a man on another nearby park bench looking directly at her over his newspaper. The little hairs on the back of her neck stood up as she realized that this was Blommaert, her MI-9 contact!

He was already here in Paris, not in Brussels as expected.

Something was wrong!

Blommaert knew that Janine recognized him and, without acknowledging her, casually got up from his bench and walked away. They understood that this would be a signal to meet at a designated safe house a short distance away.

She looked across to her sister to catch her eye and, to her shock, saw that Denise had left her bench and was intent upon walking past the café, totally unaware that Blommaert was here in Paris attempting to warn them to stay away from the café.

What the hell was Denise doing? Was she trying to protect me in case this was a trap?

Janine was horrified, she saw Denise put something in her hair and although she couldn't see what it was from this distance, she knew it was a lavender ribbon.

Denise was offering herself up to see if this was a trap!

She felt helpless, wanting to scream out a warning, but knew that would surely get them both arrested. She could not bear to lose her sister to the Nazis and was desperate to find a way to warn Denise.

In absolute panic she uttered a silent prayer to Mary, Mother of God, Our Lady of Lourdes for her intervention just as Denise approached the sidewalk entrance into the café.

At the precise moment she made the Sign of the Cross, and just before her sister would turn into the café's entrance, two German military cars pulled up in front of the entrance. Several uniformed German officers jumped out, laughing, jovial and already full of drink.

They immediately spotted this beautiful young woman with the lavender ribbon in her hair and gestured to a table obviously reserved for them. Denise gave them a brilliant smile, politely declined with a subtle shake of her head and pointed to a shop across the street. With that, all smiles, she waved goodbye to them and casually crossed the street and headed towards the shop.

Janine breathed a long sigh of relief and crossed the avenue. She walked by the shop without glancing at the window and went several blocks from the café', pausing in front of another, similar shop. She lit a cigarette, looking disinterested in her surroundings and waited for her sister to join her. When Denise came up to her, she said softly under her breath,

"That was a trap! Blommaert came down from Brussels and was here warning us off. Both Enri and Pierre must be traitors and Gestapo double agents. We must meet Blommaert and Albert Ancia and warn the others."

CHAPTER 19

OPERATION MARATHON-Paris, 30 May 1944 MI-9 safe house

Blommaert opened the door and let Janine and Denise inside. The three hugged each other for what seemed like an eternity. They had come so close to falling into a Gestapo trap.

It was now apparent that Enri Dumont, not his real name, was a double agent as was Pierre Boulain. Had they listened to Boulain and gathered fellow Comet line associates, the Nazis could have rolled up a major part of their organization.

Blommaert by this time contacted Airey Neave, his MI-9 control agent in London, to apprise him of the situation. It confirmed Neave's worst fears that double agents had again infiltrated the Comet line.

Neave learned through his intelligence sources that the man who identified himself as "Pierre Boulain" was a German double agent whose real name was Jacques Desoubrie.

Neave was concerned that as the Allied invasion took place, the Nazis' persecution of the *Réseau Comète* participants would turn even more murderous. This would likely take the form of torture and summary executions. On top of that, those Allied airmen being protected by the Comet Line would become vulnerable to similar atrocities.

In April 1944 Airey Neave conceived a plan to create remote "camps" in forested areas to house Allied airmen until they could be rescued by the allied forces invading France. They called this plan "Operation Marathon" which envisioned several remote zones in France at Chateaudun near Orleans and in the Foret de Freteval in Tours and one other to be in the Belgian Ardennes.

MI-9 chose Daniel Mouton and Thomas Rutland to be inserted into occupied France to set up the operation and security of the camps.

Rutland would run the French camps, and Mouton would take care of the Ardennes camps.

Mouton and Rutland parachuted into occupied territory during the night of April 9, 1944. Experienced agents, they hid themselves in the French countryside that night and then made their way into Paris the next day where they would contact three MI-9 Belgian operators who were setting up the forest camps to hide the Allied airmen until such time as the Allied armies could liberate them.

CHAPTER 20

EMIL'S CHICKEN HOUSE 30 May 1944 13:00 hours (1:00 PM)
Sante-Walburge, Belgium

After several hours of rocking and rolling, Jack felt the chicken truck come to a stop. He wasn't sure if this was going to be another intermittent delivery stop or, could this mean that they were being stopped by the Luftwaffe police or Gestapo?

The chickens kept up their infernal clucking and cackling so that meant that they didn't know either.

In anticipation of a possible security check, Jack placed his hand on the release latch which would allow his chicken buddies to join him in his personal space. There was no pounding on the cab wall, so he hoped for the best.

There was the distinct sound of a padlock being opened. The side cargo door swung open which caused a great deal of excitement among the chickens and their American companion.

Emil's smiling face occupied the open cargo door as he extended a hand to Jack. Emil spoke excellent English with very little accent. "Welcome to Sante-Walburge, Jack! Come! Let's get you out of the truck. You're making the chickens smell very bad." With that, he burst into raucous laughter and helped Jack unfold himself and step onto a cement floor.

Jack stood on shaky legs and removed the pieces of cloth from his ears and two smaller pieces he had inserted into his nostrils.

This got another laugh from Emil. "Ah! Very clever, my American friend! I will have to recommend that to my next passengers."

Jack smiled as he checked out his surroundings. Emil proudly told him that this two-story commercial building was built after World War I and was constructed of industrial grade cement. It occupied an entire city block.

It housed a warehouse, a large commercial kitchen and a hen brooding facility which also enabled the gathering of eggs for distribution. There were two locker rooms one for men and one for women during the busy chicken harvesting times complete with full showers for both.

Emil explained that his normal workforce was reduced almost to zero due to Nazis grabbing citizens and impressing them into forced labor camps. His current workforce consisted of himself, his wife, Miep, their twenty-two-year-old niece, Ellen and his 14-year-old nephew, Jan.

When there was a major project, usually ordered by the German occupiers, he could rely on the nearby Catholic Church for some volunteers who he paid with generous portions of chickens, eggs and byproducts.

The front of the building hosted a reception desk and business offices. There was a complete living space on the top floor with multiple guest rooms that he and his family lived in.

Jack arched his back and stretched several times. Emil motioned for him to follow him towards a door marked "Studio". He observed the American airman's slow, limping gait as he followed Emil's lead.

As they approached the door, Jack was happily surprised to be greeted by Jan, Lucien's nephew. He smiled and handed Jack a paper bag filled with toiletries and a change of clothing. He gestured for Jack to follow him into the hallway and then pointed to a washroom with a large, walk-in shower,

"Welcome, Jack! Please take some time to shower and use this soap," handing him a bar of scented soap. "This soap is very valuable, and my mother asks that you accept it as a gift from my family."

Jack smiled and accepted the soap from Jan, he was humbled as he immediately understood how valuable the soap was during the severe rationing in occupied Europe, "I thank you and your family for this gift, Jan. I will certainly use it, but afterwards there should be plenty left, and I will return it to your care if that's, okay?"

Jan smiled in return and nodded, "I will keep it safe. Please use the soap as much as possible to help with the chicken smell."

They both laughed as Jan continued, "Kindly remove the clothing you are wearing and leave it outside of the door. We will clean the clothing, and you will get it back for future use."

“Yes, of course, thank you, Jan! Where is everyone else?”

“Some of them will be here later in the day. My sister, Elise has been sent to a remote farm in the Ardennes to help our Grandparents.

Jack smiled, took the clothing and the toiletries and entered the washroom. After he stripped down, he placed the old clothing as indicated just outside the washroom door.

Overjoyed to find that there was actual hot water available, he stood under the stream for several long minutes before soaping himself repeatedly and then rinsing off.

He found a razor in with the toiletries, shaved, toweled off and got dressed. Despite lingering light-headedness and slight fever, he felt so much better. He emerged from the washroom and found Emil standing in the hallway.

“Ah! Excellent, Jack. I too have just showered and got rid of some of the chicken smell as I do each day. Come with me upstairs into the living quarters. We have a lot to do and a lot to discuss.”

CHAPTER 21

MI-9 Goes after Traitors Paris 30 May 1944 MI-9 Safe House.

MI-9 agents Albert Ancia and Baron Jean de Blommaert pleaded with Janine and Denise not to return to Brussels until they could deal with the two double agents, Enri Dumont and Pierre Boulain.

The enormity of Boulain's deception was starting to dawn on the MI-9 British Intelligence operatives. Additional sources revealed that, in addition to his real name, Jacques Desoubrie, he had many aliases including Jean Masson.

No amount of pleading, threats or logic seemed to work on these two young women. They had a sense of loyalty to their team and to the downed airmen and felt that they could avoid the Gestapo's traps now that they knew who they were dealing with.

These brave, dedicated women typified so many of Réseau Comète colleagues, many of whom had been captured, imprisoned, tortured and summarily executed at the hands of ruthless Nazi persecutors.

Ancia relayed a translated coded cable message from MI-9 senior agent, Airey Neave in London, "The Gestapo will kill you if they catch you. You both are too valuable to our mission to let you wander right into their hands back in Brussels. As you know, we have lost too many people to the Nazis already. We don't want to lose you."

Janine discussed the situation with Denise, who was anxious to return to the Ardennes to be with her son and to see her daughter who was safe and helping her grandparents at their family refuge near Bouillon, Belgium.

After much soul-searching, they finally relented and agreed that they would stay the night and evaluate the situation the next day.

Satisfied that the sisters agreed to stay away from Brussels for a little while, at least until the two traitors could be dealt with, Ancia moved them to another nearby safe house secured by British Intelligence.

Once the sisters were safely secured, he and de Blommaert met with newly arrived agents Daniel Mouton and Thomas Rutland to discuss how to deal with Enri Dumont and Pierre Boulain.

Mouton in particular was flabbergasted that Boulain was a double agent. He had worked previously with the man and together they exfiltrated several Allied airmen. Nevertheless, the evidence was now irrefutable, the Comet line had suffered greatly at the hands of Nazi double-agents and the two traitors needed to be eliminated.

Mouton, a former Belgian army commando, called in his contacts with the Resistance, the FFI, French Forces of the Interior. These were hardened, deadly men and women who were trained and capable of eliminating enemies. They immediately began the search for Enri Dumont and Pierre Boulain.

Boulain's story took a bizarre twist: FFI operatives captured a man they believed was Pierre Boulain, also known as Jacques Desoubrie. After intense interrogation, including physical abuse, the man confessed and was subsequently eliminated.

Much to everyone's confusion and embarrassment, this man turned out to be someone else, not Pierre Boulain who remained free and extremely dangerous to the *Réseau Comète*.

It wasn't until 1946 that Pierre Boulain aka Jacques Desoubrie was discovered trying to market himself as an Allied supporter. He subsequently was tried as a traitor by the French and executed.

CHAPTER 22

30 May 1944 14:00 hours (2:00 PM) Emil's Chicken House

Emil and Jack, both freshly showered, climbed up an inner stairway leading to an expansive living space on top of Emil's chicken warehouse. They reached the top of the stairs and entered a small, windowless hallway leading to an inner steel door with a serious-looking lockset.

Emil produced a key ring and opened the door leading to another poorly lit hallway. Flipping on several light switches as they entered, Emil smiled at Jack and pointed at a wooden door just to his right.

Jack opened this door which revealed a very cheerful, large sunlit living area. The smell of freshly baked bread, coffee, fried eggs and fried chicken almost overwhelmed him.

It was not lost on him that food in occupied Belgium was strictly controlled by the Nazis and people were suffering and dying of malnutrition.

Lucien greeted Jack with a broad smile and enthusiastic greeting, "Aha! Our new 'chicken man', Lieutenant Jack has finally arrived! We could tell from the smell coming up the stairs that you and Emil were near, but now you are here! Welcome Lieutenant!"

Smiling, Jack looked around the brightly lit living room. He spotted young Jan sitting next to a strikingly beautiful young blonde, blue-eyed woman with a blazing white smile. Jack guessed she was about his same age.

There was also a rough-looking man who had just risen to his feet. Before introductions could be made, a very rotund, cheerful woman with an enormous smile burst into the room from the kitchen area.

She greeted him in thickly accented English, "Welcome! I am Tante Miep, better known as 'Auntie Miep' and you are so welcome! Come, sit over by the table and we will all join you, get to know each other and enjoy some lunch."

Emil, smiling, pointed to a large table just outside the kitchen and indicated that everyone should take a seat. "Yes, let us all eat an afternoon meal."

Everyone approached the table. Jack noticed that the man had produced a makeshift cane and grimaced as he put some weight on his right leg.

Just prior to their taking their seats, Emil made the sign of the Cross, indicating that they would say *Grace.* He then smiled and addressed them all,

"Okay, let us introduce ourselves to each other. Jack, Lucien, Jan, all know each other, but we also have two others who you have not yet met,"

Gesturing first to the blonde woman, "This young Belgian beauty is our niece, Ellen. She had just finished her freshman year of study at Colombia University in New York four years ago and was back home visiting us when the Nazis took over, preventing her from returning to finish her studies."

Ellen blushed, smiled, stood up from the table and said in perfect English with only the slightest trace of an accent, "Hello, Lieutenant, glad you are with us and grateful for all you men do for us."

She sat back down as Emil pointed to the other man who stood, wincing from pain. He smiled gamely and greeted Jack with a definite Scottish accent, "Of course! My name is Ian Butler, and I'm pleased to meet you, Jack. Or should I call you 'Chicken Man'?"

That got a laugh out of Jack and everyone else at the table,

"Jack is fine, thank you, Ian. May I ask what branch of the RAF you're with? I picked up a bit of a Scottish accent. I've developed a few friends since my time in England with the Fighter Groups based at station 131 and then station 159."

Ian nodded his head, grimaced as he put more weight on his injured leg and took a deep breath, "Jack, I know both places. But I am not RAF, I'm with another branch of the military."

Ian smiled but did not go on any further.

Jack had a feeling that "Ian Butler" was not his actual name and noticed Lucien looking at Ian who gave him a slight nod, permitting him to say something,

"Jack, Ian has injured his leg as you may have noticed. We are waiting for our medical man to come look at him and to look at your wounds as well. If you recall the other day, Marcelino, Gerard and I went to check out a Brit that needed assistance?"

"Yes, I remember Janine telling me that you were going to do that."

"Well, Ian here checked out okay, but in all fairness, I should let him explain who he is."

Ian turned to Jack but at that moment, Miep interrupted the conversation with a laugh and said,

"Okay, boys, enough for now. In the meantime, let us eat!"

CHAPTER 23

30 May 1944 Lunch and Nazi's visit at Emil's Chicken House

Everyone took a seat at the table as Miep placed heaping dishes of scrambled eggs, chicken sausage, and toasted bread in front of them. Emil and Jan poured steaming hot Ersatz coffee made from ground chicory into mugs. They all settled down to a lunch aware that this meal was not available to most Belgians in occupied Europe.

There was very little conversation until the food was completely consumed. Finally, Emil stood up and moved over to a small table by the front window. He retrieved a pipe, lit it, took a deep breath and then spoke to the group still seated at the table, "Okay, Ian and Jack. You are both welcome in my home. Miep and I want to keep you both safe and out of the hands of the Nazis. We all look forward to rejoicing with you when the Allies liberate Europe and kill Hitler and all the Nazi bastards. Right?"

Both Jack and Ian smiled and nodded their agreement, as Emil continued, "In a short while, we will have a visit from a friend of *Réseau Comète*, a medical man who, at great risk to himself has agreed to look at both of your wounds and injuries and do what he can to treat you."

He continued, "So now that we've gotten that out of the way, Ian, why don't you tell Jack who you are? Things may get dangerous over the next few days, and it is better for all of us to work together and to be honest with each other.

Ian Butler just smiled, looked first at Emil then at Lucien but said nothing.

Finally, Lucien nodded and spoke, "Lieutenant Jack Dodds, United States Army air corps, meet Captain Jock Clarke, British Special Air Services".

Both men stood somewhat shakily and faced each other. Jack knew and respected the SAS's reputation for amazing commando style missions behind enemy lines and their penchant for secrecy.

He therefore was not surprised that "Ian Butler", aka Jock Clarke was a bit reluctant to share information with someone he had just met. He wasn't even sure if Jock Clarke was his real name either, but he went along with it.

Jack moved from his seat at the table, approached Clark and extended his hand. Clarke smiled, shook Jack's hand, wincing as he shifted some weight onto his injured leg. Jack looked at the leg and the cane, "How did you injure the leg?"

"Got a little hung-up with my chute on the tail of the aircraft as I jumped into the countryside the other night."

Jack and the others present were obviously stunned at the vision of someone attempting to parachute out of an airplane in the middle of the night and getting caught on the tail of the airplane. Clarke continued, "Tore a pretty good size hole in the canopy before I broke free. Damn near ruined my whole day, no, make that my whole night. Still, lucky for me, I had enough of the canopy to work for me but came down a lot faster than normal."

Clarke laughed, "I landed on top of some haystacks there at the drop zone. I was lucky and just came away with this leg injury. If not for the haystacks I would certainly not be here."

Jack was about to respond to that when Emil looked out the window, saw two German vehicles pull up and said, "Looks like we have company, some Germans. Could be routine."

Emil observed a German staff car parked outside his building with three German enlisted men standing alongside the vehicle talking amongst themselves. His niece, Ellen, who served as his receptionist left the table and went downstairs.

Emil nodded to Miep, "Miep, you know what to do." As he followed shortly behind Ellen heading downstairs.

Miep immediately went into action, "Okay, Jack, Lucien, Jan, help Ian here into the safe space, then lock yourselves in. Lucien knows what to do. Jan, once you get them in, cover the door with the tapestry and then come back here with me and help me reduce these place settings to us three. Now move!"

CHAPTER 24

30 May 1944 Germans visit Emil's Chicken House

Emil quickly descended the stairs from the living space to the ground floor of his warehouse and moved to the front office. He took a deep breath and entered the office putting on a big, jovial smile.

He was relieved to see that Ellen, fluent in German had made it to the office before him. She was putting on the charm with four young German enlisted men standing around the front of the reception desk. They, in turn were obviously enthralled with this beautiful young woman, none more than their officious leader, Corporal Karl Mueller, the senior enlisted man.

Ellen was laughing and taking notes as the Germans were intent upon placing an order. The whole conversation stopped as Emil, the proprietor, entered. He welcomed them in German. He looked at Ellen who smiled and pointed at Corporal Karl Mueller.

"Ah, yes, Uncle, Corporal Mueller would like us to deliver forty cooked chickens with side dishes to a midday luncheon reception they are having at the Liege aerodrome Monday June 5 for an important guest."

Emil's smile got even broader, "It would be an honor to do so! What kind of side dishes would you like us to prepare?"

Emil looked over to Corporal Mueller for a response. Mueller, a very large young man who stood head and shoulders above the other Germans looked at his notes then back at Emil. He grew more noticeably pompous as he responded,

"Kartoffeln, Brot and dessert of some kind. During these difficult times, it is not common to offer dessert. So, I am counting on you to make a dessert that will be a big surprise, a really big surprise. I know you can do this.

Mueller looked intently at Emil who nodded and jotted some notes on his order pad, then looked back at him with a big smile,

"Of course we can do that for you! Bread and potatoes are not a problem. Would you please confirm the time and place for the delivery?"

Mueller, referring to his notes told him, "The large hanger at the Liege airdrome. Our cooking staff don't have the facility to do the cooking themselves, so they want the chickens prepared by you and delivered on the morning of 5 June."

He looked up from his notes and then continued, "So, could you and your staff be on hand to assist in warming everything up? Once that is done, you can depart, and we can distribute the food to the guests."

Emil thought to himself that this was really a stupid way to serve the dinner as it wouldn't be freshly cooked. On top of that if they wanted to impress a very important guest, the chicken would be better served hot cut into plate sized portions and then brought to the table.

Nevertheless, he kept his big smile frozen on his face and nodded enthusiastically, "Yes, of course, Corporal. Because of the size of the order, we will select, pluck and butcher the chickens on Sunday, and then roast them slowly overnight. We will deliver them to your staff as you wish just prior to midday."

Mueller looked annoyed, "I don't really care how you do it, Emil, just get it done."

Emil thought to himself, *arrogant jerk, typical Kraut in a position of power,*

Always the good salesman he responded happily, "Certainly, no problem. It will be done. Now, may I offer you and your colleagues a few chickens to take with you now?"

The other three Germans nodded enthusiastically. Emil turned to Ellen and asked her to take the other three enlisted men with her to get the chickens while he discussed a few details with Mueller.

The three enlisted men were eager to get the chickens but seemed more eager to follow this beautiful young woman into the warehouse to get them. Emil noticed Mueller staring at her. When the others entered through the warehouse doors, he turned to Emil,

"Your niece is a very beautiful, striking woman. Is she married?"

"She is engaged."

"Hmm, too bad."

Emil purposely did not mention to Mueller that, two years ago, Martin, Ellen's fiancé' had been abducted and pressed into forced labor by the Nazis. Their sources told them that he had been moved into a forced labor camp somewhere in Germany.

Last year they were informed that he had died along with several hundred other forced laborers due to the brutal conditions there. Ellen was still mourning his loss.

He did not like the way the German was leering as he watched her disappear into the warehouse. Instead, he moved to another subject, "So, Corporal, I assume that as in previous orders, you know I will have to deal with Black Market operators in order to obtain some of the rationed goods, especially desert?"

Mueller nodded conspiratorially, "Yes, of course, I know this."

Emil smiled, "I will make the usual arrangements then and will get you the usual complimentary award delivered as per past arrangements. Can I assume that payment will be to us made in cash upon delivery?"

"Of course, just as in the past."

"Excellent! We will make this happen and your superiors will be pleased with the results. Would you care to join me in my office for a shot of schnapps?"

Mueller shook his head, "Not now. We are in uniform and on duty. Another time, Emil."

"Of course, Corporal, another time."

At that point, the three enlisted men, preceded by Ellen, came back into the front office, laughing and each holding a wire cage containing two chickens.

Emil escorted all four of them out the front door and, smiling brilliantly, waved goodbye as they climbed into their military vehicle and drove off.

He closed the door and turned to Ellen, both breathing a loud sigh of relief.

Ellen spoke first, "Glad that's over with! Can we really fulfill that size of an order? The people are starving, the Nazis regulate how many chickens we can supply to the Church, their own field hospital, and they are getting stricter."

She sighed and continued, "What about the potatoes and what about the idea of a 'special' desert? What about our ability to get some food for the poor? Forgive me, but I'm worried, uncle."

Emil smiled and shrugged it off as he and Ellen walked towards the stairs leading up to the living quarters, "No, do not worry dear Ellen. Corporal Mueller is an underhanded snake, but he has always been on the take for our Black-Market dealings, and we will make it happen. If there are complaints about the quality of the chickens, then we will get word to the higher-ups that this delivery scheme was all Mueller's idea. I have the connections."

He looked at her to see that she was following his train of thought, "We will continue to supply our friend, Father Catron with chickens, gizzards and other nutritious chicken parts for the poor and the Bosche will be no wiser. Karl Mueller will get his cut, so he won't be a problem."

Then, just before he headed back upstairs, another thought occurred to him:

Who is this "special guest" for whom this event is for? Perhaps our friends at the Resistance would like to know.

Acting on this thought, Emil excused himself as Ellen ascended the stairs while he quickly returned to his office and made a call. He left a seemingly benign coded message to some "special friends," then laughed to himself as he climbed the stairs,

Yes, maybe the Germans might be in for a bigger surprise then a 'special' desert.

Little did he know that, on that day, they all would be in for a bigger surprise.

CHAPTER 25

30 May 1944 Medical Attention for Jack & Jock

Emil returned to the upstairs living space to find Miep sitting in her rocking chair knitting something while Jan sat at the little desk by the window with his "schoolbooks."

They were obviously preparing a peaceful scene had the Germans accompanied Emil upstairs. He let out a hearty laugh, "Ah! The *sweet elderly grandmother* knitting a little-one's sweater and the *studious* schoolboy reading his 4th year primer even though he would be in 8th year if he even went to school. How lovely."

They both rose to their feet looking expectantly at him. Miep spoke first, "Well, never mind that. What happened with the Germans?"

He waved her back down into the chair, "It's all okay. Mueller was leading the others, and they were on an errand to order some cooked chicken and side dishes for some important guest who is coming next week sometime. It's all taken care of."

"How many cooked chickens?"

"Forty."

"Forty! My God! We don't have the staff to cook and prepare forty chickens. And what kind of side dishes?"

"It will be okay, Miep. We will handle it."

"I'm not sure we can, Emil. What kind of side dishes?"

"Potatoes along with bread."

"Emil, you know that each chicken will be cut into at least two, possible four servings. That means at least eighty side dishes, maybe twice that! The Germans may be planning on at least 80 to 100 guests. That's way beyond our ability to handle. Where will this be? How can we handle this?"

Emil, unfazed, smiled, "Yes, my dear, I understand your concerns.

The Boche want us to deliver these forty chickens and twice the number of side dishes to the large hanger at the Liege aerodrome. They will be honoring a 'special guest' for that luncheon. We don't yet know who that 'Special guest' is, and I don't think that that young blockhead of a corporal, Mueller knows either."

Miep just stared at Emil as he went on, "I am planning to go ahead and prepare forty chickens just in case Mueller or his bosses stop by during the process. And I will contact our black-market suppliers to start the side dishes."

Miep started to object but Emil held up a finger to silence her. "Just before I came up here, I have asked some of our 'friends' at the Resistance if they would like to 'help us' deliver a *nice surprise* to our Bosch friends and their 'Special Guest' whoever that might be on that *Special Day*."

With that, as the implication of Emil's meaning set in, Miep's eyes seemed to double in size and her mouth opened in what Emil thought might be a scream. She was interrupted by the buzzer from the front reception desk. She pushed the intercom speaker, and they heard Ellen's voice,

"Tante Miep, Herr Stark is here to see Uncle."

No response. "Tante, Miep?"

After a long pause Miep responded in a barely audible voice, "Okay, Ellen. Would you please show him up?"

In a few moments, the door swung open, and Ellen walked in leading a small man dressed in clean, pressed overalls and carrying a black leather briefcase.

Emil went over to the man and embraced him, "Kurt! I am so grateful that you could come. Would you like something to eat? Drink? A beer?" he then looked at the still stunned Miep,

"Oh! Sorry! Kurt, I think you have met my wife, Miep before and of course you've just met our niece, Ellen."

Before he could continue, Kurt, all business interrupted, "Yes, I have met Miep before and yes, I would like something to eat, as I haven't eaten anything to speak of in two days. But not until I see the patient. Where is he?"

Miep, recovering from her last conversation with Emil before this new visitor showed up, slapped her forehead as she suddenly remembered where "the patients" were. She rushed over to the wall leading to the kitchen, swept aside a large tapestry hanging on the wall, which revealed the hidden door.

She took a key hanging around her neck and knocked on the door three times in quick succession before unlocking the door leading to the safe room.

The safe room door opened, and Lucien stepped out first, loosely holding a semi-automatic carbine. After looking around the room and deciding that it was safe, he gestured inside the safe space and was soon slowly followed by Jack and Jock.

Emil laughed, "As you can see, Kurt you have not one but two patients."

Kurt, totally unfazed by this rather bizarre entrance nodded his head, gestured for both men to walk over to the kitchen table and be seated. He observed with professional interest each man's gait as they made their way over to the table.

Before they all took their seats, he gestured to Jock to remain standing.

Pointing to Jock's leg, he said, "The women can leave the room for now. I want this man to remove his trousers."

Miep retorted, "We are not leaving. You may need us for assistance, and we have already attended many sick and wounded."

Kurt snorted, a slight smile came onto his lips as he resumed his order to Jock, "Have it your way, then. Okay, *you* please remove your trousers."

CHAPTER 26

30 May 1944 Diagnosis and Treatment for Ian (aka) Jock

Jock attempted to remove his trousers while standing but started to fall backwards into the chair behind him in obvious pain. Miep and Ellen moved quickly to either side of him and assisted him into the chair. They then carefully removed his trousers.

Kurt donned a thick pair of spectacles, moved closer to Jock and gently started palpitating his injured leg. He looked to both women,

"Please help him to slowly stand up again and keep on either side of him."

Once Jock was standing up, Kurt circled around him, carefully looking at the injured leg. "I cannot completely diagnose your injury without an X-Ray, but that is impossible without the authorities being aware of the procedure. Ordinarily, I would suspect that you have a possible fracture of the tibia and the fibula. Those are the two bones in your lower leg. It is very common to break both of those bones due to some form of trauma like a fall or a car accident. Again, we cannot be certain without an X-ray. However, I doubt that this is true in your case."

Jock looked at him, "Okay, but why are you doubting that these two bones are broken without an X-ray?"

Kurt didn't respond at first, "Okay, help him back into the chair."

Kurt reached into his leather bag and extracted a thermometer, rinsed it with some alcohol and inserted it under Jock's tongue. He then continued, "I say this because someone with a broken tibia and fibula would realistically not be able to stand or walk and, even though it's painful, you are able to do both. You've definitely suffered a significant trauma to the leg, but I doubt you've broken both of these bones. So, without the benefit of X-Rays we cannot be certain as to the extent of your injury I'm afraid.

He rummaged around in his black leather case for some sterile wipes then continued, "I can come back and cast your leg in a day or two but for now, I would feel better if you just immobilized and stayed off the leg, keeping it slightly elevated and watch out for increased swelling. Under normal circumstances if we weren't under Nazi control, you should have a complete X-Ray series, and an Orthopedic expert might want to perform a surgical repair."

Jock nodded his head and laughed, "Good advice, Doctor, but I assume that we don't have too many Orthopedic experts hanging around these parts. I would like you to cast my leg when you can."

Ignoring this input from the Brit, he turned to Miep. "Can you set him up in a bed with his injured leg slightly elevated?"

"Yes, of course."

"Good. I would like you to keep an eye on his leg, looking for increased swelling or visible black and blue stains. And it is important that every hour or two, get him to sit up on the edge of the bed and let his feet hang down, but keep him off his feet. Keep his trips to the bathroom at a minimum. Is that possible?"

"Yes, Emil and my nephew can help with all that."

He disinfected the thermometer and placed it back in his bag. He then produced a vial containing a white substance.

"This is powdered aspirin. There should be enough for both patients. This man here does not have a fever, but the aspirin can help with inflammation and reduce some pain. Use it sparingly it is very difficult for me to obtain."

Miep nodded and took the vial.

Kurt grunted his approval then looked directly at Jock, "I suspect from looking at your many past wounds and scars that this is not the first time you have been injured. If you do your best to stay off that leg, you may have a good chance of healing and perhaps later seeing someone who can make sure that if there are some fractures they can be treated properly."

Jock did not show any visible reaction as Kurt continued, "In the meantime, I will do my best to help you."

He paused for effect, "And *You*, my friend have to do your best to help yourself."

Finally, Jock smiled, "Thank you. I will do my best."

Kurt nodded without further comment and turned towards Jack.

"Okay, now it's *your* turn. Remove your trousers and remove your shirt as I understand you have two wounds that need my attention."

CHAPTER 27

30 May 1944 Diagnosis and Treatment for Jack

Kurt disinfected the thermometer again and inserted it under Jack's tongue while he carefully examined the wound on his back between the shoulder blades. He then knelt on one knee and examined the penetrating wound on Jack's right leg.

Using sterile cotton swabs, he removed from a paper envelope marked "coussinets stériles" two pads and cleansed both wounds with hydrogen peroxide and then tamped them dry. He removed the thermometer from under Jack's tongue and looked at it. "This man does have a low-grade fever. Miep would you please give him a glass of water with 600 milligrams of aspirin powder now, and check it again in about four hours? Do you have a thermometer?"

Miep shook her head.

"Okay, take this one. I will get another one when I get home."

He then went into his bag and produced a packet which contained sulfanilamide. He applied the powder to Jack's wounds and then carefully patted both areas dry again with the white cotton pads. With the women's help Kurt put Jack's shirt and trousers back on.

Giving Miep several packets of sulfa, he said, "You all must keep an eye on his wounds. I believe sulfa will help with the healing of both sets of wounds, but time will tell.

Emil stood over Kurt and placed a hand on his shoulder, "Come, friend, let's get you something to eat."

He led Kurt over to the table just as Miep hurried to set some cooked chicken and warm bread down on a plate. Kurt looked at the portion on the plate and shook his head, "This is too much, people are starving. I will eat a little and then keep the rest for the poor. If you would be kind to give me some paper, I will take the extra on the plate to someone who really needs it."

Jack and Jock looked at each other, it was unspoken, but they understood that Kurt wasn't kidding, he was not going to eat all that Miep put on his plate even though, by his own admission, he hadn't eaten in almost two days.

Emil shook his head, "No, my friend please eat. I know you are always helping the church and those in need. You need your strength and so do all the people you help. My friend Lucien will accompany you home with some extra for your family. Also, let us know who you were just talking about, and we will make sure that person or that family gets some food right away. Now eat, Kurt, no argument."

"That is very kind of you. Lucien doesn't have to accompany me as I must stop at another house to check on a young woman who is about to give birth."

"All the more reason for Lucien to go with you. He will also be carrying some extra provisions for this young woman and her household. Now eat!"

No further argument from Kurt, as he gave in to his hunger and ate every morsel on his plate. When he finished, he stood and thanked Emil and Miep and promised he would be back in a day or two to check on Jock and Jack.

He made them promise to send for him if they needed him before that. Miep handed Lucien several packages of food wrapped in brown paper for Kurt and for the pregnant woman he was going to visit next.

With that, Kurt Stark said goodbye and departed with Lucien following behind him.

Jack smiled and said, "Very professional and thorough doctor. Where does he practice?"

Emil smiled, "He's not exactly a medical doctor right now. Kurt was on his way to become one before the Germans took over and interrupted his studies. He did, however complete his previous studies and is a very highly respected animal doctor."

Jack and Jock laughed at the same time as Jock said, "You mean that bloke is a veterinarian?"

"Yes," said Emil, "And a very good one. He takes care of SS-Haupt

Sturm Führer, Erik Hoeffner's personal horse and stable which explains why he has access to so many supplies. Kurt has saved the lives of many of our FFI wounded in battle and, as we just heard, he delivers the village's babies and cares for our sick."

"And I'll bet he's a good source of information being close to the head Boche in charge of that Luftwaffe airbase that got shot up recently." offered Jock

"Ah! You know about that airbase being shot up, eh?" Emil chuckled.

Jock laughed, "Oh yeah, we heard about it on the night we jumped. Good job on whoever of our flyboys did that!"

Again, Emil laughed, looking first at Jock and then at Jack, "You are sitting in the same room with one of those 'flyboys'".

Jock turned to look fully at Jack, a large smile on his face, "Good on ya, mate! Good on ya!"

Miep made it clear that it was now time for the two men to follow "*Doctor*" Kurt's advice. She pointed Jack to a large easy chair near the front window while Emil and Ellen helped Jock to a nearby bedroom and set him up as Kurt had ordered.

As he thought about the conversation that took place amongst them this past half hour, Jack remembered that Jock said that "*We* heard about the airfield on the night that "*We*" jumped. Who was **"***We*", he wondered?

CHAPTER 28

Saturday 3 June 1944 07:00 Paris to Brussels train-about a half hour outside of Brussels

Janine and Denise spent a long night hunkering down in different cars on the early morning train from Paris to Brussels. The train's unusual 04:00 AM departure from Paris was due to concern over increased Allied air attacks during daylight hours on the rail system and infrastructure. Despite overnight Allied bombing attacks on the Pas de Calais area, the train was able to get underway in the darkness.

There would still be about an hour spent in daylight as the train approached its destination, but the authorities would not allow for arrival in Brussels during the hours of darkness. No reason was given for their decision, but no one dared challenge the Nazi occupiers. All passengers were very much on edge as dawn broke nearing the Belgian border.

The conductors kept a sharp lookout for possible Allied air attacks, but it was strictly a question of saying a prayer and taking your chances to ride the rail system during these early days of June 1944.

The two sisters spent several intense days learning the alternative plans to provide safe harbor for downed allied airmen now that the European invasion was drawing near.

They exchanged valuable intelligence with MI-9 agents, Daniel Muton, andThomas Rutland, the MI-9 operatives who were responsible for the deep forest camps being established in the Belgian Ardennes and in Foret de Freteval.

Just before they crossed into Belgium, the train came to a screeching stop and the loudspeaker urged everyone to abandon the train and seek shelter immediately.

Even before the train came to a complete stop, passengers, men and women with small children, soldiers, train crew and Janine and Denise exited the train and ran to either side of the tracks seeking shelter wherever they could find it. Left on board were some elderly, the infirm and small, unescorted children crying in fear.

Almost at the same time, the air was filled with the overwhelming sound of many aircraft in close proximity to the Paris-Brussels train. Everyone hid behind whatever shelter they could find or threw themselves down on the ground and braced for the sounds of strafing from airborne machine gun and canon fire together with rockets and bombs directed at the train.

Passengers covered their eyes and ears, said their prayers and waited for the inevitable destruction coming from the sky. Mothers covered their children with their own bodies while the children screamed in terror.

And then, suddenly, the swarm of aircraft passed over the train and continued to other targets.

After waiting for what seemed like hours, but was only a few minutes, the loudspeakers ordered everyone back onto the train immediately.

Janine looked around at all the passengers, searching for sight of Denise, but there were too many people, and she was unable to see her. They had prearranged to meet at a safe house in Brussels rather than reuniting at the train station upon arrival just in case one or both may have been followed.

She shrugged her shoulders and started to move back towards the train along with the other passengers. Many were nursing bruised knees, sprained ankles and other relatively minor injuries suffered during their rapid, emergency evacuation.

Once again, the loudspeaker urgently demanded that everyone rapidly reboard the train. They all understood the implication that the Allied aircraft might return to strafe them after hitting their primary targets.

From a distance, she saw an elderly couple who were struggling to get to their feet and obviously needed help. She became angry as a young man in his late twenties, early thirties ignored their pleas for help. Instead, he looked at them disdainfully and pressed on towards the train without a second thought.

To Janine's disgust, he just walked by them and stood by the boarding steps impatiently waiting for the surging crowds to dissipate so he could reboard the train.

Enraged, she muttered under her breath, "*imbécile*!"

She stopped and helped the old woman to her feet placing her arm around her as she and the couple slowly made their way back towards the steps of the train. As they approached the boarding steps, a young German soldier quickly came to her assistance and helped them to get on board. Relieved that they were all back on board, Janine made the Sign of the Cross and silently asked God to protect them all as they resumed their journey to Brussels.

Janine helped the elderly couple back into their seats and then, as the train jolted to a start and started moving, she made her way down the aisle towards her assigned seat. She spotted the jerk who had bypassed the elderly couple to save his own ass. He was sitting in a window seat calmly reading a book.

Without showing any sign of recognition as she passed his seat, she was shocked to realize that this was the man they were supposed meet at the Café' Le Perroquet in Paris, the double agent, Enri Dumont.

CHAPTER 29

Saturday 3 June 1944 Emil's Chicken House Jack & Jock & "Doctor Kurt"

"Doctor" Kurt removed the thermometer from under Jack's tongue and after looking at it, disinfected it with alcohol. Still very serious as he put away some other items into his leather bag, "No more fever. This is a good thing. The sulfa seems to be working, and the wounds are healing nicely. I watched you walk around the room and your leg is still bothering you but is getting better."

Jack smiled as he pulled up his trousers, and joked, "So, I am good to run a race?"

Kurt wiped his glasses as he contemplated Jack's question, "Hmm, no. if you were a horse, I would have had to shoot you. So, no race for quite a while."

Lucien, Miep and Emil, sitting at the kitchen table overheard this comment. Then, it dawned on them that Kurt, always serious, had actually cracked a joke and they all burst into unrestrained laughter.

Jack joined them with a big smile, "Doctor Kurt, your bedside manner is improving nicely! When this war is over, I look forward to attending your graduation ceremony and installation as a bona fide Medical Doctor."

Kurt tried not to smile, but a thin smile flashed briefly on his tightly closed lips, "Thank you. I am not sure what you mean by "bedside manner', but I will look forward to that day if God wills it."

Jock, with his leg newly restrained in a plaster cast overheard these comments as well as he came into the room using his crutches, "So, Doctor Kurt, what about me? When will I be able to run a race? Time is slipping away from me."

Kurt pointed to the chair that Jack had just vacated before responding, "You, my British friend have a much longer way to go before you can run any race. Without any X-rays, I still cannot be certain, but any fractures of the bones in your lower leg most likely would heal better if they could be surgically corrected."

Jock winced as he lowered himself onto the chair, with his right leg extended. Just before Kurt inserted the thermometer under his tongue, he said, "That may be so, Doctor Kurt. But there is indeed a race out there and I must join it, bad leg or no bad leg."

CHAPTER 30

Saturday 3 June 1944 Janine and Denise rendezvous at Brussels Safe House

It was now two hours since she had arrived at the safe house not far from the train terminal. Denise grew increasingly worried that she had yet to hear from her sister. *Something was wrong!*

She and Janine had agreed to meet directly after arriving in Brussels. This was not like Janine who was meticulous in keeping to a plan. Denise concluded that her sister may have been stopped at a security checkpoint and may be in custody, unable to talk her way out.

Just as she prepared to depart the safe house and seek her MI-9 contacts for guidance and assistance, Janine walked in the door. Her face flushed with excitement, she embraced her sister and gushed, "I found the bastard! I followed him to his hiding place."

"Who? Who did you find?"

"The traitor, Enri Dumont. He was on the train with us. I didn't have time to alert you, or I would have lost him. I followed him at a discreet distance, paused when he paused to check if he was being followed and watched him as he produced a key and entered an apartment not far from the Place Sainte Catherine.

"I can't believe it! He was on the same train with us this morning?"

"Yes, in the car that was in between the cars that you and I were sitting in. When we did the emergency evacuation, I saw some asshole who refused to help an elderly couple regain their footing when it was time to reboard. I thought he looked familiar and confirmed it when I walked by him."

"You're sure he didn't recognize you?"

"Well, now that I think of it, perhaps I should have removed the lavender ribbon from my hair?"

"What? The lavender ribbon?"

Just as she realized that Janine was teasing her, Janine laughed, and the two sisters hugged each other. Then Denise grew serious and held her sister at arm's length. "I was so worried about you. I thought that you may have been stopped and taken into custody."

"I know, but I didn't have the time to get your attention."

Denise nodded her head and smiled, "No, I understand. You did an amazing job. Now we must alert the MI-9 and resistance to take this traitor out."

"Already done. The *Bourreau* is sitting on his apartment as we speak."

Denise felt an involuntary shudder running down her spine as the image of the *Executioner, Bourreau,* came into her mind.

CHAPTER 31

Sunday, June 4, 1944, 5:00 AM Remote farm near the Operation Marathon Ardennes refuge

British Lancaster Bombers flying a "Carpet Bagger" operation dropped leaflets over German occupied territory in Belgium and Holland and then swung over the Ardennes to a designated drop zone where they dropped weapons and supplies for the MI-9 agents and their Resistance partners.

MI-9 Agent, Daniel Muton and several FFI Resistance fighters hurried to the site to search for the supplies. Other Resistance members stood guard in case the Nazis had been alerted.

Once all the supplies had been located and removed, the chutes stowed, Daniel and the others quickly carried them deep into the forest campsite set up to house downed allied airmen.

As the Normandy invasion loomed, the mission to rescue the downed allied airmen had changed from moving them across the Pyrenees to establishing them into deep woods forest camps in France and Belgium right under the nose of the Nazis.

Daniel had assembled about 40 airmen at this early stage and by the time the allied armies liberated Belgium, he estimated that he would have about 140-150 in his Belgian refuge.

Thomas Rutland the MI-9 agent in charge of the Foret de Freteval refuge in France already had 150 airmen.

On this early Sunday morning, two days before the Normandy Invasion, Daniel met with a small group of British SAS commandos and Resistance fighters to provide intelligence, render support and plan for how best to contribute to the allies during the upcoming invasion.

He also wanted to consult with the FFI fighters to make sure that the known double agent Enri Dumont was being tracked and hopefully eliminated.

For their part, the SAS commandos were trying to locate one of their own who dropped with them several days ago, but due to a mishap when his chute got hung up on the tail of the British bomber, he became separated from them.

They were unsure if he survived the damage to his parachute, but they were unable to locate his body and were hopeful that he may have survived. Daniel and his FFI associates noted the information and promised to put out feelers among their people.

Just as they were all preparing to go their separate ways, a member of the resistance who he did not recognize came out of the darkness and handed Daniel a photograph.

The predawn light did not allow him to see the image and reluctantly he produced a small, redlight flashlight and covered everything with his jacket. Peering at the photo being shielded underneath his jacket, he recognized the pale, dead face of Enri Dumont the Nazi double agent. In this picture, it was apparent that Dumont had been killed by a single, small caliber gunshot to his forehead. When he looked back up to ask this man for some more information, he was gone.

Disappeared

It was then that he realized he had just been visited by the *Executioner.*

CHAPTER 32

Sunday, 4 June 1944 11:00 PM Preparing 40 cooked chickens Emil's Chicken House,Warehouse kitchen Sante-Walburge, Belgium

One hour before the midnight curfew imposed by the Germans, Father Corentin "Cory" Catron, the Rector of nearby Saint Thomas the Apostle Catholic Church, and four trusted women were admitted into the large, commercial warehouse kitchen by Miep. They were there to assist in the preparation of 40 cooked chickens and side dishes requested by the Germans.

Father Catron, an avid supporter of the Resistance and Comet Line, assured Miep of the women's loyalty to the cause. All four lost their husbands to Nazi brutality including torture and summary execution. They understood this effort was part of a project to get back at the Boche and further the goals of the Resistance.

All four looked earnest and ready to help. One of the women, slightly older than the other three was introduced to Miep by Father Catron as Magda DeVries. Magda was fluent in English which proved to be very helpful when dealing with downed Allied airmen.

She had a very serious, no-nonsense demeanor and was obviously their leader. Magda appeared to be in her thirties, the other three women in their early twenties. They assured Miep that they were eager to get to work and help in any way.

Miep thanked them for their willingness to work through the night and assist in this project. She introduced them to Ellen, who willingly joined the all-night effort. Ellen, always smiling, handed them aprons, and donned one herself.

Miep, in turn assured Father Catron that additional cooked chickens would arrive at his rectory in nearby Liege, Belgium once the order for the Germans was complete.

This brought great joy to the priest who struggled to feed his flock suffering from malnutrition and near starvation due to severe ration restrictions imposed by the Nazis. Many were elderly and infirm. Some were unable to feed themselves. He also harbored many newly orphaned children.

As much as he trusted Emil and Miep, he knew from experience that they, like any dedicated member of the resistance, could be subject to capture and torture.

Therefore, using the principle of "need to know", he did not reveal to them that he was hiding several Jewish families in the school and rectory of his church. In addition, some Jewish families were being sheltered in the homes of a small number of dedicated parishioners.

His brave parishioners knew all too well that the penalty for harboring Jews was punishable by torture and death if they were discovered.

He listened intently as Miep explained that they all would be working through the night. Despite her assumption that these women most likely were familiar with slaughtering, plucking and preparing chickens for cooking, she nevertheless went over her procedures for preparation and cooking in the three large commercial wood-fired ovens.

This included preserving valuable livers, gizzards and other digestible components which could be used for components in other forms of food. This would be especially helpful for feeding the poor and needy. The feathers would be washed, sanitized and set aside for other purposes as well. Nothing from these birds would be wasted.

Miep turned to Father Catron,

"Thank you, dear Father, for bringing us these wonderful sisters here to help us. As you can imagine, we have a long night in front of us. Do not worry about them, they will be safe here. I am worried about *you* on your bicycle traveling home in the dark during the hours of curfew."

He smiled and shook his head,

"The local police know me and, if stopped I will tell them that I am visiting a nearby parishioner's home to give last rites."

"But what if they ask you the name of this 'dying parishioner'?

"I will give it to them, for I am not lying, I am really going to a parishioner's home whose elderly mother is dying. I just hope I'm not too late."

He laughed, gave all the women his blessing, and departed on his bicycle into the dark streets of Sante-Walburg, Belgium.

CHAPTER 33

Monday, 5 June 1944 4:00 AM "Surprise visit at the Chicken House"

In the early hours of darkness of this Monday morning, the fragrant smell of cooking chicken filled the warehouse kitchen as Emil entered carrying two baskets of croissants prepared specially by Miep in the upstairs kitchen. He announced that breakfast was at hand.

This was ignored by the four volunteers and his niece, Ellen. Instead, they continued to cook and rotate the chicken.

Ellen looked over her shoulder, "Thank you, Uncle, but we cannot interrupt the cooking process right now."

Emil was soon joined by Miep who smiled and said, "Nonsense! You all have been doing a marvelous job! I see that you have put aside ten metal bins into which you are placing the cooked chickens. Four to a bin?"

Ellen smiled, "Yes, Tante Miep. So far, we have placed 6 bins with a total of 24 chickens in the warming tray with four more to go."

"Yes, I can see that. What about the potatoes?"

Magda smiled and said, "Already cooked and in that other bin next to the second oven. They will reheat up nicely at the venue."

Emil laughed, "You ladies have been amazing, working through the night without a break! And you have this all under control."

He expected them to laugh with him but noticed that all of them seemed to be frozen as someone entered the kitchen behind him. He turned and was shocked to see the smiling, red face of Corporal Karl Mueller.

Mueller coughed, managed a lopsided smile and said, "I agree with Emil. You ladies seem to have this all under control."

Emil and the others noticed his bright red face, slurring his words and being unsteady on his feet. His uniform jacket was uncharacteristically unbuttoned. It was obvious he had been drinking heavily through the night.

Emil thought, *Damn! Just what we don't need right now.*

He recovered quickly, smiled and greeted the plastered German.

"Corporal Mueller, what a pleasant surprise. Did the delicious aroma of cooked chicken lure you in here from your bed at this early hour?"

Emil was seething inside at the realization that *someone* must have left the front door unlocked when supplies were brought in. This oversight made it possible for this drunk blockhead to just walk right in on them.

I'll have to have a word with whoever in the family was this neglectful, he thought. He later realized to his embarrassment that *he was the one who left the door unlocked. Oops!*

Mueller laughed and steadied himself by placing a large hand on Emil's shoulder, "Well, that's not the reason I'm here, but I must admit the odor is quite compelling."

Miep smiled cordially, "Well, by all means, let me prepare a breakfast to take home with you."

Mueller, no longer smiling, slurred his response, "Thank you, but I would prefer to eat it right here," he paused as if trying to remember something profound and then continued, "With Ellen."

Ellen tried to hide her astonishment and fear, but the blush on her face betrayed her anxiety. Miep kept her smile fixed on her face and turned to Emil, "Of course! I will set six places over there in the kitchen at the large wooden table."

Mueller clumsily turned his huge body to look where Miep was gesturing to the table used by kitchen staff where they took their meals.

He stared at the table for a moment, then turned back to Miep and almost lost his balance in the process. His face reddened and his tone became harsh and arrogant, "You want *me* to sit with the *workers* and eat? Is that what you're asking me to do?"

Emil quickly tried to diffuse the situation, "Of course not! All that we meant is that the women have been working very hard all through the night to prepare your order for delivery today. Why don't we all take a break, you and I can go into my office, enjoy a little schnapps and some of these delicious croissants?"

Mueller, somewhat mollified, nodded his head, and looking directly at Ellen muttered, "That's more like it. A break in your office sounds good. I don't need to take a break with you, Delacroix, Ellen will join me.

Ellen gave her best smile, "That is so kind of you to think of me, Herr Corporal, but I must keep working with my fellow workers here. I hope you understand?"

"That was not a question or a request. It is an order! I want you to join me, and I want you to be my escort today for our luncheon at the aerodrome with a very important guest."

Miep intervened with a grandmotherly smile, "Of course, Ellen would love to join you, I'm sure. But what kind of gentleman are you? Look at her hands and her apron, all covered with chicken blood, feathers and such. Look at each one of these hard-working ladies. Don't you think that at least you can give them an opportunity to take a break and clean themselves up? After all, they have been hard at work all night on *your* project."

This seemed to get through Mueller's alcohol shrouded brain, and he made a very poorly executed bow towards the ladies, almost falling over, "Ah, yes! Please forgive me! You all can take a break and clean up."

With that, Miep gave the ladies a sharp look and they scurried to the washrooms located down the hall.

Mueller called after them as they hastened towards the restrooms, his slurred speech booming down the hallway,

"But I *only* want to eat with Ellen. You others can eat with yourselves."

Emil, barely containing his anger turned to Mueller, fixed a smile back on his face and said, "Karl, while the ladies are cleaning up, why don't you come into the front office with me now? We can go over some business, I just happen to have something for you personally and we can have a schnapps or two?"

Emil's suggestion penetrated Mueller's fog as the thought of his little *side fee* penetrated his brain, "Ja, Emil excellent idea."

Mueller staggered and followed right behind Emil as they entered his office. Emil pointed to the large office chair in front of his desk and Mueller dumped himself into it, almost flipping it over.

Emil reached into a cabinet behind the desk, extracted two sizeable shot glasses, opened a bottle of excellent schnapps and poured them both a substantial shot.

All smiles, he raised up his glass for a toast. "To better days!"

They clicked glasses, knocked down the schnapps and Emil quickly refilled Mueller's encouraging him to offer a toast.

By this time, Mueller's eyes were just about glazed over. He raised his glass, mixing spittle with words as he said, "And to a safe flight and a wonderful reception for our beloved Reichsmarschall!"

Emil hid his pleasure at this revelation and simply responded, "Prost!"

He now knew that the "important guest" was none other than Reichsmarschall Hermann Wilhelm Göring one of the most powerful members of Hitler's inner circle and a prime target for the Resistance.

Within a few minutes, the young German was snoring loudly, his head lolling to either side as he tilted back in the office chair.

Emil quietly checked him, felt that he was out for a while and exited the office. He snapped his fingers as he remembered the unlocked front door, locked it to preclude other unwelcome visitors and quickly ran up the stairs.

CHAPTER 34

Monday, 5 June 1944 4:15 AM Terror and Death at the Chicken House"

Emil took the stairs two at a time, bursting into the living space only to find everyone up there still asleep.

Miep must still be downstairs calming the women down, he thought.

14-year-old Jan got up quickly from a cot in the corner of the dining area and, rubbing his eyes, asked, "Uncle? Is everything okay?"

Emil looked at the boy, then around the living room, "Lucien? Where is Lucien?"

"I don't know, Uncle. The last I saw him he was with Father Catron bringing some food to some woman who was getting ready to have a baby."

Emil, frustrated, tried to think who he could contact at this hour to alert them to the "special guest", and, more importantly, he needed Lucien to help him with the drunk in his office. He quickly discounted the notion of using the sleeping American and the Brit to get rid of Mueller.

He now needed to focus and headed toward his upstairs study. Once there, he sat at the desk and started to investigate his coded file for a British SOE radio operator. It would be risky to ask one of their radio operators to pass this tip onto British Intelligence, but Goering was too important a target to miss.

Just at that moment, Miep came bursting through the stairway door into the room, shrieking in a high-pitched voice, "He's got Ellen! He's got Ellen!"

Emil, startled, cried out, "What? Who has Ellen?"

But he knew even as the words came out of his mouth.

"Mueller has her, Emil. He came into the ladies' washroom and grabbed her, dragged her by her hair into your office. The screams coming out of there are awful! He's going to kill her! Hurry! Do something!"

Emil ran over to the nightstand in his bedroom and grabbed his Browning Hi-Power 9 MM semi-automatic pistol out of the drawer. He quickly slid the action back to check that it was chambered with the 9 MM ammunition and turned back around, heading towards the stairs.

Miep's eyes grew wider at the sight of Emil's handgun, "Mother of God! Oh, Emil, be careful"

Emil made it down the stairs in record time and ran to his office. The lady volunteers were all pounding on the office door and yelling at Mueller to let Ellen go. Emil could hear Ellen screaming inside over the hoarse voice of the German corporal.

He pushed the ladies aside and yelled through the door, "Mueller! This is Emil. Stop this now. Let the girl go at once."

"Go away, before I kill her, Delacroix. She belongs to me."

My God! He's absolutely crazy, thought Emil. He remembered the spare keys to the building in his office located in the commercial kitchen table drawer.

More pleas and more screams coming from Ellen propelled him into the kitchen where he frantically tore through several drawers until at last, he came up with the keys.

Racing back to the front office, he fumbled through the keys until he located the office door key. With trembling fingers, he tried inserting the key into the lockset only to find that it was blocked by the key on the inside.

He took a deep breath and carefully put the spare into the lock, pushed gently and was rewarded with the sound of the key on the other side out falling to the floor.

He hurriedly turned the key, heard the lock click open and pushed the door. It wouldn't budge. Mueller must have blocked it somehow. More screams and pleading from his niece tore at his heart. He turned to the ladies and signaled them to help him push.

Magda immediately came up beside him and, joined by the other three women they managed to push the door open enough to allow

Emil to squeeze through.

The women backed away from the door and for a moment, there was muted conversation coming from inside the office with whimpering cries from Ellen in the background.

Then there was a loud gunshot followed by more screams from within. Within seconds, Emil came staggering out of the office holding his left shoulder. His face suddenly turned a ghostly pale. He took four steps away from the office door and collapsed onto the floor.

Miep arrived just in time to see Emil collapse. She wanted to yell at whoever was shrieking to shut up so she could think straight, and then realized the high-pitched screaming was coming from her own lips.

Emil lay there unconscious in a slowly increasing pool of blood. The other ladies gathered around Miep and tried to help her move Emil. There was now a chorus of hysterical, screaming women frantic to help Miep with Emil.

Amid all this confusion, no one noticed a figure slipping past them and entering the office. Suddenly, a gunshot came from within. Moments later, this was followed by a second gunshot and then, for what seemed like an eternity, all became eerily quiet.

The women froze, not sure what to do. Just then, the door to the office opened fully and Jack emerged, carrying Ellen in his arms. The young woman was clinging onto him her face buried into his chest. She was covered in blood and was weeping softly.

Magda jumped into action and ran over to Jack as he carried Ellen into the kitchen. She cleared a place on the large wooden table. Jack lowered her gently onto the table with Magda's assistance.

She appeared to have passed out but was breathing normally. Jack checked her over for the source of the blood and concluded that the blood was not hers, but it came from Mueller after he shot him.

Leticia ran into the dressing room and emerged with a blanket. She nodded to Jack as she covered Ellen up. Both Magda and Leticia were speaking softly to her, trying to comfort her.

Jack, seeing that she was being attended to by the two ladies, hustled back to check on Emil. He gently pushed Miep aside and rolled

Emil on his right side. There was a penetrating wound on his left shoulder, just missing his chest. He tore a piece of his shirt and showed Miep how to apply pressure on the wound.

Jack needed help and he needed it fast. He was at a loss as to whom he could contact, and who he could send for help. The last thing he wanted to do was to alert the authorities about this unfolding mess. The fact that he didn't speak French, Dutch, Flemish or German didn't help. At this point he wasn't too sure about English either.

Just when he was out of ideas, Lucien opened the front door and walked in followed by Father Catron, both men laughing and talking animatedly.

CHAPTER 35

Monday, 5 June 1944 4:30 AM at the Chicken house, twenty-four cooked chickens and one dead Nazi

Lucien and Father Cory were confronted by a scene of total chaos: Emil Delacroix lay on his side on the hallway floor, wounded, unconscious in a pool of blood. Kneeling next to Emil, Miep and Jack were talking rapidly and ministering to him.

Two of Father Cory's chicken project volunteers were hovering over Jack, Miep and the wounded Emil, while over in the nearby kitchen two more women were hovering over a woman who also appeared to be unconscious and covered in blood.

All of this was overshadowed by all the women sobbing and in great distress.

Before Lucien could say anything, Jack cried out, "Lucien! Thank God you're here. Can you get Kurt over here right away? If not available, can we get Emil to a hospital?"

Lucien, always calm under stress, first pointed to the kitchen and motioned Father Catron to check on Ellen then he said, "Good God, Lieutenant! What just happened here?"

"Not now, Lucien. I will explain but first Emil needs attention right now."

At that moment, young Jan appeared, having just raced down from the upstairs living area. Lucien called him over and directed his attention away from the bloody scene on the floor. "Jan, can you go quietly and calmly outside, walk to the curb and look across the street by those tall trees and give my men a sign for me?"

Jan's eyes suddenly grew larger, "Yes, of course, Uncle. What do you want me to do then?"

"Good boy! Just slowly and calmly make the sign of the Cross, turn around and slowly walk back to the front door. Turn around one more time and make the sign of the Cross again. Marcelino and Gerard will understand that signal and come to the door. Let them in immediately."

Jan nodded and hustled to the front door. While awaiting the arrival of his two trusted men, Lucien again looked to Jack for an explanation. Jack just finished pressing a clean cloth over Emil's wound and looked back at Lucien,

"Bullet wound left shoulder. He's lost a lot of blood, but I think we've stopped it now with the pressure over the wound. So, I'm hopeful that an artery may not be involved."

Lucien nodded, "Okay, who shot him?"

"That German corporal Mueller."

Seething with barely contained rage, Lucien demanded, "Mueller? That son of a bitch shot Emil. I will kill the bastard! Where is he?"

"He's dead. I killed him, Lucien. He's in the front office. I will explain later. But now Emil needs immediate attention, and Ellen also needs to be looked at."

"Ellen? Emil's niece? That's who is on the table in there?" Lucien said looking from Jack to the kitchen where Father Catron and two women were standing over Ellen. "What happened to her?"

"So far, all I know is that the German came in about a half-hour ago, roaring drunk, totally fixated on the girl, grabbed her, dragged her off into the front office and barricaded himself in there."

Lucien nodded, his face twisted into an angry snarl, "And Emil tried to stop this, I assume?"

"Yes, Emil managed to gain access to the office and tried to talk the Kraut down but got shot instead."

Just then, Marcelino and Gerard came in, and quickly took in the scene. Lucien spoke to them in rapid fire French and they moved towards the front office with guns drawn. Lucien turned back to Jack, "I just want to make sure that that Boche bastard is dead."

"Oh, he's dead, Lucien. I am an excellent shot. He's dead for certain."

Moments later, Marcelino and Gerard came out both with a grim smile on their faces. Marcelino asked in heavily accented English, "Kraut asshole is dead. I mean very dead. Who shot him?"

Lucien pointed to Jack and Marcelino asked, "Which was your first shot?" he said pointing first to his forehead and then to his crotch.

Gerard, sporting a big, toothy grin, whistled his appreciation and said, "Good shooting, Cowboy."

Jack was losing patience with all of this while Emil lay there wounded, possibly dying, but responded to these two Resistance warriors,

"The crotch first, and then I gave it a couple of seconds for the bastard to realize he had been castrated, then the forehead second. I wanted him to suffer first before I put him out of his miserable life."

Marcelino and Gerard both laughed, "You Americans are all cowboys! We should do this on all of these Nazi animals, Crotch first, head second. You are a true Cowboy!"

Despite everything that was happening, Jack couldn't stifle a laugh, then he said, "Okay, so I'm a Cowboy from *Western* North Carolina. Now, let's get Emil some help, okay?"

Lucien nodded in agreement and urgently called over to Father Catron standing in the Kitchen. "Father, please go with Marcelino and get Kurt Stark. Marcelino will be your protection and try to get any supplies that Kurt needs get back to us right away."

Within minutes, Father Catron and Marcelino left on their mission.

Lucien, taking charge of the group, then addressed Jack, and Gerard,

"Let's get Emil upstairs where Kurt, if he can get here, can get a good look at him. I know I spotted a spare door in the kitchen storage area. Gerard and I will use that as a stretcher to get him up the stairs and out of sight. Jack, if you can hold the doors open for us?"

He then called into Miep who had moved into the kitchen to check on her niece.

"Miep, if you and the ladies there can tend to the young woman, that would be very good. We are going to get Emil upstairs and out of sight. It would be wise to get her upstairs as well where Kurt can tend to her.

CHAPTER 36

Monday, 5 June 1944 5:50 AM Taking Care of Ellen & Emil at the Chicken House

Kurt Stark instructed Miep to remove the straps which secured the facemask to Emil's face. This was done after switching the ether mixture to pure oxygen at the conclusion of his emergency surgical intervention.

He carefully monitored Emil's blood pressure and heart rate during the twenty minutes it took him to surgically repair the damage done to his left shoulder by the 9mm Luger round from Mueller's pistol.

Once Kurt got a good look at the wound, he was relieved to see that there was no arterial damage. He cauterized where necessary, cleansed the wound, drew it partially together with stitches and packed it with sulfa. He instructed Miep to apply the powder every four hours as needed.

Emil was stirring and would be in pain when he was fully awake, but that was unavoidable. Morphine and other stronger pain killers were in short supply and not available to veterinarians during the Nazi occupation. The white aspirin powder might help in some small way, but Emil would just have to suffer through it.

Kurt carefully tightened the valves on the anesthesia bottles and placed them by the door leading to the stairs. He thought how lucky he was that Father Catron's influence with a mutual doctor friend enabled him to access the anesthesia bottles and additional vital supplies.

The priest accomplished all this within a very short period since Emil was shot. The last thing Kurt wanted to do was lose that valuable contact with the doctor.

He was mindful that Father Catron promised to return these items promptly before the German controlled hospital authorities did their daily morning assessment and might discover a discrepancy in their inventory.

Returning to Emil's bedside, he put his hand on Miep's shoulder, "Miep, this is the best that I can do. Unfortunately, I do not have access to plasma or other transfusion capability. The good news is that Emil did not lose too much blood before you applied pressure to the wound. That was very good thinking."

Miep smiled and nodded but knew that it was due to the advice and direction given by the American airman.

Kurt now wanted to check on young Ellen. Miep told him that thanks to the sleep aid he had provided, she was now asleep. He nodded and followed Miep into one of the guest rooms to check on her. Earlier, after the horrific attack by Mueller, Miep and Magda assisted Ellen upstairs.

As they helped her up the stairs leading to the apartment, Ellen spoke in choked whispers, more like gasps, apparently in a state of traumatic shock. This did not surprise Magda, herself a previous victim of sexual assault. That had been by a German soldier during the initial occupation of Belgium. She knew well the signs of shock and trauma.

She and Miep helped Ellen to get through a necessary clean-up and sponge bath. There was no doubt that she had been brutalized. The traumatic nature of the assault was evidenced by her two black eyes, swollen lips, and bruises on her cheek bones, neck, arms and her breasts., but Magda didn't think the creep had managed to complete his intention before he was interrupted by Emil and then killed by the American pilot who everyone was calling, "Cowboy."

Magda quietly shared her assessment with Miep after they helped her into a sleeping gown and let her lay down on top of the covers of the bed. She also shared this belief with Kurt as all three stood just inside the bedroom observing the sleeping young woman.

Kurt just nodded, shook his head in sadness and left the room. He intended to stop in the adjacent guest room to check on the Brit. Much to his surprise, the bed was empty and there was no sign of Jock.

The crippled SAS man had disappeared.

CHAPTER 37

Monday, 5 June 1944 6:20 AM Chicken Project and a Dead Nazi Sante-Walburg, Belgium

While Kurt and Miep were attending to Emil and Ellen, Jack went back downstairs to see if he could help the four "Chicken Project" ladies, Magda, Theresa, Joyce, and Leticia as they made best efforts to complete the "Chicken Project."

They all understood that the German military expected the 40 chickens and side dishes to arrive at the Liege Aerodrome before noon. Failure to comply would surely bring not only the wrath of the local German hierarchy but expose Emil and his entire operation to intense scrutiny and severe punishment. His entire Resistance organization could be uncovered.

Time was running out.

On top of that, there was the matter of a dead Nazi Corporal in Emil's office, and a cleanup of the mess associated with both his and Emil's shootings.

In a few minutes, Jack and the ladies were joined by Lucien and Gerard who were also ready to help with the project and cleanup. Marcelino was still gone, assisting Father Catron.

Lucien summed up the situation in English which they all understood to varying degrees, "We have 24 chickens already cooked. Magda tells me that they are well on their way to preparing another 16 chickens, but not nearly enough side-dishes,"

Magda nodded in agreement, Lucien continued, "Miep is needed upstairs to attend to the care of Emil and Ellen, so it's up to us gathered here to continue,"

They all agreed as he went on, "There is still the 'little' matter of removing and disposing of the body of a dead German asshole in such a way as to not create a major scandal and bring the Gestapo down here breathing on our necks."

Again, all were following his line of thinking, "It is obvious that a more thorough cleanup of the office, floor outside of the office and anything else that could be regarded as a 'crime scene" is necessary,"

Lucien looked at everyone to ensure they were still following his line of thinking and continued, "And, to top all these things off, it appears that our Brit with the broken leg has walked away. Is there anything else?"

A Scottish voice from within Emil's office replied, "Yes. You've forgotten to mention that we need to search outside the premises for the dead Nazi prick's military vehicle which will be a sure giveaway for any of the authorities looking for him."

With that, "Jock", the SAS commando emerged from Emil's office with a big smile on his face and Mueller's Walther P-38 9 mm stuck firmly in his waistband. In his right hand he held Emil's 9 mm Browning Hi Power with the slide opened indicating it was empty, and in his left hand he held his walking cane.

He hobbled over to a stunned Jack and handed him Emil's Browning. "Here, Mate, I think you dropped this with all the confusion going on at the time. You will note the open slide of this weapon which indicates that you fired the last two bullets into that asshole."

Jock smiled and repeated the last part of his statement, "The last two bullets."

Jack reacted with a start to the implications of how lucky he was that there were *any bullets* remaining in Emil's gun. In the heat of the moment, he scooped it up where Emil dropped it after being shot. He needed to beat Mueller to "the draw" before he was also shot.

He took aim at Mueller's crotch taking morbid satisfaction at the shocked look on the German's face as he felt the unbelievable wave of pain and realization of his brutal emasculation. He coldly waited for several seconds before Mueller could collapse onto the floor and carefully and deliberately put a round right in the middle of the big drunk oaf's forehead.

Jack nodded to the Brit and took the weapon, Jock grinned and continued, "If you were an SAS man in training, dropping your weapon would have been frowned upon. Would've gotten your ass kicked."

He paused as though he was deep in thought, then snapped his fingers as if a thought suddenly came upon him, "Oh, I get it now, you had to pick up the girl, but really, Yank, dropping your weapon? Failing to reload?" he tried to suppress a laugh, failed and continued, "Bad form, even for a 'Cowboy' to lose your weapon no matter how bad the situation is. Try to do better next time."

Jack smiled as he held up his middle finger.

"I hope there won't be a 'next time"

Jock's smile grew even larger as he held up his middle finger in return, "You better believe there will indeed be a next time, Mate."

Still smiling, he went on, "You realize of course that I'm just using my sophisticated British humor to lessen the tension a bit. In all seriousness, *good shooting*! I like the crotch and forehead thing. Nice touch. You can stand by my side anytime."

At that point, Janine and Denise walked in from their time in Brussels, totally unprepared for what was arrayed before them. They surveyed the group standing there in front of Emil's office including the wounded British SAS man and Lieutenant Jack. Looking directly at their brother, Janine asked,

"Lucien, what's going on?"

Lucien responded, "It's a bit of a long story."

CHAPTER 38

Monday, 5 June 1944 07:59 AM dealing with the Chicken Project and a Dead Nazi
Sante-Walburg, Belgium

Lucien briefed his two sisters on the events leading up to the very moment they walked in. Once they were brought up to speed, the very first thing they wanted to do was to see Emil and Ellen.

Denise was also anxious to see her son, Jan, who was upstairs helping Miep. They raced upstairs while the others set about tackling the tasks in front of them.

Lucien asked Gerard to carefully scout outside for the German's vehicle while the Chicken Project women busily cooked and prepared the remaining chickens.

Jack found a bucket and mop in the kitchen pantry, filled it with soapy water and carefully mopped the blood off the cement floor in front of Emil's office. Jock, still experiencing obvious pain from his broken right leg, tried to help with the clean-up.

He was eventually overruled by Lucien and the women and consigned to a chair at the kitchen table to assist in packaging up the side dishes. These consisted of cooked potatoes and some assorted bakery goods brought to the warehouse the other night by the Black-Market suppliers.

Jock grumbled at this humiliating demotion but was quickly charmed by the smiling faces of the young women volunteers who ignored his occasional sneaking of a tidbit here and there.

Gerard came back into the front of the building and reported that he had located the vehicle on a quiet side street not far from the large garage style door leading into the chicken warehouse garage.

"Perfect!" Lucien exclaimed, "If there's not any traffic to speak of, can you get the vehicle started and back it into the warehouse?"

It suddenly occurred to Lucien that they needed Mueller's keys. Gerard went into Emil's office and unceremoniously went through the dead German's pockets. He extracted a set of Mercedes keys belonging to the military vehicle.

He then slipped out the back door of the complex, moved cautiously towards the side street where the vehicle was parked. Once he was certain that nobody was in the vicinity, he quickly got in and started the vehicle.

Miep, who had just come downstairs relieved by Janice and Denise, hurried to the warehouse section of the complex to open the door for Gerard. Within a few moments, the vehicle was successfully ensconced in the warehouse and the warehouse door was closed.

Next, Lucien, Gerard and Marcelino prepared to move the body from Emil's office through the warehouse hallway and into the garage. Miep found a large rolling service cart in the garage that was used to transport multiple heavy boxes. She rolled it down the hallway to the entrance of the office and placed a small canvas tarp on top of the cart to cover the body.

They cautioned the women that they were about to bring the body out of Emil's office, and they suggested it might be better to busy themselves somewhere else to avoid being disturbed by the sight.

All four of them shrugged their shoulders and said that they did not care one bit. Leticia nicknamed "Letty" said she would like to spit on the corpse. Father Catron, who had just come downstairs with Jan, scolded Letty and said,

"As much as we have been wronged by our enemies, we must still respect the dead. We are better than that."

The Chicken Project women folded their arms across their chests in defiance. The priest just shook his head in sadness. He, of course was mindful that they all lost their husbands and the fathers of their children because of murderous Nazis like Mueller. It was not really a surprise that they didn't show the least bit of sympathy or respect for the dead man.

When the body was placed on the rolling cart, the priest stopped the men from immediately rolling down the hallway. He said a quiet prayer in Latin, sprinkling Holy Water over the body and applying some directly to the German's hands.

As he later told his Superior, the Cardinal Archbishop of Belgium, he would have also applied Holy Water to the dead man's forehead as the ritual called for, but there wasn't much left of the forehead after Jack put a bullet through it.

CHAPTER 39

Monday, 5 June 1944 11:00 AM inside Emil's Chicken House Garage Change in Plans

The four ladies who comprised the members of the "Chicken Project" smiled and hugged each other as Emil's Chicken Truck was now loaded with ten large, covered cast iron pots securely fastened with straps over the top and secured to the wooden floor of the truck. Each pot held four roasted chickens, scored and quartered for easy serving when they arrived at the aerodrome.

Also included were two large wooden crates. One held 40 baked potatoes cut in half and wrapped in parchment paper. The other crate contained 80 assorted bakery items supplied by Emil's black-market contacts.

There was an adjacent passenger van with Emil's markings parked next to the truck ready to transport the team to the aerodrome. There they would assist the Aerodrome staff to distribute the food to the assembled guests.

Magda, Theresa, Joyce, and Leticia were exhausted physically and emotionally but filled with a sense of pride and accomplishment.

Miep smiled, kissed and hugged each one of the women individually. Father Catron laughed and made the Sign of the Cross over each woman and said, "What an amazing accomplishment! You all worked so hard through the night, experienced a horrific attack on Ellen by a deranged Nazi, saw Emil get shot and yet you all persevered and came through it all! God is Great!"

Lucien clapped his hands twice for attention, "Okay! That is all true, but we now must deliver the order on time. As we get ready to proceed to the aerodrome, please remember to put on your clean aprons. Then we will be on our way."

Miep hit the switch to open the huge garage doors. Lucien started up Emil's Chicken truck and Gerard started up the van. Both drivers waited for the doors to fully open.

Just before they put their vehicles in gear, they were confronted by Janine standing outside on the sidewalk in front of the opened door shaking her head, "No!"

Lucien jumped out of the truck and looked at her as did Gerard.

She simply said, "The Allies have started bombing the aerodrome and the surrounding area!"

As she said this, they could hear anti-aircraft batteries firing, bombs detonating and sirens blaring all not far away from their location. They quickly shut down the vehicles, closed the outside door and everyone got out and headed back down the hallway to the kitchen to regroup.

Miep addressed Lucien, "You know that we have a bomb shelter underneath this building. Should we move Emil and Ellen, Father Catron, the four volunteers and our two airmen down there?"

Just then there was a loud explosion just outside the building and they all instinctively cringed. Lucien nodded, "Yes, Marcelino, Gerard and I will move Emil, you women can move Ellen. The two airmen can manage. Let's get a move on!"

Miep ran up the stairs with Janine and told Denise of their plan to move to the bomb shelter beneath the building. Within minutes, they were all moving everyone downstairs. Lucien, Marcelino and Gerard carried the makeshift stretcher with a very unhappy Emil on board who said he could walk himself. This, of course, fell on deaf ears.

Jack and Jock made it down the stairs, Jack was a lot better than Jock who was really struggling with pain.

Lucien, for his part, was first and foremost caring for his family and friends there at the Chicken House but was also worried about the team he had organized to take out the visiting dignitaries who these chickens were slated for.

It turned out that the hit team were all okay and found shelter near the aerodrome and were unscathed.

CHAPTER 40

Monday, 5 June 1944 11:20 AM Bomb Shelter hidden underneath Emil's Chicken House.

They all huddled on benches along the wall in complete darkness for a few moments until Miep was able to locate several flashlights. There was very little conversation as they all felt the vibrations of some very powerful explosions.

Denise sat next to a silent and withdrawn Ellen with her arm draped around her shoulder. She made sure she was covered with a heavy shawl taken from Miep's drawer.

Emil finally got his wish and was sitting upright next to Miep, his left shoulder immobilized in a sling.

Lucien, Marcelino and Gerard talked quietly amongst themselves over against one wall, while Jack and Jock sat near each other on the opposite wall.

Father Catron prayed quietly sitting next to Janine and the four Chicken Project ladies.

They all jumped at the sound of a very loud explosion that shook the cement walls of the shelter.

"That was close!" said Emil. In silence, they all seemed to agree.

After a while, the explosions seemed further away and then there were none.

"I think it's over. They have probably moved on." Said Lucien

Jack responded, "Yes, for now. They will probably be back for another circuit, but for now I'm willing to bet they've moved on to other objectives,"

The American airman's words hung in the atmosphere of the bomb shelter for a moment until the priest asked, "Do you really think so? You are more knowledgeable than the rest of us and know your tactics well. So should we be safe and remain in here or shall we go up and see if we can help others who may have been affected by the bombing?"

Jack thought about it for a moment, then responded, "I think that this is the beginning of the European invasion. The bomber groups are hitting airfields and infrastructure all over the occupied territories and especially along the coastline. They will circle around and hit airfields like Liege which are more inland. But I think we have some time, Father if you want to see if we can help others."

"Noble thought, Yank," said Jock, who continued, "Yes, it's certainly important to get up there to help others, but I see an opportunity here to help ourselves with this little problem of a dead Nazi, his dead Nazi staff car, and a bunch of meals that will better serve Father's poor and hungry rather than fill the bellies of some arrogant German pricks. I have an idea."

CHAPTER 41

Monday, 5 June 1944 12:15 PM, Dumping Mueller Rue Saint Nicolas near Aerodrome Liege, Belgium

Gerard drove the German staff car along the Rue Saint Nicolas approaching the aerodrome at Liege. Mueller's body slumped in the passenger seat. Gerard wore the German's blood-stained uniform jacket in case they were stopped.

He was followed at a discreet distance by a small, nondescript sedan driven by Marcelino with Jock in the right seat. There had been some fierce arguments back at the Chicken House about allowing Jock to come along, but this adventure was Jock's idea, and they respected the SAS man's expertise in matters like these.

Further back in this three-car convoy was Emil's smaller Chicken House passenger van driven by Lucien. The large Chicken House truck was intentionally left back at the warehouse.

The van's passenger seats had been hastily removed and several small, covered metal pots containing one cooked chicken in each were secured haphazardly on the floor where the seats were previously located.

Secured underneath the hood of the Chicken House van was a package containing a small plastique bomb frequently used by the Resistance courtesy of British Intelligence airdrops. There was another identical device located just above the gas tank.

Both were wired to a single detonator and battery case that Lucien would be able to activate remotely by utilizing a hand-held military radio. Similar devices were implanted in the German staff car.

All the men were heavily armed. Except "Dead Mueller" of course. Jock had the German's fully loaded Walther PPK 9 mm in his waistband and two loaded magazines in his pocket.

Following even further back were four additional members of the *Vérité Française Resistance* who were prepared to intervene if necessary. These were the men who initially had planned to greet Reichsmarschall Hermann Wilhelm Göring as he sat down for a delicious chicken dinner from Emil's Chicken House. While they were disappointed that Göring didn't show, they were enjoying this adventure.

Lucien had thoughtfully invited them to stick around as Jock's plan for disposing of the dead Nazi was unfolding.

As they drove approximately 9 kilometers towards the aerodrome from Sante Walburg, the recent bombing by the Allied Airforce had taken a visible toll. Some of the ordinance had missed the field completely and several business and residences were destroyed or badly damaged. Quite a few civilians had ventured outside, digging through the rubble, looking for survivors, pets and family valuables.

This was not the scenario that Jock was looking for. As they continued their journey, he finally came across some smoldering ruins of commercial type structures along with some heavily damaged trucks and cars. There were no people milling about at this location and Jock signaled that this was the place suited to his plan.

Marcelino pulled up next to the German staff car and signaled Gerard to pull up behind the remains of a large truck still smoldering. In a few moments, Lucien pulled in behind the staff car. They waited for a few additional minutes to make sure there were no nosy observers. Satisfied that there was still no one in sight, they proceeded with their plan.

Gerard struggled out of the Nazi uniform jacket and, with Marcelino's assistance pulled it on to Mueller and eased his body over to the driver's side. He sprinkled a cupful of petrol over the dead German's body then carefully closed the driver's side door.

He climbed into Marcelino's car and Lucien soon took the remaining rear seat. Marcelino backed the car away from the staff car and the van, turned around and drove about 200 meters away, coming to a stop.

Once they were certain there were no onlookers nearby, Lucien activated the radio-controlled remote devices and both vehicles erupted into sensational explosions.

They remained long enough to see that both vehicles were totally immersed in flames. After that, they departed the area and took a circuitous route back to the Chicken House.

Looking back over his shoulder, Jock smiled and said,

"Good job, everyone. The Krauts will think that Mueller and the Chicken van were on their way to the aerodrome to fulfill the chicken project when those nasty Allied blokes obliterated their asses."

At that precise moment, the "nasty Allied blokes" were coming back for a second attack as Jack had predicted. Two P-47's swooped right over their heads heading at top speed for the aerodrome. Marcelino pulled up adjacent to a church that was largely unscathed in the previous attack in hopes that history would repeat itself.

After several more P-47 "Jugs" flew over heading in the same direction, he decided to press on. The last thing he, or anyone else in the group wanted to encounter was the full wrath of the eight .50 caliber machine guns mounted in the wings of these fearsome aircraft.

After a slow fifteen-minute drive, they arrived in the Sante Walburg area and cautiously circled the block containing Emil's Chicken house, looking for anything out of the ordinary. Lucien spotted two trusted members of the FFI Resistance who allowed themselves to be seen. This was their signal that, so far, everything was okay.

They parked at a quiet street that bordered the Chicken House, walked fifty meters to a side entrance and quickly went in. Once inside, they all inhaled deeply and breathed out with a sigh of relief, *Mission accomplished*!

CHAPTER 42

Monday, 5 June 1944 1:00 PM- Planning Ahead at Emil's Chicken house Sante-Walburg, Belgium

Lucien and Marcelino walked down the long hallway inside Emil's Chicken House and waited patiently for Jock to painfully make his way to join them. Together, they took the stairs leading up to the living quarters on top.

Gerard, meanwhile, slipped out the side door to share information with the two *Resistance* members who were posted outside. Once Lucien, Marcelino and Jock made it up to the living space, they were greeted with subdued enthusiasm overshadowed by concern as Father Catron asked,

"Gerard?" to which Lucien smiled,

"He's fine, he's outside speaking with some compatriots."

The group issued a collective sigh of relief now that all four were accounted for. Lucien acknowledged their concern and looked around the room making a mental note of all who were present.

In addition to Emil, Miep and Father Catron there were the two leaders of Comet Line, Janice and Denise together with young Jan. Over in the far corner of the room stood a smiling Jack Dodds. Missing was Ellen who returned to her bed once she knew the four were safe. The four "Chicken Project" ladies had been sent home to rest and promised to be on hand if their help was needed with any other aspect of this mission.

All were obviously looking to Lucien for an explanation of how the mission went. He went over the damage they witnessed on their way towards the Liege aerodrome and the overview of their actions resulting in the planned destruction of the two vehicles.

Emil moved towards a nearby armchair, wincing in pain from

his left shoulder, plopped down and spoke, "Lucien, you, Marcelino, Gerard and our British warrior, Jock are to be commended not only for your bravery, but for giving that miserable German bastard the fiery send-off he deserved. I only hope his entrance into the afterlife finds him engulfed in fire as well."

That broke the ice as they all got a laugh out of that image, including Father Catron. Emil continued, "That being said, we must not assume that this will be the end of the story. The Nazis are not dumb. They've lost one of their enlisted men who they thought was leading my vehicle on his way to fulfill a project. It seems to me that the very least Mueller's commanding officer would do in this situation would be to notify his family of his death and the circumstances surrounding it. Don't you think?"

Lucien nodded, "Yes, Emil I agree that would be the normal military protocol. But I don't see the danger to us. We've made it appear that he was caught in the Allied Air Force attack on the Liege aerodrome. What's your concern?"

Jock spoke up, "I see Emil's concern and I suspect he has a lot more experience with explosives and Resistance operations than just a mere "Chicken Merchant."

He had everyone's attention as they knew this to be true, "There were several unavoidable deficiencies that may cause the Nazis to investigate further. The first and foremost is that both vehicles were destroyed by an *interior* explosion rather than an *exterior* explosion.

Emil smiled, nodded, "Yes. An exterior explosion which would have been caused by ordinance dropped during an airborne attack.

Jock continued, "The second deficiency is that if the Germans do any kind of a postmortem on the body it's possible that they will find the cause of death was two gunshot wounds and not an exterior explosion caused by the air raid."

Everyone's heads were going back and forth, from Jock to Emil as though they were watching a tennis match. Jock continued, "And there is a third problem that will lead them right here very soon to the Chicken house."

All eyes turned back to Emil as he cleared his throat and rubbed his left shoulder, "I think I know where you are going, Jock. The condition of all the human remains?"

Jock laughed, "Precisely! There was a human body in the German vehicle, but no human body in the Chicken House van. In other words, two vehicles and only one body. Where is the body of the driver of the chicken van?"

Jock went on, "On top of that, a smart investigator will have discovered that the 'Chicken Project' called for 40 cooked chickens and side-dishes. Given the short time we had to prepare this ruse, we just placed a few cooked chickens stuck in just a few pots. So, there will not be a multitude of exploded chicken carcasses found at the scene."

Jack raised a question that probably was on everyone's mind, "Do you think the Germans would really be that thorough when there was an obvious attack going on at the time?"

Jock nodded his head at the legitimacy of the question, "We're talking about *probability*, Jack. My guess is no, they *probably* won't be that thorough. Under the circumstances of the two Allied air-raids, that's the most obvious cause of death."

He paused to look at Emil who nodded for him to continue, "But as I said, we're talking about *probability*. If, for whatever reason the Germans want to investigate further, they will inevitably show up here and things could get very ugly, very fast."

CHAPTER 43

Monday, 5 June 1944 1:10 PM Next Moves Emil's Chicken house Sante-Walburg, Belgium

Emil understood Jock's point that things could go wrong very fast due to some unavoidable problems with their mission to dispose of Mueller's body and staff car. "Look, a tactical mistake was made. It was understandable given the very short time we had to act. Jock came up with a great plan under the circumstances. But, when it came to the forty chickens and all the preparation that our team put into it, we did not want to destroy so much food when so many of our people are starving. Okay it's done, we saved the food and did not place it in the van to be destroyed. Everyone understand?"

Everyone agreed. Emil then looked to Miep and Janice and Denise, "We now must make a very difficult decision. It's quite possible that the Nazis will have much more important things to do with the allied invasion imminent. It's also possible that nothing more will come out of the death of Corporal Mueller, that his death will be viewed because of the Allied air raid just as we have staged it."

All eyes were on him as he went on, "However, we cannot put our lives at risk by disregarding the possibility that the Nazis will come here and turn this place upside down. Therefore, the prudent thing to do is right now, pack up all our belongings and quietly and efficiently evacuate this place."

Father Catron cleared his throat and said, "Sorry to interrupt you, my brother, Emil. But what should we do about all the food that was part of the 'Chicken Project? I'm sure you have a plan?"

"Yes, of course, Father. I would like you to get our four wonderful women back over here right away and organize a very discreet, very orderly distribution of those meals and whatever other supplies we can give them. Can you do that?"

The priest stood up prepared to depart immediately, but Emil held up his hand signaling he wasn't quite through just yet. Catron sat back down.

Emil smiled, "There's also the problem of over 1200 chickens and roosters. We cannot have a mass stampede of people raiding my place once we depart the premises."

He laughed along with the others, "First, the sight of dozens of people running after all the birds would not only be chaotic, but it would also appear to be looting and would attract the attention of the local police and ultimately the Gestapo. So, we need to come up with a method to take care of that issue.

Janine spoke up, "Emil! This is a terrible decision for you and Miep. You've built this place into a thriving business, one that provides quietly for so many people right under the Germans' noses. And, by serving the needs of the Boche you've been able to operate on behalf of all of us. I feel terrible."

Miep interjected, "Thank you, Janine, but do not worry. There are more important things to worry about right now. And Emil and I will always land on our feet. Once this War is over and all the German occupiers are gone or dead, we will rebuild our business back the same just as we did before. Right Emil?"

"No, Miep."

Shocked, everyone looked at Emil including Miep,

"We will rebuild our business *even better than before*! Now let's get busy, we must move fast."

They all laughed and got busy coming up with alternate plans.

CHAPTER 44

Monday, 5 June 1944 6:00 PM-Preparing to depart Emil's Chicken house

Father Catron, together with Magda, Theresa, Joyce, and Leticia finished transporting the remaining cooked chickens and other perishable and non-perishable food supplies from the warehouse to secure storage at Saint Thomas the Apostle Catholic Church, his church and school. The women would oversee discreet distribution to the parish families who were all in dire need.

Several trusted older men from his parish, many of whom were not only experienced farmers but were also fiercely loyal to the resistance had agreed to supervise the removal of the live chickens over the next few days. They would be placed in backyard chicken coops being hurriedly built throughout the parish.

As Father Catron indicated, these "older" men were very capable. They were considered too old to serve in the forced labor camps by the Nazis. Most of them had served in the Belgian military during the First World War and knew their way around combat.

These same men would also do their best to protect the Chicken House property from looters. Father Catron felt that its sturdy concrete structure and bomb shelter would become invaluable as the Allied invasion "heated up".

When word got out warning that this property was protected by not only the Church but the Resistance, it would be considered off limits by most people in the area. Those who were too stupid or foolish to ignore this warning would pay a dear price.

Emil shrugged off the pain in his left shoulder and went through his business office records, burning anything that might be harmful or incriminating in the kitchen oven.

This was especially important for coded messages from some of his Black-market suppliers. He noted with satisfaction that the wonderful women volunteers had cleaned up any visible signs of Mueller's blood on his desk and office floor.

Using his hip, he carefully pushed against his large, heavy desk, moving it slightly out of position, revealing the hidden floor safe underneath. Quickly, he extracted his "going away" cash in the form of French francs, English pounds and American dollars. Using his hip again, he pushed the desk back into place and placed the money into a small attaché' case.

He checked to see that his additional Browning Hi Power 9 mm was fully loaded and secured it in his waistband holster. Jack retained the other Browning Hi Power he used to kill Mueller which was now reloaded with two extra magazines.

He was satisfied that both he and Jack were well armed and capable of dealing with any unforeseen situation. That went especially for Jack who dispatched the crazed German with ruthless efficiency.

Meanwhile, Miep collected some small family keepsakes but insisted that she and Emil travel light. She was trying to be practical and not emotional.

It was almost time to go for Emil and his group, so they hurried to say goodbye to Lucien, Marcelino, Gerard and to Jock whose SAS compatriots had contacted the Resistance and wanted to hook up with him, broken leg or not.

After much concern expressed by the others about his physical condition, he insisted that he would stay with these tough members of the Resistance until he could join up with the other British commandos. He looked at them and smiled,

"Mark my words, things will be heating up very soon, my friends, very soon. You take care and fight the good fight."

Jock's words were correct. This was the eve of "Operation Overlord," better known as "D-Day" which comprised the largest naval armada in Modern warfare history.

Poised to attack the Normandy coastline were 7,000 Allied ships and landing craft, 175,000 men, and more than 12,000 Allied aircraft which would fly over 14,000 sorties through the night and into the whole day.

On this eve of the attack, some 23,400 British and US Airborne troops were being dropped behind enemy lines. SAS commandos together with hundreds of *Resistance fighters* were setting about missions of sabotage and assassinations. Just before dawn Allied cruisers and battleships would unleash an unprecedented fierce bombardment of German defenses in the entire Normandy landing area

So as the group gathered at the Chicken House prepared to depart, Jock's words that, "*Things*" would definitely be "*heating up*" were prophetic indeed.

CHAPTER 45

Monday, 5 June 1944 8:50 PM Time to leave Emil's Chicken house

The rest of the Chicken House facility was secured and Emil's personal effects and those belonging to his group were assembled in the main hallway. Janine chatted with her sister, Denise, while the rest made some last-minute checks to ensure that they hadn't overlooked anything.

Denise had chosen to move over to Saint Thomas the Apostle Catholic church, Father Catron's parish to ensure that everything went well with the transition of food and supplies and to meet later with Janine and her MI-9 colleagues. She left with the priest and the women volunteers, promising that she would soon rejoin the family at the remote farm.

Meanwhile, Emil gave Jack a mysterious smile and signaled for him and Jan to follow him through the warehouse to a smaller garage adjacent to the much larger warehouse garage. Using his massive key ring, he selected a key and unlocked a side access door and flipped on an overhead light. All alone in the center of this small garage was an automobile covered by a canvas tarp.

Jan immediately let out a pleased chuckle, "Aha! The *Traction Avant!* I didn't know you still had it, Uncle!"

"Of course, Jan. you know I couldn't part with it."

He signaled young Jan to pull off the tarp which revealed a beautifully maintained black Citroën Traction Avant.

Jack was puzzled, "What exactly is this?"

Emil laughed, "This, my American friend is my beloved Citroën Traction Avant which I only drive on holidays and other very special occasions. It is a front-wheel drive beautiful creation by Andre Lefebvre and Flaminio Bertoni, a work of art."

"And you want to take this beauty instead of the Chicken Truck when there's a possibility, we may have to abandon it on the side of the road during any aerial bombings?"

Emil laughed, "Yes, of course! Jack. How long do you think this thing would last if we left it here alone while we took that smelly chicken truck?"

It was Jack's turn to laugh, "Oh! So, it was okay for me and other airmen to ride with the 'smelly' chickens but not for the rest of you?"

"Oh, come on, my friend, you must know I'm teasing you. First, we cannot take the large Chicken Truck as it would draw attention to ourselves especially if the Germans are looking for it. Right?"

"Right. Of course."

"Second, Father Catron had two of his men who are expert mechanics and who are very grateful for the chickens now in their own coops went over every millimeter of my car."

He continued, "They just finished cleaning and polishing it and getting it in perfect running order. They then filled it with petrol and placed two spare cans of petrol right over there secured to the side rack created just for that purpose. And one other thing,"

Jack sensed something coming, "Okay, what is that one other thing?"

"There is no way that I would dare put my Miep, my family into that 'smelly' chicken truck."

The three of them broke out in much-needed laughter. Emil asked Jan to get a rolling cart so he and Jack could retrieve the group's belongings and roll them down to this garage for loading.

While waiting for Jan to get back, Emil shared one more interesting item about Citroen,

"All of us who hate the Nazis should purchase a Citroen automobile because of the President of the company, Pierre-Jules Boulanger, who we all know as 'PJB'"

Jack, suspecting another joke asked, "And why is that?"

At that moment, Jan came pushing the cart, already loaded with the personal effects.

Emil laughed, "I will tell you later. It's a good story and it's true.

You will love it."

Jack and Jan followed Emil's instructions on how best to load up the Citroën Traction Avant and soon they returned to the main hallway to summon the others that it was time to get going.

Once they were all together, Janine joined them and, with her arm around Ellen, they all walked to the garage containing the Citroen.

While the group stood there saying their goodbyes to Janine, Emil went to the small service door leading to the street and poked his head outside briefly. Two trusted members of the Resistance came in and quietly huddled with Emil.

Jack saw with Emil's startled reaction that something significant was happening. The three men exchanged brief embraces then they stood to the side at a distance allowing Emil to return to his family while the farewells continued. Emil's face was completely neutral, stoic, revealing nothing of what he and the two Resistance men had discussed.

Janine hugged her cousin, Ellen and then kissed her aunt Miep, her uncle Emil and nephew, Jan. She planned to join them later after she and Denise met with Albert Ancia and Daniel Muton, her MI-9 contacts.

They would bring the two sisters up to speed on the status of "Operation Marathon" the establishment of the secret forest encampments being set up in France and in the Belgian Ardennes. Some downed Allied airmen were already in place in those camps and more to come with the help of the Comet line.

She smiled as she gave Jack a hug and handed him new photo ID card identifying him as Jaques Jordan, age 21 who suffered from a speech and hearing disorder. Just to the right of his photo were the words, "doofstomme"

He looked at it and laughed, "Doofstomme?"

Janine laughed with him, "Yes, Dutch, it means you are deaf and cannot speak. Might work if you're stopped."

He laughed again and put it into his shirt pocket. Janine very earnestly stepped closer to him and took both his hands in hers. She thanked him for protecting her family against the drunk Nazi corporal.

He blushed a little and, in turn thanked her for all she had done for him and his fellow airmen. He promised to do his best to protect her family on their way to the remote country farm where Denise's daughter, Elise, was waiting.

The two of them stood there in awkward silence as the rest of the group climbed into the Citroen. Just before Jack climbed behind the wheel, he again took both her hands in his and told her that he hoped her meetings with the MI-9 men would go well and that she could quickly rejoin them.

They both did their best not to become emotional. With that, Jack climbed in behind the wheel, and started the car up as the two Resistance members pulled the chain that elevated the garage door.

Before Jack put the Citroen into gear, Janine walked past them out the side door onto the street and turned right. She did not look back.

Jack cautiously pulled out of the garage, turned left and started up the side street. He had a nagging feeling that he might never see her again.

Sadly, he was right.

CHAPTER 46

Monday, 5 June 1944 9:00 PM The Night before the Big Day on the road to Bouillon, Belgium

After leaving the vicinity of Sante Walburg, Emil wanted Jack to drive a circuitous route to make sure they had not picked up a follower. Curfew wasn't until midnight, and because they would be on back roads on the way to a small remote farm near Bouillon, Belgium, he doubted that they would encounter any police or military roadblocks.

Emil and Jack noticed that the rest of the passengers remained quiet, each one apparently deep in their own thoughts as the sun just dipped below the western horizon.

Jack always loved cars, and this Citroen just made it into his list of interesting automobiles. Once he got the hang of shifting and down-shifting, everything fell into place, and it was a pleasure to drive. Emil quietly pointed him in the direction he had mapped out and there was little "small talk" between them.

They passed by towns with signs that said Hotton, Rochfort, and others.

After an hour of quiet driving, Jack looked over at Emil and said, "Emil, I love driving this Citroen! I can see why you're so fond of it. Are you going to finish telling me about your friend, PJP?"

"Ah, yes, Pierre-Jules Boulanger President of Citroen. I really don't know him personally. But those of us who know of him love him. He is totally screwing with the Nazis when they force Citroen to build trucks for the military."

"How did he do that?"

"He knew that he couldn't refuse to produce the T45 trucks for the Wehrmacht or he would be murdered along with his family and co-workers. So, he devised a clever way to sabotage his vehicles that was impossible to detect.

"How on earth did he do that without the Krauts figuring it out?"

Emil laughed, "He moved the little notch on the oil dipsticks that indicated the proper level of oil down just a bit lower."

Emil let that sink in then chuckled again, "By moving the notch down, the trucks would not have enough oil, but German mechanics would have no idea, because the little notch on the dipstick says it's just fine. Then, after the truck has been used for a while and is out deployed somewhere crucial, "*poof!*", the engine seizes up, and you've got a lot of angry, stranded, vulnerable Nazi assholes, running around in circles and cursing."

Jack and Emil laughed together at that image as Jack commented, "What an amazing act of sabotage! So simple, inexpensive to do and impossible to detect as the vehicle rolls off the assembly line."

Emil chuckled, "Yes, and the trucks will run for a while with no problem until deployed in a combat situation, then they seize up far removed from the factory and at a time and place that is most likely terrible for the military."

"Brilliant, but how is it that *you* know about PJP's antics, but the Nazis do not?"

"Those very few people who were entrusted with the responsibility for fabricating the flawed dipsticks are passive members of the *resistance.* They will proudly be on hand after the war to fabricate dipsticks marked correctly."

They both laughed and then settled down as the next 45 minutes passed quietly. Jack thought that he heard Miep snoring and a quick glance into the rear-view mirror confirmed it. He moved the mirror around a bit and observed Jan sound asleep resting on Ellen's shoulder. Ellen was wide awake and smiled at Jack through her swollen lips.

As they rounded a curve in the road with a sign that predicted 4 kilometers until "Saint Hubert", Jack braked to a stop because of a small car parked diagonally across the road blocking traffic.

Two armed men with carbines slung over their shoulders stood in front of their vehicle holding their hands up signaling for them to come to a stop.

CHAPTER 47

Monday, 5 June 1944 10:45 PM-the legend of"Cowboy Jack"and an unfriendly encounter on the road to Bouillon, Belgium

Emil cursed as one of the men unslung his carbine and approached them. "Shit, *Partisans!* Communists. Stay calm, hopefully they're part of the *resistance,* and not highway rats out to rob us. I will soon find out."

One man approached them. He sported a scraggly mustache and beard, stood about 5 feet 6 inches tall and displayed a cocky, yellow-toothed grin.

Jack noticed that he walked a bit unsteadily, apparently drunk. He approached the driver's side of the car, pointed his rifle in Jack's general direction, and spoke in some dialect that Emil understood and later translated,

"Ooh how nice! A beautiful luxury car out for a little country drive, are we? You must be very important friends of our German overlords to be out and about, aren't you? Everyone out of the car."

Jack, playing the deaf, mute just stared straight ahead, his left hand on top of the steering wheel, his right hand holding the Browning 9 mm pressed to his thigh. Emil smiled and put on his best charm as he responded in French instead of Flemish,

"No, Ami, not good friends of the Nazis, but good friends with Groupe G", referring to the combined Resistance movement.

The unsmiling man shook his head, obviously did not recognize Emil's reference to the *Resistance's* general membership. Gesturing with his hand he responded in French,

"I don't know and don't care who the hell you say you are good friends with you miserable Capitalist. Show me your ID."

Emil handed him an ID card that identified him as Frederick

LeBurton. Their antagonist gestured to Jack to hand over his ID card. All during this time, Jack continued to stare straight ahead.

All the while, he was quietly measuring the distance from the Citroen to the other man standing by his vehicle anxiously checking for any additional traffic.

Looks to me to be about 20 yards

The partisan banged with frustration on the roof of the Citroen, "Come on you idiot! Are you deaf? Show me your ID card!"

Emil, who cringed at the thought of this guy banging on his beloved car's roof, responded, "He actually is deaf."

With that, Emil tapped Jack on his shoulder and pantomimed producing the ID card.

Jack responded with a start coupled with gestures of humility and extracted his ID card, handing it to the partisan.

After reading the card, the man scoffed and then shone the flashlight once again on Miep, Ellen and Jan. "Okay, everyone out of the car with hands raised up in the air. Now!"

Before the back seat riders could open their passenger doors, Jack stepped out, doing his best to look non-threatening. He pretended to fumble, closing the driver's side door. The partisan, angered by Jack's apparent disregard for his instructions, grabbed Jack by the hair and slammed his head and face into the roof of the car, momentarily stunning him and bloodying his forehead, eye and mouth.

Emil diverted the partisan's attention by noisily getting out of his side of the car with only his right hand raised, the left still in a sling.

"Both hands, you idiot!"

Taking advantage of the guy's momentary distraction, Jack turned to his left, took a step towards the partisan and closed the distance with him. Then, wrapping his left arm around the man's shoulder, he pulled him towards him as if in a hug.

At the same time, using his right hand, he pressed his pistol into the center of the man's chest and fired one shot, tearing his heart and lungs into shreds. He let the dead man drop to the ground like a sack of potatoes and turned to face the man standing by the car blocking the roadway.

The other partisan reacted in absolute shock to this unexpected turn of events and made a desperate and clumsy attempt to unsling the carbine strapped over his shoulder, losing control of the rifle and letting it fall to the ground.

In a panic, he stooped to retrieve the fallen rifle while Jack, at the same time, took aim steadying the Browning Hi Power with both hands. He fired once, hitting the man in the upper right leg. He went down, howling in pain.

Jack cursed out loud, disappointed that he hit the guy in the leg rather than his intended target of the guy's chest. He mentally chalked it up to the stress of combat. Still holding the Browning with both hands in front of him, he cautiously moved toward the guy still rolling in pain on the ground next to his car.

When he saw Jack walking towards him, he rolled to his right and grabbed frantically at his carbine lying on the ground next to him. Jack yelled at him, "No! Don't do it!"

Obviously, the guy didn't understand English as he grabbed the carbine by the barrel and started to draw it towards him.

Jack dropped to one knee, carefully took aim and accurately shot him twice in the chest. He closed the remaining distance and kicked the carbine away from him. After checking to see that he was dead, he retrieved the weapon and started back towards the Citroen.

Emil quieted Miep, and Jan who were yelling in fear at the top of their lungs. Later, he would recall that Ellen was strangely silent.

CHAPTER 48

Monday, 5 June 1944 9:45 PM Out into the Dark of Night Allied C-47 transport at 5,000 feet Vicinity of Turnhout, Belgium

As Jack, Emil, Miep, Jan and Ellen prepared to clean up the mess on the road to Bouillon, the German Coastal Defenses were on high alert anticipating an imminent Allied invasion.

On this eve of the Normandy invasion, Allied records would show an incredible number of 464 B-17s and 206 B-24s hitting coastal defenses in Le Havre, Caen, Boulogne, and some sorties a little further north along the Belgian coast.

Over 23, 000 Paratroopers and Commandos would be dropped over the German occupied areas throughout the night into the next day. German radar showed a breakaway flight of aircraft moving inland from the Belgian coast near Antwerp and then turning sharply south back over to the French coastline.

On the heels of this heavy bomber incursion over Antwerp was a flight of three C-47 Transports. They were part of the allied military deception known as "Operation Titanic", a plan to sow confusion among the German defenders. This would cause them to divert resources away from the Normandy landing site.

Two of the C-47s had already dropped hundreds of dummy parachutists, noisemakers and empty supply cases to confuse the enemy as to where the invasion would take place. They turned and wheeled south as soon as their cargo was released.

The third C-47 continued for just a few minutes more to pass over a predesignated drop area allowing ten SAS commandos to go out the door in rapid succession. They were followed by a drop of two Jeeps armed with Vickers K machine guns.

Once on the ground, they were to hook up with local resistance and create as much mayhem as possible to divert Nazi attention from the true site of Normandy.

As Operation Overlord continued to unfold in the south, Allied command also planned to have these combined special forces and resistance fighters in the Belgium theater proceed to the vicinity of the Port of Antwerp. There they would join up with more resistance fighters to prevent retreating German forces from destroying the port.

As the commandos descended into the dark, Lucien, Gerard, Marcelino and fellow members of the resistance below awaited their landing and kept a watchful perimeter to ensure their safety.

The SAS commandos hooked up with Lucien and his men and launched a series of hit and run attacks on superior German military groups, creating havoc and uncertainty and paving the way for preservation of this valuable port.

Lucien and many in the resistance forces would soon become casualties during fierce encounters with the Nazis.

CHAPTER 49

Monday, 5 June 1944 11:00 PM Cleanup on the road to Bouillon, Belgium

Miep, Jan and Ellen exited the Citroen on the right side of the vehicle to avoid a large pool of blood and the body of the first partisan. Emil saw that Jack had just finished picking up the two carbines and was now struggling to pull the first dead criminal off to the side of the road by his feet.

It suddenly occurred to Emil that the American himself was still recovering from his own wounds. He called his young nephew, "Jan, can you please help Jack? I only have one good arm right now."

The boy was always eager to be of help, but this time, he looked very pale and squeamish. Nevertheless, he started to move towards the other side of the car.

Ellen stopped him and put a gentle hand on his shoulder, "It's okay, Jan, you, Uncle Emil and Tante Miep keep an eye out for approaching headlights. I will help Jack."

Miep, herself trembling and distraught after this brutal encounter, was surprised that Ellen was taking such a positive role after the terrible assault she had suffered just the other day. She took several deep breaths to calm herself and said a silent prayer that her niece would continue to improve.

Miep and Jan then kept a lookout for approaching vehicles. Thankfully this road was very quiet now as the midnight curfew time was almost upon them. She avoided the pool of blood left by the first criminal and went over to where Jack had leaned the carbines against the side of the Citroen and fit them into the trunk.

With the trunk open, she grabbed the bag containing spare clothes she had previously set aside for Jack and selected a pullover shirt to replace his blood-soaked shirt. She carefully walked past the pool of blood to the driver-side of the Citroen and placed the shirt on the dash in front of the steering wheel.

She was about to take a position behind the vehicle looking for any sign of oncoming traffic when something in that pool of blood caught her eye. Going over to get a closer look, she spotted the two ID cards that the would-be robber must have dropped when Jack shot him.

She thought: *It wouldn't do to leave these photo ID cards lying here for the friends of the two dead highway rats, or the police or the Gestapo, would it?*

She bent over with a handkerchief and carefully picked them up, wiped them off and took up her position keeping a lookout.

Meanwhile, Ellen moved quickly over to Jack and grabbed the other leg of the dead man. Together they pulled him off to the side of the road. One more big pull and the corpse rolled down a slight embankment out of sight.

Jack noted the determined look on Ellen's face as she followed him over to the second dead man. Ellen looked over the dead body without any emotion and grabbed one of his legs, waiting for Jack to do the same. Soon, they were able to pull him off the road and out of view as well.

He asked, "Were you seeing if you recognized him?"

Still without any visible sign of emotion, she responded, "No, I was looking at where you hit him. Two in the chest for sure, but the one in the upper right leg is kind of disappointing, because it looked like you were aiming for his crotch like you did with Mueller but missed."

Shocked, it took a moment for Jack to recover, he was at a loss for words, unable to come up with a retort, but Ellen gave a thin smile and said,

"Just kidding! You are most definitely an American Cowboy. And I hereby proclaim that you are my *personal* Cowboy, saving me not once, but now with this encounter saving all of us again!"

Ellen continued with her observation, "Good shooting under duress! I especially liked the way you hugged that first jerk and plugged him. He didn't see that coming. Where did you learn to do all this?"

"To be honest, I don't know. I was always an excellent shot with a pistol and rifle, but I did not have direct experience with close-quarter combat. Sure, I killed some German pilots when I shot them down, but it wasn't up close and personal like Mueller and now these two."

Ellen was looking at him with great intensity and nodded,

"And, I think, my American Friend, when people you cared about were harmed or threatened, you rose to the occasion. For which I am very grateful."

Emil interrupted this exchange and called out to them,

"Jack, Ellen, we need to get going before someone else comes along or these two have comrades nearby."

Jack nodded and looked inside the partisan's car. He was gratified to see that the key was in the ignition and the engine was still running.

"Ellen, do you think you could drive this thing a little further up the road until we can find a place to get rid of it? We will follow you."

Without a moment's hesitation, Ellen got behind the wheel, did a three-point turn and slowly started to drive along the road, waiting for the others to follow. Seeing this, Emil, Miep and Jan quickly took their places as Jack got behind the wheel, handed the replacement shirt to Emil and followed Ellen.

They drove about 300 meters along the road when Ellen spotted a small access road to the right hidden by tall grass. Placing the car in reverse, she backed up about 50 meters until the car was out of sight. She removed the keys from the ignition and pocketed them.

Before leaving the vehicle to rejoin her group, she went through the front and rear seats and grabbed some cartridge boxes and a small suitcase. She opened the suitcase to ensure there was nothing dangerous inside and saw nothing but old clothing. She left the suitcase behind, opened the trunk, found nothing of value and moved quickly back to the Citroen and got in.

Miep insisted that Jack get rid of his bloodied shirt and put on the replacement she set aside for him. She carefully wiped the blood from Jack's nose and eyes where his head was slammed into the roof of the car.

"It might look a bit suspicious if we get stopped by police if our deaf-mute driver had blood all over his shirt, and a bloody eye and split lip."

Jack obliged her, took his bloody shirt off and ditched it on the side of the access road, and put on the replacement. He looked back at Miep, who gave him a nod and an encouraging smile. "That's a good boy."

With that, everyone chuckled then Miep added, "Cowboy"

Jack just shook his head but had to laugh. That broke the tension and within minutes, they were back on the road heading to Bouillon.

CHAPTER 50

Monday, 5 June 1944 1:15 PM MI-9 Safe house Neder-Over-Heembeek district Brussels, Belgium

As the midnight curfew drew nearer, Denise stood amongst a cluster of small trees nestled in a little sidewalk garden just across the street from the safe house where she was to meet her sister, Janine, and the MI-9 agents.

Always alert for a potential trap, she carefully assessed the condition of the house for any telltale signs that something might be amiss. The front door light was not illuminated, which was in accordance with the black-out rules, there was a strip of a white cloth wrapped around the front door handle, and a small broom used to sweep the front stoop leaning against the side of the entranceway.

All the signals that the house was safe were in place. Still, she waited, stood motionless and watched. *Something was not right.*

Then, it suddenly dawned on her, *the white cloth should be tied around the handle of the broom, not the door handle.*

Tante Marie, better known to frequent downed airmen guests as "Auntie Marie", the owner of the safe house was sending out a subtle signal *that all was not well.*

Denise quietly moved away from her position and walked towards an alternate safe home several blocks away. She took a deep breath and made the sign of the cross as she drew nearer to the other safe house. *I hope to God, I'm wrong, but if not, I pray to God the others noticed and are safe.*

Arriving just before the midnight hour, and sensing that all was okay at the alternate safe house, she entered and was quietly greeted by two grim-faced MI-9 friends, Jean de Blommaert and Daniel Muton. Janine was nowhere to be seen

Jean and Daniel urgently but gently led her out the back door of the safe house through a back yard onto another street and walked her two blocks to an apartment building where they had another "safe space."

This indicated to her that both safe homes had been compromised, confirming her worst fears, Janine and Auntie Marie were in Gestapo custody and most likely undergoing severe interrogation and torture.

She protested to both British agents, "Marie and Janine will never talk!"

An unsmiling Jean de Blommaert unlocked the apartment door paused and placed his hand on her shoulder, "We cannot take the chance, Denise. Marie did not know the second safe house we just vacated, Janine did."

He shook his head sadly, and repeated himself, "We simply cannot take that chance."

Years later, Denise would learn that she was right. Despite hours of beatings, threats and torture, neither Janine nor Marie ever revealed anything.

CHAPTER 51

Tuesday, 6 June 1944 01:55 AM, Michel Family Refuge Remote, forest area near Bouillon, Belgium

Almost two hours after the attempted robbery, they drew closer to Bouillon and entered a section of dense forest. They had not seen any other vehicles on the road at this hour and had not spotted isolated homes or farms. They were truly in a very remote and isolated part of the Ardennes, close to the French and Luxembourg border.

Jack looked in the rear-view mirror and saw that both Jan and Miep had fallen asleep. Ellen, wide awake, made eye contact with him, acknowledging him with a slight smile then turned her gaze outside.

As they rounded a curve in the road, Emil tensed and quietly whispered that they were getting close to their destination. He instructed Jack to pull over to the side of the road. Once they came to a stop, he reached into the glove box and extracted a white handkerchief.

Jan was now awake and rested his chin on the back of the front row seats, curious as to what was happening. Looking over his shoulder at Jan, Emil handed him the white cloth and asked him to affix it to the radio antennae on the right front fender of the Citroen. The youngster was quick to oblige and hopped back into the rear seat.

Emil consulted a notepad and told Jack, "Drive very slowly, Jack. The entrance should be very close to the right, difficult to see with all this thick underbrush. Even though it appears that we are in the middle of nowhere, we are close. I have a feeling that they know we're here so do not be alarmed if someone steps out in front of us. No 'Cowboy' stuff unless I tell you, okay?"

Jack put the car in gear, and they started to roll forward very slowly, "Okay, Emil, but who, exactly are '*They*?"

No sooner had Jack spoken, when a young man who appeared to

be in his late teens emerged from the thick underbrush on the left side of the road. In his right hand he held a short-barreled shotgun. In his left hand he held a very bright flashlight. He pointed both items at Jack's head and signaled for him to stop.

At the same time, another man, much older than the young man to Jack's left emerged from the underbrush on the right. He toted a double-barreled shotgun pointed directly at Emil.

The older man had a big handlebar mustache and fierce eyes. He was not smiling. The atmosphere had suddenly grown very tense. Everyone in the rear seat was fully awake.

Before anyone could say anything, Jan addressed the older man on the right side of the vehicle and cried out in an excited voice, "Poppi!"

The older man cried out, "Janisch?"

Jan immediately responded to his childhood nickname in English, for Jack's benefit, "Yes, Poppi, it is me!"

The older man immediately broke out into a wide, smile and rushed to the side of the car, opening the rear passenger door. He cried out in heavily accented English, "Welcome, children! Welcome"

Jack looked at the unsmiling young man still standing to his left who nodded that it was okay to exit the driver's side of the vehicle. He slowly exited the Citroen and moved towards the front of the vehicle to meet Jan's grandfather. He noticed that the other guy stayed in his position to the left of the vehicle and remained vigilant, keeping a watchful eye on the road for any signs of approaching vehicles.

Very professional, Jack thought

By this time, Emil, Miep and Ellen had followed Jan out of the car and were exchanging embraces and excited conversation in French. They all turned to face Jack who stood awkwardly by the side of the car.

Emil motioned for Jack to come over to the group and then smiled and again spoke in English, "Jack, meet Raoul Michel, our host, and Jan and Elise's grandfather."

Jack took a step towards the man and extended his right hand. Raoul let out a laugh, handed Emil his shotgun and wrapped Jack up in a crushing grip. "Aha! The American Pilot! I have heard about you.

Bienvenue, Yank, welcome to my home!"

The other man standing to the left of the Citroen said, "Papa!" and gestured to the road.

Raoul grinned and nodded, "My son, Raymond is right, we must move off this road. Even at this hour it is possible for a vehicle to come. Please now put out your headlights. Our flashlights will guide you."

With that, Raoul let out a whistle and suddenly, the bushes just to the right of the Citroen miraculously parted, attached to ropes being pulled by two others on horseback. Two additional horses were tethered to trees just inside this new opening.

Once the bushes had been pulled aside, Jack observed a dirt road leading deeper into the forest. Emil signaled everyone to get back into the car. They waited for Raoul and Raymond to mount their own horses and proceeded to slowly follow them.

Jack was impressed by how effortlessly the old man mounted his big white mare as they moved through the opening and paused on the dirt road. In the rearview mirror, he spotted the two other people closing the bushes across the road behind them and then following on their horses.

Years later he would reflect with a smile on the unusual scene of Emil's beloved Citroën Traction Avant in procession with two mounted horsemen in front and two horsemen in the rear as they moved slowly ahead deeper into the Ardennes Forest in the middle of the night on the 6th day of June better known as D-Day.

CHAPTER 52

Tuesday, 6 June 1944 7:55 AM St. Giles Prison Brussels, Belgium

It was a long, sleepless night forced to stand barefoot in a tiny cement cubicle with her arms tied tightly behind her back. Janine knew that the insults and face slaps she took during her initial arrest was only the beginning of what was in store for her. Every time she felt like collapsing onto the floor, her female guard would rush in and slap her on the face and ears.

Her guard was a heavy-set middle-aged woman with her hair pulled back severely into a bun. She obviously relished her job. During that first hour after her arrest, her tormentor removed Janine's shoes, tied her arms behind her, cutting off circulation to her wrists and hands.

There were no windows to let in daylight. Janine guessed that it was now well after sunrise. Her legs were trembling, and her knees gave way, forcing her to sink to the floor.

Her guard materialized as if out of thin air, unlocked the door and stood Janine up roughly. She circled her, looking her over from head to foot with disdain and contempt, and then, without warning, smacked Janine squarely in the face.

That one punch snapped her head back and closed her right eye. Janine's head was spinning, she felt nauseous but fought to stay upright and not fall.

Sneering at Janine, the woman said, "My name is Frau Halder. You will never forget my name by the time I am finished with you. Now say my name."

Janine remained silent.

"Okay, have it your way."

Frau Halder punched Janine in the stomach, doubling her forward, then expertly raised her knee into Janine's face. Before she could collapse, Halder effortlessly stood her up and kept a hand on her until Janine regained her balance.

Looking at Janine's face, she was pleased to see a bloody nose and thought that she may have succeeded in breaking it. Then with a leering contempt, she said,

"You are a very pretty girl, aren't you? When I'm done with you, most men wouldn't want to have anything to do with you. Of course, that won't be the case with the men who are locked up in this place for rape and sexual assault. You will be a prize for them, and they will gladly tell us things we want to know just to get a chance to have you for their pleasure."

Janine shuddered at this thought but kept silent. The woman stepped closely towards Janine and looked over her whole body from her bare feet to her face. She then straightened up and started to step away but turned as if she had a second thought. Instead, she unleashed another powerful right hook, driving her fist into Janine's mouth, knocking her backwards onto the floor.

With her hands tied behind her, Janine could not do anything to break the fall, and she hit her head on the concrete floor, rendering her unconscious. A moment later, a bucket of cold water splashed on her face, and she was hauled back onto her feet.

Her jailer laughed, reached into a bag secured to her waist and produced a small mirror, holding it up for Janine to see. Her right eye was closed, her split lip was swollen, bleeding and two teeth were loose and ready to fall out. Her nose did look like it had been broken and Janine thought, *the worst is yet to come*.

Then, of all things, Janine had a funny thought, *Maybe I can get the American pilot to fix my nose like I fixed his.*

She inadvertently let out a bloody chuckle which caused the jailer to look at her incredulously,

"You think this is funny, pretty girl? I'll show you who has the last laugh you snotty bitch!"

Frau Halder smacked Janine across her face with the back of her hand and caught her before she fell again. Janine's unexpected chuckle startled the jailer and made her think that they were going to have to get much more viscous with this one than she originally thought. She left Janine standing there, promising to return shortly.

Despite her warning to remain standing Janine felt the small cubicle spinning and sank down onto her butt lest she fall and hit her head again. The room continued to spin faster and faster and then everything went black.

CHAPTER 53

Tuesday, 6 June 194410:00AM St. Giles Prison Brussels, Belgium

Janine was awakened by screams coming from some other hapless victim in another cubicle somewhere not far from hers. She regained consciousness laying on her side on the concrete floor of her cubicle. *I need to get up before that bitch comes back in here and kicks the crap out of me!*

With her arms still tied tightly behind her back she struggled to find a way to get to her feet. After repeated attempts, she simply gave up and rolled onto her side awaiting the coming of Frau Halder and another beating.

Janine was determined that she would die before divulging any information that could possibly place other members of the Comet line or the Resistance in mortal danger.

Through the night, she had already faced her Nazi tormentor with a confidence that surprised herself. Up to this point, she had not been subjected to the severe torture she knew they were capable of but steeled herself for that eventuality.

The sound of heavy boots filled the hallway and soon several Gestapo men stood in front of her cubicle and stared at this small 5ft tall Belgian woman with undisguised hatred.

Frau Halder hurried down the hall to join the men and produced a large set of jangling keys. Obviously intimidated by this group of thugs, she nervously searched for the right key.

The leader of this pack of jackals snapped his fingers in disgust, "Schnell! Schnell!"

She finally found the correct key and opened Janine's cell door. Two of the Nazis brushed past Halder and grabbed Janine under her arms. Lifting her off the floor and onto her feet, they dragged her with them as they stormed down the hall and out the basement door onto the back street.

A large, black van pulled up and two of the guards slid open the side door and literally threw Janine inside. One of the guards climbed in beside her and closed the door. The leader of the group got into the front passenger seat. He snapped his fingers, and the van lurched forward and onto the street.

He turned and looked through the steel mesh separating the front seat from the rear passenger compartment and stared at the bloodied face of the diminutive woman prisoner. He smiled at her and asked, "Verstehen Sie Deutsch?"

No response. He tried again in French, "Comprenez-vous l'allemand?"

Janine shook her head slowly, "Non, je suis désolé de ne pas comprendre la langue allemande" *No, sorry I do not understand the German Language.*

The German nodded, and said to his colleague sitting next to Janine, "Sollen wir ihr von ihrer Schwester erzählen?" *Shall we tell her about her sister?*

His German buddy understood this was an ongoing test and asked his front seat colleague, "Wann ist ihre Schwester gestorben?" *When did her sister die?*

There was absolutely no reaction from Janine whatsoever. She continued to stare straight ahead, even though her heart was burning inside her. Janine was fluent in German but chose not to reveal it to her captors.

Convinced that this prisoner did not understand German, the two men engaged in casual conversation about the rumor that the Allied invasion was underway and that soon the inferior Allied forces would all be driven into the sea.

They headed through the city and turned onto Avenue Louise. Janine knew that this was the dreaded location of the 12-story building at 453 Avenue Louise occupied by the Gestapo and Nazi headquarters in Brussels. She understood that the worst was yet to come.

CHAPTER 54

Tuesday, 6 June 1944 7:55 AM Waking up at the Michel Family Refuge at a remote, forest area Near Bouillon, Belgium

The sound of a rooster crowing, a dog barking and children laughing stirred Jack from a deep sleep. These were the ordinary sounds common to his everyday life as a boy growing up in rural Western North Carolina.

It finally penetrated his sleep-fogged brain that he was not in his bed in Deep Gap, North Carolina but in a remote out of the way family refuge deep in the Ardennes in German occupied Belgium.

He automatically looked to his left wrist to check the time on his aviator's wristwatch and remembered that he lost it in the crash of his P-51 Mustang about two weeks ago. *Two weeks ago? It felt like two years ago! So much has happened in such a short time.*

He tried to wrap his mind around it, but decided to let it go for now. He vaguely remembered meeting the rest of the Michel family just a few short hours ago. He sat up in his bed and looked at his surroundings. He was in what appeared to be an upstairs loft of some kind. There was another bed in this little space, unoccupied, unmade, and recently vacated.

Every bone and muscle in his body screamed as he swung his feet around and planted them on the wooden floor. His right eye was partly closed, and his lip was swollen. He hadn't healed from the injuries to his right leg and across his shoulder blades sustained in the crash. That, coupled with his latest physical confrontation with the roadside bandits several hours ago, added to his discomfort.

As Jack stood up, another thought hit him, *Bathroom!*

Putting on his shoes, running his fingers through his hair, he hoped that he looked somewhat presentable as he was certain he would encounter other folks in his search for a bathroom. There weren't any wash basin options in this sleeping space and no mirror. Hoping for the best, he exited the loft bedroom and started down a flight of stairs.

The stairs terminated in a large, pleasant great room lined with knotty pine walls and with many large windows letting in the bright morning sun. A large stone fireplace dominated the center wall, above which hung an impressive, mounted buck with a full antler rack.

Jack, himself a "nature lover" and an experienced hunter in the North Carolina and Tennessee woods stopped for a moment to admire this trophy before the "call of Nature" reminded him of his urgently needed destination. He moved through the great room and turned into a large kitchen. This was where all the action was taking place.

Seated around a large wooden table were his friends, Emil, and Miep together with his host, Raoul Michel. They all stopped their conversation and turned to greet him in English with big smiles. Raoul Michel spoke,

"Ah, our American friend is awake! Good morning! Come sit with us and we will have breakfast."

Jack didn't want to be rude, but he smiled and started to ask directions to the bathroom. Raoul's face brightened and he laughed,

"Oh, yes! You are looking for the loo. Of course! My friend, go out this kitchen door and you will find the 'necessary building' just ten meters from here. It contains two places for you, so you will have to choose."

He let out a hearty laugh and then continued, "We will have breakfast for you when you return."

Jack politely acknowledged the greeting, nodded his head enthusiastically and moved quickly to the exit.

He pushed open a screened wooden door and went down two steps into a grass courtyard. Over to the left was an open field of mowed grass. The entire scene confronting him revealed that this was a beautiful homestead surrounded by the tall trees of the Ardennes Forest.

Jan and his sister, Elise and another girl of the same age had been playing with a dog in the open field and waved to him. He smiled and waved back. A large Alsatian dog happily raced after a stick tossed by Jan. He laughed at himself as he now knew the source of the children's laughter and a dog barking that roused him from his early morning slumber.

Jack moved across the courtyard towards a small wooden building that he assumed was the "necessary building" housing the toilets. As he approached the wooden stoop in front of the building, Ellen came out of the front door. She descended the two steps from the stoop in front of the building and greeted him with a warm smile.

Her right eye was still sporting a big "shiner", and her swollen lip had turned a bright shade of black and blue. Before Jack could say anything, she looked at him for a moment and then broke out in a heartfelt laugh. "Oh, my American hero! My Cowboy! You look positively handsome! Who does your make-up?"

Jack instinctively reached for his own right eye which was partly closed and must have been a close second to Ellen's. His lips were also split and swollen as well, all courtesy of the roadside bandit who slammed his head into the side of the car last night.

Undaunted, Jack gave her a crooked smile and said, "You should have seen the other guy."

Ellen almost doubled over with delight and laughed, "I did! He looked a lot worse than you do especially after you finished with him and his friend.

They both had a good laugh as Ellen spontaneously gave him a big, heartfelt hug. This embrace lasted a bit longer than one would expect a "brief hug" to last. It felt so wonderful and unexpected, *and sexy* that it not only brightened Jack's Day, but he almost forgot the reason he was standing there.

Almost!

He smiled, gently separating from the hug and holding both her shoulders at arm's length, smiled and nodded towards the building housing the bathrooms.

Ellen nodded her head in understanding and returned the smile. She pointed her head toward the doors of the building and said, "See you inside the big house, Cowboy. I'm sure they're waiting to have breakfast for both of us lazy 'sleep-ins'. There's an inside space just as you come in before you enter one of two toilet options. It's equipped with a hand operated water pump and basins with soap and towels to allow a person to wash up afterwards. I would suggest you spend some extra time on that handsome face of yours. It could use a little help this morning"

Jack laughed at this suggestion but then ventured a comment, "You know, Ellen, I'm from the mountains of North Carolina. I'm not really a 'Cowboy', I'm just a "Country Boy', that's all."

She laughed, "Lieutenant, here in Europe, *all Americans are Cowboys!"*

He laughed, "Okay, have it your way."

Her eyes sparkled as she said, "Besides, the way you took care of that bastard, Mueller with two carefully placed shots in the best areas, the way you took care of those highway robbers with another amazing display of shooting under duress, that makes you a 'Cowboy' in my book. Now, go wash up and let's eat!"

She stepped forward and gave him another warm embrace.

With the memory of the wonderful hug from Ellen, Jack entered the "necessary" building and shut the door.

CHAPTER 55

Wednesday, 6 June 1944 10:00 AM Across from Nazi Headquarters 453 Avenue Louise Brussels, Belgium- MI-9 evaluates Janine's rescue

Jean De Blommaert, Janine's MI-9 contact drove past the dreaded 12 story building housing the Gestapo. His stomach was churning at the thought of Janine, yet another heroine of the Comet line caught up in their grasp.

He learned from an inside highly paid source that Janine had been severely beaten while in Giles prison and was alive but badly injured. His source told him that the Gestapo interrogators were not inclined to attempt an interview until they assessed her condition.

They also were temporarily occupied with potential evacuation plans now that the Allies had arrived in force at Normandy. This gave De Blommaert a small ray of hope. If they decided to move Janine and other high-profile prisoners, it might give them an opportunity to launch a commando mission to free Janine and others.

He passed this on to Major Airey Neave, his commanding officer in London, who immediately met with his superiors to evaluate the pros and cons of this potential mission.

While Airey Neave was working on this idea, they received word that "Auntie Marie", Marie Dumont had not survived a similar beating while in custody at Saint Giles. Marie, the owner of the safe house on the night of their capture, bravely sent out a subtle coded message to stay away from her home which had been compromised. Denise recognized it and avoided capture, but sadly, a half hour earlier, Janine did not.

De Blommaert continued down Avenue Louise, turned left and headed towards another safe house to debrief with his MI-9 colleagues Albert Ancia, Daniel Muton, Thomas Rutland and Denise Michel, Janine's sister.

Mouton and Rutland had already been hard at work setting up the remote forest camps in the Belgian Ardennes and the French Chateaudun as Operation Marathon was being implemented.

Repeated airdrops of supplies including food, medicines, clothing and even tents were consistently made and recovered by members of the resistance and delivered to the camps.

Despite her anguish at her sister's capture, Denise was hard at work coordinating all the logistics with other members of the Comet line. She told her MI-9 colleagues that she wanted to continue working the effort while here in Brussels in the hopes that she, in some way, might help in freeing her sister.

After further talks with Airey Neave, it was decided to "insulate" Denise as she was too valuable to lose to the Nazis. Neave wanted to move her to London, but Denise strictly disavowed this idea.

She was also somewhat concerned as to the whereabouts of her brother, Lucien, who she hadn't seen in two days since he went off on a mission with resistance. It wasn't unusual for Lucien to disappear for days or even weeks, but these times were unusual, and she was worried about his well-being.

While she was debating her options with her MI-9 colleagues, De Blommaert's source came back with urgent information. The source confirmed that Janine and a group of other prisoners were taken from the Gestapo Headquarters, loaded onto a convoy of German military vehicles and were racing towards the German border.

Frustrated and angry, they realized they couldn't possibly organize a rescue mission on this short notice and communicated the message to London. Denise was inconsolable. Two years before she had lost her beloved husband, Martin who had been tortured and summarily executed by the Nazis. Now it seemed she was about to lose her beloved sister, Janine, her best friend and soulmate.

The others tried to give her hope. *Janine is strong, she is tough, they will not break her!*

It had little effect on her agony, but she finally decided that the best thing for her to do right now was to rejoin her children Jan and Elise at the family refuge in Bouillon. Ancia, de Blommaert, and the other MI-9 team instantly agreed that this was an excellent idea and promised to alert her the instant they knew anything about Janine and Lucien.

Jean de Blommaert arranged for a security team to transport Denise to Bouillon to the Church of Saint John the Evangelist, which was the agreed upon drop off point for the Michel refuge. Someone from the refuge would spot her and take her from there.

Within an hour, she was on her way. The MI-9 teams breathed a sigh of relief that, at least this brave young woman was temporarily safe from the Nazi's grasp.

CHAPTER 56

Tuesday, 6 June 1944 8:35 AM "Cowboy" Jack at the Michel Family Refuge near Bouillon, Belgium

After exiting the "necessary room", Jack paused in the wash area and was pleased someone set a bowl of warm, soapy water in front of a mirror and thoughtfully placed a razor, shaving cream, toothbrush, toothpaste and face towel there for him.

After brushing his teeth, and carefully shaving around his swollen lip and dabbing the warm, moist towel over his swollen eye, he was starting to feel somewhat "human" again.

Setting the personal items aside, Jack studied himself once more in the mirror and thought to himself, *if you weren't so damn good-looking, this black eye and swollen lip might scare people off! I will say that our friend, Janine, did a good job in resetting my nose, it doesn't look half bad.*

The thought of Janine and of Denise suddenly hit him, *I hope they're both okay and safe. I hope we get to be with them again real soon.*

He shook his head, trying to get rid of any bad thoughts. He carefully drained the bowl in the sink, neatly set aside the toothbrush and other accessories and started out the door. Once back out in the courtyard, he headed to the main house and breakfast.

As he approached the house, the sounds of animated conversation and laughter emanated from the kitchen eating area. He opened the door and stepped in to a hearty greeting in English from his host, Raoul, "Greetings! Jack! We were just talking about you here with my family. Let me introduce them to you,"

Seated to his right was Raymond, the son who first emerged from the underbrush last night. Very serious, non-smiling, Raymond nodded in greeting.

To Raymond's right sat another version of Raymond, perhaps an identical twin who was introduced as Pierre. He, on the other hand, was smiling. Jack recognized Pierre as one of the horsemen that led the way to the cabins last night.

Then came Jack's friends, who felt like his family, Emil, Ellen and Jan, all smiling. Jan's sister, Elise, gave him a smile and a wave and Jack smiled and waved back, recalling how wonderful she was on the day of his crash landing and into the rain-soaked night. Completing the circle around the table and sitting right next to Elise was the other young girl he spotted playing with them and the dog this morning, Nadine. She too smiled and waved at him.

Jack was just about to ask where Miep was when she came bustling out of the cooking area carrying a large tray of steaming food followed by another woman carrying a similar tray with a big smile on both of their faces.

This jovial woman spoke in excellent English and introduced herself as Marie, Raoul's wife. She looked at Elise and Nadine and said something in French that Jack took to mean, "Let's help with the food."

It occurred to Jack that the entire group refrained from eating until he could join them. Growing up in a rural country environment himself, he knew that usually breakfast happens before dawn in most cases. He was very surprised and very grateful.

Raoul looked at those gathered around the table and, satisfied that everything was ready, he turned to Jack, "Well, my American Cowboy friend, our 'straight shooter' has finally come back to life! We are so grateful to you and all our Allied friends who fight for us, especially on this day in Normandy.

Then looking at Emil who had a broad smile, he continued, "We have heard from our friend, Emil, of your excellent marksmanship and courage and are grateful for that as well."

Jack nodded somewhat self-consciously and stood there as his host gestured to an empty seat next to Ellen and continued, "So, Jack, would you please lead us in thanking the Lord for the blessings of this table and His blessings for all of us? You may do so in English, as you can see, we have taught our family, and we all speak your language. Some better than others."

He said this last part, giving a quick glance to Raymond who averted his father's eyes.

Jack was momentarily at a loss. He grew up Catholic, but in a home that was nominally faithful in practicing the faith. He thought to himself, *Oh God! Please help me here!*

Then, calling upon his early childhood memories of dinners with his grandmother, he was able to recall some of the words as he made the sign of the Cross. "Bless us Oh, Lord for these Thy gifts which we are about to receive, Amen!" He smiled as everyone around the table echoed his prayer in barely discernible words. Then, he thought, *Oops! I forgot to add "that we receive through the bounty of Christ", but it turned out okay, so thank you Grandma and thank you Jesus*

As they passed around the food from one plate to the other, Raoul said,

"Let us enjoy this meal and then we will discuss the news that is coming to us from our sources over on the Normandy coast."

CHAPTER 57

Tuesday, 6 June 1944 10:00 AM Jack's decision Michel Family Refuge remote, forest area near Bouillon, Belgium

After breakfast, Raoul asked Jack to come and join him and Emil in a corner of the great room for a few moments. The two men sat in two large stuffed chairs smoking cigars and pointed to a third empty chair indicating that it was reserved for Jack.

Just before Jack headed over to join them, he observed a work-truck pulling out from a garage and starting down the dirt road to the paved highway.

Once seated, Raoul smiled and asked, "Jack, would you care for another cup of coffee? Real coffee, as you most likely noticed."

"I did notice, Raoul, it was amazing to have real coffee, but no thank you, I know how precious it is, and I appreciate it, but I am full."

Raoul nodded, then waved his cigar towards Jack with a raised eyebrow, again Jack declined,

"Thank you, no please, Raoul. I do not smoke."

"Amazing! An American cowboy who flies a fighter plane for the American Allies in combat and doesn't smoke cigars?"

Jack laughed, and said, "I don't smoke cigars or cigarettes either, my friend."

Raoul feigned shock and shook his head,

"As we hear in your American movies, a 'clean-cut' boy, eh?"

"So, you watch our American movies?"

"Yes, of course! How do you think we learn to speak English, American English so well?"

All three men laughed and then Raoul turned serious, "Jack, you have a decision to make and no matter which way you decide, we are your friends and will stand by you."

Emil nodded solemnly in agreement with his friend, Raoul.

Jack raised one eyebrow, the other was still swollen along with his black eye and wondered what was going on here.

"Okay, Raoul what exactly is this decision I must consider?"

"As you now know, the Allies have established a foothold on the beaches of Normandy. A full-scale invasion is taking place. Despite German propaganda that they will push the allies back into the sea, we think the end may be near for these Fascist pigs."

"Okay, I'm with you so far. What's the decision I need to make?"

Raoul looked at Emil who nodded his approval, "Jack, we understand that you will have to leave this place now that the allies are coming. They have arranged a special way to repatriate all of you airmen trapped behind enemy lines."

"Okay, what is this 'special way' may I ask?"

"They have established two camps set in remote forest areas for you and your fellow airmen. One is not far from here in another part of the Ardennes and the other is across the Meuse River into France at the Foret de Freteval.".

Jack shook his head and laughed, "Camps? You mean right under the Nazi's noses?"

Emil's turn to laugh now, "Yes Jack, very clever on the part of our friends in London. We understand that you might want to go to one of these camps and Raoul has the means to get you there once you have made your decision.

With that, Raoul and Emil started to rise from their chairs but stopped when Jack raised his hand. They both looked at him quizzically. Raoul spoke, "Yes, Jack? A decision already? Which one of the two camps do you think you would want to go?"

"Instead of the two options you assumed I would want to choose from, I have come up with a third option, a third choice for your consideration."

"Yes? What is it?" asked Raoul

"I would like to remain here with you, Raoul and with Emil and his family. I feel that I can still fight the Nazis when called upon to do so and I can be of assistance to you all. Please think about it. You don't have to give me an answer right now, but I would really like to make my decision to remain here with all of you."

Raoul nodded thoughtfully. He looked at Emil who shrugged his one good shoulder. Then he turned back to Jack with a smile, "Okay, Cowboy I understand your request. But what will you do when the Allies drive the Bosch completely out and pass by here?"

Jack laughed and said, "Then and only then will I be liberated!"

All three laughed, Raoul looked at Emil who nodded, allowing Raoul to respond. "Okay, Lieutenant. You can stay. But you cannot go into town, you must remain here out of sight as there are many traitors about. If that is okay with you then you are our guest until liberation. Agreed?"

"Yes, of course!"

Raoul laughed, "Then it is decided. This also will be good as I have a 'Medical man' of sorts coming out here to our refuge to look at Emil's shoulder and Ellen's injuries. I think it would be a good idea to have him look at you as well. So that will all work out."

Jack said, "I am very grateful for your hospitality and friendship, Raoul, thank you and your family from my heart."

Raoul put two hands on Jack's shoulders and smiled, "No, Cowboy, thank *you* and your allied brothers."

With that, they started to leave, Emil heading upstairs and Roaul out towards the kitchen, but Jack held up a hand.

They both turned to look at him with a quizzical look on their faces. Jack smiled, pointed to Raoul's cigar and said, "I guess I will try one." They all laughed as Raoul fished one out of his pocket, handed it to Jack along with several matches and they all went their separate ways.

CHAPTER 58

Tuesday, 6 June 1944 Jack and Ellen talk about the loss of their loved ones Michel Family Refuge, remote, forest area Near Bouillon, Belgium

After Raoul and Emil went their separate ways, Jack stepped outside and sat on the top of the three steps leading to the courtyard. He self-consciously stuck the unlit cigar in his mouth and patted his pocket for the matches given to him by Raoul just minutes earlier.

He recalled the times his dad and his uncle, Tim, who, when visiting with his family would smoke their "stogies" while blowing big circles of white cigar smoke. He remembered their good-natured laughter while they sat on the back porch of his family's mountain home overlooking an expanse of meadow in Deep Gap, North Carolina.

Two brothers, laughing, exchanging jokes, telling white lies and tall stories as his mom, Ann and Tim's wife, his aunt Pat were inside preparing supper and laughing, exchanging jokes, telling white lies and tall stories of their own.

Great memories, good times, wish I was there with them right now.

Sadly, that was not to be as his Uncle Tim was killed in a tractor rollover accident two years ago. Jack remembered that sad trip over to Uncle Tim and Aunt Pat's small Tennessee farm to be with her and the children. This past year, his dad passed away from a virulent form of bone cancer just days after Jack shipped out to England to join his squadron. He missed them both terribly.

His mom telegrammed him with the news about Dad's passing and told him that his dad would be proud of him and would want him to get on with his duty to serve his country.

He read her follow-up letter and smiled sadly as he could just hear her say, "Now don't you worry about me, just get over there and kick those Germans in the "you-know-where".

He laughed softly at the memory and tried in vain to strike the match given to him by Raoul.

"Having trouble there, cowboy?" Ellen said as she came up from behind him, "I thought you didn't smoke?"

He laughed, embarrassed, "I don't, really. But Raoul and Emil were puffing away, and it reminded me of my dad and my uncle smoking cigars. We call them stogies' back home."

"Sounds like a nice memory. What is your dad's name and your uncle's name"

"My dad's name is, was John, same as me and my uncle, his older brother was Timmothy, 'Tim' for short."

Ellen was quick to pick up on the past tense, "was". "I take it, since you said, '*was*' that they're both gone now?"

"Yup, both gone. I miss them both, but the cigar brought a good memory to me. What about your mom and dad?"

"Both killed last year at the end of March 1943 in the accidental bombing of a residential area of Rotterdam, the Bospolder-Tussendijken district."

She paused for a moment, trying not to get emotional, "My parents were visiting relatives and were killed along with almost four hundred residents that also left almost twenty thousand people homeless."

"Oh, my God! I am so sorry, Ellen. It was an Allied bombing?"

"Sadly, yes. It is now being called the 'Forgotten Bombardment' but it is something we will never forget.

"You all must have been furious with us, the Allies, I mean."

"Strangely, no. Devastated, yes but almost all of us realized that this was war and was an accident of war. We know that the Allies were targeting the shipyards and logistics in and around the port, attempting to destroy the Germans and free all of us from those bastards. It doesn't lessen the degree of anguish and mourning, but everyone understood it was a terrible accident.

"That's awful. Terrible. What were their names? Your father and mother?"

"Cornelius and Marie. My father was Emil's brother, and my mother was Miep's sister of the Leterme family."

"Wow! Emil and your dad were brothers and Miep and your mom were sisters. That's amazing! How close your whole family was. Amazing!"

"Yes, it was. But enough of that. Let's take a walk around these grounds. Are you up for that? Is your leg any better?"

"Sure, sounds like a great idea. Let's go."

Ellen pretended not to notice Jack's gait favoring his right leg. She made a mental note to discuss this with her uncle, Emil.

As the two of them started to walk on a clearly marked footpath leading to the nearby forest, Pierre Michel, mounted on the white mare, rode up to them and called in English,

"Hi, before you head into the forest, make sure you have a weapon with you. There have been some sanglier spotted about the woods lately."

Jack looked to Piere and to Ellen, "Sanglier?"

Ellen nodded, "Wild boar. Do you have these in America?"

"Yes, although I've never seen or encountered one."

Pierre laughed as he dismounted his horse and handed Jack one of the carbines taken from the two dead "would-be robbers" the previous night.

Jack smelled oil and noticed that the weapon was fully loaded with one in the chamber and five in the magazine. It had just been oiled, cleaned and looked 100% better than it did last night, bloody and laying in the mud on the side of the road.

"Yes, *sanglier* have a bad temper and are very dangerous. Your pistol will not be as effective as this Mauser 98. I took the liberty of cleaning and realigning the sights. It is a very fine weapon cared for very poorly by the two idiots who made the mistake of stopping you on the road last night.

He smiled and thanked Pierre, examined the bolt-action rifle and slung it over his shoulder. "It looks like you did a fine job with this weapon, Pierre. I hope you and I can shoot together, and I can sight it in."

"Oh yes, that would be fun! We are very careful to keep shooting practice to a minimum so as not to attract attention to our refuge, but there will be a time when we can do this. I look forward to it."

Pierre started to remount, then paused and turned to Jack and Ellen, "Jack, Ellen, you should be aware that we have a small bell mounted on the kitchen porch. It is for alerting all of us who do not happen to be in the main house to something important. If you hear it ring several times slowly and deliberately it usually means that one should return to the house, but there is no urgency. If it rings rapidly and multiple times, it means get your butts back to the house as quickly as you can but with caution. Understand?"

Ellen responded, "Of course. Thank you, Pierre."

With that, Jack and Ellen started down the path. To his great surprise and delight, Ellen reached for and took his hand. As they walked together holding hands, enjoying the quiet and beauty of the Ardennes Forest, he thought to himself that despite the war, today was shaping up to be great.

CHAPTER 59

Tuesday, 6 June 1944 (11 AM) Jack and Ellen on the forest path-The Bell is Ringing Michel Family Refuge,

Jack and Ellen followed the forest path for about twenty minutes. They came upon an active stream alongside the foot path. It was moving swiftly over river rocks, descending and swirling, sending up small sprays of fresh water reflecting in the mid-morning sunlight.

The stream moved rapidly past them descending to lower elevations. The hum of bees, butterflies flitting from wildflower to wildflower, birds calling to one another coupled with the warm June sunshine created a peaceful, almost surreal, idyllic scene.

Still holding hands, Ellen suggested they pause and sit on an enormous rock positioned on the bank of the stream serving as a natural bench for them. Jack let out a deep breath, relaxed and admired the beauty all around them. Ellen thought this was a perfect place for Jack to rest his leg which was obviously still bothering him.

They smiled at each other, but simply remained quiet, deep in their own thoughts, enjoying each other's company. They sat there listening to the gurgling sounds of the stream, the birds chirping all around them and enjoying the gentle breeze working its way through the tall pines.

Jack's quiet thoughts suddenly brought him back to the reality that, at this very moment over on the coast of France, men were fighting and dying. Many more were laying severely wounded on the battlefield crying for help as the armies of the Allies pressed hard ahead against the armies of the Nazis for the liberation of Europe.

He could just picture the scene of death and destruction arrayed out on the beaches and inland in the hedgerows below him. It was as though he was at this very moment flying over the battlefield in his

P-51, his brothers flying on each wing as they moved into battle like birds of prey. He started to have second thoughts about remaining at the refuge and enjoying all of this quiet beauty.

Perhaps I should be with my brother airmen in the forest instead of remaining here?

"Hello, Cowboy? Are you still with me? What's going on in that handsome head of yours?" Ellen, smiling but with a concerned look in her blue eyes.

"Oh! Sorry! I guess I was daydreaming.".

"Uh huh. You certainly were doing *something*. Is everything all right? I forget that you have been through so much yourself. Want to share?"

"I'm sorry, Ellen. Forgive me, I just was deep in thought thinking of what's going on with the invasion. How it's going. And, thinking of how wonderful all of this is here right now, the beauty of the forest, being with you, and..."

He was suddenly interrupted by Ellen moving to him and planting a deep, passionate kiss on his lips then throwing her arms around him and burying her head into his shoulder. No more words, just a close embrace.

Then, Ellen with her face buried deep in Jack's shoulder started to tremble and shake and an enormous sob leapt out of her throat, startling Jack, "Ellen? What's happening?"

Her voice, muffled by Jack's shoulder was barely discernible, "Shut up, Cowboy, just shut up and hold me."

They clung onto one another and neither one spoke. Jack just took a deep breath and kept his arms around her. An occasional sob would come from her and each time, Jack would just hold her tight and tell her that everything would be okay.

That's when they heard the Bell ringing in the distance, slowly, methodically, clearly on this June afternoon.

CHAPTER 60

Tuesday, 6 June 1944 15:30 (3:30 PM) A visit from Pharmacist Henri Charles and his assistant, Byron Champagne

As Jack and Ellen emerged from the forest path, they saw that Grandma Marie was the laughing source of the bell ringing. She stood on the porch wearing a big apron and a big smile as she spotted them and waved to them.

They spotted Raoul and Emil standing in the garden courtyard laughing and speaking with two men who had just driven into the refuge in a four passenger Renault.

Raoul waved Jack and Ellen over to them and introduced them to Henri Charles, a prominent pharmacist in Bouillon and his assistant pharmacist, Byron Champagne.

Raoul addressed Jack and Ellen, "Our friends, Henri and Byron both have a great deal of medical experience. Byron is not yet a physician although, in my opinion, he should be one. He and Henri have helped many of us in our time of need. They are both here to provide a medical assessment of Emil, you, Jack and you, Ellen.

Raoul turned to Henri and Byron. Byron spoke, "This will only be done with your permission of course, and for you, Ellen, it will be very quick and cursory and only with one of the women you trust present. Again, with your permission."

Emil, who was smoking one of Raoul's famous cigars blew out a ring of smoke from his cigar and spoke up, "Yes, I have already been subjected to a medical review by our esteemed pharmacists here and, amazingly, they have discovered that I was shot in the left shoulder."

Byron laughed, "I agree it was a challenge. It took all of my medical school training and years of experience, but I finally was able to diagnose that our friend here was the victim of a gunshot in his left shoulder. This was made somewhat easier by Emil pointing to his left shoulder and saying that there was a bullet hole there in his left shoulder.

Miep joined the group and looked at Ellen, "Byron is just going to check your head and scalp wounds and any other complaints that you might wish to address. I will be with you in total privacy."

Ellen smiled, "Okay Tante Miep. I don't think there's much to be done other than taking the time for this black eye and swollen lip to heal, but let's get it over with.

She, Miep and Bryon Champagne departed and went to one of the downstairs guest rooms for a quick check-up.

Henri Charles addressed the same request to Jack, "Lieutenant, I have been made aware that you have two areas of concern following your crash landing. Shall you and I go into a private room which will allow me to examine these wounds?"

Jack shrugged his shoulders, "Sure, let's to that."

The two men went into another guest room, where Charles examined Jack's shoulder laceration and his penetrating leg wound. Jack emerged from the back room carrying several packets of Sulfa drugs which he dutifully handed to Miep as instructed.

Henri Charles spoke privately with Jack, "Follow the instructions and have someone apply the sulfa powder on your back as I instructed. Either Byron or I will be back in about a week to ten days. If the infection has not cleared up by then, we have a real doctor who can be trusted, and we will try to figure a way for you to see him."

Jack thanked him and said, "I want to thank you, Henri, and Byron and I will do as you say, of course."

Charles nodded but wanted to impress upon Jack the seriousness of his lower leg wound, "You are a young man, Jack. You are obviously very strong since you are doing so well after some serious injuries. But you cannot ignore the seriousness of the possible infection in your right leg. I cannot emphasize enough to keep the leg as clean as possible. This means that staying in woods and forests in rather unclean conditions is not going to be safe or good for your health. I hope you understand this?"

"Staying in woods and forests, I understand."

Jack thought, *Henri Charles must be aware of the plan to hide airmen in the forest.*

Emil stepped in, "Jack, Byron and Henri need to go now."

Henri nodded and turned towards the door, but stopped for another comment, "Jack, why do they call you, 'Cowboy?"

Emil and Raoul laughed and before Jack could respond, Emil spoke up,

"Henri, it's a long story, I'll explain that later when we have some more time."

A relatively short time later, Ellen and Miep came into the kitchen. Henri and Byron were offered lunch, but politely refused, indicating that they had another medical visit to conduct and had to return to the pharmacy in Bouillon for an expected delivery.

CHAPTER 61

Tuesday, 6 June 1944 4:00 PM Jack & Ellen discuss the future
Michel Family Refuge,

Ellen found Jack sitting on the wooden porch steps deep in thought. She sat down on the steps next to him and, after a moment asked, "What did that Pharmacist say to you, Jack?"

Jack nodded his head, anticipating this question, "He said my shoulder blade wound is healing nicely. The sulfa powder is doing its job, but the wound on my right calf is still inflamed and he doesn't like the way it looks."

"I noticed you are favoring that right leg a bit and this makes sense. What did he say could be done?"

"Well, he cleaned the wound, cauterized it and reapplied Sulfa powder. If that doesn't work, he has a trusted real doctor who might want to X-ray the leg and, if necessary, perform a minor surgery to see if there isn't a piece of a bullet or shrapnel in there."

"Well, at least there's something that can be done, right?"

"Yes, it's a good thing to be sure, but…."

"But what?"

"I was hoping to rejoin my squadron once the Allies sweep thorough here and liberate everyone. Now until this infection clears up that does not look possible. I feel guilty about not rejoining the fight while so many are fighting and dying.

Ellen nodded sympathetically but internally relieved that she was not going to lose Jack so soon. This man who not only saved her life *two times* but was growing ever closer to her every day. She felt guilty about this selfish notion but secretly relieved at the same time.

Jack, sensing some of this, looked at her intently, stood up and gently put both his hands on her shoulders, turning her to face him.

Ellen seemed momentarily at a loss for words, "Jack? What is it?"

"Ellen, listen. I know we've only known each other for a little while, but I want to tell you, no I *need* to tell you that, even if I must return to service and I am gone. I promise you that I will come back."

She looked at him intently, then she smiled, "Of course, Cowboy, I wouldn't expect anything less. I will hold you to it."

As she said these heartfelt words, Ellen thought to herself, *I hope that God will allow that to happen, to let him return to me, but I have seen too many of these promises disappear in these times of war.*

With that, she drew herself to him. Jack slid his arms around her and held her in a gentle embrace. This tender moment was interrupted by Raoul's not so subtle clearing of his throat.

They all laughed, and Raoul motioned for them to come into the house. Jack held out his hand and Ellen slipped her hand into his. The two of them walked hand-in-hand up the steps and into the great room.

Raoul smiled at the sight of the two of them holding hands but shook his head sadly. He thought of his own son, Martin holding hands with Denise and made a silent prayer, coincidentally like the silent prayer that Ellen had just made to God

Lord, please don't let the devils of war tear this young couple apart!

He took a deep breath and followed Jack and Ellen into the great room.

CHAPTER 62

Tuesday, 6 June 1944 4:00 PM Jack and Ellen amid Family concerns Michel Family Refuge,

Raoul and Emil waited for Jack and Ellen in a sitting area in the great room and gestured to two empty armchairs for them. They looked at each other and took their seats. They were soon joined by Miep and Marie.

Before anyone else said anything, Ellen spoke first in English, "Okay, what is going on here?"

Miep started to respond, but Emil held up a hand, and smiled, "Ellen, Jack, as the elders in our mutual families here in Belgium, we wanted to speak with you both about our concerns for you both."

Ellen's face blushed and she angrily replied, "Concerns? What do you all mean by that?"

Again, Miep attempted to respond but held her tongue as Emil glared at her. Emil continued, "Look, we are all adults here. We can see that you two are growing fond of each other. That's a good thing and we have come to know Jack and think very highly of him. That goes without saying, but as Catholics…"

Ellen was growing angrier by the minute and now she held up her hand to interrupt her uncle, "Enough of this! I can see where this is going. You are right, we are all adults here. What exists between Jack and myself is our business, and, as much as we honor you all and respect you all, we ask you to not jump to any conclusions, and I…."

It was Jack's turn to hold up his hand, stopping Ellen in mid-sentence, "My dear friends, I can understand your concerns. You love Ellen and want to protect her am I right?"

The four senior members of the family slowly nodded as Jack continued, "Of course you do. I can see where you are concerned. Ellen and I have only known each other for a very short time. During that very short time, we, all of us have been through some extraordinary life-threatening times."

He had their rapt attention as he continued, "This is war and these terrible things happen. You are concerned, I believe that Ellen and I are caught up in the stresses of war and need time to know each other better, am I correct?"

Again, they nodded. Ellen looked at Jack intently as he went on, "I understand your concerns, believe me. I know that this concern comes out of your love for this wonderful woman. I want you all to know something,"

He paused, got up from his chair and moved over to Ellen and put his hand on her shoulder and smiled, "Look at the two of us. Both of us have black eyes. Both of us have swollen lips, and, if I can be so bold, both of us are falling in love.

With that, Ellen stood up and embraced Jack with a big smile. "Yes, it's true! Black eyes, swollen lips and all. We are in love!"

Raoul laughed, shook his head, and shrugged his shoulders. His laughter was joined by Emil, Miep and Marie.

At that exact moment, the truck driven by Raymond returned from making a run into Bouillon and in the front passenger seat sat a stone-faced Denise.

Miep and Marie let out a shriek of joy and rushed out the door with Emil and Raoul behind them.

As Jack started to follow and had one foot out the door, Ellen grabbed him by the collar of his shirt, jerked him back into the room, looked him in the eyes, and planted a big kiss on his lips, "Jack, I don't know what the future has in store for us, but let's take these days, minutes and hours together as a precious gift from God, Okay?"

Jack embraced her, kissed her tenderly and, with an unexpected hoarseness in his throat, said, "I couldn't have put it any better than that."

At that moment, they heard the women outside wailing and weeping. They turned and rushed out the door.

CHAPTER 63

Tuesday, 6 June 1944 4:45 PM Denise arrives with bad news Michel Family Refuge,

Jack and Ellen emerged from the house and saw Miep, Marie and Denise in a mutual embrace. Raoul and Emil stood awkwardly at a distance from the women. The two older women were crying, and Jack immediately thought, *someone has died.*

Denise stepped away from the women as she heard joyful cries, coming from her two children, Jan and Elise. Both teenagers were rushing to her with arms wide open.

She grabbed them to her in a long, laughing embrace. She then turned to Ellen, kissed her and then held her at arm's length. She looked her over then spoke in French, which Ellen later translated for Jack.

"You look beautiful, Ellen! After all you've been through, you still are a beautiful person inside and out!"

Finally, she turned to Jack, using her dry humor and speaking in English,

"Lieutenant, I see that you have decided to copy my cousin and have had someone decorate your face in much the same way hers was decorated. What do you have to say about that?"

Before Jack could answer, Ellen responded, "You should have seen the other guy."

It took a moment for Denise to register the humor, and then she laughed.

Ellen followed up immediately with, "No, I mean it, Denise. You *really should have seen the other two guys!"*

Denise, who ordinarily had a great sense of humor, smiled slightly but Ellen could see there was something deeply troubling her.

Ellen looked intently at her cousin, with an obvious question on her lips as to what was going on. Denise's smile was gone, and her countenance had turned deadly serious, "The reason my mother-in-law and my aunt are weeping is because dear Janine has fallen into the hands of the Gestapo."

CHAPTER 64

Tuesday, 6 June 1944 5:00 PM Denise discusses Janine's arrest and Operation Marathon, Michel Family Refuge,

With everyone still reeling from Janine's capture by the Gestapo, Denise told them of her own close call and how the safe house had certainly been compromised by a collaborator. Shock gave way to anger coupled with frustration.

In response to Raoul's angry demand that a rescue effort be mounted immediately, Denise shook her head sadly and told them that this had already been contemplated by the highest sources in British Intelligence. They were preparing to launch an immediate SAS commando operation to free her.

Just as they were starting the preparation for the raid, they found that Janine had been moved into Germany along with other high-profile prisoners. The Nazis were withdrawing many of their prisoners further inland in response to the Allied invasion.

While everyone was still digesting all this latest news, Denise turned to Jack, apparently switching gears, all business, "Lieutenant, I must discuss some important developments that will affect you as the Allied invasion continues."

Jack, momentarily shaken by this sudden change in direction, simply nodded his head in agreement, "I am so sorry for this turn of events, Denise. Do you want to take a little time to get into the house, freshen up and then talk?"

She blew out her breath, shaking her head, unwinding from her emotions and then smiled, "I appreciate your concern for me, but Janine would not want my emotions getting in the way of our dedication to the sacrifice that so many people have made serving the Réseau *Comète* mission. Let's talk and then I can rest a bit."

"Of course, Denise. Do you want to talk out here in the courtyard or someplace more private?"

"No, not necessary, Emil and Raoul already have some knowledge of what I am about to address, and Miep, Marie and Ellen are trusted and supporters of the *Réseau Comète,* so I have no hesitation in openly discussing this with you."

Denise continued, "In the early part of this year, 1944, our friends in London, better known as MI-9 contacted *Réseau Comète* to address what was to be done with all Allied airmen as the Allies advanced into the German occupied parts of Europe. It was decided that certain isolated areas in France and Belgium should be considered that would safeguard all of you from the Allied advance and from the expected German withdrawal."

Ellen asked, "Is this the plan where the 'evaders' would be hidden in the forests until they could be liberated by the allied advance?'

"Yes. It was a plan put together by British and American Intelligence in coordination with the major Resistance leadership in France, Holland and Belgium. It is known as 'Operation Marathon' and is now in place."

Jack nodded and asked, "Where, may I ask are these forested areas?"

"The plan focused on three forested areas: near Rennes in Brittany, near Chateaudun and in the Belgian Ardennes. Once the Allied liberation began, all our evaders should be moved to one of the forest areas nearest to them. This would prevent them from becoming trapped behind the front lines and not in the direct battle areas.

She looked around the room to ensure that everyone was following her, "The camp near Chateaudun was based on the 'Foret de Freteval' and known as Operation Sherwood. Well over 150 aircrew evaders from Great Britain, America, Canada, Belgium, New Zealand and Australia are already situated there."

Ellen laughed, "Right under the Nazis' noses?"

Denise smiled, "Yes, and with the cooperation of the many *Resistance* groups most local villages were kept ignorant of the men hidden in the forests while at the same time, again with the cooperation of the *Resistance*, food, medicine and supplies were delivered to the camps."

Denise looked directly at Jack, "Lieutenant, there is such a hidden camp here in the Ardennes. We can take you there, but there is a serious problem where you are concerned."

Jack, startled and asked, "Me? What is the problem?"

Emil stepped in, "Jack, according to your medical evaluations, you have a possible infected wound in your right calf that needs to be addressed. The conditions in the camps are far from satisfactory to deal with this situation."

Jack protested, "I'm sure I am not the only one of the 'evaders' who has a wound and is in the camps. I don't deserve 'special treatment, Emil."

Emil nodded sympathetically, "Of course, Jack. An expected reaction. But according to Byron Champagne, if it is not treated correctly and soon, you may not only lose your leg, but you may also lose *your life* due to the infection and the possibility of disease in the camps.

Miep and Ellen both spoke at the same time, "No!"

Then Miep took over, "Jack you must remain here for treatment."

Ellen, "Please, Jack stay here with us until we are certain that your infection has cleared up and your leg is back to full health, please."

Jack, moved by the imploring look in Ellen's eyes and seemingly outnumbered muttered a weak, "Okay, friends, but just until my leg is healed. Then I must continue to serve my country and fight for all of us. Okay?"

Miep, Marie and Ellen nodded their approval.

Raoul and Emil laughed, and Raoul spoke, "I guess that settles it! You have been outvoted my friend."

Jack shook his head in frustration, Ellen placed her hand on his shoulder and nodded in sympathy while at the same time, sporting a slight grin.

Jack turned to Denise, "Has anyone heard of Lucien, Marcelino and Gerard?"

Denise shook her head, "The last we heard of them they and other members of the Resistance joined with Jock's SAS commandos and were attacking Germans in and around the Antwerp port."

After all these discussions were concluded, Marie escorted Denise to her room to unpack. Raoul asked Pierre to drive into Bouillon and speak with Henri Charles and Byron champagne to see about further treatment for Jack.

CHAPTER 65

Friday, 9 June 1944 8:00 AM Jack and Ellen on the forest path Michel Family Refuge,

For the fourth straight day, Jack and Ellen enjoyed the solitude of their walks along the path leading to the active stream deep in the woods of the family refuge.

This morning, Ellen and Marie packed a breakfast of cheese, black bread, sausage and, of all things, a rare thermos of real black coffee laced with chicory. It was all packed into a covered picnic basket with a checkered tablecloth folded on top.

They approached the familiar bench shaped rock by the Creekside which Ellen had now named "Cowboy's rock." Jack was getting a little tired of all of his Belgian friends referring to him as a cowboy, but he took it with a good-natured smile and just enjoyed the precious time with them before he was able to return to the battle.

Jack placed the basket alongside the rock, unslung the carbine over his shoulder and spread the checkered tablecloth over a flat portion of Cowboy rock.

Usually when they began their daily morning walk, they engaged in small talk, thinking about the future, their future together. This morning, however, they were just happy to enjoy the quiet of the stream, the sounds of birds in the trees and the warmth of the June sunshine. It was hard to believe that a major war was taking place not too far from where they were.

Ellen removed her boots and waded knee deep into the stream, almost losing her balance several times in the swift moving waters. Jack watched with amusement as she held both hands out to steady herself, still almost falling and a gentle laugh each time she righted herself.

He started to carefully unpack the basket when Ellen shook her head and called him, "Forget that for now, Lieutenant. Take your boots off and get in this cold water right now!"

Jack laughed, "Yes, ma'am! Right away!"

He removed his boots and socks, rolled up his pants to his knees and waded into the water. Moving closer to her, stepping on some uneven rocks, he almost fell several times until he moved right up to her.

The cold water felt great on his right leg which had become quite sore over the past week. He was about to say something to her when she moved towards him, threw her arms around him and planted a big kiss smack on his mouth.

With that, they both lost their footing, and fell completely underwater, rising quickly gasping and laughing.

"Wow!" Jack cried, "That's one cold creek!"

Ellen laughed, I guess you will have to warm me up!"

He pulled her close to him, put both arms around her, and they stood there for a moment, saying nothing, enjoying the sounds of the swirling waters and the forest around them.

Standing there, in the cold rushing waters of the Ardennes creek, Jack thought that things could not get any better. He gently turned her towards the shore and the two of them made their way back to the bank and up to 'Cowboy Rock'.

Once out of the water, Ellen started to shiver. Jack grabbed the tablecloth and started to put it around her. She shook her head, "Listen, Cowboy, I don't want you to get the wrong idea, but I am going to remove my clothes and then I am going to put that beautiful, checkered tablecloth around me. You, my handsome pilot will not take advantage of a beautiful naked Belgian girl all alone in these Ardennes woods. Understand?"

Jack, shivering now, nodded his head, "Yes, ma'am, you will have nothing to worry about. But I need you to promise me something."

"What is it, Cowboy?"

"I'm going to remove my clothes, place them on my rock over here in the direct sunlight to dry off. I do not want to worry about this beautiful, naked Belgian girl taking advantage of this poor, wounded naked pilot all alone in these Ardennes woods."

"Believe me, you will have nothing to worry about. We are both Catholics and it is very difficult to find a priest these days. Especially one who would even consider absolution under those circumstances. So, relax and warm up."

And, within moments, warm up they did.

After a while, they lay next to each other, smiling and now completely dried off in the June sunshine. As they quietly stared up into a beautiful blue Belgian sky, they started to worry about finding a priest who might consider absolution.

That's when they heard the bell ring slowly and methodically.

CHAPTER 66

Friday, 9 June 1944 9:15 AM- Alert Bell ringing Michel Family Refuge,

Ellen and Jack hurriedly dressed, folded up the tablecloth, picked up the basket, shouldered the carbine and set out for the main house. The bell continued to ring slowly, and methodically.

"We're coming!" laughed Ellen to no one as they increased their pace.

In a few more moments, they emerged from the forest and onto the meadow. They could see the truck parked in the courtyard with Pierre standing next to Byron Champagne and his very own 1941 Citroen Traction Avant.

Emil, Raoul and Raymond stood near them talking and laughing. Miep emerged from the house and walked over to join them. The three teenagers were nowhere to be seen.

Marie spotted the duo on the meadow path, stopped ringing the bell and waved. They returned the wave and sped up even more.

As they got within shouting distance, Emil called out to them,

"Jack, Ellen, hurry! Byron has a doctor for Jack's leg, but his time is limited.

Jack and Ellen exchanged looks and continued straight towards them.

Byron smiled and nodded his head,

"Good morning, Jack! Yes, I have secured a meeting with a very trusted doctor who has agreed to meet us in a private clinic in Arlon. His time is very limited because he treats many German officers there and can fit you in this morning but has his first German in an hour and a half. Please climb into the Citroen. There is no time to waste."

Jack shook his head,

"I must change these clothes; we both fell into the stream. And I also need my ID card."

Emil stepped forward and handed Jack his ID card,

"I thought you would need this, Jack. Go now with Byron. Your clothes will dry soon enough. Remember, if you're stopped, you are "doofstom, deaf and dumb."

Jack nodded, looked at Ellen and handed Emil his carbine and the food basket. He got into the rear seat of the Citroen. Much to his surprise, Ellen jumped in there with him.

"I'm going with you. No argument."

"But, Ellen, you must have your ID also, don't you?"

"I don't care, I'm going with you."

With that, Miep stepped forward and handed Ellen her ID card and her purse,

"I thought you might need yours as well."

They all laughed as Byron put the car in gear and they rolled down the driveway.

Raymond issued a shrill whistle, and the Citroen stopped. He ran up to the passenger side and handed in the basket of food.

"We figured you'd all be hungry since you didn't have time to eat."

The group watched them drive away and turned back to the house.

Emil shook his head, "I hope and pray that this young American will not only survive his surgery but survive this whole damn war and return to our niece who has obviously fallen in love with him."

Marie responded, "Yes, Emil. But let them enjoy these precious moments they have now, because no one knows what tomorrow will bring."

None of them realized how true these words would prove to be.

CHAPTER 67

Friday, 9 June 1944 10:45 AM- Jack undergoes surgery Clinique Médicale Hospital St Joseph d'Arlon Rue Jean de Feller Arlon, Luxembourg, Wallonia Belgium

In a small examination room adjacent to the room where Jack and Ellen waited, Doctor Jacques Jansen looked over the X-rays of Jack's right calf with his nurse, Susan Heymans. Byron Champagne stood off to one side at a respectful distance.

Nurse Heymans pointed to an area just behind the tibia, "I think I see something nestled in between the fibula and the tibia. Could that be what's causing this infection?"

Doctor Jansen smiled, "Aha! Susan, you are correct. Your brother Corneille would be so proud of you. You will make a fine physician after this bloody war is over and the Krauts have been driven from our country. You, too, Byron!"

Jansen referred to Nurse Heyman's famous brother, physician Corneille Heymans, who won the Nobel Peace prize in Physiology in 1938. Susan blushed and said, "Thank you, doctor, my brother is also hoping for me to finish my medical training."

"You shall, if I have anything to do with it. And, of course, you as well, Byron. Once this war is over. Let's see what we can do for our poor friend who cannot speak and cannot hear."

"Is he really deaf and dumb?"

Jansen and Byron stifled a laugh as Jansen replied, "Of course not, but we must all play this game for the benefit of the Gestapo."

Jansen, Heymans and Champagne entered the room. Byron moved through the room and stood next to Ellen. Jansen addressed Ellen, in English, referring to Jack's false ID card,

"Madam Jordan, we believe that we have located a suspicious

fragment of some kind in your husband, Jaques' calf. I believe that you wish us to operate to remove this object?"

Ellen nodded her head, playing along with the subterfuge.

"We are going to administer a sedative to Jaques which will put him at ease and make him very drowsy for the rest of the day. He is not driving a vehicle, is he?"

"No, doctor, our friend Byron is driving."

"Excellent! Nurse Heymans will give this sedative at once to your husband. It is in powder form and will absorb very quickly into his bloodstream."

He nodded to Heymans who produced a glass of water and emptied a packet of powder into it, stirred it vigorously and handed it to Jack who consumed it in two large gulps. He turned to Byron Champagne,

"Byron, I hope you have sufficient supplies of sulfanilamide? Our own supplies are closely monitored by the Nazis and collaborators. Sadly, we do not have access to penicillin."

"Yes, thank you, Doctor. I am fortunate in that my supplies are sufficient."

Doctor Jansen smiled and continued, addressing Ellen, "Once we feel that your husband is sufficiently relaxed, we will use ether to put him into a deep sleep. He will need help walking to your vehicle. I wish that we could keep him here in the hospital but that is impossible."

Ellen nodded and thanked him, "Doctor, I cannot tell you how much we appreciate your finding the time to help my husband. I will speak to your office to arrange payment."

"There is no need to pay me for anything, dear lady, thank you. It is I who wish I could thank 'Jaques" for his service to our nation. If only he could understand us."

Jack, already starting to feel slightly dizzy from the sedative, responded with a smile, "Thanks, Doc, I know you're not buying this bullshit about my being deaf otherwise you wouldn't be talking to my 'wife' in English. I just want you to know that my friends call me Jack."

Jansen and his nurse both laughed, and he shook his head, "Be quiet, my American friend, I can see that the sedative is working, and you have lost your inhibitions. Good thing you're here amongst friends.

Now be quiet or you really might be considered the other kind of 'dumb'. Now let's take care of that leg for you so you can get back up in the air and kill some more of these Kraut bastards."

Ellen was told where to wait and she and Byron left the room and sat in an adjacent hallway. They sat there deep in their own thoughts.

Doctor Jansen nodded to nurse Heyman who slipped a blood pressure cuff on Jack's arm and placed a mask over his face. In a few short minutes, he was in a deep sleep. Both Jansen and Heymans went to work as an experienced team and soon they extracted a small, twisted piece of metal about the size of a fingernail. They cleansed the wound, applied sulfa powder and stitched up the open wound.

While nurse Heymans switched to pure oxygen in Jack's breathing mixture and monitored his blood pressure and other vitals, Doctor Jansen washed up, discarded his surgical gown and came out into the waiting area.

Ellen and Byron immediately stood up and looked at the smiling Jansen. He addressed Ellen, "Madame Jordan, everything went well, Jaques is going to be coming out of his sleep soon. Please hold out your hand."

Ellen, displaying her brilliant smile, dutifully held out her hand and Doctor Jansen dropped the tiny piece of shrapnel into her open palm. "Here is the culprit. A piece of shrapnel. It is a good thing we did this, or his infection would have become life-threatening in these times when penicillin is so difficult to obtain."

"Oh my God! Thank you, Doctor! We are forever in your debt."

"No, my dear, we are in your husband's debt and all who fight for our freedom. Now, I have another question for you in private. May we step away for a moment?"

Byron immediately moved away from them, allowing some privacy. Ellen looked at Jansen quizzically.

"I have a daughter just about your age. I am concerned about the bruises on your face, and I also noticed the bruises on your husband's face. I am obliged to ask you about how you both got them. These are stressful times. Is everything all right between you two?"

Ellen breathed a sigh of relief, and laughed, "Oh, you are so kind,

Doctor! The bruises on my face and, I must confess elsewhere on my body came from a Nazi corporal and on my husband's face from two highway robbers a day or so later."

Now it was Jansen's turn to breathe a sigh of relief as he truly liked this young couple, "Oh, I am sorry that you both went through that, I truly am. I hope that someday those cowards will get their just rewards."

Ellen laughed, "Don't worry, Doctor. That wonderful man recovering in there already took care of that. They won't be hurting anybody ever again."

She embraced the doctor who stood there for an awkward moment. They both laughed and he told her that her 'husband' would soon be able to go. Within a few minutes, they escorted a sleepy Jack to Byron's car and headed back to the refuge.

CHAPTER 68

Friday, 9 June 1944 5:00 PM- Saint Thomas the Apostle Catholic Church Liege, Belgium.

Father Catron had been sitting in the confessional since 3 PM, almost two hours. He was physically and emotionally spent, having had virtually no sleep the night before dealing with sick and dying parishioners, those families grieving for loved ones lost in the war and the added burden of keeping his flock safe.

The news coming from the Allied invasion of Normandy was confusing. If you listened to the Nazi controlled press and radio, you were inclined to think that the Allies were being pushed back into the sea and it was only a matter of time before they were defeated. Another Dunkirk if you believed the German propaganda.

That "spin" was being contradicted by reports he was getting from his contacts with the Resistance. He knew that the allies had secured a significant foothold on the coastline and were pouring men and supplies into their established areas of operation.

He also knew that the Resistance was engaged in fierce attacks on German troops, logistics and communications not just in France but now in and around the port of Antwerp. He had met with several key members of the Witt Brigade who had joined forces with other resistance groups defending the Port of Antwerp infrastructure.

Still deep in thought, he felt the confessional shift under the weight of another penitent who entered and sat on the other side. He turned and started the rite of penance,

"Au nom du Père, du Fils et du Saint-Esprit"

A rough, Scottish accent interrupted him. A familiar voice, "It's okay, Father. It's me, Jock Clarke, SAS."

"Jock! My God, you startled me are you okay?"

"Me? Yeah, I'm okay, my leg is getting better, but we need to talk"

"Yes, yes! Of course! Can you give me a minute to see if there are any other people out there who need my assistance? Then we can get together in private."

"Yes, Father. That would be fine, but I don't have much time."

"Of course, I understand. Is anyone else with you? Lucien? Gerard? Marcelino?"

"No, Father they are not with me."

"Oh, too bad. How are they doing?"

"That's why I am here, Father. They are not doing well. All three are dead."

CHAPTER 69

Friday 16 June 1944 4:00 PM Father Catron brings bad news
Michel Family Refuge, Remote, Forest area Near Bouillon, Belgium

It had been five days since Jack's surgery and the pain and swelling in his right calf had finally started to lessen. Miep and Ellen had fastidiously applied the sulfa powder as recommended by Byron and the Doctor back in Arlon, and it seemed to help the healing process.

He and Ellen had been able to take small walks just past the meadow on the forest path, but certainly not yet able to once again get to the stream and "Cowboy Rock".

He thought about that day with tenderness and love and hoped to God that he and Ellen would survive this war and share many more moments like that one by the Creekside.

As they turned around and started back home, they saw the truck pulling into the courtyard. Much to their amazement, there in the front seat sat a blindfolded Father Corentin "Cory" Catron.

As the truck came to a stop, Father Catron removed his blindfold and waved to Emil, Miep, Ellen and Jack.

Raoul approached him and offered his hand, introducing himself and apologizing for the blindfold. Father Catron, no stranger to such procedures, shook his head and smiled. "I am not offended in the least, Raoul. What I don't know cannot be tortured out of me by the Gestapo or their minions."

He then turned to Emil, Miep, Ellen and Jack and smiled. Miep and Ellen moved into him and embraced him. Emil, always alert to developing situations asked, "Father, it is certainly wonderful to see you, but I cannot imagine that you just happen to be here. What is wrong? Why have you come here?"

Father Catron nodded solemnly, looked around and spotted Jan,

Elise and Nadine riding up to them on horseback. Raymond had just emerged from the workshop covered in grease and oil after servicing a farm tractor.

"Perhaps we can go inside? Where is Denise? I thought she was here with you."

Emil nodded, "I agree that it's a good idea to move inside. Just so you know, we are here as Raoul and Maria's guests and protectees. We are all, including Jack, considered family as we consider them family. So, I understand your concern, but there is no need to withhold anything."

"Yes, I understand, but where is Denise? Is she okay? I know about Janine's arrest by the Gestapo, and we are all devastated. My sources are putting out feelers as to her locations now that the Germans have moved her."

"Yes, thank you, Father. Denise has been coming and going every day since she arrived here. I understand that she is working with other helpers of *Réseau Comète* and British intelligence on a development that is a result of the Allies' successful landings. She usually comes back to us before nightfall."

"I see. Well, then let us go inside so that we can talk."

Everyone present, including Pierre, Raymond and Nadine followed the priest led by Raoul into the Great room. The men quickly gathered more chairs and set them out.

When everyone was seated, Father Catron asked them all to bow their heads as he led them in prayer. After praying together, they looked at him expectantly. He nodded solemnly and spoke,

"I am sorry to tell you that Lucien and two of his men in arms were killed over a week ago while fighting with the *Resistance* and British commandos around the Port of Antwerp."

Miep let out a deep moan and buried her head in Emil's shoulder. Jan and Elise ran to them and hugged Emil and Miep, while Ellen stood and went to Jack who held her to him. All the Michel family made the sign of the Cross and stood up from their seats.

When things settled down, Father Catron said, "I found out about this terrible news last Friday, but I did not know until today how to find you all. I cannot be away from my parish too long. There are so many people there in desperate need. I have another priest friend covering for me. One that I trust with my life, but I still must return as soon as possible."

Emil nodded his head in understanding and Father Catron continued, "If Denise is not here soon and if I would not be imposing, I will stay the night but then I must get back to Liege tomorrow."

Raoul immediately responded, "Of course, Father! You must be our guest even under these terrible circumstances. Let me show you to the spare room and get you settled. Then we can all sit together for a meal. Denise should be here before dark."

He signaled for Pierre to get the priest's belongings from the truck. He returned with one small bag and handed it to Father Catron.

Marie spoke up, "Father, we would be delighted to have you as our guest of honor. Do you have a meal preference? No meat of course this being Friday."

Father Catron smiled, "My dear Madame Michel. I know how difficult times are. Whatever you plan for your family is fine with me, of course. Also, the Holy Father, Pius the XII delegated authority to the local bishops to issue dispensation from the eating of meat on Fridays during this terrible war. So, whatever you were going to serve will be just fine."

"Okay, thank you dear Father. It will be chicken and vegetables then. Can I ask you for a favor?"

"Yes, of course! What can I do?"

"After dinner, could you hear confession from those who would like to receive the sacrament?"

"Absolutely! It would be my honor to do so. I would also be obliged to offer you all the Mass and Eucharist. Anything else?"

Ellen spoke up, "Could you also marry Lieutenant John Dodds and me?"

That broke the tension. Everyone, except Ellen and Jack, broke into uproarious laughter.

Ellen said so softly it was drowned out by the laughter, "I wasn't kidding."

Just then, Denise walked into the side door, having been quietly dropped off by Henri the Pharmacist, she stood there for a moment with her eyes wide open at the sight of Father Catron standing there laughing with all of them.

"Father! My God, so great to see you!"

She looked around the room at all the smiling faces, and asked,

"What's so funny?"

CHAPTER 70

Friday 16 June 1944 6:00 PM Father Catron True Confessions Michel Family Refuge, Near Bouillon, Belgium

Over by a large storage barn just outside of the courtyard, Denise sat on a long wooden bench, hewed out of a large oak tree by someone years ago. Jan leaned against her left side; Elise leaned against her right side. All three had been mourning the loss of Lucien and wept in an exhausted silence.

Subdued conversations and the smell of roasting chickens wafted out from the kitchen screened door. Inside the kitchen, Marie, Miep, Ellen and Nadine all hustled about setting the table and preparing the evening meal.

Inside the far corner of the great room, Raoul set up a makeshift altar and Jack and Emil assisted by draping a white linen sheet over the table and placing two candelabras on either end. Pierre and Raymond turned all the sitting chairs around to face the altar and then added extra chairs to accommodate everyone.

A large walk-in storage closet was situated just behind the altar and Raoul and Father Catron carefully moved items located on one wall of shelves to increase the floor space. Two wooden chairs were set facing each other and Raoul and the priest draped a white sheet in between the chairs, suspended by a section of clothesline thus creating a privacy screen of sorts.

Father Catron turned to Raoul and nodded in satisfaction, "Thank you, my brother. You have created a perfect confessional setting. For those who wish to remain anonymous and for those who wish to make a face-to-face confession. God is good."

Raoul closed the door of the home-made confessional and looked intently at the priest. Catron paused and, seeing the emotions just barely beneath Raoul's grizzled face, he gestured to one of the chairs. Raoul pulled aside the sheet separating them, "No need to preserve anonymity, Father."

"No, certainly not. Go ahead, my son."

Both made the Sign of the Cross and Raoul began in French, "Bless me, Father, for I have sinned. My last confession was a lifetime ago, during that time…"

Inside the kitchen, Marie and Miep saw that everyone was awaiting their turn to receive the sacrament of Penance. They shrugged their shoulders and placed the roasted chickens in a warming tray in the back of the ovens and carefully covered up the side dishes.

Marie looked at Miep and smiled, "It may be a while before anyone gets to eat."

Miep agreed, "Yes, but once all of us have our time with Jesus in confession, then that will be the time to have Mass and consume Him in communion. Dinner, my dear sister can wait."

The two women embraced, entered the great room and took their place in line.

CHAPTER 71

Friday 16 June 1944 (8:00 PM Father Catron hears more True Confessions at the Michel Family Refuge,

After Jan and Elise came and went from confession, Jack was the second to last penitent to enter the makeshift confessional. Only Ellen remained. Denise was nowhere to be seen and was still outside somewhere mourning the loss of her brother and possibly her sister.

Miep marveled at Father Catron's patience and his endurance to hear almost two straight hours of this relatively small group's confessions.

After ten minutes passed, Jack exited the little room and went outside to pray for his assigned penance. Ellen made the Sign of the Cross and went in. Miep looked at the far corner of the great room at the Grandfather Clock's pendulum slowly swinging away the hours and minutes. It was now 8:15 PM and she figured Father would soon be done.

She heard Maria inside the kitchen, rattling dishes, pots and pans and got up to give her a hand. Together they prepared the side dishes, checked that the kettle was on for tea and noted that they would soon have to "borrow back" some of the kitchen chairs brought into the great room for the upcoming Mass.

Marie smiled and said, "At this rate, when Father finishes confessions and starts in on Mass, we probably won't eat until midnight and all of this food will be cold and tasteless."

Miep nodded her head in agreement, "Well, I think that everyone will understand. We are so lucky that Father Catron is here during these terrible times considering all he must do back at his parish in Liege."

Marie glanced into the great room and saw Ellen and Father Catron emerging from the little room.

"Ah! He's just finished. Let's keep everything on warm and join them for Mass."

At that point, Denise came in from her long sabbatical outside and approached Father Catron, who put his arm around her shoulder and guided her into the confessional.

Both Marie and Miep groaned and then laughed, Miep spoke, "God has decided to guide our Denise back into His arms. Let us rejoice and be glad!"

Marie nodded solemnly "Amen, Sister. I just wish He had given us all a little time to feed these multitudes." Again, they laughed.

Ten minutes later, Father Catron emerged with Denise who went outside to pray. Catron looked at the two elder women and called them over to him. "My dear sisters, I can see that dinner is fully prepared and has been awaiting us to fulfill our sacramentary needs. I cannot abide during these times of starvation and deprivation to allow this food to go to waste. Therefore, I propose that we celebrate Mass tomorrow morning at first light. Would that be okay with you and my hosts?"

There was immediate agreement and some loud rejoicing as the kitchen chairs were brought back from the great room and everyone, including Denise, sat at the table. Father Catron asked Jan if he would like to say Grace to which he agreed.

Jan did a splendid job in Father Catron's opinion, thanking God for the blessings of the food, the hands that prepared it, for the poor, the starving, the men and women who fought for freedom and for his Uncle Lucien, Marcelino and Gerard and finally, for his aunt Janine. Catron wondered if this young man might have a vocation to the priesthood.

Time will tell, he thought.

Then the sounds of low-key laughter, clinking of cutlery on ceramic plates and quiet conversation filled the kitchen air as everyone settled down for their evening meal.

The Grandfather clock in the great room rang out its chime. Miep noted that it was 21:00 (9:00 PM)

CHAPTER 72

Friday 16 June 1944 11:30 PM Jack and Ellen, Late night meeting with Father Catron Michel Family Refuge

All the women worked together to clear and wash the last of the dinner plates. The table was covered with a clean tablecloth in anticipation of a large group breakfast with their visiting guest, Father Catron.

The men, except for Pierre, Raymond and Jan sat in the great room. Jack figured the two older sons were out there somewhere keeping a watchful eye for intruders. Jan was extremely tired, worn out with grief and went to his bed.

Father Catron, Emil and Raoul sat quietly smoking Raoul's cigars. Jack respectfully declined and just sat there quietly. Conversation in the great room and, for that matter, in the kitchen was quiet and subdued considering the loss of Lucien and his compatriots and for Janine, whose fate was still unknown.

When the kitchen tasks were completed, Marie, Miep, Denise and Ellen came into the great room, and each took an empty seat. Ellen chose the one closest to Jack. Elise and Nadine, the two teenage girls, said their "goodnight wishes" and went to their beds.

Father Catron tapped out his cigar in the ashtray and made eye contact with Ellen. A silent signal was transmitted between the two of them which was not lost on Jack, or for that matter, on any of the others who pretended not to notice.

Father Catron cleared his throat as he rose from his chair. He motioned the others to remain seated as they were rising out of respect, "No, please my friends, remain seated. Enjoy what's left of this evening. I wish to discuss a few things with this young couple. Jack and Ellen, if the mosquitos are not too bad, shall we sit outside in the garden?"

Ellen rose immediately, followed by Jack and all three of them exited the great room and went out to the garden area. Raoul excused the intrusion but hastened out in front of them and lit several lanterns in the garden area and then went back inside.

Father Catron took a seat on a concrete bench facing an adjoining concrete bench now occupied by Jack and Ellen. He looked at Ellen and nodded, "Ellen, why don't you tell me what I can do for you and for Jack?"

Ellen laughed and turned to Jack. She started to speak with a little tremor in her voice, "Jack, this is kind of awkward, but I have to ask you something…"

Before Ellen could go any further, Jack held up his hand to stop her, "Ellen, with all due respect, I need to stop you right there."

Her blue eyes got narrow, she was getting emotional, and she looked as though she was going to explode with anger for being cut off. Jack ignored it and smiled, rose to his feet, turned and faced her and got down on his good knee.

Ellen's mouth became wide open as she started to grasp where this was going, but Jack continued, "Ellen Delacroix, in front of Father Catron as my witness, will you consent to be my wife?"

"Wait! What?"

"Ellen, will you marry me?"

She jumped up from the bench and threw her arms around him, kissing him on his mouth, his cheeks and his forehead.

Father Catron laughed, "I guess that means 'Yes!"

With that, there was an explosion of joy and laughter coming from the kitchen screened door as Marie, Miep and Denise who were obviously listening in, raced out into the garden and hugged everyone within reach, including the priest.

Father Catron smiled and said, "Children, we have a lot to discuss and a lot to work out before a marriage can take place. I suggest we go to sleep now, if that's possible for you, Ellen and for you, Jack. We will sit down after early morning Mass and go through the details and the obstacles. Is that agreeable with everyone?"

Everyone agreed and within a half hour the house became dark, and people went to their respective bedrooms. Soon everyone in the house, except for Jack and Ellen, was fast asleep.

CHAPTER 73

Saturday 17 June 1944 7:00 AM Early morning Mass with Father Catron Michel Family Refuge

Jan helped Father Catron set up for Mass by lighting the candles on either end of the makeshift altar and preparing a ceramic bowl of water and hand towel for his hand purification. Father Catron brought along his own travel vestments, unconsecrated hosts, chalice, altar linens and a small supply of red wine to be consecrated during the Mass.

In a very short time family members, including the two older boys, Pierre and Raymond came in and took their seats. Raoul remained standing by the screened door of the great room looking out to the meadow and the forest periodically.

All the women sat in the chairs closest to the makeshift altar with Jack and Emil sitting just behind them next to Raymond and Pierre.

In a few minutes, Father Catron approached the altar and everyone who was seated rose from their chairs. Mass at the Michel Family Refuge had begun.

Shortly after the Mass concluded, Father Catron watched as Jan tidied up the altar, extinguished the candles and carefully folded the altar linens that he brought with him from Liege. He smiled at this young man and asked, "Jan, have you ever thought about becoming a priest?"

Jan jerked around as though poked with a sharp stick, then smiled, "Yes, Father, all the time."

Catron smiled and went over to him and put his hand on the boy's shoulder, "Let's speak with your mother, Denise, and see if we can't get things moving in that direction for you. Would that be okay/"

Jan, smiling from ear to ear, nodded his head enthusiastically, "Yes, Father! That would be wonderful."

The priest looked for Denise and discovered that she had joined the other women in the kitchen preparing to serve breakfast to the group. He would speak with her and Jan after spending time with Jack and Ellen.

Father Catron smiled and then turned to see Jack and Ellen standing nearby waiting for him. "Jack, Ellen, let's go back out to the garden and discuss your plans."

The two of them accompanied the priest out into the garden and assumed the same positions on the two concrete benches as the night before.

Once seated, Father Catron said, "Okay you two, let's see how we can move things along for you both. But first, let's pray."

He made the Sign of the Cross as did Jack and Ellen, led them in prayer and then started to lay out before them all the hurdles and obstacles that were in their path on the way to Holy Matrimony.

CHAPTER 74

Saturday 17 June 1944 9:00 AM Office of Edouard Degrelle, Pharmacist, Degrelle Pharmacy Rue des Casernes Bouillon, Belgium

In his office above his pharmacy in the village of Bouillon, Pharmacist Edouard Degrelle and his trusted assistant, Paul Bouchard met with three members of the paramilitary wing of the *Formations de Combat*. They were part of a Rexist assassination squad.

Degrelle, brother of Leon Degrelle, founder of the pro-Nazi Rexist Movement, was himself a devout Nazi and head of a unit of the Rexist party in the Ardennes. The men were discussing a failed assassination attempt on his famous brother, Leon and were trying to determine if there were any members of the Resistance in the Bouillon area or elsewhere who might have been involved in the attempt.

Edouard opened his desktop drawer and withdrew a note pad. Putting on his reading glasses he gave the names of several men who were local or otherwise within the boundaries of occupied Belgium. All were prominent opponents of "the Rexist cause."

The list included the local priest, Father Michel Masson, Pastor of Saint John the Evangelist, Bouillon who publicly embarrassed Edouard by denying him communion twice in recent weeks at Mass while vocally citing his Rexist affiliation. Also included was Pharmacist Henri Charles, a competitor located on Rue Georges Lorand in Bouillon.

The killers wrote down the names on their own pad: René Pierlot, Louis and his brother Henri Bodart and Father Michel Masson. Degrelle's assistant Buchard, was shocked at the mention of the priest, but showed no emotion or reaction at the mention of the priest's name who happened to be his wife's brother.

Bouchard was secretly a double agent, a fervent anti-Nazi and member of the Resistance who had successfully infiltrated Degrelle's inner circle and earned his trust. He proved to be a terrific inside source of intelligence for the Resistance.

Marco, the self-identified leader of this three-man commando group looked at the names and whistled, "The local priest, had the audacity to deny you communion? He will pay for that! What about this pharmacist, Henri Charles?"

Edouard nodded, "Yes, Charles is an outspoken critic of my brother and of me. He is often seen in the company of men who are reputed to be in the Resistance. His death will send a clear message to those who oppose us."

Marco nodded and continued to review the list, much to Edouard's annoyance. "René Pierlot, isn't he the brother of that minister who is in exile in London?"

Bouchard nodded, "Yes. You are correct."

Marco went down the list, then addressed Edouard, "Louis Bodart was at one point very close to you and your family, wasn't he?"

Edouard, growing frustrated at this man's questioning said, "Yes, at one time he was also close to Father Degrelle in the Catholic Party but is now our enemy."

He paused, then continued, "Why do you ask Marco? Do *you* have a problem with me mentioning his name? Perhaps we have the wrong people sitting here. Perhaps I should ask my brother for his recommendation. Do I have to speak to someone else?"

Marco decided to back off. He did not want to insult Leon Degrelle or, for that matter, his brother, Edouard, who struck him as an arrogant bastard.

"No, of course not. I just need to get all the background I can before we move on these men."

"Yes, of course you do. Just so you know Louis' brother, Henri is a municipal administrator who is now fervently opposed to us. He is an enemy. He is very visible publicly. Perhaps this might be a bit too challenging for you?"

Marco was growing increasingly annoyed with the sarcasm and getting a little disenchanted with this pompous, self-important jerk but held his tongue. His two henchmen knew Marco's short temper and were worried that he might "blow a fuse," and then there would be Hell to pay. But Marco just shrugged it off for the time being.

"No, certainly not we will take care of all of them."

Edouard nodded in satisfaction then turned to Bouchard who produced the addresses of the new targets. He and Bouchard rose from their chairs and immediately the three commandos did as well.

He looked at them dismissively and said, "This meeting is over. Now go and take care of this."

The three killers rose, muttered their goodbyes and left.

Once they left the office and exited onto the street, Degrelle looked at Bouchard, laughed and said, "Scary bunch, don't you think?"

Bouchard, laughed, nodded in agreement, "Yes, Edouard, scary indeed."

CHAPTER 75

Saturday 17 June 1944 Early morning-after Mass Jack and Ellen in the Garden with Father Catron Michel Family Refuge

Father Catron observed the two young people as they took their seats on the concrete bench opposite his own. He thought to himself, *"how young they looked.*

He reflected that by standards that existed outside of a time of war the Church would have a different set of guidelines for couples who aspired to receive the sacrament of Holy Matrimony.

But this is indeed a time of war, men and women are fighting and dying, things and standards are changed.

"Father?" It was Jack looking intently at him.

"Oh! Sorry, Jack. I was deep in thought there for a moment. I'm back with you now."

They all shared a nervous laugh and Father Catron started the conversation, "Okay. Jack, Ellen, how long have you two known each other?"

Ellen responded, "A little over two weeks."

"I see. Two weeks ago, you two did not know each other, and in that short period of time you both have decided that you wish to spend the rest of your lives together, is that right?"

They both nodded and grasped each other's hands. Father Catron nodded and continued, "I hope you can see that the Church would consider this far too short a time to make such an important, life-changing decision. Normally the Church would want a couple to know each other for at least six months."

Ellen started to object, but Catron silenced her by holding up his hand, "Be patient, Ellen, let me continue."

"Sorry, Father, but."

Again, he raised his hand and patiently continued, "During that time, the Church would meet regularly with the couple both together and individually to discuss many of the important issues that come with marriage."

He paused to see that they were totally involved in what he was saying then went on, "That being said, these are not '*normal times*', this is a time of great turmoil, life, death, grief and tragedy. You two are not alone in discovering another person during these times and falling in love, love 'at first sight' if you will."

They both smiled and nodded enthusiastically,

"Okay, I understand what is happening here with you both. But I must tell you that, as a priest, I have grave concerns for the durability of such 'instant' romances and relationships. They heat up quickly and they cool off quickly. Do you understand those concerns?"

Jack spoke up, "Yes, Father, certainly we do. We also understand that in these times of war, life can be very short. Ellen and I have fallen in love. We don't know what the future holds for us. None of us do. But one thing is certain. Whatever time we have in this life, we want to spend it together and we want to bring God into our relationship through Marriage."

Father Catron was impressed. He held up his hand indicating that he needed a moment. He lowered his head and stared at the top of his shoes, deep in thought.

Jack and Ellen patiently waited. Finally, he lifted his head and looked at them. "Okay, I understand. First, a few questions for you, Jack. I have a pretty good idea of the answers that Ellen might have. Here are the questions and I don't want you to respond immediately, just listen and then respond afterwards, Okay?"

Jack took a deep breath and nodded. Father Catron began, "I want you to write these answers down after you've thought about them and if you forget, I'm sure Ellen will refresh your memory. First, you must attest that you have been baptized, received your First Eucharist, Holy communion you would say in the States, and have been Confirmed. With me so far?"

"Yes."

"If you cannot recall receiving any of these sacraments, we will have a problem getting wartime permission from my bishop. I don't know your family situation back in the States but then they would have to help with that, for example providing the name of the Catholic church where your sacraments of Initiation took place."

Jack responded immediately, "No, I am certain that I have received those sacraments. To the best of my knowledge especially about Baptism, all my sacraments were done at Saint Matthew Catholic church in Charlotte, North Carolina when my dad worked there."

Father Catron nodded, smiled and gestured for Jack to continue.

"My confirmation name is 'John' after John the Baptist, and I can give approximate dates. Plus, my mother doesn't even know if I'm alive after I got shot down."

Both Father Catron and Ellen were surprised by this revelation, which made sense considering his recent crash and survival. They both looked at Jack with a mixture of shock and sadness. The priest nodded,

"When the time is right, Jack, I think we can get word to the American military that you are alive. Let's continue. Have you ever been married before?

"No, never."

"Okay, same for you Ellen?"

"Yes, I mean no I've never been married before, I said 'yes' in response to Jack's answer, I…"

Catron laughed, and waved his hand to calm her down, "That's okay, relax. Do you both consent to the possibility of having children, and if so, do you consent to raising them Catholic?

Two affirmative responses.

"Okay, a couple of other things. In Belgium and in most other countries in Europe marriage occurs in two parts. First a civil union approved by the local civilian authorities, then a Sacramental Marriage in the Church. In the eyes of the civil authorities, you two wouldn't be considered married without the civil union."

Jack started to object, but the priest waved him quiet as well.

"We obviously cannot submit Jack to the civil authorities until and unless the Allied forces kick the current civil authorities in their rear-ends and we have been liberated. That will be a bridge to cross downstream."

They both nodded their understanding. Catron went on, "I am going to pray for all these issues and concerns. I suggest you two do as well and talk things out as best you can. I have very pressing obligations at my parish in Liege. I am going to consult with my Bishop at Saint Rumbold's Cathedral in Mechelen. With his approval I should be able to offer a Sacramental union of Holy Matrimony for you both.

They stood up and hugged each other, but then observed the priest waving them back down into their seats.

"If, however, he does not approve, then I am powerless to perform the ceremony."

Ellen nodded, "What do you think he will say?"

"I simply don't know. I will meet with him sometime next week and get back with you."

With that, they stood, and Father Catron said a prayer over them and blessed them with the Sign of the Cross.

In a few short minutes, he said his goodbyes to everyone gathered there in the house, got into the truck with Pierre. This time he was not given a blindfold. He waved to everyone as they drove down the road to the gate and then they were gone.

Jack looked at Ellen and smiled,

"A lot to think about. But a lot to be thankful for."

She hugged him as they walked towards the house,

"John the Baptist? You chose a saint with the same first name as yourself?"

"No, apparently my Mee-Maw chose it for me."

"I see, "said Ellen.

Jack laughed and asked her as they entered through the kitchen screened door, "Any other questions?"

"Yes. Who or what is a Mee-Maw?"

CHAPTER 76

Saturday 17 June 1944 US and Allied operations Battle of Normandy and Rexist Commandos prepare their plans.

Pierre Michel dropped Father Catron off at the residence of Father Michel Masson, Pastor Saint John the Evangelist, in Bouillon where he had parked his trusted Renault. Constance Rademacher, Father Masson's parish secretary, said that he was in the church hearing confessions. She would tell him that Father Catron came by to pick up his car and would call him when he got back to his own parish in Liege.

On the evening of the day that Father Catron drove back to Liege and Jack and Ellen were deep in thought about their future lives together, American operations in the Cotentin Peninsula to cut German lines continued.

Several villages and towns on the road to the 7th Corps were freed, the town of Magneville and Néhou by elements of the 60th US Infantry Regiment. At the same time, the 47th American infantry regiment entered the town of Saint-Sauveur-le-Vicomte.

Meanwhile, back in Bouillon, Marco and his two Rexist compatriots scoped out the pharmacy owned and operated by Henri Charles. They also went to confession and attended daily Mass, receiving Holy communion from Father Michel Masson whom they intended to murder the next day or so.

Their attendance at Mass was observed by Paul Bouchard who sat quietly and unobserved in the rear row of pews. When the killers departed the Church, Bouchard entered the confessional jumping ahead of others waiting in line.

This angered many of the people who had been patiently waiting to have their confessions heard. One older lady glared at him and resolved to declare her anger to her favorite priest as soon as she entered the confessional.

Much to her surprise and to those also waiting, Father Masson abruptly left the confessional, briefly apologized to those in line, doffed his beretta, explaining that there was a sacramental emergency that needed his immediate attention.

The parishioners did not see him again until the second week of July. He did not explain the reason for his abrupt disappearance.

CHAPTER 77

Monday 26 June 1944 5:00 PM Saint Thomas the Apostle Catholic Church Liege, Belgium.

Father Catron was exhausted. His day had been full of the things that every parish priest faces from time to time but especially during the Nazi occupation of Belgium. At 3 AM he provided the last rites for a dying parishioner.

Next, in defiance of the curfew restrictions, he drove to the Liege University Hospital for a parishioner badly beaten by Nazi thugs who mistakenly took him for someone else. No sooner did he return from the hospital; he received an urgent call to baptize a newborn in danger of death. He raced to the family's home only to find that he was too late, the infant died just minutes before he arrived.

Nevertheless, he prayed over the child with the grieving family and asked the husband to come in when he could to make the arrangements. When he finally returned to the parish office, Magda DeVries, his newly appointed parish secretary, told him that Cardinal Van Roey's office had called and would like a return call as soon as possible.

Catron tried several times to return the phone call but each time the call was interrupted or failed. This was not uncommon during the war, especially since the Allied landing in Normandy.

He advised Magda that he needed to look in on his "special guests", meaning the Jewish families he had secreted throughout the parish in "safe homes." He held up his military grade walkie-talkie which was illegal for a civilian to possess.

He said, "If the Cardinal calls back, tell him I am available to see him at once at his pleasure, then just press the button on the side three times." Magda looked at her duplicate walkie-talkie and saw the button.

Catron continued, "That is the so-called "squelch" button and will emit a low volume screeching sound. This will alert me to return to the office at once. Do not transmit over the radio, just the button on the side."

Magda shrugged her shoulders and turned to answer the phone, which had just started ringing. Catron turned on his heels and started rushing out the door before she could stop him.

He made it halfway down the hallway leading to the outside when his walkie-talkie screeched. Catron whipped around and was back in the office within seconds. Magda handed him the phone and said simply, "For you."

Catron brought the receiver to his ear, expecting to speak with the Cardinal Archbishop's secretary. Instead, none other than the Cardinal himself was on the other end.

"Father Catron, good to hear your voice. Listen, I know how busy you must be but is there some way you could join me for dinner this evening? We have a great deal to talk about."

Father Catron thought he would burst. He was so delighted that the Cardinal Archbishop would not only speak with him directly but invite him to dinner with him.

"Of course, Your Eminence! It would be an honor. What time shall I be there?"

"Whatever time you can make it, Father Catron. We will have dinner when you can get here."

"Yes, Your Eminence, it is about 85 kilometers from here to Mechelen and given the strict travel restrictions, it takes me up to two hours."

"I understand. And Corentin?"

Catron's mouth fell open in shock, the Cardinal Archbishop had just called him by his first given name, an incredible honor. Startled, he heard the Cardinal's voice,

"Father Catron? Are you there?"

"Yes, Your Eminence, a bad connection. Did you have something else you wished to say?"

"Yes, Corentin, pack a bag for one to two night's stay. I will send a covering priest to cover for you. Now, you take your time and drive slowly and carefully so as not to attract attention from our German friends. Understand?"

Yes, your Eminence."

"Good! See you soon."

Catron looked around his room for his notes, scooped them up and started for his quarters. Halfway down the hallway towards his room, he met Magda who handed him his overnight bag with a big smile.

"Go in safety, dear Father. I've already spoken with young Father Joseph who filled in for you a few weeks ago. He is on his way. And don't worry. All the troubles will still be here when you get back. Now go!"

Catron laughed, "Magda, God bless you! Ever since the 'Chicken Project' I knew you were someone special. I am so grateful for you!"

Magda blushed and joked; "Okay then why don't you just double my salary?"

They both laughed, as Magda was not being paid and two times zero was still zero.

Catron went to the garage, retrieved his beloved 1939 Renault Juvaquatre and headed out towards Mechelen, Brussels and St Rumbold's Cathedral.

CHAPTER 78

Monday 26 June 1944 7:30 PM Cardinal Archbishop's residence Near Cathedral of St. Michael and St. Gudula Brussels, Belgium

After two hours of driving, Father Catron pulled his Renault Juvaquatre up to the large wrought iron gates with the seal of the Cardinal Archbishop affixed to each side. An armed guard approached the driver's side of the vehicle and Catron rolled down the window holding his credentials out for the officer's review.

The unsmiling guard read his credentials very carefully and then handed them back to him. He turned to two other guards standing just inside the gates and nodded. They opened the gates and Catron proceeded into the cobblestone courtyard, pulling up next to an older Citroen sedan and parked.

As he shut down the engine of the Renault, a young seminarian wearing a black cassock approached the driver's side door and opened it for Catron. Smiling, and speaking in French, the young man said,

"Greetings, Father Catron! I hope you had a safe journey. Let me take your things and bring them to your room. The Cardinal Archbishop is waiting for you."

Nodding his head towards another seminarian approaching the vehicle, he said, "Georges will escort you to the dining room."

Georges, also wearing a black cassock, acknowledged Father Catron with a smile and led the way into the residence. Catron had only been here one other time years ago when he himself was a young seminarian on summer duty. He continued to follow Georges and eventually they entered a brightly lit dining room where several religious sisters were busy bringing glassware and dishes to several place settings.

The only other person in the room was The Archbishop of Mechelen and primate of the Catholic Church of Belgium, Jozef-Ernest

Cardinal van Roey. Cardinal van Roey rose from a large padded easy chair and greeted Catron with a big smile and open arms.

"Father Catron! I am so glad you have made it! Come, let us take a seat over here" pointing to two easy chairs facing each other, "this way we can talk about things while the good sisters prepare our meal for us."

Catron crossed over the carpet to the Cardinal Archbishop, took his extended hand and kissed his ring, bowing slightly. Cardinal van Roey smiled and guided Father Catron to the sitting area, indicating an armchair for him and took the one opposite it for himself. Suddenly, a thought jolted the Cardinal, as he voiced concern, "Are you very hungry? Forgive my lack of consideration with all the rationing and lack of food, would you prefer to eat first and talk afterwards?"

In truth, Catron had not eaten but a piece of bread and cheese earlier in the day. He was ravenously hungry, but he shook his head, "No thank you, your Eminence, I am fine and would most certainly prefer to talk now if it is okay with you."

Cardinal van Roey smiled and nodded, indicating that Catron should start talking. Catron discussed the growing number of Jewish families he and his parishioners were hiding. He explained the incredible demands that that humanitarian effort placed on him, his parishioners and his all-volunteer staff to provide food and shelter.

The Cardinal listened intently, nodded a few times, asking a question or two but signaled Catron to continue. Father Catron talked about the recent bombing of the Liege aerodrome, and briefly discussed the attempted rape and the young Airman's intervention which led to the dead Nazi at the Chicken house. This latest revelation visibly shocked the prelate, prompting him to ask for a bit more detail.

Catron described the bravery of the young American pilot, John Dodds, who was seriously wounded while attacking a German aerodrome and crashing near the Ardennes Forest. He went on to explain how, despite his wounds, he saved Ellen Delacroix not once but almost certainly twice.

The Cardinal Archbishop was visibly moved by these revelations and signaled Catron to continue. Catron then related how Lieutenant

Dodds and Ellen Delacroix came to him and told him that they had fallen in love and expressed their desire to be married as soon as possible.

Just as the Cardinal was about to respond, a religious sister stood near them and waited to be recognized. As soon as the Cardinal looked at her and smiled, she announced that dinner was ready. The Cardinal rose and gestured for Father Catron to follow him. To Catron's surprise, they bypassed the large table elaborately set and moved into the kitchen where a smaller table was set for just two places. The Cardinal smiled, "I will explain later."

CHAPTER 79

Monday 26 June 1944 9:00 PM Cardinal Archbishop's residence Near Cathedral of St. Michael and St. Gudula Brussels, Belgium

"So, Corentin, you are wondering who all the people are for these place settings, aren't you?"

Catron nodded his head. The Cardinal pointed to the sisters working away in the kitchen, "Our good sisters will go out tomorrow and quietly bring some homeless and poor into the residence here and we will serve them. They are a remarkable group of religious and they help me to help others. Now, let's eat."

After the meal, the Cardinal gestured to the same two chairs, and they resumed their seats. Catron accepted the offer of a cigar which the Cardinal lit himself. He then started the conversation, "Father Catron, I must commend you on all you are doing to serve God's people from the evils brought to us by the Nazis. Your efforts in arranging safe homes for the Jewish families is outstanding. "

He took another long draw on his cigar then continued, "Please keep this going, but be *very careful*, as the Nazis have no compunction about putting priests and religious behind bars and into the worst of the concentration camps. I have a very good feeling that soon the Allies will push through and liberate all of us. Then we can truly rejoice."

Father Catron thanked the Cardinal. Then he leaned forward, "Your Eminence, I don't mean to be impertinent, but I am so anxious to know your thoughts about the young couple? The American pilot and the young woman who I have known for so many years?"

Cardinal van Roey smiled, took another long draw on his own cigar, and blew out a perfectly concentric smoke ring and said, "This is an emotional situation, Father. On the one hand they obviously have great affection for one another. They realize that life during these times of war can be very short and want to enjoy each other for whatever time God grants them, am I right?"

Catron nodded and the Cardinal continued, "On the other hand, they have only known each other for two, almost three weeks according to you. They both have experienced great trauma; his flying into combat, getting shot down, crashing and surviving and then feeling overwhelming gratitude for not only surviving the crash but being rescued by members of the *Réseau Comète*."

The Cardinal paused, drew a deep intake from the cigar and this time, blew out four perfectly round smoke circles. Much to his own delight and Father Cory's.

"Ha! I am getting better at this. I will have to try it with the Holy Father when, and if I get to see him after liberation. But, enough of that, let's continue."

Catron smiled and gestured for him to continue, "The young woman has also survived trauma and near-death experiences according to your account. Her reaction and attraction to this young man as her hero is only to be expected. It doesn't surprise me. Do you think it is temporal?"

Catron thought about it and shook his head, "No I have known her for quite some time. She has always been levelheaded and mature in my opinion.

Catron continued, "I also understand that when they were accosted by the two highway bandits it was almost certain that they would all be victims of far more than just robbery. This was according to other occupants of the car who have experience in these things."

The Cardinal nodded, "Yes, I've heard of similar events."

Catron went on, "Faced with that inevitability, and immediately after being brutally assaulted himself, the American was forced to shoot them before they shot him and the others. He killed both men."

The priest shook his head in sadness, "In the aftermath of that traumatic event, Ellen showed a strength in spirit that amazes me. Again, according to others who were present, she didn't hesitate to assist the American to remove the bodies from the road. Displaying a characteristic toughness that I've come to expect from her."

This got the Cardinal's attention, "Remarkable. What these young people and so many others have gone through in these terrible times is truly incredible. I have heard enough for this evening, and I will make you a promise."

This got Father Catron's attention. "Yes, your Eminence?"

"First, we will pray the last of our seven canonical hours together with the two young seminarians, the Compline."

"Okay, I understand."

The Cardinal Archbishop rose from his chair as did Father Catron. "Then, Father Catron, after Compline I am ordering you to bed to get some much needed and well-deserved rest. I have a suspicion that you have had very little sleep.

"Yes, Your Eminence."

"Then, I will pray on all these things, and we will meet at first light for Lauds. Again, with our young seminarians and this time with our sisters religious. With me so far?"

A slightly exasperated Father Catron nodded his head, "Yes, your Eminence."

"After I have prayed on this during the night, and after Morning prayer and after a healthy breakfast, I will give you my answer about your American pilot and your young Belgian woman. Now, let's go pray."

CHAPTER 80

Tuesday 27 June 1944 6:30 AM Lauds, Morning Prayer followed by Mass in the Private Chapel Cardinal Archbishop's residence Near Cathedral of St. Michael and St. Gudula Brussels, Belgium

After Morning Prayer and Mass, the two seminarians and three Sisters of Saint Mary repaired to the kitchen to prepare breakfast.

At the request of the Cardinal Archbishop, Father Catron remained in the sanctuary while he and the Cardinal bowed before the Blessed Sacrament. The Cardinal motioned Father Catron to follow him.

They moved through a hallway past the bedrooms and out onto a balcony overlooking the courtyard below where Father Catron's Renault was parked. The Cardinal gestured to two wrought iron seats and took one himself. He offered Catron another cigar which he politely declined. After lighting his cigar and taking a few puffs, he turned to face Catron,

"Father Catron, I have prayed about this American pilot and this young, Belgian woman. As I'm sure you have already pointed out to them, two weeks is hardly enough time for a man and a woman to get to know one another well enough to formulate a plan to spend the rest of their lives together in Holy Matrimony. Am I correct?"

"Yes, your Eminence." Catron responded while at the same time thought t*his is not sounding good for Jack and Ellen.*

The Cardinal nodded and continued, "Of course, there is the added complication of not having definitive proof of this young man's sacramental records. Then, his government and even his family are not even aware if he is still alive."

Another long puff on his cigar as he paused for a moment watching the rising sun illuminate the Belgian sky. He then continued, "All of that, coupled with keeping the Nazis in the dark about the American's existence while still trying to satisfy the civilian requirements for a civil proceeding. How am I doing so far?

"You have summed up the case accurately your Excellency."

Another puff on the cigar and the Cardinal smiled, "Yes, I have."

Then, as though a thought just occurred to the Cardinal Archbishop, he snapped his fingers and said, "Oh! And there is also an added, somewhat personal complication. If I were to give you permission to confer the sacrament on an enemy combatant of the German occupiers, a man who was, with our knowledge collaborating with the *Resistance*, I would effectively be assigning the death penalty to you and to me."

Catron was crushed, *what a fool I am!* This unanticipated consequence hit him like a ton of bricks. He hadn't worried about the implications that he would personally face, *but* he had not thought of the danger that this would confer upon the *Cardinal Archbishop!*

He was already mentally formulating the best way to break this news to Ellen and Jack when the Cardinal Archbishop, the prelate of Belgium blew out four perfect rings of smoke and turned to face him with an enormous grin,

"I like it! Let's do this. We'll give old Adolph something to complain about. Can you somehow get this couple here to the Cathedral safely?"

"Yes, your Eminence, I believe I can."

"Okay, Father Catron. Do it as quickly as possible. Bring them to see me right here in my residence. Only two trusted witnesses. Then, I will arrange from my contacts after the deed is done to alert the Allies of this pilot's existence and that he is now married to a wonderful Belgian woman. We will work out other details later. Now get moving!"

Without further ado, the Cardinal Archbishop, known among his admirers as the "Iron Bishop" for his hatred of the Nazis, the pro-Nazi Rexists and collaborators had decided true to his fearless nature.

Within ten minutes, Father Catron was in his Juvaquatre on his way back to his parish in Liege with an enormous smile on his lips for the entire two-hour drive. About a half hour out of Liege, it suddenly occurred to him that he had rushed to his car and totally forgot the breakfast that the good sisters had waiting for him. *Darn!*

CHAPTER 81

Tuesday 27 June 1944 10:30 AM Office of the Civil Administrator Nazi occupational headquarters 12-story building at 453 Avenue Louise Brussels, Belgium

The Reichskommisar for Belgium and Northern France, who, basically was the German Civil Administrator for both territories, was a longtime Nazi and fervent anti-Semite by the name of Joseph Grohé. Grohé had just been briefed about the worsening situation the German forces faced in the wake of the Normandy invasion. He brushed aside all the propaganda nonsense that the forces of the Fatherland were about to push the Allies back into the sea. He was many things to his many enemies, but he was not stupid, he knew better.

Grohé ordered his personal assistant to quietly draw up plans for what amounted to a general retreat from the entire country of Belgium in anticipation of the arrival of Allied forces. These plans were to be kept "Top Secret" as Hitler would regard this as a total capitulation and betrayal of Germany which would lead to his own execution as a traitor.

As the Allies increased their intensive bombing of railway junctions and transport networks across northern France and Belgium, Grohé knew the "handwriting was on the wall." Being a practical man, he issued immediate orders for a severely reduced curfew, closing things down now for most civilians at 21:00 Hours (9:00 PM) instead of the customary 00:01 hours (Midnight) lasting until 07:00 (7:00 AM) instead of 6 AM.

In conference with senior military officers who were worried about increased defections, Grohé ordered roadblocks and detailed, careful inspections of all drivers and passengers into and out of the city.

When pressed by the sympathetic Belgian pro-Nazi press as to why the increased security and patrols, Grohé responded by citing "concerns" for the safety and security of Belgian civilians considering thousands of civilian casualties due to the Allied bombings. The fewer civilians on the road, the fewer casualties, he proclaimed.

He even cited the condemnation of the intense Allied bombing by Cardinal van Roey, the outspoken Cardinal Archbishop and prelate of Belgium who appealed to Allied commanders on Belgium radio to stop the indiscriminate bombing which rarely hit their intended target and killed and wounded countless innocent civilians.

It didn't take long for "special interest groups" like the Catholic Church and Red Cross workers to register their concern about these newly increased restrictions. These protests largely fell on deaf ears, but Joseph Grohé, recognized that he personally might just need some protection by these organizations once Germany withdrew and was defeated which he knew was now inevitable.

He therefore took an unprecedented step and reached out to the office of the Cardinal Archbishop and requested an appointment at the Cardinal's Cathedral office instead of demanding van Roey come to Nazi headquarters.

The Cardinal Archbishop's secretary immediately responded and within an hour, the most powerful Nazi in Belgium was seated in one of the same upholstered chairs occupied by Father Catron less than four hours earlier.

After some preliminary "small talk" during which Grohé politely declined the offer of one of van Roey's cigars, the German Civil Administrator tried to explain the sudden increase in security, and travel restrictions that would affect the ability of many priests, sisters religious and others to serve their communities. He offered to issue newly minted ID cards which would go a long way to expedite their travels and would also permit some extension of the new curfew hours.

The Cardinal Archbishop saw right through this self-serving overture but smiled and nodded appreciatively as though he was buying the explanation this German was spewing. He pushed for assurances that these new restrictions would not end up with scores of his priests and religious sisters being detained and even arrested as they tried to carry out God's work.

Grohé assured him that this would not be the case and, if for some reason there was a "mix-up" he would personally intervene on behalf of the Church. He promised to get out the word to all the security forces entrusted with the new roadblocks and inspection sites to allow unencumbered access to priests and religious.

Cardinal van Roey thanked him and mentioned that he thought highly of the Administrator's concerns for the Belgian people and walked him out to his car. As he watched the German's departure, he turned to his personal secretary and said,

"Get me Father Catron on the phone. There's been a change of plans."

CHAPTER 82

Thursday 29 June 1944 1:00 PM Father Catron and the Hidden children Saint Thomas the Apostle Catholic Church, Liege, Belgium.

It had been two days since returning from his visit with Cardinal Archbishop, van Roey. Father Catron was anxious to get together with the American Pilot and Emil's niece, Ellen Delacroix. He had good news for the young couple once he came to a decision as to how to implement their marriage in secret.

Unfortunately, his visit to the Michel family refuge in Bouillon was delayed out of necessity. He was immersed in continual crises raging among the Religious Sisters and the people of his parish concerning the issue of the "hidden children."

These were the Jewish children that several communities of Religious Sisters together with members of the Resistance were hiding in the various convents, his school and the safe houses provided by several brave parish families sheltering them from the Nazis.

The continued onslaught of Nazi arrests and persecutions of the Jewish people in Belgium continued even though the Allied invasion made it clear that Germany was going to lose this war.

It was apparent that the search for Jews, especially those children and adults being harbored in "safe houses" were increasing as the Allied advances seemed imminent. People of his parish who were housing young Jewish children and Jewish adults on behalf of their families were growing increasingly desperate as collaborators were denouncing many of them to the Gestapo.

Despite repeated warnings from the *Resistance* that these traitors would be made to pay dearly for their collaboration, Gestapo agents were still knocking on doors, searching homes and had raided Father Catron's school dormitories several times looking for these sheltered innocents.

Entire families throughout Belgium who were harboring these little ones were being arrested along with the Jewish children and sent off to concentration camps. Many would not survive the experience and many, especially Jewish children were murdered in the camps.

With all of those innocents weighing so heavily upon him, Father Catron knelt all alone before the Blessed Sacrament, praying silently for guidance. He was physically and emotionally exhausted, worried about his "flock", the people entrusted to his care as shepherd of his parish.

Deep in thought, he sensed the presence of others standing silently at a respectful distance from him. He turned to see his parish Secretary Magda DeVries standing alongside 80-year-old Mother Philomena, the Mother Superior of the Sisters of Immaculata de Namur.

During these times of great persecutions of priests and religious it was very unusual for this wonderful leader of the Religious Sisters to expose herself to the possibility of arrest, detention and even extradition to the infamous concentration camps.

Father Catron literally sprang to his feet and moved quickly to greet her with such haste that it clearly surprised Mother Philomena. She clasped his hands in hers and laughed, "It is good to see a young man leap to his feet and rush towards this old woman! It's been so long before any man, young or old has paid such attention to this old lady."

Father Catron, laughed, kissed her hands and said, "Mother Superior! It is such a wonderful surprise to have you here to brighten my day! To what do I owe this honor?"

"Well, I can assure you, Father Catron that the honor is all mine, especially given the wonderful courage that you and your people have shown with taking care of our 'special guests', but I'm not so sure you will consider my visit a 'wonderful surprise' when I tell you the reason I am here."

CHAPTER 83

Thursday 29 June 1944 The Dutch Pickle Truck- Father Catron, Mother Philomena- Saint Thomas the Apostle Catholic Church, Liege, Belgium.

Father Catron gestured to the first set of pews, and he and Mother Philomena sat facing one another. He looked at Magda as if to suggest that she should give them some privacy but Mother Philomena, anticipating his concern, waved him away. Instead, she turned to face Magda who smiled as Mother Philomena continued, "I know your secretary, Magda very well. I was involved with consoling her and her family over the murder and death of her husband, Phillip who was a respected member of the Resistance. I have complete confidence and trust in Magda. Anything I must discuss with you is perfectly safe with her being present."

Father Catron smiled, "Thank you, Mother, as you can see, I have complete trust in Magda as well. Please continue."

"I am here under the protection of the Resistance. They have driven me here in a large delivery van marked with the name of a Dutch Gerkin company which is sanctioned by senior Nazi bureaucrats who enjoy the product and who are currently occupying their headquarters in Brussels. It is commonly seen driving from Holland into Belgium and is almost never questioned. This vehicle is currently backed up to your parish garage. How we got possession of this vehicle is not important."

Catron nodded his head and wondered where all of this was going, but he chuckled, "I see, let me get this straight, you, the Mother Superior of the Sisters of Immaculata have arrived here in a large, Dutch pickle truck. I think I understand."

Magda stifled a slight laugh herself but managed to keep the rest bottled in.

Mother Philomena, not amused, all business, continued, “So far, we have driven right though the new road blocks without much trouble. It has also been helped by possessing my newly issued ID under the direction of ‘The Reichskommisar for Belgium and Northern France, Joseph Grohé.’ Which you should soon have in your possession, Father.”

At this signal, Magda stepped forward and presented Father Catron with an Envelope from the Cardinal Archbishop containing his own newly issued ID Card.

Both Catron and Mother Philomena laughed, and she said, “Good timing!”

She continued, “Now, I have been trying to get a severely wounded member of the Resistance to a hospital or a doctor. I have found this to be just about impossible without risking his summary execution at the hands of these soulless devils. Two things that I need your help with.”

“Yes, of course, Mother! How can I be of assistance?”

“The first of these requests is that this brave man is obviously in imminent danger of death. If he hasn’t died already while we’re sitting here ‘*idling away the time*’, I would like you to hear his confession, anoint him with the Sacred Oils and give him *Viaticum,* food for the journey.”

Father Catron hid a smile and shook his head at the Mother Superior’s crack about ‘*idling away the time*’. He thought,

Mother must be one ‘tough cookie’ running her Holy Order of Consecrated Women.

Laughing inwardly, he responded, “Of course! I will go see this man immediately. Where can I….”

He stopped when the Mother Superior raised her hand, “The second thing may obviate the first thing. I understand you have access to a medical doctor who might help this man, saving his life?”

“Well, it’s possible if we can get this doctor to cooperate. He has been frightened before when he helped us, and may not be inclined to help us again, but I can always see him.

She nodded thoughtfully, “Yes, of course, I know you will do your best. Perhaps a visit from friends of the Resistance might help?””

"Of course, it couldn't hurt. Now please give me this man's location and I will go at once to give him the sacraments. Where can I find him?"

"He's outside in our delivery van."

Shocked at this revelation, Father Catron, with Maga's assistance quickly retrieved the sacred oils and his Book of Rites and followed Mother Superior out to the van which was backed up to the parish garage.

Two members of the Resistance dressed as delivery men greeted the trio and opened the rear door of the van revealing the inside to the priest and Magda. Mother Philomena remained inside the parish Garage seated in a metal chair just out of sight.

Inside the van, the first thing they saw was another armed member of the Resistance guarding two young men who were blindfolded, gagged and whose wrists were tied and bound behind their backs. Just behind them in the large delivery van was an improvised curtain shielding whatever or whoever was behind it.

He nodded, and spoke in Dutch, "Ah, the real delivery drivers. I trust they will not be harmed when you are through with this van?"

The Resistance man guarding the two prisoners knew that Catron was saying this for the benefit and intimidation of the prisoners and responded in Dutch,

"They will not be harmed if they cooperate and forget everything, they may have heard this afternoon."

The two prisoners nodded their heads vigorously in agreement.

The two phony "Delivery Men" nodded to their compatriot and the two prisoners were carefully lifted out of the van and guided into the garage where they were seated in two metal chairs right next to Mother Philomena who remained expressionless.

The guard pulled back the makeshift curtain which revealed a stretcher resting on two crates secured to the wooden floor. On the stretcher was a man who was semi-conscious and moaning in obvious pain and distress. What was left of his right arm and right leg were wrapped in bloody bandages. His head and face were similarly wrapped in blood-soaked bandages.

It was obvious to Father Catron that he had lost a lot of blood and most likely was in traumatic, life-threatening shock.

Magda moved up to the left side of the head of the stretcher with Catron on the right side. She held onto the sacred oils and his book of prayers as Catron donned a purple stole. He looked at Magda with concern,

"I must carefully remove the bandages covering his face and head to anoint him and see if he can accept even a tiny piece of the Eucharist. This may be difficult for him and also for you to see."

Undaunted, Magda reached forward herself and expertly and carefully removed the bandages covering the victim's face.

And there, to her shock and that of Father Catron lay Lucien Leterme, brother of Janine & Denise who they all thought was dead.

Magda cried out in French, her hand to her chest, "Lucien, my God! You're not dead!"

This got Lucien's attention as he tried to sit up and failed, falling back down onto the stretcher. He coughed up blood, "No, my dear not quite dead, but close."

Father Catron looked at Lucien and said, "Lucien, my friend, you may be close, but we're going to fight for you to spite the Nazis who think they can kill a good man like you. I still want to anoint you and give you some time to spend here on Earth, but I think I should take your confession and give you communion. What do you think?"

Just at that moment, the air raid sirens throughout the whole region went off at precisely the same time the roar of four engine bombers and bombs dropping and exploding nearby overwhelmed all other sounds. They all instinctively ducked.

Lucien again coughed and laughed at the same time, "You better hurry up, Father or we will all be facing Jesus sooner rather than later."

CHAPTER 84

Thursday 29 June 1944 3:00 PM, Lucien Alive, Bombs dropping Father Catron, Mother Philomena at the Liege University Hospital Liege, Belgium.

The scene at the Emergency reception at the Liege University Hospital was chaotic. The Allied bombers had once again largely missed their targets of the railway transfer yards and the Liege Aerodrome. Instead, much of their ordinance fell onto civilian and commercial areas causing numerous civilian casualties.

The wounded and the dead were being transported to area hospitals by ambulance and a multitude of civilian vehicles, overwhelming the emergency reception staff at the medical centers.

With all the confusion, and all the different vehicles arriving at the various emergency reception areas, it was not surprising that one of the vehicles used to transport victims of the bombings to the Liege University Hospital, was a Dutch Gerkin delivery van.

Amid the chaos, there was virtually no German military presence at the reception area for the casualties coming in from surrounding civilian areas. They were involved in search and rescue and were not concerned with the hospital arrivals. Father Catron made his way into the depths of the hospital without being challenged.

He arrived at a closed door marked "Professor Phillipe Vanden Boeynants, Orthopedic Surgery." Doctor Vanden Boeynants was the source of the medical supplies obtained by Kurt Stark when Emil was shot in the shoulder several weeks ago. He and his wife and children were also occasional parishioners of Father Catron.

Father Catron did not knock despite a posted note on the door requiring it. Instead, he turned the handle and entered upon another chaotic scene. Several doctors, nurses and other medical assistants were gathered around a large conference table shouting over one another and trying to determine available beds and alternate medical facilities.

Because of the confusion, the noise and the frenetic environment there in the room, no one noticed the priest at first. Finally, a middle-aged woman in a blood-stained nurse's uniform rushed over to the priest and angrily demanded that he leave the room at once. Catron ignored her and searched for Doctor Vanden Boeynants, spotting him wearing a surgical gown in a far corner of the room on the telephone.

Vanden Boeynants spotted Father Catron at the same time and hurriedly finished his call, hung up and rushed over to the priest. Catron noticed that the doctor's surgical gown was blood-stained and well-worn.

The doctor's face was white with fear at the sight of his parish priest and angrily pushed aside the nurse who was still trying to evict Catron. Shocked, she immediately backed away from them.

"My God! Father Catron? Is my family, okay?"

Catron had not anticipated this understandable reaction and placed his hands on the doctor's shoulders nodding his head with a reassuring smile.

"Yes, Phillipe, I can assure you that they are all okay and have come into the Church bomb shelter." He, of course, had no real knowledge of their well-being but he needed this doctor's immediate cooperation.

"Oh, thank God!" but then expressing continued alarm he asked,

"Why are you here, Father? What's wrong?"

"Do you remember the man who was with me and Kurt Stark several weeks ago when we needed some supplies which you graciously provided?"

Vanden Boeynants' face went slack for a moment as he tried to wrap his brain about all this information, then suddenly, he recalled Lucien who was a well-respected and feared member of the Resistance. His eyes widened,

"Oh, yes! Of course, I do remember him, but not his name. Why?"

"He is badly wounded. Missing part of his right arm and right leg. In traumatic shock, loss of blood, close to death in my opinion. We have him in a delivery van outside the Hospital doors."

Vanden Boeynants reacted as though he had been slapped in the face,

"Oh, I am so sorry to hear that, Father, but you can't expect us to take him in here? The authorities will soon discover who he is and all of us will pay the price for accepting him. I'm sorry, but it's impossible."

"Ah, Phillipe! You should know that nothing is impossible with God!"

The unmistakable voice of Mother Philomena, Superior of the Sisters of Immaculata de Namur who just appeared alongside them in this crowded room. She was accompanied by one of the tough-looking members of the Resistance who was not noticeably armed this time.

She smiled at the priest and the doctor, "Phillipe was one of my prize students when he attended one of our schools in Namur. I thought I recognized the name on the door. And now look at you! A successful and well-respected professor of surgery here. I am so proud of you as I'm sure your parents are as well looking down on you from heaven.'

She turned to Father Catron, "Phillipe came to us as a six-year-old boy who was orphaned because of the pandemic. I think that this is what motivated you to get into medicine to cure those who were infected by the 'Spanish Flu' isn't it, Phillipe?"

A shocked Vanden Boeynants just nodded his head.

"Now, I'm sure that you can find some way to help our friend who is languishing out in the van outside, can't you?"

The middle-aged nurse who just moments before was the antagonist who berated Father Catron, suddenly was all smiles and embraced Mother Philomena.

"Mother! Do you remember me? I am Katrina! You and the sisters took me in when my whole family died in the pandemic."

"Katrina! Of course I remember you! My God how fortunate to have two of my former students doing so well."

Katrina smiled and turned to the doctor. "I think I have a way to help Father Catron here and Mother. Give me a minute." Katrina ran over to the phone and spoke urgently to someone on the other end.

Mother Philomena said, "Please hurry dear, our friend is in very bad shape."

After nurse Katrina hung up the phone, she asked Mother Philomena where the patient was and what type of vehicle he was located in. Two orderlies entered the room, and Katrina gave them the location of the Gerkin truck and told them to bring the patient past the Triage section and right into Operatory assessment, which was Doctor Vanden Boeynants' operatory.

She then addressed the doctor and Mother Philomena,

"Your patient's name is now 'Gaston Eyskens.' He is 28 years old, and our records have been updated to indicate that he has suffered the loss of his right arm and part of his right leg. Doctor, I will assemble a team for you right now."

Doctor Vanden Boeynants turned to Father Catron and smiled, "I realize you and nurse Katrina got off on the wrong foot, but as you can see, she kind of runs things around here for me. I'm glad she's on our side."

Catron nodded, "I am quite amazed, doctor. But I don't understand, who is this, Gaston Eyskens?"

Doctor Vanden Boeynants looked at a note handed to him by nurse Katrina just before she left the room in a hurry. Then he smiled and laughed,

"Gaston Eyskens, may his soul rest in peace, was a DOA, 'Dead on Arrival' just recently processed. No known family members. Katrina is on a roll."

Vanden Boeynants turned to leave and prepared to race down to surgery.

"Father, please go to the parish with Mother and I will get word to you about your patient."

Then, as an afterthought, "Oh, do you wish to give him his sacraments?"

Mother Philomena smiled, "Good thinking, Phillipe. Already done. Go with God."

With that, the doctor ran from the room.

Father Catron and Mother Philomena turned to leave. She looked at her Resistance escort and nodded her head. He smiled and left the room.

Catron asked her, "Where is he going, Mother?"

"To find out all he can about Gaston Eyskens, Lucien's new name."

CHAPTER 85

Thursday 29 June 1944 9:15 PM- Lucien out of surgery, Liege University Hospital Liege, Belgium

After four and a half hours of surgery, Doctor Phillipe Vanden Boeynants and his entire team were exhausted. They worked feverishly repairing what was left of Lucien's right arm and right leg, treating and cauterizing the gaping wounds caused by an explosive detonation of what surely must have been a mortar shell.

The team had given Lucien a life-saving transfusion of type O blood during the surgery. He was also given penicillin, which was so difficult to obtain during these war-time restrictions.

Doctor Vanden Boeynants was relieved that Lucien's Blood pressure and heartbeat remained stable despite the terrible trauma he had undergone in an incident that certainly must have occurred several days ago.

The greatest risk to Lucien was the possibility of infection and other complications from this massive trauma. Most Antibiotics had yet to be invented in 1944. He made the Sign of the Cross and said quietly, "Sleep well, my friend and know that many people are praying for you."

With that, the doctor departed the operating room and left the cleanup and transport of the patient to a bed for the rest of the staff. Two orderlies and a medical assistant carefully rolled Lucien out into the hallway and towards a wing of the hospital where post-surgery patients went for recovery.

There wasn't a vacant bed to be had in the entire hospital, so they positioned the gurney near the nurse's station, and locked the wheels. Not finding any nurses on this wing, and under pressure to assist other patients, they departed except for the medical assistant who was still wearing his surgical mask. Once the orderlies moved away, he removed the mask to reveal the grim face of Herman Van Dam, a senior member of the Resistance.

Van Dam was not surprised that the nurse's station was currently devoid of nurses. The entire Liege University hospital staff had been overwhelmed by the influx of casualties suffering from the Allied bombing which, regrettably, had largely missed their targets.

Throughout the hospital he observed numerous exhausted doctors and nursing staff slumped into chairs and gurneys in the hallways leading to the "Post Operation Recovery" section.

His concern was that Lucien, and other patients were not being properly monitored after surviving the initial trauma that brought them into the hospital. There was no one who was circulating among these patients monitoring their vital signs.

Van Dam, a seasoned member of the Resistance and a battle-hardened veteran of World War One, had been an infantry man in the Belgian army and had seen his share of wounded and dying. He knew that these patients lining the hallways of the hospital were in a critical phase of recovery.

He entered the nurses' station and searched through a small, ransacked supply cabinet. He eventually located a blood pressure cuff and, after a further search, found a small bottle of isopropyl alcohol, cotton swabs and an unopened cellophane envelope containing a thermometer.

He turned to leave the station and return to Lucien when he was confronted by a short, stocky middle-aged nurse with her hands on her hips. Her operating room gown covered in bloodstains was loosely tied around her nurse's uniform.

She looked and sounded exhausted and spoke to him in Flemish,

"Who the hell are you? What do you think you're doing?"

"Relax, nurse. I was simply looking for this blood-pressure cuff and a thermometer to check on my patient."

He hoped that he wouldn't have to restrain this hard-working woman to prevent a problem with any member of the police or German authority when he recognized her as the hard-charging nurse he had encountered earlier along with Doctor Vanden Boeynants.

"Nurse Katrina? I met you earlier when Mother Philomena and I brought in the patient missing his arm and leg. I was just with you and Doctor Vanden Boeynants during his surgery."

Katrina's face lit up with recognition, "Of course, I knew I had seen you before. Where is the patient? That is why I am here. I had to clean up the operating room to get it ready for the next surgery and couldn't be with him when he was taken away."

Katrina accompanied Van Dam to Lucien's gurney, took the blood-pressure cuff and thermometer from him and checked Lucien's vitals.

"This young man is amazing. His vitals are holding strong despite all he has been through. Follow me back to the station, I want to make sure that 'Gaston Eyskens' is properly noted in the nurses' register."

She turned and headed back to the nurse's station, found a clipboard and entered Lucien's alias on it. Once that was completed, she suddenly realized that there were numerous patients who were similarly unattended. Cleaning the thermometer off with alcohol, she took the clipboard and turned to Van Dam,

"Okay, you, whatever your name is, come with me. Let's check the vitals of these other patients and get their names properly entered here so that loved ones waiting in this hospital or arriving here soon will have some idea of how they are doing."

She turned, took two steps back towards the hallway and collapsed into Van Dam's arms. He gently carried her over to a corner behind the nurses' station and propped her up in a chair.

He found a folded gurney blanket, opened it and put it on the floor, carried nurse Katrina over to the corner and gently lowered the unconscious, and extraordinarily dedicated nurse onto the makeshift sleeping mat.

He then took the clipboard, the blood-pressure cuff, the thermometer and alcohol swabs and started down the hallway, taking the vitals of the other patients on their gurneys.

When he finished doing this as best he could, he returned the clipboard to the nurses' station and went back over to Lucien's gurney. He sat on the floor next to him. He noted the time 23:00 hours (11:00 PM) on his wristwatch and slipped into an uneasy sleep himself.

CHAPTER 86

Friday, 30 June 1944 5:45 AM, Jack and Ellen Michel Family Refuge, Near Bouillon, Belgium

As night faded into day, a sleepless Jack listened to the morning sounds outside the bedroom window he shared with young Jan. Early morning songbirds conducting their ritual greetings, the Michel family rooster announcing the impending dawn and the winnowing of one of the horses all brought back memories of waking up in the summertime in the mountains of North Carolina.

Careful not to awaken Jan, he rolled out of bed, slipped on his trousers, socks, and carried his boots so as not to make a 'clunking sound' walking down the wooden stairs. He gathered up a change of clothes including shirt, socks and boxer shorts, together with a small bag of toiletries all thoughtfully provided by Miep and made his way quietly down the stairs.

At the bottom of the stairs, he sat on the last of the steps, pulled his boots on and made his way quietly to the screened door and out into the courtyard to the bathroom facilities.

Bracing himself for the cold-water shower, he quickly soaped himself, rinsed off, brushed his teeth and toweled off. Exiting the shower area, he almost bumped into a sleepy Ellen, herself carrying her change of clothes and toiletries. They exchanged smiles and a "good morning" kiss.

After a brief embrace, she looked at him, "Good morning, Lieutenant. So nice to see your handsome face this morning."

"Why thank you, Ma'am. Do you come here often?"

Ellen, not quite up to speed on American humor, asked, "What does that mean?"

Jack laughed and shook his head, "Never mind, silly American humor. I was thinking about today. What do you think about..."

His thought was interrupted by a single ringing of the bell. They both stuck their heads out of the shower facilities to see Marie looking at Pierre on Horseback leading a truck driven by the pharmacist assistant, Byron Champagne.

Ellen tightened her robe around her and followed Jack into the garden courtyard. Miep, Denise and Raoul came out into the garden as well, soon followed by Emil. Champagne nodded to all of them and handed Raoul an envelope. He greeted the group and said, "Good morning, everyone, we received a telephone call from Liege early this morning and Henri wrote this all down and insisted I bring this notification to all of you immediately."

Everyone looked at Raoul as he hastily opened the note. He read it carefully and smiled. "It is from Reverend Father Catron. It says, there is no other way to get a message to you but through the pharmacy.'

Lucien alive. Seriously wounded with life-threatening injuries, but alive and in hospital. I will keep you informed.

Please do not attempt to come and visit him due to increased security. I repeat, I will let you know when it is okay to come and how he is doing. Do not try to come and see him. He has been badly wounded but so far has survived successful surgery.

I cannot be with you all right now due to this development and other serious issues at the parish. But please know that there will be more information to come.

May God bless you all, Reverend Corentin Catron"

The whole group erupted into shouts of joy and the women hugged each other. It then became apparent from the look on Raoul's face that there was something else in the note from Henri Charles. They stopped hugging and laughing and looked at him expectantly. He nodded solemnly and continued,

"There is a little footnote here, shall I read it now, or wait until after breakfast?"

Marie knew when he was being a tease and just about yelled at him, "Of course! Read it right now, Raoul."

It says, "*Please tell Ellen and Jack, I met with the Cardinal Archbishop*

Joseph Ernest Van Roey, and he has given me permission to bring you both together in the sacrament of Holy Matrimony. As soon as I can get away from here, I will come to all of you and make the necessary arrangements."

With that, another eruption of joy and jubilation. Jack smiled and looked at Ellen who appeared stunned at first then overjoyed. They hugged and Jack twirled her around once to everyone's delight.

Marie and Miep looked at each other, "Come, sister, let's have a celebratory breakfast together for our engaged couple. Oh, and Ellen?"

Ellen detached herself from Jack and looked at Marie, "Yes, Marie?"

"Why don't you finish what you started to do before Byron showed up?"

They all laughed as Ellen moved quickly back into the shower facility and Byron, his mission complete, prepared to return to Bouillon.

Denise came running back out of the house with a packed bag, "Byron, wait! I'm coming with you."

Emil, startled said, "Denise, you heard Father Catron's caution to not come right now. I understand you're wanting to be near Lucien, but we should exercise restraint."

"Yes, of course I heard his note of caution, but I have contacts there that he does not have and in addition I must also coordinate with our friends across the channel with respect to all our people entrusted to *Réseau Comète*. In addition, I want to check with them if there is any new information they might have about Janine. I promise I will be careful. I love you all, please look after my children."

With that, Denise climbed into the truck with Byron, and they departed.

CHAPTER 87

Monday 3 July 1944, 7:45 AM, Jack and Ellen on their way to "Cowboy Rock" discuss the future and the War, Michel Family Refuge,

Jack and Ellen walked hand in hand on the path leading from the meadow into the forest area. It was a pleasant, warm July morning and Jack found it difficult to think about what his fellow aviators were experiencing right now.

As much as he loved spending time with the love of his life, Ellen and all his wonderful friends, he knew in his heart that he should be back in his P-51 contributing to the war effort. He hoped that Father Catron would soon arrive and allow their marriage to take place before he was able to return to combat.

Ellen sensed that Jack was deep in thought as they approached the unique rock that she had dubbed as "cowboy rock." She smiled as they immediately sat and took off their shoes and socks,

"You, Lieutenant, are not quite here with me this morning. What's troubling you? What's on your mind?"

"I'm sorry! You're right, I am a bit distracted. Thinking about our upcoming wedding, making sure you're taken care of when I am called back into active duty. How Lucien is doing, all of that."

Ellen nodded as she stood up and waded into the water, "Jack, I will understand if you decide against marrying me now. I will not like it, but I will understand. Is that what's really behind this? Would you prefer to wait until this war is over? Or are you having complete second thoughts?"

This startled Jack to his core, "Wait! What? Heavens no! I love you and want to marry you absolutely! The sooner the better."

Ellen smiled, "Glad to hear it, Cowboy, so that's a good thing. Then tell me what is bothering you?"

"I just worry what will happen to you if, God forbid, I do not make it back to you. This is, after all war."

Ellen, standing in knee-deep water, looked at Jack with big, blue eyes,

"Now listen to me, Jack. I do not want you to worry about that! Do you hear me? When it's time for you to get back up into the air the only thing I want you to worry about is doing your best to end this war. I can take care of myself, and I will be here in Belgium waiting for my American husband to take his 'war bride' home to America. Got it?"

"Yes, Ma'am. Got it."

"Good! Now get those legs going and get into this cool water with your future wife."

"On my way."

That's when they heard two consecutive rifle shots, followed by the ringing of the bell.

Within minutes they were both moving quickly back down the path towards the house. Jack had unshouldered and double-checked his carbine. He carried it in both hands, making sure Ellen remained close to him but one step behind him, shielding her with his body.

CHAPTER 88

Monday 3 July 1944 8:30 AM, Jack and Ellen "Sanglier on the loose" Michel Family Refuge

Jack and Ellen departed the forest area and entered the path at the beginning of the meadow. At first, they couldn't see where the shots had come from and then, suddenly Ellen pointed to the truck in the middle of the courtyard about 100 meters away with the three teenagers standing on top of its hood, roof and open cargo area.

Two large black animals were ramming the truck, and one was trying to jump into the flatbed causing Elise and Nadine to scream. Jan was on top of the cab holding his leg in obvious pain.

Jack moved towards this chaotic scene with Ellen close behind him. They were closing the distance between them, but it was difficult to get a clear picture of exactly what was going on. As he drew closer, he gained a new perspective and saw someone lying underneath the truck writhing in pain. To his shock, he realized it was Raoul. The two sons, Pierre and Raymond, were nowhere to be seen.

At this moment, Emil came running out with his handgun clasped in his good right hand and promptly tripped and fell on the ground. Miep and Marie were screaming at the animals while at the same time, Marie was ringing the bell frantically.

Jack, taking this scene in a few mere seconds, raised his Mauser to his shoulder and sighted in on the one beast trying to jump into the truck. He took a deep breath and squeezed the trigger. The animal fell immediately and stopped moving. Jack quickly chambered another round.

The second, much larger animal stopped butting the truck and turned to face Jack and Ellen. It stood there snorting and grunting and then charged straight for them, covering the distance at an incredible speed.

He instinctively knew that he needed to aim just in front and slightly below the chest of this enraged animal as it would then run right into his bullet. He drew a bead on his target and touched off another shot, hitting the animal smack in the middle of its chest and killing it instantly.

It tumbled and rolled almost right up to their feet. Taking a deep breath, "What the hell are these things?" he yelled.

Ellen, barely able to speak choked out, "Sanglier, sanglier. Wild boars."

CHAPTER 89

Monday 3 July 1944 Wild Boars, the aftermath-Michel Family Refuge

Jack and Ellen, accompanied by Miep, Marie, Nadine and Elise, helped Raoul and Jan into the kitchen. Emil made it into the house on his own. He had taken a fall as he ran out to help those being attacked by the wild boars, but despite the pain in his left shoulder was otherwise okay.

Raoul was in pain but visibly angry. He spoke in French which Ellen interpreted for Jack.

"I've never seen these creatures do anything but tear up our garden and make a mess. I cannot believe they would be so aggressive as to attack our young people and then, instead of running away when I fired a couple of shots over their heads, they charged me."

Emil noticed that the teenagers were strangely silent when they heard Raoul's complaint. He spoke to them in English out of respect for Jack.

"Why do you think the beasts reacted as they did?"

Jan, who was very stoic despite his pain, looked accusingly at the girls. "I think that Elise and Nadine have the answer to that question, Uncle."

All eyes turned to the two young girls. After a short pause, Nadine spoke up,

"We were going into the garden to pick tomatoes. We saw two baby pigs nestled in a clump of grass over by the corn. They were just recently born. We each picked one up and hugged them and started walking to the truck, thinking we could keep them as pets. That's when the beasts attacked us."

Marie put her hand to her chest, "Oh my God! They were newborn pigs. The two boars were obviously the mother and the father protecting their young. You girls should never have touched them. Were there only two?"

Elise sheepishly said, "I think so, we didn't see any others. I guess we weren't thinking."

Jan snorted, replied in French, "You could say that again!"

Miep shook her head, "All right enough is enough. What is done is done. Let's get the wounds treated."

Marie treated a deep gash on Raoul's right leg and cuts to his hands received as he tried to fend off the beasts. She was relieved that there was no uncontrolled bleeding and, after cleaning the wounds with some clean soapy water, she asked Nadine to apply pressure over the leg wound with a clean cloth.

A quick examination of Jan's wound revealed a slightly less severe gash on his leg and did the same cleansing procedure on the wound, asking Elise to press another clean cloth over the area.

Miep went to the shelves where she and Marie stored the sulfa powder brought to them by the pharmacist. They applied liberal amounts to both Raoul and Jan's wounds.

Jack and Ellen suddenly looked at each other and then at the teenage girls, "Wait! Where are the piglets that you carried in your arms?"

They both looked shocked at this question then blurted out, "Oh! I think that they may still be in the bed of the truck."

Jack and Ellen rushed out to the truck and, sure enough, two tiny piglets were curled up in the front of the bed, sound asleep, nestled against some burlap bags. They got up into the bed of the truck and checked the little ones out.

Just then Pierre and Raymond came rushing up at full gallop and dismounted. They had obviously been riding hard judging from the lathered and panting horses.

Raymond shouted, "We heard the gunshots and the bell, we were up on the high ridges, patrolling, what is going….."

He never finished the sentence when he saw Ellen and Jack both holding tiny, newborn old piglets in their arms.

Ellen smiled, "Nice of you boys to show up. The excitement is pretty much over thanks to the cowboy and his trusty Mauser. Better late than never. Aren't these little ones cute? We were thinking of calling this one little Pierre and the one in Jack's arms, little Raymond.

Just then, Pierre looked over at the vegetable garden and pointed. Two more tiny piglets emerged from the thick underbrush and started crying for their mother.

Ellen gasped, "We'd better check and see if there are still more."

Miep, Marie, Elise and Nadine joined in the search for other piglets.

By the time the search was complete, the Michel family refuge had five tiny feral piglets installed in a box in the barn with no way to feed them.

CHAPTER 90

Tuesday 4 July 1944, 5:45 AM, Lucien in Recovery- Liege University Hospital Liege, Belgium

Nurse Katrina Simone carried a tray of medications and moved down the hallway to the large clinic recovery room where several of her assigned patients were placed.

She approached the bed of a heavily sedated "Gaston Eyskens" better known as Lucien Leterme. Checking his vital signs, she was startled by a sleeping figure on the floor just to the side of the hospital bed. It was Herman Van Dam, who had not left Lucien's side since they brought him in almost a week ago.

Katrina became concerned that this tough, grizzled member of the *Resistance* did not awaken at the first signs of someone approaching Lucien's bedside. This was out of character for Van Dam who always seemed to be one step ahead of everyone else.

She let him sleep while she circulated among the other patients in the clinic taking their vital signs and distributing medications. When she finished with her duties, she noticed that Van Dam was now standing shakily and seemed disoriented.

Nurse Simone moved quickly towards him and pushed him into the chair next to Lucien's bed. She felt his forehead and quickly determined that he was raging with fever which she confirmed with the thermometer. She whispered harshly to him,

"Van Dam, you are sick! Stay here while I get you some penicillin and some aspirin."

He started to protest, but just nodded his head in acceptance.

Within a few minutes, Nurse Simone returned with some water, aspirin powder and two pieces of bread which she took from her lunch box.

"Here, drink this water first, then eat a slice of bread."

She watched him as he followed her instructions. Then she poured a packet of aspirin powder into the glass and refilled it halfway with water, handing it back to Van Dam. Without comment, he consumed it. When he finished, he smiled and looked at her. "Thank you, Katrina, I appreciate your kindness."

Katrina smiled, looking at the room to ensure that all were still asleep, then turned back to Van Dam. "Okay, now that there's no one here awake but you and me, stand up and lower your trousers. I'm going to give you a shot of penicillin."

Van Dam, World War 1 combat veteran, deadly assassin of the *Resistance* shook his head, and whispered hoarsely, "No thank you, I will be fine."

Another voice, "Bullshit! Drop your drawers, Van Dam. Let's see your ugly butt."

Lucien rolled to their side and smiled.

Startled, Van Dam complied, and Katrina gave him the jab.

They all started to laugh, then quickly stifled it lest they draw attention to themselves.

Lucien received a sip of water from Katrina and said, "Sorry you had to see that ugly butt of this ugly Dutchman. I know you were just doing your job."

Katrina smiled, "Well, Mister Gaston Eyskens there's two things I have to say."

He and Van Dam looked at her as she continued, "The first is, when you've seen one ugly butt, you've seen them all."

They laughed quietly, "What is the second thing?"

"I think our patient here is 'turning the corner."

They laughed as Lucien asked, "Which one?"

"Both of you."

CHAPTER 91

Tuesday 4 July 1944 Pigs out for Adoption-Michel Family Refuge

Raoul Michel lit up a cigar and sat on the porch overlooking his garden and meadow. He was worried about his two sons, Raymond and Pierre. He understood both young men had been meeting secretly with members of the *Resistance* and were planning something "big" to happen.

Raoul served in the French military during the First World War and saw a lot of action. He himself was closely connected with the *Resistance* but was concerned that some of the younger members were becoming increasingly anxious and impatient to strike at the German occupiers and their collaborators sooner rather than later. All this sentiment was inspired by the impending Allied victory just around the corner.

He cautioned his sons and their peer group to be patient. The right time will come, he told them, but right now the Germans and their collaborators were becoming like a cornered rat growing more, not less dangerous. He feared that his counsel was largely falling on deaf ears.

The episode with the Sanglier, Wild Boar attack provided a much-needed distraction. First, the family was suddenly confronted with two recently killed feral pigs which meant ample supplies of fresh pork. Food was too precious to allow to go to waste and the Michel family would not allow those who were hungry and starving to go without.

He instructed his sons, experienced hunters to "field dress" their carcasses which meant to remove the pigs' entrails, wash out their bodies and prepare them for butchering. He gave them the address of a local farmer friend who also was an experienced butcher. This man would prepare the meat and work with the local churches to distribute it to the needy, also saving some for the Michel family refuge.

The next mission he designed to keep his sons out of trouble was to figure out what to do with five baby piglets who were still nursing. The two teenage girls, Elise and Nadine, felt terrible at being the primary cause that these little ones were now orphans. Raoul knew that he could butcher the babies for food but decided instead to see if any of the local farmers had a nursing female pig, a sow that might give these little ones a fighting chance. Raymond and Pierre looked at their father like he was crazy but shrugged their shoulders and agreed to give it a try. They loaded up the piglets and Nadine, Elise and Jan in the truck and headed out in search of a foster momma pig for the piglets.

Years later, both Raymond and Pierre would reflect that this "adventure" had most likely saved their lives.

CHAPTER 92

Saturday July 8, 1944 Father Catron and Denise on their way to Bouillon

Saint Thomas the Apostle Catholic Church, Liege, Belgium - Father Catron finished lunch with his friend, Father Michel Joseph, who was sent there by the Cardinal Archbishop, to relieve him while he conducted Church business elsewhere.

In particular, the Cardinal Archbishop wanted Father Catron to try to locate the whereabouts of Father Michel Masson, the Pastor of the Church of Saint John the Evangelist Bouillon who had apparently gone missing. Repeated phone calls to the parish office, town officials and the local pharmacy went unanswered, which was not completely unusual during wartime.

What was unspoken but understood, was his mission to visit with the American Army Air corps pilot, Lieutenant John "Jack" Dodds and his fiancé Ellen Delacroix, a Belgian woman at the Michel family refuge near Bouillon.

Father Catron and Father Joseph walked from the kitchen eating area to the nearby office to speak with Magda DeVries, his parish secretary and invaluable assistant. True to form, Magda prepared a small 'overnight bag' containing vestments, sacred oils, a Mass-kit and other necessary items for a traveling priest.

"Magda, you are amazing! What would I do without you?"

She smiled, handed him the bag and said,

"Flattery will get you far in life, Father Catron. Now, please go and be safe. Remember that you have a quick visit to the University Hospital to check on Gaston Eyskens at the request of Mother Philomena."

"Yes, of course I remember. Thank you, Magda, I will see you soon, God willing."

He embraced Father Joseph and headed down to the garage. Once there he opened the outside door, climbed into his 1939 Renault Juvaquatre and pulled through to the outside street. He got out of the Renault and went back to shut the garage door.

A woman's voice close by startled him,

"Good afternoon, Father Catron! May I come along with you on your journey to Bouillon, with perhaps a stop on the way to University Hospital?"

Turning around, he saw the smiling face of Denise, sister of Janine and Lucien.

"Denise! What a surprise! Why didn't you come upstairs instead of hanging out here by the garage?"

"Too many eyes on you and your parish, Father. Plus, I didn't want to put Magda or your priest friend under any pressure if they were questioned about my whereabouts. You know the story, 'Only those who need to know.' So, I just waited to see if the garage door would come up and here you are."

"Always the cautious one, Denise, and rightly so. I take it you want to go and see Gaston Eyskens?"

She laughed,

"Is that his alias? *Gaston Eyskens*? Where on earth did you come up with that name?"

"It's a long story, Mrs. Eyskens. Come, hop in let's go visit your 'husband'. Gaston will be so glad to see you."

Denise got in and they headed towards the University hospital.

CHAPTER 93

Saturday July 8, 1944, 1:00 PM the Murder of Edouard Degrelle at the Degrelle Pharmacy Rue des Casernes Bouillon, Belgium

Pharmacist Edouard Degrelle hung up the telephone with disgust. He looked at the three Rexist commandos sitting before him with equal disgust, hurling insult after insult at their "stupidity and ineptitude." He held the telephone receiver in his hand, waiving it as he spoke to make his points.

"You idiots are so lucky that I could not get through to my brother right now, this phone line is always being interrupted. When I do speak with Leon, I will tell him what a bunch of fools he sent me.

Degrelle was furious at the team for failing to kill even one of the people on his list. Even the local priest who had publicly humiliated him had not been touched.

Marco, the leader of the three-man team was not one to be easily intimidated but kept quiet during Degrelle's rant. This man was the brother of Leon Degrelle, powerful leader of the Rexist movement recently awarded accolades by Hitler himself. With that in mind, he just sat there quietly fuming. Marco's teammates, Michael and Rogier, always remained quiet, preferring that Marco do the talking and take the verbal abuse.

Marco looked at Edouard waiting for the onslaught of yelling and hysteria to end so that he could explain that the priest had suddenly left town and was nowhere to be found. He was quickly reaching his limit to this abuse, clenching and unclenching his hands, he thought: *Just keep it up, Edouard, I am fast approaching a time when I might level some abuse at you just before I cut your miserable throat.*

Marco felt that he should exercise constraint and not lose his temper with Leon's brother as arrogant a jerk as he was. But he knew himself and knew that there was a time looming soon. Deep in thought, he suddenly realized that Degrelle's rant was currently directed at him, personally. "Did you not hear what I was saying, Marco? Have you suddenly gone deaf as well as dumb? You are a complete, worthless idiot as are your two imbeciles sitting here with you. You all three are a disgrace to my brother and all Rexists."

Marco finally had enough, much to the delight of his two compatriots.

"Okay, Edouard, *enough*! You sit there behind your big desk issuing orders and insulting me and my team who have shed more blood, killed more enemies of the Fatherland than you could ever imagine. Yet you sit there like some kind of king or dictator. I respect your brother, Leon so I will not kill you for all your crap, but understand this, *we will not take any more of your bullshit.* We will do our best to eliminate those on your list, but as of this moment me and my team are through with you."

Degrelle, shocked by this unexpected tirade, was speechless. He also was a bit terrified because he knew what Marco was capable of. Yet, he had to show that he was still a powerful man to be feared and respected. He reached for the phone with a snide look on his face.

"So that's how it's going to be, Marco? We'll just see what my brother Leon thinks about your little outburst. A voice on the other end asked him what number he was trying to connect with."

He looked at the note on his desk to find Leon's latest contact number and did not see Marco pull out his silenced Ruger 22 caliber semi-automatic pistol, move around to behind Degrelle and press it to the back of his head, firing a single shot into his brain.

Degrelle did not have time to react, in fact, for Degrelle he did not have "time" for anything else, for Edouard Degrelle *time* no longer existed.

Marco pushed the dead pharmacist off his chair and, using his foot, rolled him under his desk. He used the pharmacist's shirt to wipe the blood off the silencer on his Ruger and slipped it back into his shoulder holster.

He then stopped to look at his two team members, who remained seated with their mouths and eyes wide open.

CHAPTER 94

Saturday July 8, 1944, 2:00 PM Office of Edouard Degrelle Marco's plans

Marco fixed his eyes on both of his teammates, then looked at the empty chair recently occupied by the now very dead Edouard Degrelle. "Any one of you have a problem with this? If you do, you can leave now and get out of my sight. I will not hold it against you."

They both were in shock, but shook their heads, "no." Instead, Michael and Rogier both started to laugh. Michael said, "Never did anyone need that more than that asshole. I'm glad you did that, Marco. But what do we do now?"

He laughed and shrugged his shoulders, relieved that he didn't have to kill the two men who had served so well with him up to this time. "Well, we will continue to look at the names on the list and do our best to eliminate them. I will report to Leon myself and pretend that we have no idea what happened to his little brother. Someone will discover this guy sooner or later and they'll think it was the *Resistance*. Let's leave his list on the desk for the Krauts to find. Maybe the Germans will do some of the work for us."

The trio left the office and took the back stairs down exiting out the back of the pharmacy. Downstairs the pharmacy was open, and people were submitting requests for prescriptions to the clerks who were totally unaware of what had just transpired in the offices above them.

Marco laughed and felt safe that no one had seen them arrive or depart from the pharmacy. They got into their car, backed out of the parking space and headed out of Bouillon. They knew they would be back in town very soon once Leon Degrelle heard the terrible news about the murder of his brother.

When he told the other two that they would be back in the next day or so in search of the "Killers", all three broke into uncontrolled laughter.

CHAPTER 95

Saturday July 8, 1944, 2:15 PM Office of Edouard Degrelle Bouchard's revised list

One person who was watching them drive away was not laughing. Paul Bouchard had listened to them interact with Degrelle from an empty office across the street, using a hidden microphone. He knew what had happened even though Marco's gun was silenced. He took a deep breath and muttered to himself, *Time to go and discover the body of that pompous jerk and report it to the police and his brother*.

Steeling himself for the task, he moved across the street, passed through the retail section of the pharmacy and up the front stairs. He ignored the dead body of Edouard partially pushed under the desk. Instead, Bouchard focused on the telephone receiver out of the cradle on the desk. Turning the telephone receiver over, he carefully unscrewed the mouthpiece, disconnected two wires and removed the small microphone provided to him by MI-6, British Intelligence. *Probably an unnecessary precaution, but why take chances?*

He pocketed the device then turned his attention to the handwritten list of potential targets that Degrelle had him draw up to give to the Rexist commandos. They, the real killers, left that on the desk to be discovered and, he assumed to be acted upon by the police and German authorities.

He sat on the edge of the desk and thought he should compose a slightly different list. There were many friends on that list, including his brother-in-law, Father Michel Masson. He wished he could remove them all but knew that the killers had seen quite a bit of the list and would know something was wrong.

After careful thought, Bouchard re-wrote the list, eliminating his brother-in-law and several other close friends, including Raoul Michel and his sons who were very close to his family. He placed the revised list on the desk and dialed the local police.

Within a few minutes, the pharmacy was swarming with the Ordnungspolizei (Orpo or order police) who served as the local police. Because of the prominence of the victim, several key members of the Gestapo were also present. The conclusion was inescapable, Leon Degrelle's brother was unquestioningly the victim of the French, Belgian Resistance.

Bouchard made sure that the retail section of the pharmacy was empty of customers and staff and secured the front door. Within a half hour, police orderlies placed the dead body of Edouard Degrelle onto a stretcher and carried it down the back stairs and into a waiting police van.

Bouchard, clinging to his role as Edouard's trusted aide and confidant told the officer in charge of the police investigation, Oberleutnant Kurt Schmidt that he was about to call Leon Degrelle personally and notify him of his brother's death.

Schmidt reacted with surprise and deference that Herr Bouchard had the ability to speak directly to the great man, Léon Degrelle personally. Bouchard invited the Oberleutnant to remain with him as he reported the sad news, and the German actually took off his cap out of respect and sat in front of the desk as Bouchard made the call.

As expected, Degrelle was heartbroken and devastated. Above all, he was angry, he wanted revenge, and he wanted it fast. Bouchard asked Degrelle to kindly hold for a moment while he retrieved the information requested. He covered the speaker and asked the Oberleutnant for his contact information. A humbled Schmidt wrote it down on a notepad and handed it to Bouchard who relayed the information to Degrelle.

After several more seconds, Bouchard promised to keep Degrelle up to speed on his end and hung up. He looked at the Oberleutnant for a long moment and then slid the notepad with 42 names over to him. "These individuals are ones that Edouard Degrelle wanted investigated. They may not necessarily have anything to do with his death, but now his brother, Léon Degrelle wants you to investigate them forthwith. Do you have a problem with that, Herr Oberleutnant?"

The German stood abruptly, looked at the note, barked a quick acceptance of the assignment, clicked his heels and departed, bringing all of the remaining police with him.

After everyone had departed the pharmacy, Bouchard lowered his head and took several slow and deep breaths. He made the sign of the Cross and said out loud to the empty room, "*Now, what the hell am I supposed to do?*"

CHAPTER 96

Saturday July 8, 1944, 5:15 PM The hunt for Degrelle's killers Office of Ordnungspolizei 1 Place Ducale 6830 Bouillon

Oberleutnant Kurt Schmidt, the officer in charge of the investigation into the murder of Edouard Degrelle divided up the 42 names of the individuals on Bouchard's list among his troops. With typical German efficiency, four groups of five officers each left the station in four multi-passenger vans borrowed from the prison in Arlon. They were given instructions to make best efforts to arrest these men suspected of being members of the *Resistance* without violence, but to use whatever force was necessary.

Schmidt assembled four lightly armored staff cars with five heavily armed combat troops in each one, thereby creating a formidable force if any of the alleged members of the *Resistance* had thoughts of resisting their arrest. In addition to the troops, each vehicle contained a local collaborator familiar with addresses and locations of those on the list.

At the same time, Schmidt had a squad of enlisted men circulate flyers throughout Bouillon demanding that all bicycles and personal radios be surrendered at the Office of Ordnungspolizei no later than 17:00 hours the following day, Sunday, July 9, 1944.

The Germans went to the various homes of the individuals on the list and knocked on doors demanding entry. If entry was refused, the door was summarily smashed in and anyone in the way of the arresting troops would be taken into custody as well.

At the infamous Arlon prison six hours later, Schmidt checked off the last of the four vans and stood impatiently next to his senior enlisted man as he tallied up the total in custody. He turned to the Oberleutnant, "We have 49 prisoners in total, Sir. 39 men who are on the list, those in custody but not on the list are 6 young men ages 14, 15 and 16 and 4 women."

Schmidt took this information in and then asked, "So, Korporal the 6 teenagers and the 4 women taken into custody. What is the reason they are included in this lot?"

"According to the arresting officers, Sir they resisted the effort to take the man on the list into custody."

"I see. I would like you to do something once the 39 men on the list are processed and incarcerated."

"Yessir, of course."

"Find out from the arresting officer exactly how these people were resisting and if they assaulted our men in a serious way. If you determine that they were simply family members reacting to a loved one's being arrested, then we will take those people into Bouillon and place them in custody at our headquarters for their intransigence. Do you understand?"

"Oh, Yessir. Completely."

Schmidt nodded and continued, "The 39 men on the list will naturally remain here at the prison where their punishment most likely will be death. That brings up another point. Who are the 3 men on the list that were not available for detention?"

The Korporal consulted his notes then announced their names, "René Pierlot, Louis Bodart and his brother Henri Bodart."

"Hmm, I see. Please make sure that the search continues through the night if necessary. I wish to report to Brigadier General Leon Degrelle that we have successfully accomplished our mission of finding the killers and those who supported the killers."

The Korporal saluted the Oberleutnant. Schmidt returned the salute and headed back to police headquarters.

He would not be aware until the following morning that the three missing men were already dead at the hands of Marco, Michael and Rogier who were operating from memory on the previous list.

CHAPTER 97

Sunday, July 9, 1944, 8:00 AM Pharmacy of Henri Charles Rue des Champs Bouillon, Belgium

Pharmacist Henri Charles opened his pharmacy and set up the prescription orders for the day to come. His staff, all loyal employees of long standing, were atypically late in arriving for work this morning.

He attributed this to the unusual police activity that occurred last evening and throughout the night. He didn't know the reason for this increased presence of military and civilian police but hoped it was because of the impending Allied liberation of the countries occupied by the Germans.

Marta Hingis, his first employee to show up, arrived at 08:20, a full twenty minutes behind her normal time. Flustered, she complained that the police intercepted her on her bike as she headed to work and seized her bicycle without explanation. She observed the same inexplicable event occurring throughout Bouillon.

Soon after Marta's arrival, two other women employees came in, also devoid of their bicycles as well. Charles was now sufficiently alarmed at what was happening that he excused himself and walked up the stairs to his office to make a few discreet phone calls to see if he could make sense of all of this.

He spent the next hour patiently calling those of his close contacts in the Resistance who had telephones to see what was happening. His internal alarm bells were going off when absolutely none of his trusted contacts answered their phones.

At 09:20, Marta buzzed his intercom from downstairs,

"Professor Charles, there is a man downstairs who has an injured person out in their car needing immediate medical attention. Can you come down, sir?"

"Yes, Marta. What about Mr. Champagne? He hasn't arrived either?"

"No, sir. If I recall, I think he was scheduled to go to the Clinique in Arlon early this morning."

Charles slapped his forehead, "Of course! I forgot. Tell them I will be right down to see how I can help."

"Yessir, of course."

Charles went over to the closet in his office and extracted his medical bag which he always kept well stocked. He thought to himself as he descended the stairs, *Both Byron Champagne and I need to complete our medical training when this war is over. This town really needs some doctors.*

Henri Charles would never get that chance. He stepped outside and was greeted by Marco who promptly placed his silenced 22 caliber Ruger to his head and fired a single bullet into his brain. Marco was following a last-minute request from Leon Degrelle to eliminate his brother's primary competitor in Bouillon.

Degrelle ordered Charles's murder not just out of revenge, he couldn't stand the idea that Henri Charles' business would prosper now that his competitor, Edouard was murdered by members of the *Resistance* with whom Charles was likely associated with.

Several things happened all at once:

A woman passerby screamed at the top of her lungs as she witnessed Charles' cold-blooded murder in broad daylight,

An armored staff car with five combat troops just happened to be returning from their night-time mission of rounding up suspected members of the Resistance and came to a stop after hearing the woman's scream.

Five combat hardened men jumped out, leveled their weapons at Marco, the murderer of Henri Charles and placed him, Michael and Rogier under arrest.

The town of Bouillon, Belgium was now down to one pharmacist, Byron Champagne.

He was currently in Arlon, not far from the prison which now housed 39 new prisoners, citizens of Bouillon.

CHAPTER 98

Sunday, July 9, 1944, 8:00 AM Jack finishes follow up review with Doctor Jansen Clinique Médicale Arlon, Luxembourg

Jack, Ellen and Byron Champagne walked out of the clinic. A few minutes earlier, Doctor Jansen removed the stitches on Jack's right calf and pronounced in French to Ellen, Byron and Nurse Susan Heymans that the leg looked very good and was fully recovered.

He smiled, turned to Ellen and said in English, "Ah, too bad this poor, deaf lad can't hear me, but he is fully capable of returning to the skies when he's repatriated and can kill more Nazis for all of us."

All of them, including Jack, laughed who responded, "Thank you, Doctor Jansen and you, too Nurse Heymans. It's a miracle, but my hearing has suddenly been restored."

They all laughed, and Jack continued, "I hope that I can get back into the air soon before this war is ended so I can get a few more Germans sent to their 1000-year-old Reich in the Sky."

They all laughed at this humor from the American. All of them, except Ellen, who suddenly was confronted with Jack's imminent departure to return to active duty once he was repatriated.

Doctor Jansen shook Jack's hand, "Go with God, my friend. I hope we can meet again during better times."

They said goodbye and headed towards the parking lot.

As they drew closer to their vehicles, Champagne noticed Pierre and Raymond sitting in the front seat of the family truck and Jan, Nadine and Elise laughing and jumping around in the truck bed like typical teenagers. He turned to Jack and Ellen,

"Why don't you two jump into my car and I'll take you back to the Michel farm? The truck looks a bit crowded. I do have to stop by there anyway to drop some more sulfa packets that Henri wanted to give to

Marie to replenish her supply, and to see how Emil's wound is healing. I also understand that Raoul needs a bit of attention, something about an incident with a pig."

Ellen laughed and thanked Champagne, "Thank you, Byron, it's a tempting offer, but we promised to ride with the teenagers when Pierre takes all of us to collect some butchered pork and check on five little piglets."

Champagne laughed, shook his head, "Piglets? Pork? An incident with a pig? What's that all about?"

"A long story, we'll tell you later. Regards to Henri."

Within minutes, Pierre turned to the right to go into the outskirts of Luxembourg and Champagne turned to the left to head back to the Michel family refuge.

Little did he or the others know that they would never see Henri Charles alive again.

CHAPTER 99

Sunday Morning, July 9, 1944, Denise & Father Catron Prepare to move Lucien

Denise and Father Catron decided on Saturday afternoon to stay overnight in Liege after their visit with Lucien in the hospital took up a great deal of time. Father Catron had Magda prepare a guest room for Denise.

In the meantime, he and Mother Philomena worked out the best way to move Lucien and his protector, Herman Van Dam, to a safe location where Lucien could continue to recuperate, and Herman, a respected member of the Belgian Resistance would avoid any further exposure to detection by the authorities.

Much to their surprise, and the disappointment of Doctor Phillipe Vanden Boeynants, Nurse Katrina Simone, the doctor's invaluable and dedicated trauma nurse, insisted that she would go wherever they decided to situate Lucien.

It was apparent to Father Catron and Mother Superior that Nurse Simone was not only dedicated to serving the medical needs of her double amputee, Lucien, but also had grown fond of the grizzled Van Dam who was himself recovering from a bout of a serious head cold and sinus infection.

After some frantic searching for a suitable location, and in consultation with friends and neighbors of Emil and Miep, it was decided to move Lucien and his medical entourage back into the Delacroix "Chicken House." It seemed that concerns about an investigation into the real cause of death of would-be rapist, Korporal Karl Mueller failed to materialize.

According to veterinarian Kurt Stark, SS-Haupt Sturm Führer, Erik Hoeffner, who was Korporal Mueller's commanding officer, had no time for any follow up investigation. To him Mueller died in the

Allied bombing of the Liege aerodrome, case closed. He was otherwise occupied trying to figure out how to send his prize horse safely back to Germany.

Kurt Stark was completely in favor of moving Lucien to the upstairs living quarters and assured everyone that he could provide limited medical assistance utilizing his access to medical supplies in his role as veterinarian.

Father Catron and Magda DeVries spoke with the neighborhood group of volunteers who were keeping watch over the "Chicken House" and explained the situation. Everyone signaled that they were all "On Board", and quickly went to the Delacroix building and prepared it for re-opening.

Several men made sure that the water and electricity were functioning while the women stocked the cooler and refrigeration units with limited supplies of food and drink scraped together during these "bare boned" times of severe rationing.

With all these logistics falling into place, Father Catron, Father Joseph, Denise and Magda settled down to a quiet dinner and a peaceful overnight rest. Mother Philomena, Mother Superior of the Sisters of Immaculata de Namur promised to assist in any way possible on Sunday morning and would be accompanied by two of her Religious Order sisters.

At the same time, once Doctor Vanden Boeynants was convinced of Nurse Simone's earnest desire to go with Lucien, he resolved to help in getting Lucien transported and to keep a close eye on his recovery.

In recognition of his offer to assist in a big way, the doctor made Nurse Simone promise that, when things got better for Lucien, she would ultimately return to him as his valued nursing assistant. Simone quickly made a promise with one hand behind her back, fingers crossed and a big smile on her face.

Early Sunday morning, once word came back to Father Catron and Magda that the building was up and running, he contacted Doctor Vanden Boeynants at his home to let him know what was happening. Vanden Boeynants expressed his commitment and surprised Father Catron that he personally intended to drive a hospital transport van.

When Father Catron and Denise arrived at University Hospital on Sunday morning, the good doctor, accompanied by two trusted orderlies, themselves members of the Resistance, placed a heavily sedated Lucien on a rolling gurney and along with Van Dam and Nurse Simone, headed down to the discharge bays of the University hospital.

Within a half hour, Lucien, Van Dam and Nurse Simone were on their way towards Liege and Emil and Miep's "Chicken House."

Father Catron, Mother Philomena and Denise went slightly ahead of the hospital van and were on hand when it arrived. Catron directed them into the open garage and closed the door behind them.

Doctor Vanden Boeynants together with Nurse Simone supervised the careful movement of Lucien through the hallways on a rolling gurney and held their collective breath as the two very strong orderlies managed, with the help of several strong men to get Lucien up the stairs and into the living space.

When she entered the upstairs living space, Denise immediately noticed the flowers in the vases, the freshly made hospital bed in the larger of the guest rooms and an additional two beds in the other guest rooms for Van Dam and Nurse Simone. This made her smile, and she turned to Father Catron,

"I feel so thankful about everyone stepping forward to take care of my brother. Everyone here is a true blessing."

Father Catron agreed, nodded his head and turned to the gathering of neighbors and supporters around Lucien's hospital bed.

"Let's all take a moment to pray to God certainly for Lucien's quick recovery, and for all those who have given the ultimate sacrifice for all of us."

He saw that all eyes were on him as he continued, "I also would like to pray for all of you who have gathered here to support Lucien and, in a very special way for Doctor Vanden Boeynants, Nurse Simone and Herman Van Dam for providing so thoughtfully and professionally for his well-being."

All present bowed their heads as Father Catron led them in Prayer. When they concluded with the Sign of the Cross, Mother Philomena spoke, "I would now like to offer a prayer for Father Catron, your wonderful priest and pastor of your church."

Everyone bowed their heads in prayer. Afterwards, Mother Philomena continued, "I know, Father that you have an important mission to accomplish that will take you out of town for a few days starting tomorrow, Monday, so please know you are in our prayers in a very special way."

Mother then smiled as two sisters of her order entered the upstairs living space, carrying two small overnight bags and some other supplies. "I would also like to introduce Sister Alicia and Sister Marjorie. Both wonderful sisters are trained as nurses' assistants and will be here for the next few days to assist Nurse Simone. In another two days, two other sisters of my order will be here to rotate care."

Father Catron thanked everyone, "I am truly blessed with having such wonderful and devoted friends. I know that many of you were not able to attend Mass this morning offered by my colleague, Father Joseph, because you were either with us as we relocated Lucien here or working hard to set up his bedroom and those of all the volunteers who will be here assisting in his recovery. I therefore propose, with your indulgence, that I set up Mass for us right here. What do you think?"

Everyone there, including Mother Philomena and the two sisters visiting, thought that this was a great idea. Magda quickly headed back to the parish and returned with additional supplies to set up for a Mass in the dining room.

The only one not attending and receiving communion was Lucien who was still in a deep, drug-induced sleep. Shortly after Mass concluded, most of the volunteers including Doctor Vanden Boeynants and the two orderlies departed.

Father Catron was anxious to get on the road to Bouillon. He noted that it was 1 PM and looked over to Denise who was huddled with Mother Philomena and Sisters Marjorie and Alicia. They appeared to be in deep prayer which pleased him. *Denise needs Spiritual support and guidance and what better person to provide it to her than Mother Philomena.*

He caught Denise's eye and signaled that it was time to go. She went over and kissed the still sleeping Lucien on his forehead. She smiled, embraced Mother Philomena and the two Sisters. She said goodbye to everyone around her and together she and Father Catron descended the stairs, threw their bags into his Renault Juvaquatre and headed out towards Bouillon.

It was at least a two-hour drive to Bouillon during war-time conditions and, at the Cardinal Archbishop's request, Catron agreed to first make a stop and check on the whereabouts of Father Michel Masson the missing priest assigned as Pastor to Saint John the Evangelist, in Bouillon.

CHAPTER 100

Sunday, July 9, 1944, 10:00 AM Office of Ordnungspolizei
1 Place Ducale 6830 Bouillon

Oberleutnant Kurt Schmidt went through the list of the men taken into custody and placed in the Arlon prison. He had little doubt that the nasty members of the Strafbataillone (penal battalions) who were in charge at the prison would exact terrible and sinister punishment on these unfortunate individuals.

In Schmidt's opinion these Strafbataillone officers were a sadistic and rather creepy bunch of human beings. He knew the allies were gaining more ground each day and the Wehrmacht was losing the war. He doubted if they would be here in this area before the end of the year to liberate the prison. *Too bad for those incarcerated there, it will be too late for them,* he thought.

Not one to be too sentimental, he shrugged his shoulders and continued to look through his field action reports. He recalled that his men were unable to locate three of the men on the list provided to them by Bouchard. He searched for their names and found them circled with red pencil by one of the enlisted men on the task force:

René Pierlot, Louis Bodart and his brother Henri Bodart

He was confident that they must have fled the area or just were lucky to not be at their homes when his men knocked on their doors. He made a note to have a follow up visit sent to their homes once his men had sufficient rest after their all-night searches.

Just then, his staff sergeant downstairs buzzed his intercom, "Herr Oberleutnant, I have Sergeant Stephan on the radio with an urgent message for you."

Schmidt sat up, Stephan was a trusted, battle-hardened warrior, a no-nonsense soldier. He responded, "Yes. Ask him what's going on, I'll hold on."

After a brief pause, the intercom came back on, "Yes, Herr Oberleutnant, Sergeant Stephan reports that he and his men were just returning from their mission when they came upon the murder of another pharmacist, a Henri Charles. They apprehended the perpetrators, three members who are likely members of the resistance."

"Excellent! Tell Sergeant Stephan to bring them here and secure them in a holding cell, I will interrogate them. He and his men are to be congratulated."

"Yessir! I will tell them. Oh, and sir?"

"Yes, what is it?"

"Another team returning from the night raids just radioed in while we were speaking. My assistant took the information."

Schmidt was losing patience with this drawn-out delivery, "Yes, yes, go ahead. What is it?"

"A Sergeant Kohler reports they came across three civilians murdered execution style, with their hands tied behind their backs and a note in one of their pockets."

"A note? What did the note say?"

Another long pause, then, "It said, for Edouard Degrelle."

Oberleutnant Schmidt was flabbergasted. "Did Sergeant Kohler know the names of these murdered men?

"Yessir, hold on. Here it is, the three victims were identified by family members who had gathered there as René Pierlot, Louis Bodart and his brother Henri Bodart.

Schmidt thought, *the missing three. What the hell is going on here?*

CHAPTER 101

Sunday, July 9, 1944, 5:00 PM Saint John the Evangelist Catholic church, Bouillon

The Catholic Church became a gathering place for many of Bouillon's citizens who were reacting to the seizure of over 40 men by the Gestapo and members of the Ordnungspolizei in the wake of the murder of Edouard Degrelle.

Over one hundred people who were comprised mostly of younger mothers with children and elderly men and women. sought shelter and comfort from one another

Rampant anger and fear caused by the brutal seizure and arrest of many of the local men during the night prevailed over those gathered there in the church.

There was also considerable upset and grief over the execution style murder of three well-respected local men coupled with the rumor of another brutal murder in broad daylight of the popular pharmacist, Henri Charles.

Meanwhile Father Michel Masson the priest assigned to the Church as pastor had disappeared and was nowhere to be found. The absence of their local priest increased the feelings of abandonment and desperation among the people.

There was no one in a position of civilian leadership and those gathered there were starting to panic as to what the next step of the Nazis might be. Rumors abounded about entire villages being slaughtered, men, women and children by the Nazis. These rumors were not without foundation as the Germans were fully capable of such atrocities.

Constance Rademacher, the woman who served as the Pastor's assistant and receptionist attempted to calm the people down and tried calling the Cardinal Archbishop's office in Brussels all to no avail. It was, after all, a Sunday.

She finally got through to a woman who didn't seem capable of taking a message and gave up hope when the call was cut off.

Constance herself was no stranger to tragedy as her only son, 18-year-old Eduard was among those seized by the Nazis last night and her husband, Thomas was kidnapped and sent to the labor camps in Germany where he perished two years ago.

This murder of Henri Charles was confirmed by the tearful arrival at the Church of Byron Champagne, the well-respected assistant Pharmacist.

Anger, fear and resentment, coupled with loud outbursts of crying were growing rapidly among the people and Champagne realized that he needed to offer some guidance and advice to calm things down and to prevent further tragedy and reaction from the Nazis.

Acting on impulse, he went to the front of the Church, entered the sanctuary and got behind the podium used to proclaim the readings and announcements. He used a ruler he found inside the podium to pound on the wooden structure to get the people's attention. He took a deep breath, looked out on the desperation of the people gathered there and started,

"Dear Friends, please listen to me. I too am in mourning and concerned about all that has happened here today. I know many of you have had a family member arrested last night and have also heard of the violence that has befallen four of our citizens, which include my mentor, Professor Henri Charles. I understand that you are frightened and want to know what has become of those arrested, I also understand that..."

He was interrupted by an angry outburst from an elderly woman holding a baby,

"Stop with your stupid speeches! I am holding my granddaughter here who lost her mother, my daughter-in-law, in childbirth. Now, last night the Nazis took the child's father, my son for no reason and he is most likely dead by now."

Champagne was stunned by this outburst and thought that

everything was spiraling out of control when, suddenly there was an outcry from the back of the Church,

"The priest! The priest is here!"

And in walked Father Corentin "Cory" Catron, accompanied by well-known former resident Denise Michel.

CHAPTER 102

Sunday, July 9, 1944, 9:00 PM Office of Ordnungspolizei
1 Place Ducale 6830 Bouillon

At the end of another long day of cleaning up the mess that started with the murder of Léon Degrelle's brother, Edouard, Oberleutnant Kurt Schmidt had just about had enough. He buzzed down to his desk sergeant, Sergeant Nicholas Mannheim. "Yes, Herr Oberleutnant?"

"Those three men who were caught in the act of murdering the other pharmacist. Are they still here or did we transfer them to Arlon?"

"They are still here in the holding pens, sir. All our transport is currently tied up, so they will be here overnight.

"I see. Are they still demanding to speak with Herr Degrelle, the victim's brother?"

"Yes, one of them, the obvious leader is. He is not asking, he is demanding."

"I see. Is he locked up with his two accomplices or are they separated?"

"No, Sir. They are all in the same holding cell as all the others are currently filled with the women and young children you did not want sent to Arlon prison."

"Naturally that would be the case. Okay who is the Captain of the Guard on duty right now?"

"Sir, I sent Sergeant Josef Stefan to his barrack about an hour ago. As you are aware, Sergeant Stefan was the arresting officer of the three men who killed Henri Charles the other pharmacist."

"I see. He was in the rotation to be Captain of the Guard tonight?

"Yes, Sir. But he was, in my opinion, his Command Sergeant, at a point of exhaustion. I ordered him to return to his barracks over his protest and he is resting, sir. I am now the acting Captain of the Guard.

Schmidt, himself, near total exhaustion from lack of sleep during the past twenty-four hours, replied, "Okay Sergeant Mannheim, I agree with your decision to send Sergeant Stefan for a rest. We all could use a rest after these past twenty-four hours. When you yourself are rested, please evaluate the women and young children in our custody to see who we are comfortable with returning to their homes."

"Yes, sir. I have already taken the time to do that. I believe that we could release all of them sir. The only problem is that all the transport vehicles are still not here."

"Ah, I see, Sergeant Mannheim. You are keeping them under lock and key because we cannot deliver them to their homes? The very homes we took them from in the late hours of the night?"

Mannheim, sensing that perhaps this might not be the correct answer, replied tentatively, "Yes sir?"

"Okay, enough of this bullcrap, Sergeant, turn them loose. I guarantee they will find their own way to their homes. And Sergeant?"

"Yes, Herr Oberleutnant?"

"Make sure that the three killers are separated once the other holding cells are emptied. Far enough away so that they can no longer compare notes. Tell them they will be there until I decide to interview them. Feed them a decent portion of a meal. Can you accomplish this task without any trouble?"

"Yes sir! I will get my men to release the women and children and then do as you suggest, sir."

"Excellent. Also, Sergeant?"

"Yes, Herr Oberleutnant?"

"When you have accomplished all of these things, I order you to get some rest yourself."

"Yes, Herr Oberleutnant! Thank you. Herr Oberleutnant."

"You are welcome. I will be up here taking a rest on the cot in my office. I will talk with you in the morning, unless there are any problems."

"Yes, Herr Oberleutnant."

CHAPTER 103

Sunday, July 9, 1944, 9:00 PM Parish Hall, Saint John the Evangelist, Bouillon

After Father Catron said Mass for the people, Constance Rademacher, the Pastor's assistant, Denise and Byron Champagne ushered them into the parish hall. There was no food to be had, and Father Catron was very concerned about the nursing mothers and the young children.

This concern also extended to several quite elderly men and women, all caught up in this horror visited on them by the German military police in the wake of the murder of Edouard Degrelle.

At the conclusion of Mass, while the people were moving into the parish hall, after repeated attempts, Father Catron was amazed that he was finally able to connect with Cardinal Archbishop Joseph Ernest Van Roey himself.

He quickly brought Cardinal Van Roey up to speed about all that transpired in Bouillion and the current desperate situation developing with the displaced families gathered in the Church. The Cardinal asked several questions about the whereabouts of Father Michel Masson, possible sources of food for the families and Catron's own well-being. Assuring Father Catron that he would get back to him, the Cardinal Archbishop terminated the call.

Catron went to the Parish Hall to see what could be done for the people and was gratified to see that Constance, Denise and Byron had moved tables aside and set up blankets and chairs for the families. He noticed Champagne speaking with another man who had just entered through a side door of the Hall. After a brief conversation, the two men left through the side door.

Denise made eye contact with Father Catron, and he signaled her to join him in a small anteroom adjacent to the Hall. As soon as they were together, and out of sight of the others, she burst into tears,

"Father, this is so terrible! I cannot believe what is happening to our people. We now have over 40 families who have been ripped apart by these crazy Nazis all over the murder of that traitor, Degrelle's brother. On top of that, our dear friend Henri Charles has been murdered in some twisted form of retaliation. I am at a loss as to what can we do."

Catron held out his arms, and Denise clung to him, burying her face into his chest and sobbing uncontrollably. He knew that all the events of these past few days, including finding Lucien alive but seriously maimed had taken its toll on this ordinarily stoic and brave woman. He let her cry herself out and wondered himself as to what they could do. He offered up a silent prayer for guidance and deliverance for these people. He immersed himself in deep prayer.

While still holding the crying Denise in an embrace, he heard someone clearing his throat and looked over to the doorway into the anteroom to see Byron Champagne standing politely awaiting his attention. He patted Denise on her head, and she broke off the embrace and turned to face Byron. She was still crying softly and did not seem to focus on Byron.

He was visibly moved by the anguish on her face and waited for her to regain her focus. When she finally acknowledged him, he addressed them both,

"My friend, Paul Bouchard has a temporary solution for feeding the people here. He has located a great supply of canned goods but needs assistance in retrieving them and then we can prepare something for the people to eat."

Within a few minutes, Denise, Byron, Constance and Father Catron organized a group of people, especially some of the teenagers, to assist in retrieving the much-needed canned food.

The Parish Hall had a small kitchen with a wood-fired stove being stoked and lighted by the other man that Catron previously observed working with Champagne. He had been introduced to as Paul Bouchard, who had been Edouard Degrelle's assistant.

This seemed very strange to Father Catron, to have this man working so diligently on behalf of townspeople whose husbands, fathers and sons had been arrested for suspicion of complicity in Degrelle's murder. He was about to say something when Constance Rademacher called him aside,

"Bouchard's wife is Father Masson's sister. He is not a collaborator although some people might wrongly accuse him of being one. He is taking a great chance being here with us. Not so much from the families here, but from the Rexists who think he is on their side.

Just then, Denise approached Catron,

"Father, I know you must stay here at least through the night, but I really would like to get out to the refuge to see my family, especially my children, to make sure they are all right and to fill them in on Lucien. I think that I can drive Byron's car, or he could drive me in a little while."

Bouchard overheard this from Denise and spoke up,

"Denise, I really don't think it's a good idea to drive on this night either with someone or alone. The patrols are back up and running and you would be subject to arrest as the authorities have imposed a curfew. The police are from the Sicherheitdienst and are a nasty, sadistic bunch. Please stay here for the night. My wife has a spare bedroom if you would feel more comfortable."

For a moment, Denise did not say anything. She overheard Constance imply that Bouchard was a bit more than met the eye and was trustworthy.

"I will think it over. But I am very concerned for my Father-in-law and my two brothers-n-law. They may be a target for assassination like the three earlier today and my friend Henri who was your competitor."

"I understand your anxiety. Raoul, Pierre and Raymond are friends of mine. I was able to quickly modify the list that Degrelle was going to supply to the Rexist commandos, so I removed their names. The Rexist commandos are the ones who killed Degrelle, not the *Resistance*."

"I see. Wow! I'll bet his brother has no idea that his team took out his own brother. And all these people are paying the price. Thank you, Paul. That does make me feel a little better. I still feel the need to get out to the refuge as soon as possible, but I see your point. I also want to thank you for your very kind offer of hospitality. I will remain here however to be with these people."

"Of course, Denise. I will be on hand first daylight to bring you out to the refuge. By then I should have a better feel for where things stand with the police, Gestapo, Sicherheitdienst. I will have a pass for you as well. Do you have a preference of which name you would like to use?"

"Yes, thank you, Paul. Hmmm… let's see… how about Theresa Avila?"

Paul laughed, "You're joking right? Saint Theresa Avila?"

"Nope. I am not joking. First, I've always hoped to become a saint and second, most of these idiots are born and bred atheists. They wouldn't know a saint from a woodpecker."

They both laughed, Paul promised to be back before dawn, and he departed for his apartment.

On his way to his car, he wondered how Marco and crew knew about the three men and the pharmacist since he eliminated them from the second list he reproduced. Then it hit him, *Marco has his own list!*

He decided to bring two pistols and a shotgun with him in the morning. He might just need them.

CHAPTER 104

Monday July 10, 1944, 7:30 AM Office of the Civil Administrator Nazi occupational headquarters 453 Avenue Louise Brussels, Belgium

Joseph Grohé as the Reichskommisar for Belgium and Northern France was privy to unadulterated reports from the German Army units fighting a desperate but losing battle against overwhelming Allied forces. He was briefed on the intense, bloody fighting around the northern section of the city of Caen. It was apparent that the German defenders were being forced to withdraw and that the city would soon be liberated.

There was no doubt that the Allies despite being bloodied, suffering severe casualties would triumph and soon there would be a "break-out" which meant his command over France and Belgium would be short-lived. He knew he had little time left.

Grohé and his top aides met in the middle of the night with General von Falkenhausen, head of the military administration and his staff to arrange the transition of power to Grohé as civilian administrator under the power of the SS.

This change was to be effective in three days' time and came about at the direct request of the Führer who expressed his confidence in Grohé. This made Grohé the new strong man of the occupation, though it wouldn't be long-lasting with the almost certain defeat of the German forces.

The Führer would not be too pleased with Grohé if he knew that he had secretly started the process for setting up an orderly and general retreat from all of Belgium. He laughed inwardly as he thought, *No fighting to the death for him, sorry, Adolph! I will salvage as many of our troops as I can together with equipment and then we can live to fight for another day.*

Grohé was many things, a fervent life-long Nazi, a flagrant anti-semite, a brutal dictator and murderer, but he was not stupid, and he was very interested in self-preservation.

He had carefully cultivated a quiet "back-door" relationship with Cardinal Joseph Ernest Van Roey-the Cardinal Archbishop of Belgium. Over the past several weeks, he would meet with the Cardinal Archbishop at his residence near St. Rumbold's Cathedral and sometimes at an office the Cardinal maintained at the Cathedral of Saint Michael and Saint Gudula.

Grohé clung to the hope that Hitler would be able to "pull something out of his hat" and miraculously overcome what seemed like an imminent defeat, but, as a pragmatist, he recognized that this was a false hope. Instead, his instincts inspired him to curry favor with powerful figures like the Cardinal Archbishop who might prove to be useful for his own personal survival in Post-War Europe no longer dominated by Adolph Hitler and the Nazis.

He went out of his way to issue protective ID passes to members of the Clergy and Religious communities. These passes with his personal signature would go a long way to ensure that those members of the Catholic clergy and Religious orders could travel within Belgium with very little chance of harassment during ever increasing roadblocks and security checks.

This pleased the Cardinal Archbishop greatly and furthered the growth of a guarded relationship. For his part, Cardinal Van Roey saw right through Grohé's efforts but felt it was important to maintain communication with him as things deteriorated with the Nazis' collapse of control.

Grohé was starting to enjoy his get-togethers with the cleric and looked forward to their occasional meetings. He had yet to have had the opportunity to grant something truly big that would hopefully incline the powerful, well-respected prelate to assist him, put in a "Good Word" for him if he became subject to prosecution in post-war Europe.

He was pleasantly surprised when his personal assistant buzzed his intercom,

"Sir, Cardinal Joseph Ernest Van Roey-the Cardinal Archbishop of Belgium for you."

"Oh, very good, please put him though." A momentary pause then,

"Uh, sir? The Cardinal Archbishop is not on the phone, he's downstairs in the waiting area.

"I see. Please tell him that I will be right down. Would you kindly show him into the meeting room and offer him something to drink, Tea, coffee, water?"

"Yes sir, right away, Sir."

Grohé hustled over to the bathroom right across from his office, combed his hair, splashed water on his face and straightened his tie. One last check in the mirror and he started down the stairs, thinking to himself, *I hope that the Cardinal presents me with a problem that he has encountered that is something that is within my power to grant.*

Grohé was right, the Cardinal had a problem that was too big for him to handle and, once he, Grohé came to fully appreciate its implications he had significant doubts as to whether he himself would have the power to solve the Cardinal Archbishop's problem.

He reached the bottom of the stairway, walked across the marble floor and into the conference room. The Cardinal stood up and smiled, "Herr Grohé I hope I didn't come at an inconvenient time?"

"Why no, your Eminence. I always have time for you. How can I help?"

Fifteen minutes later as he ushered the Cardinal Archbishop out the front door to his waiting car, Grohé thought, "*I may have gotten my wish for a complex problem, but I may not have the ability to solve it for the Cardinal or for me.*

He entered his office reception area on the way to his inner office and asked his personal assistant, Rolf Mannheim, to get Leon Degrelle on the phone for him right away.

Years later, while hiding out in the Ore Mountains near the German Czech border, he would sometimes reflect about that heated and contentious exchange he had with Degrelle who was mourning the loss of his brother, Edouard.

Grohé recalled that despite the uncertainty of the outcome of his call, it may have been possible that the Cardinal Archbishop was nevertheless grateful for his efforts. He hoped that it would possibly mitigate severe punishment when he faced the inevitable arrest and trial by the Allies.

CHAPTER 105

Monday, July 10, 1944, 11:00 AM Office of Ordnungspolizei
1 Place Ducale 6830 Bouillon

Oberleutnant Kurt Schmidt had a very contentious and emotional conversation with Léon Degrelle when he placed a call to update him and offer his personal condolences.

Degrelle seemed to imply that the Office of Ordnungspolizei was somehow negligent in not preventing Edouard's murder. Degrelle condemned Schmidt for releasing Marco and his two accomplices without first consulting him.

This came as a complete surprise to the Oberleutnant as these three were clearly carrying proof that they were Rexist commandos working for Degrelle. He wondered if Degrelle may have new information that his brother might have been killed by them rather than members of the Resistance?

Degrelle confirmed this suspicion when he told Schmidt that "there is a possibility that they know a lot more about who killed Edouard than they're letting on."

Schmidt, bristling at the implication that he was somehow derelict in his duties, reminded himself that Leon Degrelle was the equivalent of a Brigadier General with the Iron Cross and Oak Leaves bestowed on him by none other than the Fuhrer himself.

He calmed himself down and patiently explained that he had attempted to reach Degrelle five times before releasing the trio. None of his calls went through. In the meantime, Marco kept demanding release and insisting that he was working directly for Degrelle.

Schmidt took a different approach and asked Degrelle if he would share with him as the officer in charge of the ongoing investigation into his brother's murder, the reason for his belief that he should have retained custody of Marco and his two associates.

Degrelle declined to answer that query, instead he changed direction and asked the Oberleutnant to confirm that 46 members of the Resistance were currently in his custody. Schmidt corrected the number to 42 members, explaining that three were found executed on the outskirts of town while the pharmacist Henri Charles was murdered outside his pharmacy. He added that Charles was murdered by Marco and his team, who were caught red-handed.

He sensed that Degrelle was writing these details down as they spoke. Degrelle then asked him if all the men in custody had been sentenced yet. Schmidt replied that there had not yet been a review of everyone by the prison review board.

Degrelle knew that Schmidt had the authority to overrule the board's findings and insisted that, no matter what their decision, he wanted a guilty verdict and death sentence imposed on everyone in custody.

While the Oberleutnant was digesting this demand, Degrelle dropped a bombshell on him by revealing that earlier this morning, he received a telephone call from a "Very high-ranking member of the party" expressing outrage and condolences for his brother's murder. This important official insisted that no executions were to be enacted until he personally arrived at the prison to show his respect for the Degrelle family.

Schmidt asked Degrelle, "Sir, who is this 'high-ranking member of the party' that we are to wait for? Before Degrelle could respond, Schmidt heard someone talking to Degrelle who quickly responded to Schmidt's question,

"It is the Reichskommisar for Belgium and Northern France; I must terminate this call Herr Oberleutnant as I have another call of great importance. I will expect your full compliance, Goodbye."

Frustrated, Schmidt sat there wondering who the hell this "High-Ranking Party Official was"

It didn't take long for him to find out.

CHAPTER 106

Monday, July 10, 1944, 11:10 AM Office of Ordnungspolizei 1 Place Ducale 6830 Bouillon, Schmidt speaks with Joseph Grohé

Oberleutnant Schmidt was buzzed on his intercom by his desk sergeant, "Sir? I have a person on the line who has been trying to reach you from Nazi Headquarters in Brussels. He says it is extremely important."

Schmidt had a feeling he knew who it was, "Who is it, Sergeant?"

"It is the Reichskommisar for Belgium and Northern France."

"His name, Sergeant?"

"Joseph Grohé"

Joseph Grohé spoke urgently but politely with Schmidt and repeated Degrelle's emphasis that no executions were to take place unless he personally was present. He informed Schmidt that he was recently appointed to this powerful post by Hitler himself and would consider it a great service if Schmidt made sure that this request was honored. He then abruptly terminated the call, leaving Schmidt to his own resources.

A stunned Schmidt, to his credit, made sure that Grohé was who he said he was, by contacting his close friend, Oberleutnant William Hoeffner, a classmate who was the chief of staff of General von Falkenhausen, head of the military administration over Belgium and France.

His friend quickly told him that the General was removed from office by Hitler and Grohé was now the most powerful Nazi official in all of Belgium and France. He did not want to know the specifics of Schmidt's conversation with Grohé, but he told him that he had better pay attention to him.

When Hoeffner was done explaining this recent development, he asked Schmidt if he was alone in the room. Schmidt said that he was and Hoeffner whispered into the phone,

"Kurt, you didn't hear this from me, but you better enact a back-up plan if you know what I mean." He then hung up, leaving Schmidt staring at the telephone receiver.

Schmidt knew exactly what his friend meant.

Germany is losing the war, and Germany is going to fall.

He hung up the phone, then picked it up again and dialed the prison, speaking to the officer in charge, his subordinate. He gave strict instructions that no executions were to be done without his approval and not until Herr Joseph Grohé was physically present.

When asked who Joseph Grohé was, he responded as if everyone knew that he was the newly appointed Reichskommisar for Belgium and Northern France.

He then buzzed his desk sergeant, "Yes, Sir?"

"Those three men we just released. I would like an alert put out over our radios and to our roadblocks to seize them and place them under arrest with a caution that they are heavily armed. If necessary, they are authorized to shoot to kill if there is any resistance from them."

"Sir? We just let them loose, I don't understand."

Schmidt erupted with pent up anger, "Sergeant! It is not up to you to understand! Just follow my order!"

"Yes sir, sorry, Sir, right away, Sir."

Schmidt released the button, took off his eyeglasses, rubbed his eyes and searched his desk for a bottle of aspirin. This had all the earmarks of another long day. He no sooner downed four aspirins than his intercom buzzed again, he sighed and pressed down on the button, "Yes, Sergeant, what is it?"

"Sir, sorry to bother you, but I have one of our security checkpoints on the radio who are responding to the alert we just put out."

Schmidt sat up excited, "Yes, yes, go on!"

"Sir, they reported that not 15 minutes ago, the three men we put the bulletin out on passed through their checkpoint after showing them their paperwork. Do you want them to give chase?"

"Which way were they headed?"

A brief pause as the sergeant spoke to the security team. "Sir, they were headed towards Luxembourg and probably are about 20 kilometers ahead of the team right now."

Schmidt thought for a moment, sighed and then pressed back, "No, Sergeant. Tell them not to worry and call all our security teams back to base. Everyone including you and I need a bit of a rest. And thank you, Sergeant."

"Yes sir, thank you Sir."

All the roadblocks were dismantled, and the security teams headed back into headquarters.

Meanwhile about 20 kilometers away from the last checkpoint outside of Bouillon, Marco, Michael and Rogier having just passed through unchallenged, continued east towards Luxembourg.

Michael asked, "I guess we are not going after the Michel family on our list and the priest who we met a few days ago?"

Marco laughed, "No, we will count our blessings. That Oberleutnant is no fool, by this time he has already put out an all points alert for our heads with a shoot to kill order. I know that's what I would do."

With that, all three killers laughed and continued down the road toward Germany and beyond.

CHAPTER 107

Monday, July 10, 1944, 11:10 AM Parish Hall
Church of Saint John the Evangelist, Bouillon

Father Catron joined by Constance Rademacher, Denise Michel, and Byron Champagne set out bowls of hot soup derived from the last of the canned vegetables brought by Paul Bouchard.

Just when they were wondering where the next meal would come from, Bouchard came in through the side door accompanied by several tough-looking men all carrying boxes of canned food, containers of freshly acquired milk and, last but not least, Father Michel Masson, Pastor.

The entire hall erupted with shouts of joy when they saw Father Masson, who, despite looking malnourished, haggard and ten kilos lighter, joined in the celebration of his return.

Father Masson and Father Catron smiled, embraced and were quickly surrounded by small children and their mothers. He explained to the crowd that his brother-in-law Paul Bouchard was able to get word to him that he was a target of the Rexist killers, and he wanted to get far away from the parish to prevent harm to anyone near him if he was targeted and attacked. He hid in the forest with the help of those members of the Resistance who were not scooped up by the recent raid.

The Resistance men continued to unload the canned goods with the help of

Constance, Byron, Paul and Denise while Father Masson asked Father Catron if he would hear his confession. "Of course, my brother. It would be an honor, let's go."

The two priests excused themselves from the crowd, moved into the Church and Catron heard his brother priest's confession. A few minutes later the two priests returned and were ushered to a table to enjoy some soup.

At noon time, Father Catron announced that he and Denise were going to take their leave and gave all of them a blessing. They moved towards Father Catron's Renault followed by Byron Champagne who planned to accompany them.

Three Resistance fighters jumped into an old farm truck and insisted on leading the way, just in case those Rexist fighters were lying in wait. Father Catron knew it was useless to decline the kind offer, shrugged his shoulders and they fell in line behind the truck. Within minutes, they were on their way to the Michel family refuge.

As they approached the section of heavy brush that shielded the entrance, the guys in the farm truck hit four quick blasts on the horn. Within seconds, Pierre popped his head over the hedges and smiled.

He pulled the brush aside and opened the gate admitting Father Catron's 1939 Renault Juvaquatre followed by Byron Champagne in his Citroen.

CHAPTER 108

Monday, July 10, 1944, 12:30 PM Reunion Michel Family Refuge

Good news was hard to come by in war-torn Belgium. As was so typical during these times, good news was usually mixed with bad news. This was most certainly the case with the "good news" attached to the joyful reunion of Denise with her children, of Father Catron with all the Michel family, and especially with Jack and Ellen. All of this coupled with the miraculous survival of Lucien and his recovery and the reopening of the "Chicken House."

But the bad news that was brought to them was sobering. The execution-style murder of the three men and the cold-blooded murder of their friend, Henri Charles was devastating. This coupled with the late night round-up of 42 Bouillon men torn from their families and placed in the dreaded Arlon prison served as a cruel reminder of the horrors that existed under the Nazi Occupation.

Raoul Michel suggested that with Father Catron's approval they all gather in the great room for prayer. Almost the entire group agreed to this suggestion except for Byron Champagne. He apologized, delivered more packets of the sulfa drugs, but indicated that he felt pressed for time to get back to Bouillon.

He was anxious to assist the families dealing with the loss of the men taken to Arlon prison. He was also interested in getting at least one pharmacy reopened with the assistance of Paul Bouchard.

Before returning to do all this, he would like to take care of the medical assessment of Emil's shoulder wound and Raoul's wounds received from the attack by the Sanglier. This brought everyone back to quietly reflect on the pressing needs of the community and the dedication of this humble pharmacist.

Father Catron spoke up, breaking through the moment, "I have a better idea. Bear with me. Byron, please take Raoul and Emil into the house and do what you must do for them. Jack and Ellen, please take a walk with me. We need to talk. The rest of you, do not go anywhere, we will have a Mass in a little while and then I too have pressing needs back in Liege."

Marie, Miep, Nadine and Elise hustled to the kitchen and grabbed chairs and moved them into the great room in anticipation of the Mass. Denise brought her suitcase into her guest room and then joined the women.

Jan in the meantime set up the table which would serve as the altar and Pierre and Raymond resumed their security patrols on horseback until such time as the bell rang, calling them to come for Mass and, hopefully, dinner afterwards.

Just as Champagne finished examining Raoul and Emil, Father Catron returned with a smiling Ellen and Jack. He called everyone to listen as he had a special announcement.

"There will be a slight change in plans regarding the Mass. We will indeed have a special Mass this afternoon. A Nuptial Mass."

It became so quiet at first, one could hear a pin drop. Then the realization of what Father Catron just said sunk in and there was joyous laughter and hugs among the women. Smiles abounded all around. He addressed the group. "I have been authorized by Cardinal Archbishop Joseph Ernest Van Roey to perform the sacramental ceremony for the American Airman, Lieutenant John "Jack" Dodds and Ellen Delacroix."

Laughter and clapping of hands ensued as Father Catron continued, "Jack and Ellen have expressed their desire that Emil Delacroix and Denise Michel serve as their primary witnesses, as Best Man and Maid of Honor."

He paused and looked at Emil and at Denise, "Emil and Denise, do you accept this honor?"

They both laughed and instantly replied with a big "Yes!"

Father Catron continued, "Excellent! There are a few more issues I would like to address."

CHAPTER 109

Monday, July 10, 1944, 1:15 PMWedding Plans Michel Family Refuge

Once Father Catron secured the affirmation from Emil and Denise to serve as Best Man and Maid of Honor, he continued, "Now, it is the normal practice in most European countries that a civil wedding takes place first before the sacramental union occurs in the church. But this is a time of war. We Belgians do not recognize the current administrators of Civil authority, the Nazis."

He had everyone's attention as he went on, "Therefore, the Cardinal Archbishop will coordinate with the appropriate Allied Military authorities to confirm that an approved sacramental union of these two wonderful young people has occurred with his permission"

He let this unconventional tactic sink in, then, "In the meantime, an upstanding member of the civilian community will be chosen to represent the legitimate civil authorities in absentia. I believe that Mr. Byron Champagne will adequately fulfill this objective. Is this okay with you, Mr. Champagne?"

Byron smiled and nodded his head. Father Catron continued, "We now come to the blessing of the rings. Because this is very short notice, the groom, Lieutenant Dodds did not have time to go shopping in downtown Bouillon for a wedding and engagement ring for his beautiful bride and the bride, Ellen Delacroix likewise did not have the time to go shopping for a wedding band for the groom."

Everyone chuckled at his attempt at humor as he continued with a big smile,

"Therefore, by the power vested in me by the Cardinal Archbishop of Belgium I temporarily will use these rings." He held up two paper cigar rings taken from Raoul's supply of cigars which caused an uproar of laughter.

This was interrupted by a loud protest from Denise, "Oh no you don't Father! As the Maid of Honor, I will provide actual rings for my Bride and her Groom."

With that, she rushed into her bedroom and within a few minutes returned and handed Father Catron two wedding rings. Ellen immediately recognized what Denise had done and cried out,

"No, dear Denise! We cannot let you do this. These are your wedding rings for you and for Martin."

"You absolutely must accept these my dear cousin. Martin left behind his wedding ring on the night when he went on his last mission. He would want a fellow warrior like Jack to honor this ring by wearing it."

Then pointing to her wedding ring in Father Catron's hand, she said, "I, for one never plan on remarrying anyone ever again. I have spoken with Mother Philomena, Mother Superior of the Sisters of Immaculata de Namur and with the approval of my children, Jan and Elise, I will profess for her Order."

This came as a shock to everyone including Father Catron. Denise smiled and continued, "I would be so proud to know that you, my dearest friend and cousin will think of me every time you look at that ring."

Ellen, moved to tears embraced Denise as did the other women gathered around the pair. Father Catron, a little uncomfortable with these emotional moments cleared his throat and suggested, "Shall we get started with the Mass?"

Miep, Maria and Denise stopped what they were doing and looked incredulously at the priest. Denise spoke up, "Are you kidding? *Get started with the Mass*? Father Catron, with all due respect, you are not only a wonderful priest, but you, most definitely are a *typical man*! As Maid of Honor, it is my duty to take this bride, get her properly dressed ready for the wedding ceremony, and Emil, as the Best Man you must find some way to get our American Flyboy looking a little more presentable. No offense, Jack"

Jack laughed as Emil signaled to follow him, "None taken." As he followed Emil to another bedroom. Father Catron sighed and sat down with Raoul and Byron Champagne as the women and the two teenage girls went out into the garden to pick flowers.

The priest accepted a cigar from Raoul and laughed, "There is something to be said about the priestly celibate life without women to boss them around."

Raoul lit his cigar, then Father Catron's cigar and lastly Byon's cigar and laughed, "Really?You must remind me some day."

CHAPTER 110

Monday, July 10, 1944, Mr. & Mrs. John Dodds Michel Family Refuge

The great room was set up facing the makeshift altar. In front of the altar Jan set two folded carpets with a pillow on the top of each one as per Father Catron's instructions. These would serve as "kneelers" for the Bride and Groom during the wedding ceremony.

Jan placed candles on either side of the altar table and placed the standing crucifix from Father Catron's Mass kit in the center. While all this was going on, Marie and Miep together with Nadine and Elise started to cook vegetables and bake bread for the evening meal.

Raoul and Byron prepared several chickens to be roasted once the Mass was finished. Father Catron prepared his liturgy and arranged his vestments. As events were moving into the late afternoon, he accepted Raoul and Marie's invitation to spend the night rather than attempt the long drive back to Liege, tired and in the dark with uncertain safety on the roads. Everyone breathed a sigh of relief when he announced that decision.

Byron insisted that he would have to return to Bouillon later that evening, but the group were holding out hope for his personal safety that he too would change his mind.

Emil and Jack emerged from Emil's guestroom, both clad in dark slacks and jackets. Jack squeezed into one of Emil's suits and, in the opinion of the women who inspected him thought that he looked presentable except for his scuffed boots. They all understood that there wasn't any other option available to him on such short notice. Still, everyone thought that he looked very good.

All eyes turned to Ellen as she walked in with Denise. There was a noticeable gasp when Jack laid eyes on her. She looked beautiful! Denise had found a white dress and white shoes somewhere and had skillfully placed Ellen's blonde hair in a bouffant style on top of her head.

Later, Denise revealed that the white dress was her own pre-wedding dress worn at the civil ceremony, which would be replaced with the formal white wedding gown at the church ceremony. She quickly modified it to fit Ellen and It looked great on her, in Jack's opinion and everyone else's as well.

Marie recognized that Mass would soon be starting now that the bride and groom were ready, so she stepped out on the porch and rang the bell one time, signaling Pierre and Raymon to return to the house. Within minutes the two young men rode up in their horses and tied them up. As they approached the kitchen door Marie pulled them aside,

"Boys, please do me a favor. After dinner and before we serve desert, would you kindly go over to the spare guesthouse and make sure that it's presentable for the bride and groom? Nothing fancy, just swept out. Miep and I will come over and make the bed and dress it up with flowers afterwards for the newlyweds."

They both smiled and told her they would do it immediately. The two boys hustled over to the guesthouse and were back within ten minutes signaling that the initial clean-up mission was accomplished. Marie then called Elise and Nadine over and handed them two flower vases filled with freshly picked flowers from her garden and a freshly cleaned set of bed linens.

"I trust you girls to get over to the spare guesthouse and make it into a welcoming honeymoon cottage just like you would want for your own weddings in the not-too-distant future. Can you do that before Mass starts?"

They both smiled and nodded, took the vases and the linens and started out the door. Marie called to them, "If Father gets ready to start, I'll ring the bell. Right now, he's going over what he is going to do with the bride and groom. I think you'll have about 10 minutes, so hurry!

Fifteen minutes later, Father Catron called out to everyone that they were ready to start. Marie held up her hand asking for another few minutes and Father smiled and went back to speaking with the Bride and Groom. Another ten minutes went by, Nadine and Elise came running back in, red cheeks, big smiles and nodded to Marie who signaled Father Catron.

Father Catron started, "Let us begin. In the name of the Father, and of the Son and of the Holy ghost...."

Thirty minutes later he turned Jack and Ellen around and said with a big smile on his face,

"Ladies and Gentlemen, allow me to introduce Mister and Missus John Dodds."

CHAPTER 111

July, August 1944 Jack & Ellen Michel Family Refuge

The downed "Evacuees", Allied airmen were still being sheltered in their forest refuges awaiting the Allied forces to liberate all of France and Belgium and, of course, them. Until such time as the Allies came through and liberated the forest refuges, Jack remained at the Michel Family refuge with his new Bride during July and August.

This gave the newlyweds time to enjoy their new life together. Ellen loved the way that the women decorated the guesthouse. It was converted from a rustic "bunk house" to a delightful 'honeymoon haven" as she liked to put it. For his part, Jack loved *anything* that Ellen loved so he wasn't troubled by all the "frilly" stuff.

On a day-to-day basis, the able-bodied members of the family, which now included Jack, slaughtered chickens and rabbits, worked the fields, and harvested vegetables in season. They also helped in preparing the food for families and those in need in and around Bouillon.

Jack was still being hidden from the Nazis, so it was not possible for him to assist in the distribution of food. Instead, he took turns with Pierre and Raymond riding horseback on security patrols. After the recent incidents with wild boars, German would-be rapists, and highway cut-throats, everyone respected his abilities with the Mauser K98 carbine and the Browning Hi Power 9 mm.

When not working the fields or assisting in some other way, Jack and Ellen continued their daily walk along the forest path to "Cowboy Rock" and some laughs and splashing for a brief time in the fast-moving creek.

Jack also did his best to get back into shape by running, doing push-ups, and all the other calisthenics he had been taught during his basic training. Ellen knew that he felt obligated to return to active duty and serve until the war was over. She resolved to enjoy each day that they had together and not worry about what the future held.

Years later, they would often reflect on these days at the Michel Family refuge as not only beautifully idyllic, but the beginning of a wonderful life-long love affair.

There was still no word on the fate of the over forty men seized by the Gestapo and being held in the Arlon prison.

Father Catron, during a brief return visit provided them with a beautifully printed "Certificaat van Heilige Huwelijken" which meant "Certificate of Holy Matrimony" in Dutch, signed by him as the Presider of the Marriage liturgy and counter-signed by none other than Cardinal Joseph Ernest Van Roey-the Cardinal Archbishop of Belgium.

The Cardinal informed British Intelligence and Allied command through his resources about Jack's survival and his marriage to Ellen. He also related that he received word about the Bouillon men at the Arlon prison about a delaying tactic from another important contact, a senior German official.

This official, who was later revealed as Joseph Grohé, was desperately trying to curry favor with the Cardinal Archbishop in post-war Europe. Grohé informed the Cardinal that, as a delaying tactic, he demanded that no executions were to be performed at the prison unless he was personally there to oversee it.

Grohé further told the Cardinal that he had no intention of going to the prison and the hope was that the Allies would be there and liberate all the prisoners soon. Everyone held their breath and offered continual prayers for the well-being of these men.

Denise made frequent trips into Liege and Brussels. She met several times with Mother Philomena to discuss the possibility of pursuing a life as a consecrated Religious Sister.

She also met with her MI-9 colleagues at various safe houses, coordinating the repatriation of the downed Allied airmen being protected in the forest camps under Operation Marathon. With Jack's permission she informed MI-9 that she was responsible for the protection of 2nd Lieutenant John Dodds at an off-camp location.

Unbeknownst to Jack, Denise added that the American Airman had been working closely with Belgian and French Resistance and was greatly respected by the "Secret Army." Proud of Jack, she told them about how quickly and professionally he took out the would-be rapist, German Corporal Mueller and then the two partisans on the road to Bouillon.

This impressed Albert Ancia, Jean de Blommaert and Daniel Muton, all MI-9 Operators. They quickly relayed this information to Airey Neave in London, who, in turn shared Jack's name with senior Special Operations Executive Leader Hardy Amies.

Rather than lose this valuable resource, Neave argued for a commando mission to liberate Lieutenant Dodds. After careful consideration Hardy Amies gave it a "thumbs down" as he felt the Allies would soon be able to liberate all of Belgium. In the meantime, he reached out to his contacts in the French and Belgian Resistance to keep an eye on this American Airman.

CHAPTER 112

Early September 1944, Liberation of Belgium, Michel Family Refuge

Early each morning, Raoul would adjust his illegal radio as the others clustered around him in the Great Room. On the 2nd day in September an excited woman on the radio shouted "La Belgique Est libérée,"

They shouted out in English for Jack's sake, "Belgium is Free!" Allied troops crossed the Belgian border at several places. The 1st U.S. Army crossed the Belgian border in the hamlet of Cendro on the 2nd of September."

The broadcast informed the listeners that 2nd British Army at Douai, France was ordered to march on to Brussels and the British forces arrived in Belgium on September 3rd. On that evening, together with the Belgian Brigade Piron, they entered Brussels, the capital.

It was obvious that liberation was moving fast. Joseph Grohé implemented his secret withdrawal plans and the German authorities and a multitude of Nazi collaborators packed their bags and fled east towards Germany.

The Belgian and French Resistance were extremely active, assisting in the rapid liberation, chasing down and executing many collaborators, and preventing a "scorched earth" destruction by the withdrawing Germans. This was especially important when it came to Antwerp, which was essential to the continual flow of logistics to support the Allied invasion.

British Intelligence Officer, Airey Neave MI-9's chief operating officer for France and Belgium set up MI-9 field operations in France. He followed the Allied advances looking to repatriate downed Allied airmen who were secured away deep in forest redoubts during Operation Marathon as well as those who were being given safe harbor in citizen's homes.

His request to American commanders for logistical and armed support in finding MI-9 Agents and Allied airmen was initially met with skepticism. There were still armed German units in various stages of withdrawal and the situation was deemed too dangerous to put out a "scouting Party," especially if the airmen were still sequestered in safe environments.

Finally, when it became evident that Neave was "for real" he obtained an armed escort to the Foret de Freteval. Much to the surprise of the Allied Commanders who first turned Neave down, he retrieved 152 airmen who were ensconced there under the supervision of MI-9 Agent Thomas Rutland. Neave was able to beg, borrow and "steal" several buses to transport these airmen to safety under armed escort.

A further search with an enhanced armed escort to the Belgian Ardennes camp under the supervision of Daniel Mouton produced another 145 airmen who were likewise transported to safety.

Airey Neave continued his search for MI-9 agents and downed Allied airmen throughout liberated Europe. By now he was recognized by many Allied commanders and was able to hitch rides with American and British occupation troops. A gifted speaker, he was often able to convince commanders to release platoons to help him in his search to track down his people.

Jack was kept privy to Neave's search and knew that Neave was aware of his location and would send for him in two days' time. He took the limited time he had left to brief Ellen about his understanding of Military codes and procedures to bring dependents back to the States. He also wrote down a complete list of his American family and their contact information to the best of his memory.

He and Ellen put together two complete duplicate portfolios which proved they were married: the Wedding certificates signed and provided by Father Catron and cosigned by the Cardinal Archbishop, several photographs of the actual wedding ceremony taken by Elise using her 35-millimeter, Argus C3 camera. (Developed in his pharmacy by Byron Champagne.)

Finally, several signed and notarized statements by the witnesses,

Emil Delacroix and Denise Michel and Byron Champagne. Jack placed one portfolio in his personal luggage and Ellen kept hers in a safe place.

As the day drew near when he would be picked up by the MI-9 search party, he made a promise to Ellen: "I will be back for you, Ellen. No matter how long it takes, have faith. You and I are destined to spend the rest of our lives on this earth together. I promise you I will be back."

A tearful Ellen smiled and said, "I will hold you to that promise, Cowboy."

They spent the next two nights in the 'honeymoon' bunk house curled up in each other's arms, talking in soft whispers about their plans for the future.

CHAPTER 113

Early September 1944, 9 AM Jack goes back! Michel Family Refuge

After an early morning breakfast with the Michel family and Emil, Miep and a visiting Byron Champagne, Jack and Ellen took one last walk to "Cowboy Rock." Both had been told by Denise, who was in close contact with her MI-9 colleagues that the MI-9 armed escort would most likely arrive at the entrance to the Michel family refuge somewhere around 11 AM.

They walked hand in hand and sat on their rock in quiet harmony. They said very little, each one deep in their own thoughts. Jack wrestled with an enormous series of conflicting thoughts and emotions. On the one hand he felt duty bound to return to fight for his country and for his Allies. On the other hand, he deeply felt the impending separation from Ellen the love of his life.

Ellen, for her part would later admit to much of the same series of conflicting emotions. She understood this man who she lovingly referred to as "Cowboy", was almost certainly going to put himself in danger and might not ever return to her despite his promises to the contrary. Ellen knew that he was an honorable man and would, of necessity put himself in harm's way for the good of others just as he did on that terrible early morning at the Chicken House and then shortly thereafter on the road to Bouillon.

The thought of losing him was almost overwhelming, but she reconciled those thoughts with the realization that they were both lucky during this time of war to have had the time together over these past several weeks. She determined to be positive and to think that there would be a day soon when they would be reunited and able to embark upon a new life together.

Their thoughts were interrupted by one solitary ringing of the bell. Jack looked at his new wristwatch, a wedding gift from Emil and Miep. "Darn! It's only 10 AM, I was hoping that Denise's prediction of 11AM was more in line with our plans this morning."

They both stood and started walking back to the house. As they approached the meadow, there was no sign of an armed escort awaiting his arrival, just Denise with two bags in her hand. As they drew nearer, she smiled,

"Sorry to interrupt you two love birds, but the escort will indeed be here soon, and I thought that Jack might like to wear this."

Denise held up the larger of the two bags and withdrew and held up Jack's flight suit, the rips and cuts sewn and repaired.

He smiled, "I thought you and Janine destroyed my flight suit."

"No. we were going to, but we decided to remove your name tag and anything else that might be an identifier for you, and we stored it at that first safe house in the forest that Lucien took you to that first day. We hid it under the floorboards behind that swinging pantry door."

She then held up the second bag and withdrew his flight boots. "Sorry, that Elise and I didn't buff these up for you, but we did repair some of the tears and cleaned them up. If you decide to wear these things, you better hurry up as the escort will be here in short order."

Jack embraced Denise, thanked her and Elise and took the clothes and boots into the "Honeymoon house" to change. He emerged a few moments later dressed as 2nd Lieutenant John Dodds, US Army Air Corps, except there was no name tag on his flight suit, previously removed and destroyed by Janine and Denise. Denise then reached into her purse and produced Jack's "dog-tags" which she placed over his head.

"There! You now look the part, Lieutenant Dodds, except that the suit is a little too big on you right now as you obviously have not enjoyed our Belgian cooking and have lost about 5 or 6 kilos in my estimation."

Just as the entire Michel Family gathered in the open garden area, Pierre and Raymond led two armed Military vehicles with big white stars on their sides down the dirt road towards the house. Both vehicles had a mounted 50 Cal machine gun each manned by a soldier.

Airey Neave was in the first vehicle with a driver and Daniel Mouton who ran the camp in the Ardennes was in the second vehicle along with four other soldiers. All the soldiers, including the sergeant in charge were combat hardened, heavily armed members of the 1st US Army that had recently crossed into Belgium on the 2nd of September.

Everyone disembarked and greeted the Michel Family and friends. The soldiers went over to the horses and asked Jan, Elise and Nadine many questions about the horses, about how they were doing and about the surrounding countryside which they found to be beautiful.

They went back to the vehicles and signaled the teenagers to follow. Reaching into several boxes inside the vehicles, they produced large piles of chocolate, chewing gum and other goodies. They handed them American cigarettes for the adults and some playing cards. All to the delight of Jan, Elise and Nadine as well as the adults who laughed and smiled in appreciation.

Airey Neave spent a little time speaking with Raoul and Emil, who he apparently had a working relationship with as members of the resistance. After a few more minutes had transpired, he looked at Jack and nodded. Jack turned to Ellen, and they embraced, which was soon followed by the entire Michel family and friends embracing him. The soldiers laughed, whooped and hollered much to the amusement of Airey Neave and Daniel Mouton. Neave commented,

"Looks like this downed airman had a slightly better time of it than those lads hunkered down in the woods."

He nodded to the sergeant in charge, and they all piled back into their vehicles. Within minutes they were rolling back down the dirt road with Jack looking back at his Belgian family and friends. They, in turn were looking back at him and holding their hands up to their foreheads in a salute. All except Ellen.

Denise moved quickly over to Ellen and put her arm around her. Ellen buried her head in Denise's shoulder and tried but failed to suppress huge sobs emanating from deep within her chest. Denise spoke soothingly to her in French.

"It's okay, Ellen. You had a chance to express everything in your heart. He will be back, I feel it." Ellen looked up at her with big blue eyes, in between sobs, she said, “No, I didn’t express everything in my heart.”

“That’s okay. You’ll tell him the next time you see him, and I believe that won’t be too long especially once the Nazis are defeated.”

“No, Denise it’s not okay I should have told him everything in my heart.”

“Well, I don’t want to get personal, but what is so pressing on your heart?”

“I’m pregnant.”

CHAPTER 114

September 1944, Airey Neave Debriefs Jack MI-9 HQ location Brussels, Belgium

Six hours after leaving Bouillon, the MI-9 escorts dropped Jack, Airey Neave and Daniel Mouton off at a small, nondescript two-story brick building in downtown Brussels. There were no signs that this building had any special designation other than two gruff-looking men standing outside the wrought iron gate leading into the front courtyard.

Neave shook hands with all the military escorts and thanked them. Jack also thanked them, and they surprised him by saluting him. As he returned their salutes and watched them pull away, he thought that they still had a long way to go and a lot more fighting until they reached Berlin.

Neave and Mouton smiled and directed Jack's attention to the gate as the two vehicles pulled away.

"Come on in, Lieutenant, let's talk a bit about your time behind lines while we work on getting you a change of clothes."

"Thank you, sir, but I'm fine with what I'm wearing."

Without acknowledging Jack's comment, the two MI-9 men led him inside and opened a doorway halfway down a long hall. As Neary gestured towards a vacant chair next to a long conference table, he said,

"Jack, we are not going to take this suit away from you, but tomorrow we are planning to take you to Le Mans Airfield just south of here into France where elements of the 357 Fighter Group are temporarily staged."

Jack reacted with great excitement, "My fighter group is here, in France?"

Neave smiled, "Yes, Jack. Just so you know the normal protocol would be to ship you over to the UK to be debriefed at the Special Reception Center in London. This is a lengthy, rather cumbersome practice which normally results in your being shipped back to the United States. I don't think that would tie in with your aspirations to return to active duty, does it?"

"No sir! Absolutely not!"

"I didn't think so. Jack, we've been appraised of your conduct behind enemy lines, interceding on behalf of Belgian citizens, protecting them from Nazis and Partisan highway robbers and cutthroats."

Jack shook his head and laughed, "It sounds like Denise has been speaking with you."

"Denise Michel? Yes, of course, we are very fond of Denise and proud of her service, she has had very good things to say about you, but your praises come from a very influential source."

Jack reacted with surprise, "Really? Who might that be?"

"Cardinal Joseph Ernest Van Roey-the Cardinal Archbishop of Belgium. Oh, and congratulations on your marriage to Ellen Delacroix. I see that you didn't waste your time behind enemy lines. Sorry we had to interrupt your honeymoon."

With that, both he and Daniel Mouton erupted in laughter, Neave continued,

"The Cardinal Archbishop's influence here in Belgium and his kind words about you have had a great effect on the Allied command. This is especially true as we are all sorting through our continuing progress in defeating Hitler and all the Nazis."

He glanced at a notepad in front of him, "Jack, we have set up a meeting tomorrow mid-morning with you and Lieutenant Colonel William, "Bill" McKenna, Deputy Group Commander of the 357th Fighter Group. He will interview you and evaluate the possibility of returning you to active duty."

For once, Jack was speechless as Neave continued, "So, now you can understand that getting thoroughly debriefed, you will need to wear a proper flight suit with your name and rank on it. It's already being prepared for you. Please be assured that this suit you are wearing, and your boots will be returned to you to do with as you see fit."

"I see, sir, sorry I didn't mean any disrespect."

"Oh no, Jack, please just relax, no disrespect was inferred. Let's go upstairs, check you into a guest room and give you a chance to shower, change have a bite to eat. Daniel and I will join you for a meal. We will talk a little more about your experiences behind the enemy lines. This will take the place of dealing with the bureaucrats at the Special Reception Center in London."

He looked at Jack to make sure he was following him, "You will spend the night here with us and then tomorrow you will be turned over to the 357th. Any questions or comments for now?"

"Yes sir, thank you very much for picking me up and setting up the meeting tomorrow. I do have a question for you, has there been any word about Janine, Denise's sister?"

Neave shook his head, "Sadly, no. We are doing all possible to locate her whereabouts, but so far, nothing. She is likely at one of several concentration camps in Germany, but nothing yet. On a positive note, I do have some good information about her and Denise's brother, Lucien.

"Really? What is it?"

"He is recovering very well from his terrible injuries, and we have just received permission to fly him to the UK for ongoing treatment and rehabilitation. All the green lights of approval for this are based on his heroic service in trying to preserve the integrity of the Port of Antwerp."

"That is very good news, sir. Thank you for letting me know."

After settling into his guestroom, Jack showered and put on a pair of slacks and an Olive-drab T-shirt left for him by Neave. He left the guestroom and followed the smells downstairs to a dining area where he found Airey and Daniel waiting for him.

Two Belgian women who looked like a mother and daughter, smiled at him as he entered the dining area and began to set the dinner table. Once that was done, they departed the room and left the men to eat and talk among themselves.

After dinner, Neave and Mouton went through a series of questions about all that Jack could remember from the very first days following his crash landing, his being rescued by Lucien and the other members of the Comet line and the Belgian resistance right up to his joining up with them this day.

They were very interested in more details about Emil's Chicken House, Father Catron's involvement and the disposition of the dead German corporal who was allegedly killed during the Allied bombing of Liege aerodrome. They already knew about the murder of Leon Degrelle's brother, Edouard, the retaliation and murder of Henri Charles and the three other men who were murdered execution style.

Jack mentioned the devastating effect on the Bouillon families of the arrest and detention of the 42 men by the Gestapo and expressed concern about the trio of the Rexist commandos who might come back to seek revenge on the Michel family and the priest, Father Michel Masson.

Neave looked at Mouton and nodded his head. Daniel looked at Jack with a grim smile, "They have been neutralized, Jack. The resistance caught up with them and they died. I might add they died in a most unpleasant way. Raoul and his family and Father Masson have nothing to fear from them."

This caused Jack to breathe a great sigh of relief. From the detailed questions that they both leveled at him, Jack was convinced that they had already ascertained a lot of what happened through Denise who was privy to almost everything.

After another hour of conversation and an offer of an after-dinner drink, which he politely declined, they bid him goodnight and told him that there would be an early morning breakfast call around 4 AM for the 510-kilometer drive to Le Mans.

Jack thanked them and returned to his guestroom. After stripping down to his boxer shorts, again provided by Neave, he got down on his knees and prayed. He prayed for the safety of Ellen, and for all his loved ones.

Climbing onto his bed, he smiled and tried to quell the hundreds of thoughts swirling around in his over-tired brain, especially as they applied to the events that the next day would bring. Exhausted, he finally fell fast asleep, protected by armed MI-9 guards outside the MI-9 Safehouse in liberated Brussels.

CHAPTER 115

Friday, September 15, 1944, On the road to the 357 Fighter Group, Le Mans, France.

Jack sat in the right passenger seat of the Jeep as it made its way towards Le Mans Forward airbase for the 357 Fighter group. He was wearing the brand-new US Army Air Corps flight suit with his embroidered name tag given to him by Neave earlier this morning in Brussels.

The Staff Sergeant behind the wheel figured they had just about another hour to go. Airey Neave sat slumped in the rear seat, fast asleep. They had been on the road since 04:00 hours and watched the night turn into an overcast day.

For the past two hours they passed scores of military vehicles, civilians on foot or on bicycles and even some on horseback, all moving in one direction, North towards Brussels.

"Refugees returning to their homes." Said the sergeant. "Damn pity what these people have gone through."

Neave told Jack that once he arrived at the field, he was on his own. Neave planned to bum a ride back over to the UK to take care of some pressing MI-9 business. At 10:00 AM the jeep turned into a roadblock manned by several MP's standing in front of a sign that said,

"Le Mans Airfield Advanced Landing Ground (ALG) A-35 Joint Allied Air Command Home of the 357 Fighter Group"

Jack felt his heart and his breathing accelerate as he heard the familiar sounds of P-51 Mustangs warming up getting ready for take-off even though a light mist was falling. There were several DC-3s (C-47s) parked near the entrance that were in the process of loading passengers and cargo.

Everyone except Jack showed their Military ID's. Airey Neave showed his British SOE ID (British Intelligence Special Operations) and pointed to Jack who produced his dog-tags as previously instructed by Neave.

The MP checked off the names on his clipboard which included Jack's name. He signaled to the other MPs to raise the hand operated gate. Just as the jeep started forward, the MP held up his hand requesting a momentary stop.

He smiled at Jack and gave a crisp salute, "Welcome back, sir! We're glad to welcome all our men returning to us from behind enemy lines. We're glad you're back with us!"

The other three MPs saluted as well, and Jack returned the salute with a big smile on his face.

As they entered the service road running alongside the active runway, Jack noticed that the P-51's were the newer dash D's. Most of the P-51s were clad in an overall coat of "RAF green" (olive drab) with gray undersurfaces, but several were in bare metal with olive drab tails and upper surfaces. He didn't care which one would be assigned to him, he just wanted to get his hands on one of them.

They approached a series of newly erected Quonset huts and pulled up to the first one marked "Operations Center." Airey Neary hopped out, grabbed his bag, shook Jack's hand, and handed him a business card. "This is where I get off, Jack. Good luck to you! I will keep an eye on things as to your progress and you can contact me at the number on this card if you need anything. The sergeant will drive you over to that other Quonset hut a little further on."

"Thank you, sir and thank you for your service and especially for your efforts with regard to Lucien."

Neave waved to him as the jeep pulled off and headed to another Quonset hut about a half mile down the taxiway. They pulled up to this building marked "Command and Operations" and came to a stop. A corporal whose nametag identified him as "J.C. Smythe" came right out of the center and greeted Jack with a crisp salute, which Jack returned.

The corporal smiled while taking his bag from his hands, "Welcome,

Lieutenant Dodds. Follow me, sir. The Squadron Wing commander is waiting for you."

Jack followed the corporal down the hall past a series of cubby-hole offices hopping with enlisted men and officers all engaged in a flurry of activity. They stopped at a closed door.

A sign fastened to the middle of the door was marked,

357th Fighter Squadron
Squadron Wing Commander
1st Lieutenant Robert Murphy

Jack's eyes must have bugged out of his head as he laughed out loud, "Murph? Wing commander? You've got to be kidding me!"

The corporal knocked on the door and a voice from within called out,

"Corporal Smythe, I hope you were able to delouse and disinfect the Lieutenant. If so, send that poor excuse for a runaway pilot in here pronto!"

Smythe looked at Jack and smiled, "I see you know each other, sir."

CHAPTER 116

Friday, September 15, 1944, 357th Fighter Squadron Wing Commander, 1st Lieutenant Robert Murphy Forward Airbase Le Mans

Jack moved into Murphy's office just as he came around the desk to greet him. His intention to salute 1st Lieutenant Murphy was interrupted when "Murph" placed him in a great big, bone-crushing "bear hug." Murphy laughed and cried out,

"You stupid son of a bitch! I thought you were dead. Now all of that crying and moaning I did all those nights was for nada!"

Jack, trying to regain his breath laughed, "2nd Lieutenant John Dodds reporting for duty, sir."

Again, Murphy laughed, "2nd Lieutenant? Bullshit! I have here your silver bar and this afternoon after your medical exam clearance our CO, Group Commander, Lieutenant Colonel Spicer is going to personally pin them on your uniform collar, 1st Lieutenant Dodds."

Jack was momentarily at a loss of words, but quickly recovered, "Murph, it's so great to see you. I worried so much about you that day, wondering if you made it back to base."

Murphy grinned, "Let me get this straight. *YOU WORRIED ABOUT ME?* This coming from the guy who crashed and burned into a field in the Ardennes?"

"Well, I knew that you probably would get lost. I kept telling you that England was due West, not East but you never got the hang of it."

Murphy laughed, "Okay, enough of this bullshit. Sit down for a moment and let's go over a few things that the CO wants to clear up before Captain Meyers gets hold of you.

"Who's Captain Meyers?"

"Oh, he's better known as 'Doc Meyers', our own 'sawbones', our flight Surgeon who has been traveling with us even to this forlorn airbase stuck in beautiful Le Mans, France. Don't worry, buddy, he's a good guy. You should get through with no problem."

For the next hour and a half, after going through everything that Jack experienced, including marrying Ellen, which got a tremendous laugh out of Murphy, the two friends went over the flight maneuvers that Jack was to accomplish with Murphy flying wing and observing.

Jack was getting truly excited and looked forward to climbing back into the cockpit. Murphy handed him a list of the flight maneuvers for Jack to study and just when they were going to go over them one more time, the intercom buzzed.

"Sir, Captain Meyers just buzzed me. He is ready for Lieutenant Dodds."

"Okay, thanks Corporal, I will send him out. Will you direct him to the Med-Unit?"

"Yessir. Right away."

Murphy smiled at Jack, "Relax, buddy. You will do fine. When you're finished, I will have Smythe transport you into town where we have taken over an old hotel. The CO and other brass want to have dinner with you tonight and greet you formally. I have ordered a complete set of uniform shirts, slacks and flight gear for you. All of that will be waiting at the hotel."

Within a few minutes, Corporal Smythe guided Jack to the Med-Unit Quonset Hut where he was confronted by a smiling man, clad in scrubs.

"Welcome, Lieutenant Dodds, I'm "Doc" Meyers your host for this medical adventure. Come in, take all your clothes off and relax."

With that, both he and Jack laughed, and the medical evaluation began in earnest.

CHAPTER 117

Friday, September 15, 1944, 357th Fighter Squadron, Passed Med Eval with "Flying colors", Captain Meyers Flight Surgeon Forward Airbase Le Mans

"Doc" Meyers was a true professional, very calm and very thorough. He was assisted by 2nd Lieutenant Lynn D'Aloia, an experienced member of the Army Nurse Corp (ANC). Also present was 2nd Lieutenant Terry Griffin, a brand-new member of the ANC in her first duty assignment. She was following Nurse D'Aloia on her rounds and taking notes.

Because of the presence of the nurses, Jack was able to retain his boxer shorts for most of the examination. Meyers joked with Jack to put him at ease, "Relax, Lieutenant these are not women in the absolute sense. They are hard core medical professionals who are wholly unattractive *while in uniform*."

The two nurses smiled, ignored the inuendo and stayed above the conversation. Instead, they focused on the progress of the test results and made appropriate notations in the chart.

Nurse D'Aloia asked Jack, "Lieutenant, what was the cause of this penetration wound on your right calf?

"It turned out to be a piece of shrapnel about the size of a pinky fingernail."

She made a note of that information, then asked, "Who, may I ask, located this tiny piece of shrapnel and who performed the surgery to remove it? There is little evidence of sutures, and the incision and removal of the sutures appear very professional."

Jack thought about not revealing the names of the doctor and his nurse until they were truly liberated by the allies but decided that they would be protected and received assurances from "Doc".

"It was done by a Doctor Jacques Jansen assisted by his Nurse,

Susan Heymans. This was at the Clinique Médicale Hospital St Joseph D'Arlon. They both snuck me into the clinic at great risk to themselves."

Doctor Meyers agreed that whoever treated Jack's wounds did a first-class professional job. He made a note to share this team's name with Military Intelligence for their protection and for recognition and an award of appreciation.

Meyers examined all of Jack's vitals, including neurological evaluations, especially as they applied to balance and coordination. He concluded by asking Jack to stand on one leg with his eyes closed to see if he would lose his balance.

"Well, Lieutenant, you've passed the Romberg test with flying colors. Did you study for this test or do you simply like standing on one leg for long periods of time with your eyes closed?"

Again, more subtle laughter from the two ANC professionals. Nurse Terry Griffin understood that the Romberg test was looking for balance issues but asked the doctor for a more scientific explanation.

He turned to Jack and said, "Why don't you tell her, Lieutenant?"

Before he could answer, a laughing Nurse D'aloia turned to Nurse Griffin and responded, "As Lieutenant Dodds will surely tell you, the Romberg test measures a person's sense of balance and proprioception by comparing standing with eyes open and closed. It can diagnose sensory ataxia, central vertigo, and head trauma, but it is not quantitative or reliable. Wouldn't you say so Lieutenant Dodds?"

Jack said, "Yes, I agree completely except I need a little help with explaining proprioception, sensory ataxia and the rest of all that stuff."

Nurse D'Aloia started to explain, "Proprioception is the feature mediated by proprioceptors, which are sensory receptors and..."

She stopped when she saw the doctor grinning ear to ear, "Oh, Screw it, Doc! You're just messing with us poor little nurses. Let's pass this guy and head into Le Mans for a drink at the Officer's Club."

Meyers laughed and turned to Jack, "What do you say, Lieutenant? I think you can stumble into an airplane and do a halfway decent job of flying against the Krauts. Get yourself dressed and let's head into the Hotel and the Officer's club. Any questions?"

Jack, a bit stunned asked, "You mean there really is an Officer's club?"

Doc Meyers turned to the two nurses and smiled, "I think our boy here is catching on. C'mon ladies, last one into the Jeep is a rotten egg."

With that, Doc Meyers, Nurse D'Aloia and Nurse Griffin made whooping noises as they headed towards the front door of the Quonset hut. Suddenly, Meyers snapped his fingers and turned to Jack,

"In case you didn't get it, Lieutenant Dodds, you passed your physical with flying colors. You are cleared to get into the aircraft and fly around, impressing everybody with your skills and kills. Now, unless you want to meet the CO and other brass in your boxer shorts, I suggest you get dressed and meet us outside. Our Jeep awaits you."

Just then 1st Lieutenant Bob Murphy stepped into the room with a big smile, "You go ahead with the Nurses, Captain Meyers, I will help our boy here relearn how to tie a tie."

Twenty minutes later, Jack and Murph climbed into a jeep and headed into downtown Le Mans.

CHAPTER 118

Friday, September 15, 1944, Hôtel Concordia Le Mans "Meet & Greet"

Murphy and Jack arrived in their Jeep in front of the Hotel in the Old Town section of Le Mans. Two MPs pointed them towards a parking spot, and they parked and got out.

Jack looked at the entrance to this magnificent old hotel and remarked,

"Wow! This is one beautiful old hotel. This is where we are staying?"

Murphy laughed, "No sorry, old boy. This is where the brass are staying. Doc Meyers and the Nurses are also staying here. You and I and the rest of the squadron are staying in those last two Quonset huts running alongside the runway back out at the field."

Jack laughed, "I thought this might be too good to be true. So why, exactly are we here then?"

"We are here so the senior guys can formally welcome you back from behind enemy lines. After which, they will settle down for a delicious dinner, and you and I will return to the mess hall and join up with the rest of the guys.

"Well, I actually would prefer to be with the squadron, and I don't care if we are in a Quonset hut or anywhere else."

"Good, because as the Allied forces advance, there's always the possibility that the 357th will relocate to an advanced temporary airfield as well. This place here at Le Mans is pretty good and you'll like it."

They entered the main lobby of the hotel and were shown to the large meeting hall where they were warmly greeted by 357 Group Commander, Lieutenant Colonel John Spicer, Deputy Group Commander Lieutenant Colonel William McKenna and Operations Officer, Lieutenant Colonel Thomas Graham.

After jack shook everyone's hands, Lieutenant Colonel Spicer smiled,

"Lieutenant Dodds, we are delighted to have you back with us. Our men have just returned from today's mission, they are debriefing right now back at the field and the ground crews are readying their aircraft for tomorrow's missions. They are looking forward to seeing you for chow, so we won't keep you very long. Just a quick greeting from all the command staff and one little extra event."

Spicer looked at Murphy who smiled and handed him an envelope. The Colonel opened the envelope and removed the silver First Lieutenant Bar, signaling Jack to move closer to him. He deftly removed the gold-colored 2nd Lieutenant bar from Jack's uniform shirt and replaced it with the First Lieutenant Bar. Standing back from Jack, the Colonel smiled and saluted,

"Welcome back 1st Lieutenant John Dodds! Now you go fly with the team and kick some German Ass."

Everyone present returned Jack's salute and with that, Murph started to lead Jack back out to the Jeep. But the Colonel was not quite done,

"Hold on just a moment, 1st Lieutenant Murphy. I think I may have forgotten something." He made a show of searching through his pockets until Operations Officer, Lieutenant Colonel Graham stepped forward and handed him another similar envelope. Lieutenant Colonel Spicer smiled again,

"Almost forgot this. 1st Lieutenant Murphy please step forward."

A stunned Murphy stepped up to the Colonel who removed his 1st Lieutenant bar and replaced it with the double bars signifying the rank of Captain.

"Congratulations, Captain Robert Murphy. Now you go with 1st Lieutenant Dodds here and *you* kick some German Ass."

Murphy laughed, smiled and saluted, "Yessir!"

After much hand shaking and back slapping, Murphy and Jack climbed back into the Jeep and made it out to the field just as the chow-lines were opening.

When Jack walked in, everything stopped, there was a great uproar of jeering, cat calls and laughter as the 357th welcomed one of their own back home.

CHAPTER 119

Saturday, September 16, 1944, 357th Fighter Squadron Jack Back in the Saddle Forward Airbase Le Mans

Dawn at the airfield found Jack in the cockpit of a P-51D running through the pre-flight checklist while the maintenance crew below ran through their own checks. Darkness was giving way to daylight when Seargeant Jan Rogowski the crew chief climbed up on the wing. Rogowski, a member of the Polish Air Corps contingent spoke with heavily accented English which, to Jack's ear sounded something like this: "How's it go-ink, Lieutenant? "Every-think" look good down here."

Jack smiled, he was getting used to this likeable sergeant's accent, "Good, thanks, Sergeant. Just trying to get familiar with this K-14 gunsight. I was used to the N-3B reflector sights. I guess I'll figure it out."

"Yes, you figure it out okay. No doubt. You had three kills already when you took time behind enemy lines," He laughed then continued, "But everybody like this new sight. You will like too."

"Thanks, Sergeant. I guess I'm ready to start this bird up and get up over the channel to do some air work.

"Roger Lieutenant! We stand by."

Within a few moments, Jack ran through the checklists, fired up the Merlin Engine and clicked his microphone button three times. The clicks were acknowledged with three clicks coming from the handheld microphone by one of the two sergeants acting as controllers in the portable wooden tower in the middle of the field.

Brand new Captain, Bob Murphy had already completed his preflight and warm-up and clicked his readiness to fly "wing" on Jack's P-51 and would observe Jack going through his maneuvers and familiarization flight.

The tower controllers were aware of the dual Mustang flight preparing to taxi and fly out to a designated training area over the English Channel. The protocol before a major mission launch was to keep radio communications to an absolute minimum, hence the "Mike clicks"

The controller directed his powerful signal light towards Jack's Mustang and then Murphy's P-51, gave them a steady green light for about 15 seconds. Jack started taxiing to the "run-up" area and once there, spun his Mustang around into the wind and ran the engine through the required series of checks.

Murphy did the same and awaited Jack's signal that he was ready for takeoff.

Satisfied that everything checked out okay, Jack clicked his mike twice followed by another two clicks. He got the flashing green light, and he taxied into position slightly to the left of an imaginary centerline with Murphy getting into position slightly to the right.

Both pilots were given a steady green light, meaning "okay to take-off."

Jack's P-51 accelerated quickly down the northbound runway and within seconds, Jack was airborne, wheels up and into a climbing turn with Murphy tight by to his right, flying wing. Both pilots climbing in formation heading west towards the designated practice area over the English Channel.

Once he reached ten thousand feet, Murphy called Jack, "Okay Jack, I'm moving out of your way while you run through the maneuvers delegated for your work-out. When you're done, we will do some formation maneuvers with you on my wing this time."

Jack responded, "Roger. Here goes."

He executed a series of 45-degree steep turns left and right and was pleased that he still had "the touch", rolling out precisely on the compass heading he had when he entered into the maneuver each time.

Next, he did some "slow flight" with and without flaps and landing gear, some power on and power off stalls, and was ready to do some formation flying with Murphy and then return to base and do some "touch and go's" and landings to a full stop. He was enjoying the feel of this remarkable aircraft when Murphy's voice broke in,

"Coming up on your Six, Jack. Maintain your heading." And within seconds, there he was in his P-51D,

"Line up on my right wing, Jack and let's do a little formation flying and simulated attacks in tandem."

For the next half-hour the two aircraft performed in tight formation, climbing, diving, turning in either direction in perfect concert. Murphy's voice came back on,

"Okay. You're good. Follow me back to base and we'll do a low pass, break left over the runway, and I will make a complete full stop, and you can do a series of touch and goes."

"Roger!"

For the next 45 minutes, after Murphy's full stop landing, Jack practiced his "touch-and-go" landings, which meant bringing the aircraft down and making a perfect landing on the main gear but accelerating for another rolling take-off before allowing the tailwheel to touch down.

On his last approach, the tower operator called him to request that this be his final landing and to report to Operations. After landing and taxiing to his tie-down area, he waited for Sergeant Rogowski's signal to "cut-engine" and shut it down. Within seconds the Sergeant was up on the wing and assisted him in unstrapping and exiting the cockpit.

When they were both on the ground, Rogowski smiled and said, "You 'look-een' good, Lieutenant! Nice 'land inks' now report to Operations."

Jack laughed and thanked the sergeant. He noticed that the squadron was mounting their Mustangs and that a mission was about to be underway. Excited, he prepared to rush over to Operations to see if he was going along. As he turned to leave, Rogowski called to him.

"Lieutenant, I receive permission from Captain Murphy to place three dead German swastikas on aircraft. I know you will get two more soon and then I place more dead German swastikas on aircraft. I also have permission for you to name aircraft. What name you like?"

Jack smiled and laughed out loud as he prepared to run over to Operations,

“Great! Thanks, Sergeant! How about ‘Ellen’s Cowboy’ that would be great, got it?”

Rogowski replied that he got it, but, as it turned out, he didn’t quite get it exactly the way Jack said it.

CHAPTER 120

Saturday, September 16, 1944, 357th Fighter Squadron Operations Brief Forward Airbase Le Mans

Jack entered the front door of the Quonset hut marked **"357 FG Command Center".** The place was a virtual "beehive" of activity, enlisted men and several officers busy going over charts, speaking on several telephone lines and one or two wearing earphones communicating with people by radio.

He approached one enlisted man with his head buried in a map and asked if he knew where he was to go and who he was to see. Startled out of his intense concentration, the corporal looked up quickly and took in Jack's nametag.

"Oh! Good morning, Lieutenant Dodds. Hold on one moment, sir, let me check for you." The young corporal picked up the phone and spoke to someone, then nodded and hung up. "Sir, if you would go down this hall and enter the first room on your left, Lieutenant Colonel Graham is waiting there for you."

Jack thanked him and soon found himself standing in front of a door marked **Lieutenant Colonel Thomas Graham, 357 Operations Officer**.

He knocked and a gruff voice inside said, "Come." He entered and saluted Graham, "Second Lieutenant John Dodds, Sir."

Graham smiled and returned the salute, "Relax Jack, at ease. I realize we just bestowed the upgrade on you last night, but it's '*First Lieutenant'* Dodds now, isn't it?" He laughed, pointed at a chair in front of his desk and walked around his desk taking a seat opposite him.

"We're a bit more informal at these Forward Airbases, unless of course some General or other Big Wig shows up. How did it feel getting back into the Mustang?"

"Excellent, sir, absolutely excellent."

"I thought you'd take right back to it, kinda like riding a bicycle, right?"

Jack smiled and gave him a "thumbs up" but before he could respond, Graham got serious,

"Jack, just so you know up until a few months ago we would not have been able to put you back in the cockpit. There was a very strict rule prohibiting airmen who returned from behind enemy lines from getting back into service. Did you ever get to know Chuck Yeager?"

"No, sir. I've heard of him but never met him."

"You will definitely meet him. He's at another forward airbase right now but raising Holy Hell among the Krauts. Last March on his 8th mission, he and Group commander Col. Henry Spicer were both shot down. Spicer was captured, but Yeager was helped by the Maquis, resistance and ultimately made it back to England just this past May."

"Oh, that's terrific! He obviously got permission to return to active duty, I assume."

Graham laughed, "Oh he got permission all right, from none other than General Dwight David Eisenhower himself!"

"The Supreme Allied Commander?"

"Yes, none other. He bugged 'Ike' so much that he finally relented in June and Chuck is out there kicking ass. You hopefully will get to meet him and his 'ride', *Glamorous Glen,* his assigned P-51D apparently named after his girlfriend. The point of all of this, Jack is the concern that if Yeager or you or another 'evader' gets shot down again behind enemy lines the Krauts may torture information about the resistance out of you."

"Yes, sir I can see that would be a concern." He wondered where this was going, but Graham continued,

"British Intelligence, especially MI-9 through their own channels have alerted all of the people you may have encountered that we're putting our valuable assets back into the air. They have assured the Brits and us that they have taken the necessary precautions to protect their people. So, Jack please try not to get your ass shot down again, Okay?"

Jack laughed, "Yessir! Will do."

Graham stood to signal that the meeting was ending, but smiled, "Now, we don't have the ability with all the air traffic over the channel to give you the opportunity to do some actual shooting practice. Still, get with Murphy who is an expert with the newly installed K-14 gunsights. They're almost intuitive and you will come to love the technology. For your first missions, we're going to put you onto raids into Holland and keep you away from Germany for at least a little while. So, like we said last night at the hotel, go kick some Kraut ass. Dismissed, *First* Lieutenant. And fly safe, Jack."

Graham returned Jack's salute and walked him to the door.

"Go over to the main room here and get one of the Intelligence officers to go over the current Allied lines, the status of our offensive and what our current objectives are."

"Yes sir, will do."

Jack spent an hour with 'Intel' and got a feel for the locations of the front lines and what his Flight Group were doing. It was approaching lunch time, and he realized from the growling sounds emanating from his stomach that he forgot to eat breakfast in his excitement to get back into the Mustang.

He got into line at the food commissary and took a seat with his ground crew. He noticed that Sergeant Jan Rogowski wasn't there and was just about to inquire as to his whereabouts, when he came in, got on the "chow-line' and took a seat across from Jack.

Rogowski smiled, parked a Brownie hand-held camera on the table in front of him and said, "Loo-ten-ant! Wait till you see your bird! One of our kids is excellent artist and your bird is decorated and ready to roll. I have Brownie camera to take pictures for you."

Jack grew very excited and said, "Sounds terrific, Sergeant! As soon as you've finished your lunch, let's go out there and take some pictures."

Sergeant Rogowski wolfed down his food and grabbed his Brownie camera and said, "We go!". They exited the building, got into Rogowski's jeep and drove over to Jack's Mustang. A young corporal smiled and held a sheet over the nose cowling so Jack couldn't see it immediately.

As they approached the aircraft, Jack was able to see his name stenciled just under the cockpit entrance, "1st Lieutenant J. Dodds" and broke out in a big smile.

Rogowski instructed the corporal to remove the sheet which he did with great dramatic flourish revealing a large cartoon sign bearing the title, "Ellie's Cowboy" in cartoon letters across the cowling.

Jack kept the big smile frozen on his face. He didn't have the heart to correct Rogowski's misunderstanding of "Ellen" as opposed to "Ellie." Instead, he thought to himself, *Maybe Ellen will change her name to Ellie.*

As he posed for the camera in front of the Mustang it would later turn out that, much to his surprise, she did.

CHAPTER 121

September through November 1944
18 September 1944: Mission 639 Mighty 8th Air Force 357th Fighter Squadron
Jack on the Attack Forward Airbase Le Mans

Dawn was just appearing in the Eastern sky. Jack was officially on his first mission since climbing back in the cockpit of the P-51. He wouldn't ever admit it, as he taxied out onto the runway at Le Mans, but he was as nervous "as a cat."

He was positioned just to the right side of the runway as Bob Murphy readied himself just slightly forward and to his left. The nervous tremors dissipated once he poured the power to the big Rolls-Royce Merlin engine and "Ellie's Cowboy" together with Murphy's "Lucky Lady" leapt forward down the runway.

Both P-51s entered a steep, climbing left turn in perfect unison with Jack tucked right in on Murphy's right wing. They joined with other members of their squadron forming up at twenty thousand feet over the English Channel.

This was going to be an immense mission. Their squadron would soon join with over 500 other fighter escorts which included P-38s, P-47s, and their group of P-51s protecting 248 B-24s and a flight of C-47s.

The B-24s were preparing to drop supplies to the First Allied Airborne Army in the Netherlands. The C-47s carried the second troop echelon to be dropped into the Netherlands to join the heavy fighting around the Arnhem area.

Jack's fighter group strafed rail and highway traffic while other fighters bombed flak positions. Over 100 Luftwaffe fighters entered the fray and Jack, and the others didn't have time to think or worry about anything other than staying alive and killing the enemy.

Amid the melee, Jack saw a BF-109 lining up on another P-51 and rolled hard left for a long 300-yard deflection shot. He fired a controlled burst of his six 50 caliber Brownings and observed his burst walking up the nose of his target and into the cockpit.

He didn't have time to rejoice at his 4th kill as several rounds of 20 MM cannon fire whizzed past his cockpit from another BF-109 who jumped on his tail.

Jack turned hard right, with the Messerschmidt turning hard with him and soon the two aircraft were engaged in a tight right-turning circle known as the "Lufbery Circle."The two enemy combatants were both attempting to get in firing position on their opponent's tail.

Jack did not like this "knife-fight" tactic especially in the midst of all the other dogfights going on and so he suddenly rolled sharply left, catching the inexperienced German pilot off guard. No sooner did he do this than he rolled right again and had an excellent deflection shot at the BF-109 who moments before had been on his tail.

He watched his tracers walk onto the German's aircraft and was surprised to see another group of tracers coming from another P-51 who had jumped into the fray to protect Jack. Before he could identify his fellow P-51 driver, the Messerschmidt burst into flames and exploded.

Jack returned to Le Mans at the conclusion of this "free-for-all" and was number ten to circle and land. As he shut down his engine, he was helped to unstrap in the cockpit by an enthusiastic Sergeant Rogowski, "Look like Eileen's Cowboy saw some action today Loo-tenant. We fix her up okay. Do not look seer-e-us. You okay, Loo-tenant?"

Jack smiled and thought, *I'm starting to understand this guy.* Then he laughed, "Yes, Sergeant, I'm okay."

When he stepped out of the cockpit onto the wing, his legs almost gave out from under him, and he quickly grabbed onto the side of the cockpit to steady himself. Embarrassed, he stood there for a moment to regain strength in his legs before descending the rest of the way to the ground. Rogowski had seen this before in returning pilots who had been engaged in life-or-death aerial dogfights. He moved close to his pilot, protecting him from the sight of others, "It is okay, Loo-tenant.

No worry. Happen to everyone. Take breath."

Jack nodded his head and suddenly turned away from Rogowski as he vomited onto the ground. The Sergeant looked away from his pilot as did the other members of the ground crew who had all seen this before.

Just then, a smiling Murphy pulled up in his Jeep, "Hey, Ace! Quit the dramatics and get your ass in here we have to debrief."

CHAPTER 122

September through November 1944
18 September 1944: Mission 639, 357th Fighter Squadron Mission 639 Debrief Forward Airbase Le Mans

The men of the 357th took their seats and talked amongst themselves. Jack sat next to Murphy who was in constant motion, asking and answering questions from the guys in the squadron.

Jack just sat back and took some deep breaths, trying to get his heartbeat down and relax his tightened leg muscles and lower back. It started to dawn on him that he almost certainly could claim one BF-109 and possibly a second one which would put him over the top with 5 kills making him an Ace. He tried not to think about it.

He looked up to the front of the room and saw 357 Group Commander Lieutenant Colonel John Spicer, and Operations Officer Lieutenant Colonel Thomas Graham huddled together.

After a few minutes passed by, Lieutenant Graham signaled Major Joe Carson, 362nd Fighter Squadron and newly appointed Captain Bob Murphy, 363rd Fighter Squadron up to the front with them. Jack noticed Murphy and Carson reading from something on a clipboard and looking his way, several times and Murphy smiling and nodding his head over something that Carson said.

The "Brass" took their seats facing the men and Major Carson took over. Jack's nervousness heightened as he was sure to be singled out as a brand-new Ace and just wasn't sure how he would react. Major Carson called everyone to order, and the room got quiet.

"Okay gentlemen, here is the after-action report on Mission 639. Initial B-24 force was 252 with 4 returning to base with maintenance issues. 7 B-24s down, 6 damaged beyond repair and 154 damaged. 1

airman is KIA, killed in action, 26 WIA wounded in action and 61 MIA missing in action."

"As you guys know we had greater than 500 fighter escorts comprised of P-38s, P-47s and our P-51s coming from 377th FG and us at the 357th. We thoroughly pissed off the Krauts who sent up over 100 BF-109s and a bunch of Würgers."

He smiled and added, "For those of you who have been 'out of touch' hiding behind enemy lines, drinking Belgian beer a Würger is just our affectionate way of describing the beloved Focke-Wulf 190." There was a breakout of laughter as everyone turned to look at Jack.

Carson then got serious, "Okay, here's the bad news. We lost three of our own, Joe Pollock, John Beaudoin and Paul Gaucher. We believe that they all got out of their aircraft, as we observed chutes deployed. That's all we know for now. They are currently listed among the 20 MIAs.

The bottom line here is that out of 500 fighter escorts deployed, the Allies lost 20, 9 damaged beyond repair and 46 damaged. I don't have the breakdown of which types are which. We had one pilot KIA, killed in action, still waiting on more details there and as I said before 20 MIA, missing in action."

He handed the clipboard to Murphy who flipped the page and started in,

"The good news is that the AAF claims 29 enemy aircraft in the air and several on the ground. Our own Jack Dodds on his first mission back with us is credited with taking down one BF-109 which we verified, and he gets credit for ½ of another BF-109 which is a shared kill with 2nd Lieutenant Joe Pollock, who as you know bailed out of his aircraft after it caught fire. So that puts 1st Lieutenant John, 'Jack' Dodds' one half of a Kraut short of an Ace."

The group which had been subdued at the news of the KIA, and MIAs whooped a bit for Jack and were interrupted by Colonel Graham who smiled and waved his hand for them to be silent.

Murphy continued, "Okay, men, let's not get too carried away or Dodd's head might explode."

The meeting broke up after that, and a very subdued Jack headed back over to look at any damage that "Ellie's Cowboy" incurred from his "go-around with the other BF-109. He was not thinking about almost becoming an Ace, he was only thinking about Joe Pollock, John Beaudoin and Paul Gaucher and hoping that they would be okay.

CHAPTER 123

18 September 1944, Leaving Michel family refuge

On the same day that Jack flew his first combat mission after his return, Denise met with Raoul, Maria, Emil and Miep to discuss Ellen's "Situation." It was decided that the safest and best place for her to go through her pregnancy would be as close to Brussels as possible.

The family was still in deep mourning over the news that, despite the best efforts of the medical teams attending to Lucien in England, he developed a severe, uncontrollable infection and succumbed to his wounds. Because of the War, no one from the family was able to attend his funeral and burial. There would be many memorial services and plaques for him and for all the brave men and women in the Resistance who fought against the Nazis.

The family now shifted their attention and their love for Ellen's care and the pressing need to move her to a safe place. Emil, ever pragmatic, pointed out that the Chicken House had been successfully reopened for Lucien and was now available. Both he and Miep insisted that Ellen accompany them there and take up residence. There was greatly improved access to medical care and other support from the neighbors, including Father Catron, Mother Philomena and others.

Denise felt that Elise, Jan and Nadine would also benefit from the availability of school through the good offices of Father Catron. Raoul and Maria seconded the idea for Nadine. Once this course of action was decided upon, things moved quickly. Emil drove into town and asked Byron Champagne for his help to which he readily agreed. Using Byron's telephone, he called Father Catron's Church office and spoke with Magda DeVries who promised to send someone over to the house to ensure that all would be ready for their arrival.

At the conclusion of the call, Byron pulled his Renault around and followed Emil back out to the refuge. Within two hours, they were packed, said their goodbyes, promised to stay in close touch and then they were on their way to the Chicken House in Sante-Walburg near Liege.

Two hours later, as they pulled up to the Chicken House, they saw a smiling Father Catron and Magda Devries opening the garage door for them. Once they were unloaded and everything was placed in the guestrooms upstairs, they sat in the great room and caught up with one another.

Father Catron smiled and handed Ellen an envelope addressed to him and marked with the stamp of the United States Military Armed Forces Postal Services. She smiled, looked at him and he encouraged her to open it.

"It's really for you. Jack did not know how to address a letter to you at the refuge, so he entrusted me with that job. I am so glad you're here, because I was not able to immediately head out to deliver it to you. It just arrived today. Don't worry, there's nothing in there too personal."

They all watched Ellen as she read Jack's note and then, to her surprise, a photograph popped out showing Jack in front of a P-51 Mustang with the nose-art proclaiming "Ellie's Cowboy" on it. Ellen was absolutely flabbergasted by this photo, she cried out with a mixture of joy and confusion, "*Ellie's* Cowboy? Why *Ellie* and not Ellen's Cowboy I wonder?"

Emil offered an explanation, "Maybe another pilot had an 'Ellen' on his airplane?"

A whole host of different ideas followed, but then all of them just smiled and focused on the picture of US Army Air Corps Lieutenant Jack Dodds in his flight suit standing proudly in front of a magnificent P-51 Mustang aircraft with a big smile on his face.

Laughing, Ellen shrugged her shoulders and said, "From now on my name will be Ellie." They all laughed, but didn't realize that Ellen, now "Ellie" was serious.

An overall atmosphere of good humor and hope for the future prevailed. This feeling of happiness would not last long as they, like most Belgians failed to realize that the Nazis still had a reign of terror planned for Belgium with the V1 and V2 attacks. Had they fully appreciated the danger they were heading into, they might have opted to remain in Bouillon.

Of course, as they would later relate in their reflections after the war, "hindsight is always 20-20" and they would have also faced a reign of terror in December of 1944 during the Nazis' last offensive in the Ardennes known as the "Battle of the Bulge.

CHAPTER 124

October through December 1944, V1 &V-2 Terror-Belgium, Bomb Shelter hidden underneath Emil's Chicken House Sante-Walburg, Belgium

On 18 December 1944, three months passed after leaving the Michel family refuge. After arriving in Sante-Walburg at the Chicken House, the entire group felt happy that they were now relatively safe in liberated Belgium. There were occasional blasts from these infernal "Rocket Bombs", V1s but they seemed to be focused way to the west on the entrance into the port of Antwerp.

Most Belgians felt that the Nazis would be defeated, and the war would come to an end by the end of 1944. They did not know that the Nazis had another, even more terrible secret weapon of terror: the V2 ballistic missile

The Allies realized as early as 1943 that the Nazis were working on "Weapons of Terror" designed to demoralize the civilian populations and military personnel as well. In August of 1943, Allied intelligence discovered that these weapons were being developed and tested at a base in Peenemünde, near the Baltic Sea. They launched an enormous attack involving over 600 Allied bombers which, while it left the test center mostly intact, caused the Nazis to realize that they had been discovered and there would be more attacks.

In response, in January 1944, the German Supreme Command decided to transfer the production of V-weapons to an underground complex near Nordhausen. This was where the infamous Mittelbau-Dora concentration camp was established, and forced labor was put to work excavating mineshafts that already existed.

Post-war Allied intelligence revealed that more than 60,000 prisoners were forced to work there under indescribable conditions. It was estimated that over 20,000 prisoners died of malnutrition, disease, work related accidents or harsh punishment for failure to achieve goals.

Antwerp became a major target of the Nazis due to its function as a primary port of entry for the Allied logistics supplying the war effort. V1 bombs were launched from catapult ramps mostly located in parts of France and areas west of the Netherlands still held by the Nazis. The V2s were initially launched from launching bases and bunkers in northern France, but were switched to mobile units in the Netherlands after the Allies discovered the fixed sites and attacked them with great success.

Post war analysis revealed that more than 22,000 V1s were fired. Over 6,000 reached England and approximately 7,000 fell within Belgium. 11,000 victims of whom 4,000 were Belgians were claimed by these V1 bombs, the first weapons of Mass Destruction.

The V2 attacks numbered about 4,000, 1,135 hit England and 1,664 Rockets fell into Belgium with 1,610 on Antwerp. Approximately 3,000 Belgians and others were killed and 3,000 victims in England.

Instead of enjoying relative peace and comfort back in the spacious, bright upper rooms at the Chicken House, the family spent most of their daylight hours in the well-constructed bomb shelter beneath the house, worrying about the V1 Bombs and still unaware of the V2s.

Father Catron's School did not offer adequate shelter from these attacks and therefore most of his students were secured in better shelters. Despite all of the fear and concern on the part of the adult populace, the teenagers, Jan, Elise and Nadine often plead with Denise for an opportunity to go to a popular movie house in Antwerp called the Rex Cinema.

"They show Cowboy Westerns there! In English with French subtitles," Jan and Elise pleaded, "We can all practice our English."

She kept shaking her head, "Not yet, children. It is not yet safe. Soon it will be safe for you to go."

On 16 December 1944, they received a surprise visit from their friend, the pharmacist, Byron Champagne. Byron dropped off some much-needed medical supplies and told them that he was meeting a woman friend to go the Rex theater in Antwerp to see a "Cowboy Western".

He laughingly invited Ellen, now "Ellie" and the teenagers to accompany him and his date. He had also invited Father Catron, who, at first agreed but then had to decline due to some pressing issues that had just cropped up at the parish.

Finally, Denise shrugged her shoulders and relented. Most of the V1 and V2 attacks were well west of the city of Antwerp aimed at the port itself. She waved goodbye to them as they piled into Byron's Renault and set out to pick up his girlfriend. After they departed, she helped Emil and Miep tend to their growing flock of chickens which kept her mind off her concerns for their safety. After an hour had passed, she settled into working with her friends, laughing at Emil's corny jokes.

Their laughter ended abruptly when they looked up and saw an ashen-faced Father Catron and a weeping Magda DeVries standing in the entrance to the chicken coops within the Chicken House warehouse section.

Denise cried out, "What? What has happened?"

Father Catron spoke in a shattered voice, "The Rex theatre has been bombed by one of these 'flying trees', a V2 bomb. There are a lot of casualties. Did the children and Ellen go with…"

He didn't finish his question when Denise let out a scream of terror and collapsed to the ground.

CHAPTER 125

October through December 1944
357th Fighter Squadron Mission 639 Debrief, Forward Airbase Le Mans

December 1944. 1st Lieutenant Jack Dodds flew a total of 21 combat missions in the previous two months of October, and November 1944. He was credited with two "Kills" in each month which officially made him an Ace with 8 confirmed kills.

Jack also had one half of a kill shared with another airman, 2nd Lieutenant Joe Pollock who was listed as MIA after bailing out of his P-51 on 18 September 1944 Mission number 639.

His crew chief, Sergeant Jan Rogowski proudly added the Swastika emblems to "Ellie's Cowboy" each time a downed German airplane was credited to Jack. For Jack's part, he was unaffected by the notion that he was now officially an "Ace" with five plus "Kills." His goal was simply to do his duty and hoped that the war would soon be ended both here in Europe and out in the Pacific against the Japanese.

He received a letter from Ellen, who now called herself "Ellie." She described their return to Sante-Walburg and to Emil's Chicken House. Ellie was so joyful at receiving his picture standing in front of his P-51. He could almost hear her laughter when he wrote previously explaining how Rogowski screwed up the names.

The biggest "bombshell" for Jack was Ellie's announcement that she was pregnant. She hadn't seen a doctor yet, but the older women in the family estimated that she was 4 months along with a birth in mid to late Spring, 1945.

Despite his anxiety about her safety and the safety of her surrounding family and close-knit friends, Jack felt that Emil's bomb shelter would provide adequate protection and was glad that she was safely ensconced there.

That all changed when recent intelligence briefings alerted the pilots to the presence of the V1 and V2 attacks on the Port of Antwerp and on Liege where his loved one was currently living.

During the first two weeks of December 1944, he and his fighter group were assigned the task of escorting the bombers and assisting them in hitting marshalling yards, bridges and targets of opportunity inside of Germany.

Together with Ninth Air Force assets he and his squadron escorted the RAF, divebombed targets in cities and supported the 3rd Armored Division in the Echtz-Geich area, the 104th Infantry Division at Merken, the 9th Infantry Division at Merode and Derichsweiler, and the 83rd Infantry Division at Strass.

On the 14 December, bad weather grounded the bombers, so Jack joined with other fighters to fly armed reconnaissance, hitting rail targets and bridges and provided support for the US 2nd and 99th Infantry divisions in the Monschau Forest, the 8th Infantry Division in the Bergstein area, the 78th Infantry division in the Simmerath-Resternich area and the XII and XX Corps around Habkirchen and Saarlautern.

Each night after his operations debriefs, he would chow down with the men, check with his ground crew and sit down to write Ellie a letter. He wasn't sure how many she would receive, but it felt good expressing his love for her and letting her know what he was doing. His letters were careful not to reveal anything that might trigger the censors to prevent it from being sent.

16 December, was the same day of the V2 attack that hit the Rex theater in Antwerp and was the beginning of the Battle of the Bulge, called *Unternehman* Wacht am Rhein in German with meant "Operation Watch on the Rhein. Jack and the men of the 357th were not yet aware of both events and the loss of life associated with each.

Bad weather canceled the 9th Air Force bombardments and caused many aborts for the 8th Air Force as well. Fighters from both the 8th and the 9th Air Force did their best to support US First Army elements in the Ardennes in Belgium as Field Marshall Gerd con Rundstedt continued with his all-out counter offensive.

CHAPTER 126

16 December 1944, Rex Theater Disaster at De Keyserlei 15 Antwerp, Belgium

At 3:00 PM a frustrated Byron Champagne cursed under his breath and pulled over to the side of the road in the little town just north of Antwerp. He handed his written instructions to his new girlfriend, Linda's home to Ellie, sitting in the front passenger seat of the Renault. She laughed and gave him a gentle jab,

"So typical of all of you men, so stubborn. If you had just given me these instructions a half hour ago, we would already have found your girlfriend Linda's apartment and we would be eating popcorn and candy in our seats by now."

The three teenagers in the rear seat chimed in, Jan speaking the loudest, "It's already too late! Gary Cooper and Jean Arthur were supposed to kick off the cinema at 2:30 and it's now 3:00 PM"

Byron felt guilty but defended his actions, "I still think we will be okay. Several of my friends told me that even though the cinema is supposed to start at 2:30, it never does. They said the theater shows a movie reel of the progress of the Allied armies and their battles against the Germans and they really didn't get going until a little after three PM. We're only ten minutes away."

Just then, Ellie who had been studying the map cried out, "Byron you are right! We are just a few minutes away. Pull up to this next corner and turn right."

Within 5 minutes they pulled up to the front door of the apartment indicated in Linda's notes. Three things happened in quick succession:

Byron beeped the horn to alert Linda they had arrived,
Linda ran out with a big smile on her face,
and Ellie threw up.

Shocked, they all looked at Ellie who got out of the car and was dry heaving on the side of the road, trying to talk at the same time, "Sorry, sorry, sorry! I don't know what came over me. One minute I was fine and the next, I was overcome with nausea."

Elise and Nadine quickly got out of the car and went over to Ellie. Elise handed her a handkerchief while Nadine rubbed her back as Ellie continued to gag. Up until this point no one said hello to Linda who had gone a bit pale herself.

Byron spoke up, "Everyone, this is Linda. Linda, this is everyone. And the one throwing up is my dear friend, Ellen, who now goes by the name, Ellie. Ellie is 5 months pregnant, and her husband is off fighting the Krauts."

Linda, to her credit, laughed and said to Ellie and the girls, "Nice to meet you all, now let's get this poor woman into the house. I am a student nurse in training, and I have seen this form of nausea many times in pregnant women. It is sometimes called 'Morning Sickness' but doesn't necessarily happen just in the morning as we see here. There is no way Ellie should be sitting in a movie theatre right now."

Everyone except Jan and Byron agreed with this assessment. That is to say, all the *women* present agreed. The two guys groaned. Being rather thick-headed at moments like this, they even contemplated going to the theater without the women but, common sense and an instinct for self-preservation prevailed. They correctly decided that they would never live it down if they displayed such insensitive behavior.

Ellie protested, "No, please just give me a moment. I don't want to ruin your afternoon. I like Gary Cooper… I should be okay. Perhaps a drink of cold water might help?" With that, she gagged again, and Linda took charge.

"Yes, of course. Let's go into my apartment. My mother is there, and she will have some suggestions for you. After all she has given birth to eight children."

Byron and Jan shrugged their shoulders in defeat. Byron parked the Renault and set the parking brake. They went inside with Linda, Ellie and the two teenage girls. With all the commotion as they entered the apartment and greeted Linda's mother, they did not hear the distant thunder coming from the Rex theater as it suffered a direct hit by a V2 rocket bomb with 1,120 people inside.

As it turned out, Ellie's "Morning Sickness" did more than just prevent them from seeing Gary Cooper and Jean Arthur in the "*Plainsman*" it saved all their lives.

The V2 Rocket launched that afternoon by the Nazis in Hellendoorn, the Netherlands attained a height just touching the edge of space in under one minute. Just as it reached its zenith, its engine went silent, which tipped the 15 meter long 17,000-pound missile over into its downward arc. Attaining supersonic speed the V-2's terrifying plunge towards the theater below was not heard or seen at 3:20 PM as it entered the roof of the Rex Theater at three times the speed of sound, followed by the sonic boom.

The theater exploded in a blinding detonation, sending ceiling, balcony and walls tumbling inward on the theatergoers. The movie screen fell upon those in the front seats, and a suffocating cloud of pulverized cement and ceiling plaster engulfed the entire district in a blanket of powdered debris.

To those who were just outside the theater and somehow survived the explosion, at first there was silence. Then came the screams and moans of victims inside and outside the theater, many caught underneath concrete and steel. Rescuers later would find some of the victims had been sitting quietly in their seats, killed instantly by the blast wave and concussion.

To add to this "Horror Show", an enormous steam boiler used to supply heat to the theater suddenly gave way to the heat of the detonation and the boiling water within exploded, lifting the rubble pile and burning alive would-be rescuers and many of the victims who were still trapped in the rubble.

Rescuers would work for the next week in their recovery efforts. 567 people died in this devastating attack from one V2 rocket and almost another 700 were injured. The fear of this evil terror weapon would drive many Belgians out of the city. Others would spend most of their days in shelters, venturing out only when necessary. The original joy of liberation and freedom was torn to shreds by the Nazis' one last deadly onslaught.

Byron and his group of would-be movie-goers knew little of what had just happened in downtown Antwerp. They knew there had been an explosion of some kind but wouldn't realize the full horror of what occurred until days later. Because Ellie was not feeling that well, they decided to drive back to the Chicken House and introduce Byron's brand-new girlfriend, Linda, to everyone there.

Jan, ever the enthusiast cried out, "Boy, will they ever be surprised!"

And when, at the Chicken House they walked in on all their family and friends, including Father Catron all somberly gathered around a distraught Denise, it turned out that Jan was right.

CHAPTER 127

April 1945, Jack moves as Squadron Commander to 354th Fighter Group Ober-Olm Germany

1st Lieutenant John "Jack" Dodds, newly appointed Squadron Commander of the 353rd Fighter Group led his flight of P-51s to join in the attack on airfields, oil and munitions depots, and explosive plants in Central and North Germany.

During an April 7 mission, they met over 100 conventional German fighters and 50 or more of the new German jets. The Germans downed 15 heavy bombers while the Americans downed 104 German aircraft including a few jets.

Upon return to Ober-Olm on that day, Jack found out during his Operations debrief that his buddy, Captain Bob Murphy, Squadron Commander of the 355th Fighter Group had incurred some flak damage and crash-landed somewhere in Central Germany.

He, and two other P-51 pilots, were declared MIA. Jack knew that if anyone could evade capture and get picked up it would be Murph. One week later, his intuition was proved correct; Murphy was repatriated with his squadron and was recovering from some non-life-threatening injuries back in England.

By the fourth week of April 1945, Jack had flown 65 plus combat missions and was eligible for leave and transfer back to the United States. He requested deferment of a return to the States and instead asked for and was granted permission to take a one week leave to visit his pregnant wife in Liege, Belgium.

On April 30, he caught a ride on a C-54 from Ober-Olm to Brussels. When he arrived at Belgian Air Force (BAF) outpost Brussels, he used the Military Operations phone and dialed the number he had for Father Catron.

After several rings, someone answered in Dutch, but as soon as he said, "Hello?" in English, Magda DeVries laughed and said,

"Oh My God! Is this Lieutenant Jack?"

Jack laughed, "Magda? Is that you? Wow! Listen, is there anyway someone can pick me up at the joint Air Force base here in Brussels? I have some leave, and I want to go and surprise Ellen."

"Oh, do you mean, 'Ellie?', because if you do there is going to be a huge surprise."

Jack chuckled, "I know! It will be a surprise for her, Emil, Miep and the rest of the gang."

It was Magda's turn to laugh, "Oh no, Lieutenant it will be a big surprise all right, but the surprise will be on you!"

"Surprise? Did she know I was coming somehow?"

"No, Lieutenant this will be a great surprise for both of you."

Jack was losing his patience, but did not want to offend this wonderful woman, "Magda! Please can you take me to the Chicken House so I can surprise my wife? Please!"

"No, Lieutenant, I will not take you to the Chicken house to see your wife, because she is not there."

Magda was thoroughly enjoying herself as she awaited the American's reaction.

"Not there! Not there? Where is she?"

Magda laughed, "She is at the Liege Clinic giving birth to your baby. Shall I take you there?"

Magda left a note for Father Catron, climbed into her five-year-old Renault and headed to the airport. She hadn't had that much fun in a long time.

CHAPTER 128

April 30, 1944, A Child is Born, Liege University Hospital Liege, Belgium

Magda pulled her Renault into a parking spot marked "*clergy* "and put a sign in her visor that identified the name and address of the Church. As they exited the vehicle, an armed guard approached them, recognized Magda and smiled. He then looked questioningly at the US Army Air Corps Lieutenant standing next to her.

She laughed and spoke in English, "Gerard, this is Lieutenant John Dodds. He is here to surprise his wife who is in labor, Lieutenant this is my cousin, Gerard Simone."

Gerard smiled, "It is nice to meet you, Lieutenant. Come with me, I will take you to the waiting area for expectant fathers. Magda, are you coming?"

Magda laughed, "I wouldn't miss this for the world. Of course I am coming."

Gerard took them through the back doors by the loading dock and led them through a labyrinth of hallways and offices and into an area marked "maternity".

They were led to a room filled with families, mostly nervous men who were waiting for their spouse or girlfriend to deliver a newborn into the world. Jack looked around the room, "I want to see Ellie! She doesn't even know I am here."

Gerard counseled him, "I'm sorry, Lieutenant. That is not possible, the man must wait. It is a longstanding policy that only nurses and doctors can be with women in labor. Your wife will soon know of your presence."

With that, Gerard wished him luck and departed. Once he was out of sight, Magda whispered to Jack, "Shh, Lieutenant, I have a plan. Stay here. I will be right back."

Magda departed the waiting room and returned a few minutes later escorting a bewildered doctor wearing surgical scrubs. The nametag on his blouse said "Professor Phillipe Vanden Boeynants, Orthopedic Surgery"

Magda brought the good doctor over to meet Jack and some awkward handshakes later, the two men came up with a plan for him to briefly see Ellen.

CHAPTER 129

April 30, 1944, Jack & Ellie, Liege University Hospital Liege, Belgium

Ellie's labor pains were becoming more frequent. Each time she let out a gasp or cry of pain, she would receive calm reassurance from Sister Marjorie, one of the Religious Sisters of the Immaculata de Namur who were volunteers in the maternity ward. Miep was also there, helping whenever she could and holding Ellie's hand.

Doctor Eric Harmel, Professor of Obstetrics, met briefly with Ellie as she was being prepared for delivery. He offered her some options for anesthesia during Labor. He explained that its application would offer some relief from the pain of labor but might delete any memory of the labor and delivery itself.

After thinking it over and discussing it with Miep, she agreed on the mildest form possible. The doctor administered a mild combination of morphine and scopolamine and turned Ellie over to the good Sisters until she got closer.

Ellie prayed a rosary with Miep and, as each contraction seemed to become more frequent, fought to remain conscious. Just before she slipped into a form of "Twilight sleep" another doctor, wearing scrubs and a surgical mask appeared and kissed her on her forehead. In her "brain-fog" state, she thought that it was a bit strange that a doctor would kiss her on her forehead, but, since his eyes were so much like her Cowboy's eyes, she relaxed and let herself drift off into the "Twilight sleep" that the doctor had described.

Through her sleep-shrouded state she thought she could hear her nurses, Miep, the sisters of Immaculata all encouraging her, but it was all like a dream. She thought she heard a baby crying and then didn't remember anything for a while until she woke up as Sister Marjorie handed her a little baby boy.

"You did a good job, Ellen," said Sister Marjorie, "He is a healthy baby boy! What will you call him?"

"I think I will wait to surprise Jack and then we'll decide. What a surprise that will be!"

"How about Lucien?" said Jack, clad in scrubs stepping into her line of sight sporting an enormous smile from ear to ear. That was a surprise indeed.

CHAPTER 130

2 May 1944, Baptism of Baby Lucien, Emil's Chicken house Sante-Walburg

Late afternoon on May 2nd, Jack, in his US Army Air Corps Pilot uniform got Ellie, and the baby discharged. Magda's cousin, Security Guard Gerard Simone guided Jack, Ellie and baby Lucien to the rear parking lot. There, Father Catron waited in his 1939 Renault Juvaquatre.

Father Catron smiled, got out of the car and assisted Jack in getting Ellie and the baby safely into the rear seat, then he and Jack secured themselves into the front of the car as he carefully backed out of the parking space and got on the road.

Father Catron told them that they were going to make a brief stop at his Church for a "Special surprise." They laughed and were eager to see just what Father had in mind for them as they pulled up in front of Saint Thomas the Apostle Catholic Church, his parish. Father Catron smiled and said, "C'mon, get out, you'll enjoy this, I promise."

As they approached the front of the Church, the doors were opened by Pierre and Raymond Michel with big smiles on their faces. Once they entered, Jack and Ellie were astounded to see all their Belgian family and friends: Emil and Miep, Denise and Jan and Elise, and the rest of the Bouillon family and friends, Raoul, Marie, Nadine together with Pharmacist Byron champagne and his new girlfriend, Linda.

Magda greeted them with a broad smile and held up a beautiful white lace baptismal gown as Marie proudly proclaimed, "This is the Baptismal gown that all my children wore on their day of Baptism. We would be honored if you would allow baby Lucien to wear it as well."

Ellie smiled and burst into tears. Just then, Mother Philomena, Sister Marjorie and Sister Alice entered from a side entrance with some flowers and big smiles.

Ellie cried out, "Mother Philomena and Sisters, I cannot believe that you were willing to take time out from your busy schedule to be here for this child's Baptism."

"Well, my dear, it's true that we have very busy schedules. But we wouldn't miss this for the world. Besides, I see from the car that just pulled up in front of the church that someone who is even busier than us has found the time to come here."

Ellie couldn't see who was in the car at first. Then, she gasped as Cardinal Joseph Ernest Van Roey-the Cardinal Archbishop of Belgium together with Father Joseph came walking up the pathway to the main doors of the church.

The Cardinal Archbishop greeted everyone and spotted Jack who was unmistakable in his Army Air Corps uniform. He moved towards Jack and smiled as Jack reached out and shook his hand. This shocked some of the Belgians gathered around them as they would have kissed the cardinal's ring. The Cardinal did not seem to notice this lack of Belgian protocol since he grasped Jack's extended hand with both of his,

"It is a pleasure to meet you, Lieutenant Dodds, a pleasure. I am so glad that you have survived your experiences here during the Nazi occupation and want to thank you and your fellow comrades for putting yourselves on the line for our freedom."

Jack was speechless, but recovered quickly and said, "Thank you, your Eminence, and thank you for all you did for Ellie and for me."

The Cardinal, always sharp said, "Did you say 'Ellie', I distinctly recall signing a marriage certificate using 'Ellen' for this beautiful young mother's name."

Father Catron laughed and said, "It's a long story, your Eminence. Perhaps we can go into more detail at dinner at the Chicken House."

Cardinal Van Roey laughed, went over to the baby who had just been dressed by Magda and Marie and held out his arms for the child,

"Okay, agreed. You will explain this to me over dinner, then. Let's get this child born into Christ, shall we?"

Jan and Byron took pictures with their cameras as the liturgy of the Baptism for Lucien Emil Dodds took place, presided over by none other than Cardinal Joseph Ernest Van Roey, the Cardinal Archbishop of Belgium also known as the "Iron Bishop."

CHAPTER 131

May 5, 1944, Gathering for Dinner Emil's Chicken House Liege, Belgium

The Cardinal Archbishop led the assembled group in a prayer of thanksgiving for all of God's blessings, especially for all those who gave the ultimate sacrifice for the freedom and well-being of all their brothers and sisters.

He thoughtfully made special mention for the repose of the soul of Lucien and prayed for the well-being and safe return of Janine and all those still in Nazi captivity.

The dinner at the Chicken House that followed the Baptism included Roast Chicken, Deep Fried Chicken with an appetizer comprised of fried chicken livers and vegetables together with freshly baked bread. This was accompanied by homemade Belgian beer supplied by several of Father Catron's parishioners and Blue Berry pie made from blueberry preserves.

The Cardinal joked, "Blueberry Pie? Here at the 'Chicken house?' I would have thought it would have been *chicken-pot pie!*"

There was much laughter and friendship as the evening approached the hour before the temporary curfew imposed by the military authorities for the safety of the populace. The Cardinal thoroughly enjoyed himself as did Mother Philomena. He insisted that he and Father Joseph drive the Mother Superior and the two Sisters home, and, after several warm farewells, they departed.

Shortly thereafter, Byron, Linda and Raoul and his family said farewell as well. Jack and Emil made a thorough security sweep downstairs of the Chicken House, ensured all the doors were locked and the emergency lights for the bomb shelter below were in working order.

By the time they returned to the upstairs living area Miep, Denise and Jan finished cleaning up after dinner while Elise helped Ellie put little Lucien into his Bassinet which had been decorated for the Baptism and set up for them in the large guest room.

Jack and Ellie said good night to the others, closed their door and changed into their sleeping clothes: a nightgown for Ellie, boxer shorts for Jack. They held hands and stood over the bassinet looking at their newborn baby, sound asleep.

After saying their prayers for baby Lucien and all their intentions, exhausted from the day's activities, they climbed into bed. Immediately Ellie curled up in Jack's arms placing her head on his chest. She softly whispered, "I just nursed him and so, I hope we will have a few hours of quiet time in each other's arms. I can't tell you how many hours at night I've spent dreaming of being right here in your arms again, Cowboy."

"Me, as well, dear Ellie. I can't begin to describe how happy I am today. To be with the woman I love in my arms, to be with my miraculous son, Little Lucien, to have spent the entire day with my Belgian friends and family who have meant so much to me."

After a pause, he continued, "Actually, since that day that seems so long ago when I was catapulted into all your midst, my entire life has taken on a new dimension. I honestly would be content to spend the rest of my life with you in my arms, with little Lucien asleep next to us right here in Emil and Miep's Chicken House."

He stared thoughtfully up at the ceiling and smiled before continuing, "Of course, we will go back to America first so that you and Lucien can meet your American family. Then I think we will come back here to Belgium and see about making our life here. What do you think?"

Ellie didn't respond, the sound of her soft breathing said it all. In moments, Jack's eyes flickered closed and he, too was soon smiling in a peaceful and deep sleep, breathing softly with Ellie in his arms, safe and secure in Emil and Miep's Chicken House.

CHAPTER 132

Dodds Family-Present day- Arriving twin Baron Palm Beach County Park, Lantana Airport Palm Beach County, Florida

55-year-old Air South Express Captain, Emil Dodds turned his family's Twin Beech Baron G-58 from the base leg to the final approach leg for runway 34 at Palm Beach County Park Airport at Lantana, Florida. Retired Air South Express Captain, Lucien Dodds, age 75, sitting in the right seat pressed the "Mike" button on his control wheel and reported,

"Lantana, Twin Baron 23 Victor turning base to final, runway three-four, Lantana. Full stop."

Emil put the Baron down with three soft squeaks of the tires and took the first turn off onto a taxiway. Lucien reported, "Twin Baron 23 Victor clear runway three-four, Lantana, taxi to Airmax." While Emil "cleaned up" the aircraft, raising flaps, adjusting the trim, Lucien switched to the Fixed Base Operator's (FBO) frequency and requested parking instructions.

Airmax CEO, Dara Weinstein responded, "23 Victor just taxi up to the front of the office and we'll park you there and then move you into the hangar after we've fueled you and checked everything else out. Welcome guys!"

Lucien smiled, "Roger Dara, thanks."

Lucien turned to rear-seat passenger, 89-year-old Belgian Priest and friend, Father Jan Michel, "That landing that was made by my show-off son is called a 'Grease job', but we won't let it go to his head."

Father Jan laughed, "You didn't think I knew that? I hung around your dad and you guys too long not to pick up a little 'Aviation speak.' Nice landing Emil. Not bad for a 747 pilot."

The other rear seat passenger, 25-year-old William Dodds laughed and patted the priest affectionately on his shoulder, "You tell him, Father Jan"

Emil laughed then got serious as he saw Dara come out of the office with a young female ramp attendant to guide them into a parking spot right in front of the Airmax offices. The ramp agent, who's nametag identified her as Alice Robinson, expertly guided them into their parking spot and then crossed her hands over her head, signaling to come to a complete stop.

Once they shut down, and performed all the necessary checklists, they opened the door and, before they could offer to assist the 89-year-old priest, he was out the door and stepped carefully onto the tarmac.

Dara greeted the group with an always bright smile and pointed Alice, her young ramp-hand to the baggage compartment. She hugged the Dodds family and offered her hand to the priest who introduced himself.

"Welcome, everyone, Alice here will take your luggage out front to your rental car which is parked just outside the rear entrance of the office. Come on into the office. We have three hotel rooms set up for you guys' right next door at the Hilton PBI at Palm Beach International airport. "

Lucien smiled, "that's great, Dara! Always a full service FBO for sure."

She laughed, "Lucien, there are several messages for you: one from that doctor at the VA hospital. He says that it is not urgent, but very important. He says you have his cell number, but I took it, just in case.

She looked at her I-pad, "There are three messages from an Emma Guarneiri, pronounced "Gwah-Nairy" I believe. I think she's same reporter from the *Sunshine times* that wrote that nice article about your dad. I told her I was not sure when you would land even though I suspect she has the usual flight following Apps and might be aware that you're arriving here."

Lucien laughed, "That's okay, Dara, thanks for being protective of our privacy. Emma's a good and honest reporter. She did do a nice job writing about Dad's story and we will work with her. But first things first, we all need to get to the VA hospital and see Dad."

Dara smiled, "Yes, while I was on the phone with her, I heard you guys report ten miles out. Reporters can be a royal pain in the… "

Dara trailed off as she realized the priest was following her every word. Father Jan filled it in with a big smile,

"Yes, I know. Reporters can be a *pain in the ass*."

They all laughed just as a very attractive young woman in her early to mid-twenties came around to the front of the building and added to Father Jan's comment, "Yes, we can be *royal* pains in the asses but, you have to admit that was a great article I did about your dad last month, right?"

Then with a big smile she turned to Dara, "And Dara even though you told me you weren't sure when these guys were landing, that wasn't entirely true, was it? You forget that I am a commercial rated pilot, and I have all the 'flight following apps', so there's that."

Dara laughed, "Busted, Emma, but we take care of our customers here at Airmax."

The two women laughed as Lucien chimed in, "Hello, Emma! Everyone, please say hello to Emma Guarneiri who did indeed write that excellent article about my dad, Jack Dodds in the *Sunshine times.* Emma, let me introduce you to…"

Emma smiled and interrupted, "Wait, let me see if I can fill in the blanks. We have here with us, in addition to retired Air South Express Captain Lucien Dodds, current Air South Express Captain Emil Dodds, up and coming First Officer for Air South Express Bill Dodds and none other than the famous Belgian priest, Father Jan Michel. How am I doing?"

Father Jan looked surprised. "*Famous*? What makes you think I'm famous?"

Emma smiled, "Well, *famous* in the sense that you played such a primary role as a 'young teenager' during Jack's time in occupied Belgium according to his interview and time spent with me."

Lucien caught Emma's eye, and she immediately stopped talking and looked to him, "Yes, Lucien?"

"Emma, listen. We, as you know, just got in after flying here from North Carolina. I know you're anxious to speak with us about Dad's condition and his prognosis, but we honestly don't know anything other than he is still in and out of consciousness. I will speak with his doctor soon and I promise I will keep you in the loop. Okay?"

"Promise?"

"Yes, of course I promise. You did such a nice job bringing Dad and Mom's life into the world in a sensitive and touching way. It also brought to life all the brave men and women and their sacrifices made during the Nazi occupation. So, I want you to do a follow-up as, I'm sure, the whole Dodds family does as well. Can I call you later after we hopefully can see Dad and meet with his doctor?"

"Yes, of course Captain Dodds, by all means. I will let you guys get settled and will wait to hear from you."

Lucien laughed, "Thanks, Emma and it's Lucien, you don't have to call me Captain."

Emma smiled, said her goodbyes to the group and left.

Dara handed Emil the car keys and said, "Let me know if there is anything else I can do and know that my family is praying for Jack and all of you."

"Thanks, Dara. I will keep you posted. Not sure how long we will be here."

They piled into the rental car and headed over to the hotel, with Emil behind the wheel so Lucien could give the doctor a call.

CHAPTER 133

Present Day Dr. Timothy Schneider MD West Palm Beach VA Medical Center

Doctor Tim Schneider, Board Certified Neurologist, waited with a cup of coffee at the ER department of the VA hospital in West Palm Beach. He told Lucien Dodds over the phone that, since it was after visiting hours, they should meet him there and he would brief them on Jack's condition and escort them to his room.

Right on schedule, a Gold Chevy Tahoe rental pulled up to the ER drop off as directed. Schneider had already arranged with Stephen Robinson and Lou Thedy, the two uniformed guards on duty for the family to leave the keys with him while they visited his patient.

Lucien, Emil, Bill and Father Jan exited their vehicle and walked up to Doctor Schneider. After the introductions were made and the keys turned over to Stephen, they followed Schneider to a nearby elevator and went to the 2nd floor.

Exiting the elevator, they followed the doctor down a hallway and entered an office marked "Neurology." Doctor Schneider pointed them to several chairs arranged around a low coffee table and they took their seats as the doctor addressed Lucien,

"Lucien, as we discussed over the phone, John is in and out of consciousness. For a while, we were amazed at how, at almost 100 years of age, he was tolerating the trauma and emergency surgery. But recently we see John starting to decline. To put it simply, he's slipping away."

Lucien nodded, "So, he's in a coma now? He won't know that we're all here?"

Tim Schneider shook his head, "No, not exactly, but close. He may have a moment of awareness, not sure about his lucidity, but you might have a moment or two. My PA Tony Riso is checking on him right now and…"

Schneider's cellphone buzzed and he glanced at the screen. "Tony's just now in there with your dad and he says he's awake. Let's go see him."

CHAPTER 134

Present Day

Jack awakens as Family visits- VA Medical Center West Palm Beach

"John? You're awake! Excellent! Welcome back!"

Jack's eyes slowly opened, and he was staring at bright overhead lights and what appeared to be a white, acoustic ceiling. It had all the appearances of a hospital room.

How could this be? Where the hell am I?

He slowly realized that someone was talking to him in a calm, quiet voice. Jack squinted his eyes and tried to focus. He attempted to speak but his throat was painfully sore. He nodded his head to indicate that he heard this person and tried to sit up.

The voice quickly interrupted, "No, it's okay, John. Just stay as you are. You've been asleep for quite a while and we're so happy that you're now awake. Do you have any pain right now?"

He slowly shook his head from side to side.

"That's okay, John. You are currently in the VA Medical Center in West Palm Beach, Florida. Do you remember any other times you were here for routine medical tests?"

Jack didn't answer. He fixed his eyes on the person leaning over his bedside.

"it's okay, John! It's perfectly understandable. First, I'm Doctor Tim Schneider, the "doc" assigned to your case. I'm a board-certified Neurologist here at the VA Center. Do you have any memory of what happened to you and why you're here?"

Jack slowly shook his head from side to side again.

"Not surprising, John. You had a nasty fall about two weeks ago after leaving your dentist's office and hit your head. You had a closed head injury with what you might say was a "brain-bleed" and you were taken by the paramedics to a nearby Trauma center. With me so far?"

Jack swallowed and, in almost a whisper, said, "Where are my family?"

"They're just outside your room and quite anxious to see you, John. I'm just about to send them in."

"Is my wife, Ellie there?"

"No, it's your son, Lucien your grandsons and a Catholic Priest friend of yours. Anything else before I bring them in?"

In a voice so low and hoarse, Doctor Schneider had to lean over and almost place his ear next to Jack's mouth, "Yes. My friends call me Jack."

Schneider smiled, "Okay, Jack! I'll send them in."

CHAPTER 135

Present Day
Lucien, Emil, Bill and Father Jan gather around Jack –
VA Medical Center West Palm Beach

Lucien, Emil, Bill and Father Jan gathered around Jack's bed. His eyes were closed, and he appeared to be in a deep sleep. Physician's Assistant, Tony Riso said, "Try talking to him. He just was awake and spoke a little with Doctor Schneider."

Lucien tried, "Dad? It's me, Lucien. Can you open your eyes?"

When there was no response, Emil tried, "Grandpa? Can you hear us? We're here with you, Dad Lucien, my son Bill and Father Jan.

Jack's eyes fluttered open and to everyone's amazement slowly said, "Father Catron is here? Can I get his blessing?"

Father Jan said, "Of course, Jack, but it's Jan, now Father Jan. Our Dear Friend, Father Catron could not be with us today, but he's near-by. I will not only give you a blessing, but I will give you the sacrament of healing with the sacred oils and the Eucharist as well." He turned to Riso, "Can he swallow a tiny bit of the Eucharist?"

Riso, himself a Catholic, nodded his head, "Yes, I think so. Just try a tiny piece and I will have some water here to help him swallow it."

Riso signaled to Anne Marie Frumenti, the charge nurse standing just outside the patient room, and she retrieved a cup of water. She had just come on duty for the night shift and stood nearby to assist if needed.

Father Jan motioned for quiet and asked, "Jack, would you like me to hear your confession?"

No response. He then quickly reached into his pocket and produced his Pastoral Care of the Sick kit. He invoked the sacrament of healing, performed the anointing with the sacred oils and provided an Apostolic Blessing. He then opened a pyx containing a consecrated host, the Blessed Sacrament, and broke off a tiny piece. He tried once again to get Jack to respond, "Jack, can you stick out your tongue for the Eucharist?"

Everyone stared at Jack who did not respond. Just as they were about to conclude that he had slipped back into a deep sleep, Bill Dodds, cried out, "Look! His tongue is out!"

Father Jan placed the tiny piece of the Eucharist on Jack's tongue and watched him take it in and swallow it. Tony Riso signaled to Anne Marie who gave Jack a tiny sip of water which he also swallowed.

Father Jan smiled, "Well our brother, Jack has just had *Viaticum, food for the journey*. Now I will fraction the remainder of this Eucharist and provide it to whoever wishes to receive it."

Lucien, Emil, Bill and Anne Marie all consumed the remainder of the Eucharist. Tim Schneider and Tony Riso who had moved back from the bed and were watching from the doorway, made the sign of the Cross and watched as each member of the Dodds family kissed a sleeping Jack on his forehead and departed. Father Jan lingered for just a moment, said an additional prayer over Jack and made a full Sign of the Cross over his whole body.

They thanked Tony Riso and Nurse, Anne Marie for their caring and sensitive attention to Jack as they all followed Doctor Schneider down the hall to the elevator.

Just before they got into the elevator, Bill Dodds turned and asked, Doctor Schneider, "Look, I know it's probably against VA protocols, but is there any way that I could quietly spend the night with Grandpa just being there with him? I promise I won't be any trouble."

Lucien was about to say something but observed Doctor Schneider, Tony Riso and Nurse Anne Marie exchanging glances. Something unsaid transpired between the trio.

Schneider addressed Bill Dodds, "Look, Bill, I am on a 12-hour shift and plan to be here through the next few hours. Tony is just coming off shift, but Anne Marie will be here through the night. They have nodded their agreement that you can stay. If you promise to be silent, no matter what you see happening by any of the medical staff. I will stick my neck out and you can stay."

Bill smiled, "Thank you so much, Doc!" but Schneider raised his hand, "that being said, if anyone else in authority so much as raises one 'squawk,' you will have to leave. Understood?"

"Absolutely! Thanks."

With that settled, Doctor Schneider bid the others good night. They indicated that they would be back in the morning to see Jack one more time. Lucien told Bill to call him if he needed to be picked up or if anything important happened.

Tim Schneider stood there with Tony Riso and Anne Marie and watched them get into the elevator. His intuition told him that Jack would probably not make it through the night.

He was glad that someone from the family would be with him.

Tim Schneider was an excellent and caring physician. His experience and his intuition would prove to be right.

CHAPTER 136

Present and Past come together
Jack & Ellie time to go-
VA Medical Center

Jack woke with a start, he thought he heard the baby crying then went silent. He recalled Ellie saying that she had just nursed him, so he needn't worry.

He rolled to his right, but Ellie wasn't there, *she must have gone to check on Baby Lucien,* he thought.

He smiled at the beautiful memory of her head on his chest and her arms around him as they made their plans for life after the War. Her soft, quiet breathing as she fell asleep snuggled up with him filled him with overwhelming joy and peace.

Then, through the quiet of his dream, in the middle of the night, he heard Ellie calling to him, "Jack, come here and join me. I need you in my arms."

For some reason, he couldn't open his eyes, he struggled to stay awake, but sleep was softly restraining him. "Ellie?" he whispered, "Where are you? I can't seem to see you. Why aren't you back with me with your arms around me and your head on my chest? Like just before?"

Her soft laugh filled his heart, "Honey, my dear 'Cowboy', I'm close by and, even though you can't see me, I am right here with you."

His whispered voice was growing ever softer, sleep was overtaking him more rapidly now, "I want you back with me, I don't understand. Where are you? I can't see you."

Again, that soft laughter, just like she did when they walked by the stream at the Michel family refuge in Bouillon. "I'm right here next to you, but for now, you can't see me because I've been called home to be with God and His angels. It's time for you to join me."

Jack knew that he must be dreaming but there was something about the way Ellie's voice penetrated deep into his heart. He felt like he was drifting up off his bed. His heart started beating faster, "I don't understand, you're saying that you're with God and His angels? You mean that you are dead? I don't understand. That can't be, I must be dreaming, our friends just left after the dinner, we were just cuddled up together and the baby was just Baptized and…"

Again, that soft laughter, putting him at ease, "No, sweet Jack. I am not dead, I am very much alive but in a fuller, more beautiful life. It is now time for you to move into that life with me."

"To be with you? You mean it's my time?"

She laughed a bit more heartily than before, "Boy, you cowboys sure are slow. Yes, it is time for you John Dodds."

Now it was his turn to laugh, "You know all my friends call me Jack. Is Cowboy Rock there where you are?"

"Yes, Jack, come with me, and you will find out. It's easy, Cowboy, just surrender and open your heart."

And that's exactly what Jack did.

EPILOGUE

Four weeks after Jack and Ellie are reunited

The South Florida National Cemetery is a 338-acre United States National Cemetery located in Lake Worth, Florida. As is the case with most National Cemeteries, great honor and respect is coupled with peaceful repose for the men and women who served their country and a place where their families can visit, gather and reflect and pray for their loved ones.

This is where I would have committed the fictional character, 1st Lieutenant John, "Jack" Dodds and his beloved spouse, Ellen, "Ellie" Dodds had they really existed. This place is truly a lasting memorial to the men and women who have selflessly served their country.

Jack and Ellie embody the example of real-life men and women who were caught up in a time of war and tragedy for humanity. Those who fought and put their lives on the line for freedom and those who awaited their safe return and sometimes answered the knock on the door only to be confronted by an officer and a chaplain and the realities of war. Heroes are buried in this place and many other places dedicated to those who served their country.

Throughout France, Belgium, Holland, Spain and elsewhere in Europe similar places abound that offer a lasting memorial for the many brave men and women of the French, Belgian, Dutch and Spanish Resistance, for the Réseau *Comète*, the Comet Line who put their lives in danger and who sacrificed themselves for the protection and safety of Allied Airmen and others.

Just as Jack, Ellen and the entire family and friends I've created for this novel are fictitious characters, so are the characters that populate the Resistance groups largely derived from this author's imagination.

The Real-life central figures who are portrayed by my fictitious characters are largely based on some of the following brave people: André de Jongh AKA "Dedée", the young woman who is largely regarded as the founder of the Comet Line, Frederic de Jongh Andrée's father, Elsie Maréchal and many others, too many to list here. Dedée" was betrayed by Nazi double agents and underwent brutal treatment in Nazi concentration camps. Miraculously, she survived and was liberated by Allied forces. Many others did not survive.

Cardinal Joseph Ernest Van Roey-the Cardinal Archbishop of Belgium was a real-life, well-respected figure in the Catholic Church's resistance to Nazism in Belgium. He was, in fact a fervent anti-Nazi who in the beginning of December, 1941 said,

> *"With Germany we step many degrees downward and reach the lowest possible depths. We have a duty of conscience to combat and to strive for the defeat of these dangers...Reason and good sense both direct us towards confidence, towards resistance"TIME Magazine Prelates Against Hitler, 15 December 1941*

He did not hesitate to intervene and openly rebuke the Rexist, pro-Nazi leaders who aspired to gain control over the Belgian peoples. Not one to suffer fools, he was known as the "Iron Bishop".

I simply had to include this staunch defender of human rights into the story. I took the author's liberty of giving his Eminence a significant role in his interactions with my fictitious characters in this book. This was based on his strong persona, his fervent stance against Hitler and his Nazi thugs, and love for his laity, clergy and religious sisters and brothers. His words and actions with my characters are completely derived from my imagination.

Father Corentin "Cory" Catron, who played such a central role in my story is, again a fictitious person but based on real-life priests who served the faithful during the Nazi terror and occupation. So too is Mother Philomena, Mother Superior of the Sisters of Immaculata de Namur and her fictitious order. Her character portrays the immense sacrifice and great risk that the religious orders took to shield Jewish families and especially Jewish children.

Many Jewish children were entrusted to their care by terrified mothers and fathers who knew they were destined to suffer torture and death at the hands of the Nazi brutes but hoped that their children would be protected and spared. There are many stories about these "Hidden Children" shielded and protected by Catholic priests, nuns and laity.

Where possible, I have included conversations and actions that spring from my imagination but are attributed to actual people both famous, infamous and little known.

For the conclusion of this Epilogue, I thought we should hear from one of my favorite fictitious characters, the young teenage Jan Michel who was involved in so many aspects of Jack's adventures behind enemy lines. Young Jan becomes "Father Jan" at the end of the story. When attempting to address the bravery and sacrifices of real-life heroes, the incredible stories that took place during the Nazi occupation, I imagine Father Jan's character would say something like this:

"Yes, it was amazing. Especially the bravery of so-called ordinary people. There are literally thousands of stories about all that went on. Many stories will be told, many will be written, and many will not be revealed even in novels that were based on truth but offered as fiction."

Much like this one.

ACKNOWLEDGEMENT

The “Cowboy and the Chicken House”, an unlikely adventure in historical fiction could not have been written without the help and encouragement of a close circle of family and loyal friends.

This is especially true for my best friend and my high school sweetheart, Alice who has been my patient listener, my “down-to-Earth” editor and encouraging counselor throughout our lives together.

Just as I assembled a cast of characters who brought to life Jack Dodds and his adventures during that time behind enemy lines, so was I fortunate enough to assemble another cast of characters who provided me with some much-needed editorial insights and encouragement.

They are listed here in gratitude:

Bill Bond, Barbara, “Barb” Johnson, Clint Johnson, Lee Edward Levenson, Anne-Marie Levenson, Marjorie and Stephen Robinson, Alice Robinson, Marjorie Siegel, Brian Siegel,Theresa Griffin, Patrick Griffin, Herman and Ellen Lustig,Tom Schneider, Bill Sunter, and Lou Thedy,

Now, if I have forgotten to mention anyone here, you have my permission to place me underneath an upside-down P-51D Mustang deep in the Ardennes Forest.

Provided, of course, that it is no longer burning!

With great appreciation and affection, I am thankful for each and every one of you.